Praise for *Louisiana Catch*

"*Louisiana Catch* is perfectly relevant and lovingly bottom lines the urgency to become involved in the feminist agenda, all the while being a deliciously romantic and hopeful story. Sweta proves, yet again, her ability to illustrate all the nuanced layers of a woman's experience and honor her power to create change in the world."

PALLAVI SASTRY, Actress (*Blue Bloods*)

"*Louisiana Catch* is a compelling read! I was swept into Ahana's world as she struggles to find a path forward after a turbulent and violent marriage. Sweta raises an interesting question—are we destined to be defined by our choices? Read and find out for yourselves!"

VANDANA KUMAR, Publisher *India Currents* Magazine

"A moving, modern story about letting go of the past in order to find true empowerment. As a longtime advocate of women in need, Sweta Vikram doesn't shy away from difficult topics. *Louisiana Catch* deals with the complexities of love, loss, history and home."

GEORGIA CLARK, author, *The Regulars*

"Utterly unique, insightful and clever. Enthralling and confronting at the same time, *Louisiana Catch* draws the reader in and ultimately provides hope."

BARBARA BOS, Managing Editor,
Women Writers, Women's Books

"In *Louisiana Catch*, celebrated author Sweta Vikram reminds us that violence against women should never be acceptable and it's not the victim's fault. The sudden loss of a dear one and a divorce from an abusive marriage force Ahana to emerge from her sheltered life and re-build her confidence to organize the largest women's conference. While she is determined to help other women, she once again faces love and deceit along the way. Will that help her or deter her from sharing her story of abuse with other survivors?"

DR. SHRUTI KAPOOR, Founder and CEO, Sayfty

"A very compelling read! I am in awe of Sweta's ability to intelligently capture, blend and integrate pertinent psychological issues that face society today."

SUNITA PATTANI, psychotherapist,
author, and trauma specialist

"*Louisiana Catch* is the story of a woman finding her voice and learning to listen to it. Sweta's descriptions paint a rich picture, capturing the complexities of relationships, culture and abuse, drawing you in and painting a vivid picture in your mind. A thoroughly enjoyable read that draws you in."

KIMBERLY CAMPBELL, Executive Director, Exhale to Inhale

"This is a powerful story, using the romantic formula to advocate a message the world needs to hear: that it is never alright to abuse women. If you like romances, you'll enjoy this one. Even if you don't, you'll find the story worth reading, for its exciting plot twists, for a look into the culture of India, and above all, for the message it shouts."

BOB RICH, PhD, author, *Anger and Anxiety*

"*Louisiana Catch* perfectly captures what it means to be human in a digital world, where support groups meet online, love interests flirt on Twitter, and people get confused with personas. Equal parts tender and playful, moving and hopeful, Vikram's prose connects us with timeless truths about grief and redemption in a satisfyingly modern way."

STEPHANIE PATERIK, Managing Editor, *Adweek*

"*Louisiana Catch* is a triumph. In Ahana, Sweta Vikram has created an unforgettable character —strong, wise and deeply human, who'll inspire a new generation struggling to come to terms with their identity in a world of blurring identities."

KARAN BAJAJ, New York Times bestselling author,
The Yoga of Max's Discontent

"In *Louisiana Catch*, Sweta Vikram brings life to the complex human rights issue of violence against women. Through one woman's journey to make sense of her past and ultimately heal, Vikram shows us that yoga can reconnect us to ourselves, and that by empowering others, we transform our own lives."

ZOË LEPAGE, Founder, Exhale to Inhale

"Kudos to Sweta S. Vikram for penning a powerhouse of a book! This novel is a must-read for women (and for supportive men). I hope she wins an award for this incredible book!"

SUSAN ORTLIEB, *Suko's Notebook*

louisiana catch

Sweta Srivastava Vikram

Modern History Press
Ann Arbor

Louisiana Catch

Copyright © 2018 by Sweta Srivastava Vikram. All Rights Reserved.

1st Printing – April 2018

This is a work of fiction. Names, characters, businesses, places, events, and incidents are either the products of the author's imagination or used in a fictitious manner. Any resemblance to actual persons, living or dead, or actual events is purely coincidental.

Library of Congress Cataloging-in-Publication Data

Names: Vikram, Sweta Srivastava, 1975- author.
Title: Louisiana catch : a novel / by Sweta Srivastava Vikram.
Description: Ann Arbor, MI : Modern History Press, [2017]
Identifiers: LCCN 2017025072 (print) I LCCN 2017027742 (ebook) I ISBN
   9781615993543 (ePub, PDF, Kindle) I ISBN 9781615993529 (softcover :
   acid-free paper) I ISBN 9781615993536 (hardcover : acid-free paper) I
ISBN
   9781615993543 (eBook)
Subjects: LCSH: Man-woman relationships--Fiction. I Divorced women--
Fiction.
   I GSAFD: Love stories.
Classification: LCC PS3622.I493 (ebook) I LCC PS3622.I493 L68 2018
(print) I
   DDC 813/.6--dc23
LC record available at https://lccn.loc.gov/2017025072

Distributed by Ingram (USA/CAN/AU), Bertram's Books (UK/EU)

Published by
Modern History Press
5145 Pontiac Trail
Ann Arbor, MI 48105

Tollfree: 888-761-6268
FAX: 734-663-6861

www.ModernHistoryPress.com
info@ModernHistoryPress.com

"To find yourself, think for yourself."

~ Socrates

DEDICATION

For Rashi Singhvi Baid, Nirav Patel, and Jaya Sharan

This one's for you. And you know why.

Also by Sweta Srivastava Vikram

POETRY

Kaleidoscope: An Asian Journey with Colors

Because All is Not Lost: Verse on Grief

Beyond the Scent of Sorrow

No Ocean Here: Stories in Verse about Women from Asia, Africa, and the Middle East

Wet Silence: Poems about Hindu Widows

Saris and a Single Malt

FICTION

Perfectly Untraditional

Dramatis Personae

Ahana Chopra............Women's rights advocate in New Delhi, India

Amanda......................Member of the online therapy group

Athena.......................Ahana's Shih Tzu

Baburao.....................Ahana's driver in New Delhi

Megan Black ....PR Head, *Shine On*

Chutney ....Mumma's youngest sister, who lives in New Delhi

Crystal.......................Rohan Brady's assistant

Jay Dubois.................Ahana's colleague in online therapy

Sarah Goldstein..........Professor at Columbia University

Dev Khanna ....Ahana's ex-husband in New Delhi

Lakshmi ....Domestic help at Ahana's parents' house in New Delhi

Masi...........................Mumma's sister, who lives in New Orleans

Mausa ....Husband of Masi

Michael Hedick..........Rohan Brady's boss in the US ("Dracula")

Naina ....Ahana's cousin, daughter of Masi

Rohan Brady ....Publicist in NYC and NOLA, and Ahana's conference colleague

Josh Rossi...................Cop in NYC and Naina's fiancé

Shelly Roy ....Executive Director, Freedom Movement

Socrates.....................Rohan Brady's Golden Retriever

Tanya ....Member of the online therapy group

1

My name is Ahana Chopra, and I was born and raised in the most ludicrous city in the world: New Delhi. Sometimes, I feel New Delhi doesn't understand me. Other times, I don't understand it. I don't think I've ever found a way to bridge the differences between what I was and what I was expected to be in this city.

In Delhi, you find the majority running away from something, stashing away some secret but pretending to be happy. In Delhi, you always need to be on your guard.

Thirty minutes ago, when I was out for an evening run close to my office, a group of men sitting on their motorbikes and sipping tea in small glasses started whistling and making loud kissing noises, "Baby doll, 36 DD!" I covered my chest with my arms and looked around. The streets weren't empty, but harassers in New Delhi fear no one—neither the police nor the pedestrians. Two of the men got down from their bikes and started to walk toward me. I moved away from them and scoped out a different route mentally. I could taste bile in my mouth; my running route and routine represented a small zone of freedom for me, and I could feel it being stolen away. I pushed my glasses closer to my face and noticed a small path across the street where no automobile could enter. I didn't think when I sprinted through the moving traffic—with the cars honking, people rolling down their windows and cussing at me. I fell down a couple of times and bruised my shin. But I got up and wiped myself off. I ran until I couldn't see the harassers.

Because of the thrusting aggressiveness of the people here, I find myself making extra effort to go unnoticed. At work parties, I hide in a quiet corner with a glass of wine. On Monday mornings especially, I try to reach work when no one is around—discussing weekend debauchery isn't my thing. At social gatherings, I want to disappear and become invisible. I don't care whether others chat with me; it is equally fine if I am alone with my thoughts. I can just as effortlessly look outside and observe everyone as I can look inside to see all my thoughts and emotions. But, oh, the New Delhi elites, so preoccupied with everyone else's business!

It must have been February 2013 when I was crossing the park to my parents' house—troubled by everything and thankful that my mother's bridge partners seemed to have deserted the place already. *No one in this park knows about my life. I am safe.*

"You Kashmiri?" It was one of several old women clad in *salwar kameez*—their long, full-sleeved shirts below their knees and baggy trousers were ill-fitting. They had wrapped their bodies in shawls and well-worn colorful sneakers. I sighed inwardly looking at the unfamiliar faces. Often these random "aunties" pretended to go for morning walks, using the opportunity to scope out future daughters-in-law or bicker about their current daughters-in-law.

"Huh?" I unwillingly pried the headphones out of my ears.

Sucking their teeth and shaking their heads, they gathered around me. "Kashmiri pundit or Muslim?"

"Excuse me?" But before I could get a word in, they interrupted.

"Afghanistan?"

"No. New Delhi," I said, conscious of my slight British accent. It was left over from my university and MBA years in London, and I knew it made me sound like a snob. "Where we all are right now." I used my index finger to draw a circle over my head. "The capital of India." And, of course, I wasn't exactly trying to fit in anymore, either.

"What is your height?"

"Five feet eight inches," I blurted out, and hated myself for not staying quiet. I simply didn't know how not to answer when someone asked a question. My childhood manners clung to me even now.

"Are you married?" one of the aunties asked sharply. I guess she noticed that I didn't wear a wedding ring, have *sindoor* in my hair, or a *mangalsutra* around my neck. The lack of the ring, the vermillion in my hair, and the missing beaded necklace must have made her assume I was single.

I readjusted my glasses. "No." I tried not to raise my voice. I was taught to be respectful to the elderly. But my throat felt dry suddenly. I rubbed my feet against the earth.

"Finding a boy will not be easy at this height. You will stand out." Half-a-dozen heads bobbed in rhythm like a pendulum.

With straight hair seven inches below my shoulder, I literally stood out from other women. It was normal; I've been questioned in languages that have far more syllables than Hindi and English. I am fluent in French, but I would bet my favorite wine that the strangers giving me the third degree knew nothing beyond French *paarphuumes*, or, as the rest of us pronounce it: perfumes.

"You are so fair. *Gori girl*. And so, tall and thin—like a pole." At least a couple of portly aunties nodded their heads and spoke with a thick accent. They muttered in mutilated English, "No hips. How will she carry children? Maybe she is the kind of woman who doesn't eat

3

or know how to cook. But she is *gori*. Light skin color and good looks make everything easy. She can be taught these homely chores."

"Excuse me, but I have to go." I rushed off.

People have made up their minds, which I can't change. New Delhi resents me for not embodying its spirit. What would these women say if they knew the worst of my secrets: that I was newly divorced from my college sweetheart Dev Khanna?

* * *

A few weeks prior to my filing for divorce, Dev turned into a psychotic stranger in an alley and forced me while I was asleep. This was a new low even for him. When I met with my parents for dinner at The Delhi Golf Club that evening, Mumma cupped my face, "*Beta*, you have become quieter than usual. What's going on?"

People still called me *beta*, an endearing term for a child, even though I was well into my thirties. If only I could tell Mumma that her *beta* was living in hell. If only I could share with her what happened in our bedroom every night after sundown. Dev was so charming around everybody—Mumma too had approved when Dev proposed to me. People wanted to be him and with him. Dev, with his long face, breezy eyelashes, and sharp features, was the life of every party.

Me? I was so timid in my own marriage and life.

I didn't say anything to Mumma.

She ran her hands through my hair. "Whenever you are ready to talk, I will never judge you. You know that, right?"

Dad poured me a glass of French pinot noir and he ordered Mumma a Glenlivet Single Malt straight. I knew they were stressed; the only time Mumma didn't have her whiskey on the rocks was when her yoga and meditation couldn't help her decompress.

My parents let me be, which not many understood. I still remember the day I left work early and showed up at my parents to tell them, "Mumma, I took your suggestion. I asked Dev for a divorce this morning."

Mumma heard me patiently.

I sobbed inconsolably. "He is upset and I am scared how this will all pan out, Mumma." My tongue still tasted bitter from licking the envelope for the divorce proceedings.

"We know the judge, *beta*. Everything will be sorted out in six months, maximum."

The day Mumma's lawyer finally got Dev to sign the divorce papers, I had laughingly told her, "Ma, I am so good at setting boundaries for other people and at advocating women's rights. But in my own life, I failed."

"It takes courage to put a bad marriage behind you."

"Oh well." I dug my feet into our living room carpet as I thought about how Dev made me watch disgusting porn videos. Even after sex hurt, I witnessed how it turned him on, but I was unable to draw a line. I used to feel inconsequential in that seven-bedroom ancestral house of his. I couldn't fight off Dev. I was ashamed to talk to anyone about it.

Mumma stroked my hair. "No one has any right over your life. Now find the inner strength to fight for yourself and your happiness."

Even though I was unable to confess the extent of Dev's sexual and emotional dominance over me, I felt Mumma understood my pain. She had seen me turn quieter around him. I had lost weight and couldn't sleep. I squirmed when Dev touched me in front of Mumma.

She cradled me in her arms. "You are safe with us, *beta*. Your dad and I will always be there for you." She kissed my forehead. "Let's go collect your things."

* * *

When I moved back in with Mumma and Dad and started to call their house my home, Mumma brought me Athena, a Shih Tzu, as a welcome home gift. Athena's little bed was set up in my bedroom, which had enough space for a study, a swing with extraordinary craftsmanship, a kingsize bed, a dresser, a small library, a recliner, a couch, a meditation and yoga space, and two nightstands.

Mumma made me a mug of hot chocolate every single evening. Sometimes, I would put my head in her lap and she would run her fingers through my hair. "Time makes everything better, *beta*. Just don't expect things to get better overnight."

"I hate the ugliness of it all. The papers. Who owns what? Looking for ways to avoid running into Dev. That's not how I envisioned my life, Mumma." Dev had sent me a text message earlier that day that said: "You're one of those bitches who accuse men of rape because they're so afraid to say they want it."

"I know, *beta*. I have faith that there is something better waiting for you."

* * *

In May 2013, one day at breakfast, Mumma announced, as she sipped on her apple and celery juice, "Let's all make a trip to New Orleans."

5

"They have bugs the size of elephants during summer," I said without looking at her or Dad. Much as I loved New Orleans, Masi—Mumma's sister—and my cousin Naina, I didn't want to go anywhere. I was divorced from Dev and I didn't want to see anyone. Our wedding had been such a lavish affair with over 2,000 invitees. Masi and Naina had made multiple trips to New Delhi to help us prepare for the wedding. Ten years later, nothing existed. All the bruises and soreness were gone, but sometimes I still felt them. I saw a shadow on my arm and expected to be reminded of a humiliating fight. It was not easy getting used to freedom.

"Okay, then maybe when it gets cooler? We must help with Naina's wedding preparations, *beta*. She lives in New York, but the wedding is in New Orleans. That *badmaash* has a long list of things she wants done." Mumma laughed thinking about our family's favorite brat aka *badmaash*, Naina, as she cut slices of apple and put them in my and Dad's plates.

Maybe New Orleans wasn't such a bad idea after all. "Mumma."

"Ya, *beta*." She looked at me.

"With everything going on at home, I guess I didn't mention it..."

"What, *beta*?"

"Remember the Annual Women's Conference in NOLA I told you about?"

"The one in autumn of next year? What about it?"

"The board accepted my proposal for *No Excuse*—the core theme of the three-day event. They invited me to be the local point-person in New Orleans. I can actually live in New Orleans for a few months next year while we put our conference together."

Mumma lit up with pride. "This is perfect. Let's go this summer. You can do some work, and I will take a few months off from my hospital, and travel with you. It'll be fun. We can help Masi. And then we can go back next year for the conference and Naina's wedding."

"Are you sure you can leave your patients?"

"No one is more important than you, *beta*." Mumma cupped my face. "And I need to save my sister, too."

"What's wrong with Masi?"

"Nothing yet, but once her in-laws show up, she will turn into a chimney."

"Meaning?"

"Remember when we visited them for Naina's medical school graduation—the more her mother-in-law bragged about your masi's $2 million home and her son's career as the leading cardiologist of NOLA, the more my sister cringed and smoked."

6

"Oh, yes. And when Masi bought her new house and we went all for the housewarming, her mother-in-law insisted Masi and Naina not enter the kitchen or do any religious rituals if they were on their period."

Mumma burst out laughing. "Of course, I remember. Your masi got so tired of her tyrannical mom-in-law that she maintained she was always having her period because of menopause and didn't enter the kitchen at all during their visit. She would sit in her huge bathtub and smoke like a diva."

We both laughed, thinking about Masi.

Masi and Naina were thrilled that my work would bring both Mumma and me to New Orleans. "I am taking you to Marie Laveau's House of Voodoo when you visit this time," Naina insisted in the video chat. "I am going to put a hex on that fucking Dev." The two dimples, one on each side of her cheek, became deeper, as her eyes twinkled with determination.

My heart uncurled a little more. I was grateful for Naina. Even though she didn't know the harrowing details of my marital relationship with Dev, she was firmly on my side. Her larger-than-life personality and protectiveness beyond all rationality were reminders of the good in my life. How easily she could say whatever was in her heart, even though she was a year younger than me.

* * *

Two weeks after the board accepted my proposal to host the conference in NOLA, Mumma and I were sitting in our patio, getting ready to drink our morning tea. It was hot and Mumma was fanning herself. But she insisted that we didn't pull the temporary roof we normally used for summer days. I switched on the desert cooler.

Mumma said, "Thank you." She took a deep breath. "What does the theme *No Excuse* represent, Ahana?"

"You know my organization is bringing together world leaders, advocates, activists, feminists, nonprofits, corporations supportive of women's safety and rights at one conference to fight violence against women? *No Excuse*, my brainchild, is the core theme of the three-day event. No excuse for rapes, policing, or any kind of violence against women."

"Oh, I see." She didn't probe further. A few minutes later, she sighed, "Promise, you'll believe in sunrise again."

"Whaaaat?" I rubbed my eyes, pretending the morning sun and scorching temperatures were hurting them. But it was a ruse to pretend I didn't understand Mumma's advice. I stretched my arms over my head and let out a yawn.

7

"Promise me, Ahana. That you won't just give up on love. You are only thirty-three, *beta*. You have your whole life ahead of you."

"Where is all this coming from?" I poured tea into the cups and looked at the high iron fence surrounding the patio. It was covered with creepers. The front of the house had high, cemented boundary walls. No one from the outside could see inside our home. I was safe from Dev here. Two days earlier, he had shown up at my office car park and made a scene.

Mumma asked the gardener to water the morning glory and zinnia pots. She turned to her tea and stirred it. "Can't a mother worry?"

"Yes, she can. But my mumma doesn't worry so early in the day." I gave her a kiss on the cheek.

She hugged me tightly. "Let go of the things that do not serve you, Ahana."

I noticed my mother was addressing me as "Ahana" as opposed to "*beta*." It confused me.

"Sure thing, Yogini Mom." I bowed. Athena came running to me and I played with her.

Mumma brought her eyebrows together. She spoke in a determined voice. "I won't be around forever. I want you to promise me that you will consciously harbor thoughts that bring joy to your life." She gently ran her hands over my ring finger, which was now empty.

"So now I am a negative and depressed woman?" I pulled my hand away.

"No one is saying that. But you have never bothered to matter in your own life."

I tried to interject but Mumma raised her voice. "Dev was an unfortunate chapter. I am sorry we didn't see it sooner. But you can't let a bad marriage stop you from living your life fully. If I hadn't stepped in, you probably wouldn't have even left him, Ahana."

Mumma was different today. She was a big believer in learning from experience. She was a professional woman who was excellent at her job, and she had never quite mastered the grace in the kitchen that characterizes women who always work at home. There were little burn scars on her hands and arms from cooking. But she was proud of the scars. "Burn and learn," was her mantra. It was more Dad who would try to talk sense to me.

I quietly got up from the coffee table in our patio and asked our housekeeper, Lakshmi, to bring me my yoga mat. Lakshmi replied, "Wokay, *didi*," in a heavy South Indian accent. She loved to call me *didi*, even though I wasn't her older sister.

"I am serious, Ahana." Mumma stood up.

8

"I know you are. That's why I need to breathe so I don't stress out. I don't want to be reminded what a fool I have been." I put Athena down.

As soon as Lakshmi brought the mat, I laid it out and got into a headstand. Some people turn to wine, others to cigarettes, and a few to pot. I have always turned to yoga to find peace. Being upside down with my feet straight up toward the sky and heart over my head, I felt I could deal with the moment. Athena tried to lick my face but Lakshmi picked her up. "No disturbing Ahana *didi,* wokay?"

Mumma's tone changed. "I am not trying to hurt you, Ahana."

"I know."

"You will open yourself to the idea of a partner and love, Ahana. Promise me." Mumma started to leave as it was getting hot outdoors.

"I promise." I closed my eyes.

Little did I know that my mother, who'd taught me everything in life, would not teach me one thing: to learn to live without her. And that was the day that, for me, time began all over again.

≉ 2 ≉

When I joined Freedom Movement as a women's rights advocate, I didn't need to travel much. For the most part, I had a non-demanding 9-5 desk job where I didn't need to encounter people at work. On occasions, I was expected to mingle with the New Delhi socialites and help raise money, which I did successfully. Classic case of secret introvert—hiding inside an extroverted shell that is required to do her job well enough. But with my promotion to head of communications and fundraising, a leadership position which I initially resisted, things changed. As a high-powered official, my work was to build stakeholder and donor relations, raise funds for the organization, manage all the marketing, events, public relations and corporate communications for the nonprofit, and overlook all the internal communications aspect. I was new at all of this and hadn't excelled yet.

I had left home early that morning because one of our rural sister organizations wanted us to showcase their work at the conference in New Orleans; they represented female workers in India who were scared to use unisex public restrooms because of the rise in sexual assault cases in these spaces. So they had invited me to their office for a site visit.

I was two hours away from the Indian capital, stuck in a tiny, hot car in the month of June, when I got a call from Dad, "Your mumma is in the intensive care unit."

I couldn't believe him. How could Mumma be fighting for her life when her morning was full of action verbs—she had done an hour of yoga and drank her green juice. She had rearranged her closet. She wrote a list for our New Orleans trip.

Dad went on to share the details. "She passed out while she was in the shower. I called the ambulance. I don't think she has much time." Dad sounded robotic.

I thought of the right things to say and ask. But I couldn't. Mumma had been different today. She had scolded me for not living my life. She hated the summer heat, but she had chosen to sit in the patio, instead of the sunroom with the air conditioner on, and drink tea. She had taken the day off from her hospital, very unlike her to abandon her patients, because she felt she hadn't been able to see some of her close friends. "Life is so unpredictable, *beta*. I don't want to have any regrets." What did she mean by any of it?

* * *

I remember every detail. When I got to the hospital, several of my parents' friends were waiting in the lobby. Had it not been for the strong "hospital smell," you could have confused the place for a five-star hotel: the amenities, posh clothes, the crowd, the gift store, and the restaurants.

I tried to avoid them, but many aunties formed a group and hugged me tight. "Nothing will happen, Ahana. We are here for you." I didn't blink or cry as they stroked my hair. This was the hospital where my mother worked. This was the space where she saved lives. The hospital aimed to bring India the highest standards of medical care along with clinical research, education, and training.

I politely excused myself and went to the washroom. There was no food in my stomach, yet I felt nauseated. After throwing up bile and retching for a few minutes, I splashed water on my face. I wiped myself with my *dupatta*—the long scarf over my *salwar kameez* covering my big chest since I was in rural parts of New Delhi earlier that day and didn't want to draw any attention to myself—and bought a lemonade from the cafeteria to rehydrate myself.

My phone rang: Masi calling from New Orleans. "Naina just reached NOLA from New York. We are on our way to Delhi, *beta*. Don't let anything happen to your mother."

I got to Mumma's room and stood at the threshold for a few moments. *This can't be happening.* Normally, Mumma's face glowed, but I could barely see her features since she was hooked onto a ventilator. Mumma, the person who was our lifeline, needed help breathing. *Wake up, Mumma.*

My feet didn't want to move, but I slowly walked inside Mumma's room. Dad was sitting next to her in a chair; he looked lifeless.

"Can I get you anything?" I rubbed his shoulders. He didn't respond, just stared at Mumma.

I ran my eyes over her: Mumma in the hospital with tubes and machines attached to her. Despite being a doctor's daughter, I didn't recognize many items of medical equipment. A rough blanket was placed on her body. I wanted to cover her toes. Mumma often complained about her feet getting cold. Was she cold now? *Can you feel anything?* Monitors around her beeping. Needles and pipes poking through her once enviable skin. She looked like a frail, pale shadow of her former self. I couldn't see Mumma like this. I started dry heaving again.

Suddenly, one of the monitors began to beep and distracted me. The nurse pressed a call button and spoke with urgency. It didn't sound good. "What's happening?" I touched her arm. The nurse ignored me, saying, "Everyone leave the room," and ushered us to the bench outside Mumma's room. Two doctors and three nurses flooded in. After screaming, "Wait outside," they closed the door. I saw through the glass window that Mumma was having difficulty breathing. I started to shake. Mumma's youngest sister, whom Naina and I called Chutney, hugged me.

Dr. Murty, Mumma's colleague and chief of cardiology, stepped out of the room after a few minutes. He turned to Dad, Chutney, and me, "The leaks through her heart valves have flooded her lungs."

Mumma's heart failed us all.

"Will Mumma be okay? Can we see her?" I asked with my eyes flooded with tears. The noise from the heart monitor affirmed she was still alive, with its consistent, rhythmic beeps.

"Even if she survives, she'll become a vegetable." Dr. Murty patted my shoulder.

My heart sank. In that instance, I knew Mumma wouldn't survive. She'd often said, "Dignity and independence are important to me. The day I must depend on anyone, physically or financially, that'll be the end of it."

I pleaded with Dr. Murty, "Can you keep her alive until Masi and Naina arrive? Please? Just a little bit longer?"

Even before he could respond, the nurses called out to Dr. Murty. Too many people moved rapidly inside Mumma's room; it didn't look good. I panicked. I peered through the windows again; they were trying to revive Mumma. They were doing some procedure. Dr. Murty attempted chest compressions a few times. Finally, I saw him remove the surgical mask from his face and shake his head. He said something to the head nurse—I couldn't read his lips. I looked at the heart monitor; Mumma had flat-lined. The head nurse pulled a white sheet over Mumma's face. My body sank to the floor. I had seen darkness before in my marriage with Dev, but it was nothing compared to what I felt in that moment. My life felt over without my mother in it.

Dr. Murty stepped out of the room and removed his gloves, "I am so sorry. We tried our best."

I sat still.

"When did she pass away?" Chutney asked.

"Time of death: 7:17 p.m."

Dad saw me, but he didn't see me. He said nothing; just cried.

* * *

Time vanished. Grief came in waves—in some instances, I was calm and got all the paperwork in order; in others, I felt completely overwhelmed. Bills. Death certificate. Nurses paying their condolences as Mumma was their boss. Notifying friends and family.

At one point, I begged the guy on guard duty to let me into the morgue. He asked for five hundred rupees as a bribe. It was cold inside unlike the dry, sweltering Delhi streets. The morgue had an eerie vibe. He handed me a mask. His instructions were crisp, "Not more than ten minutes, OK? I am doing you a favor by letting you inside. Use the sanitizer before you leave."

I covered my face with the mask. He pulled out the drawer in which Mumma's body was kept. She looked so peaceful; it made me angry. How could she be OK? How could she leave us without any notice? With her gone, I was lost. I touched Mumma's body. I poked her gently, hoping she would sit up. When she didn't respond, I lay on the floor in a fetal position. I wailed silently and grabbed my chest. The guy asked me to leave.

I was alive but felt dead. Life wasn't supposed to happen this way. Mumma was my best friend. I wanted to run away from everything, especially the aunties. "So what if your Mumma is gone? Think of me as your mom," so many said as I stepped outside the morgue. "Did you take a picture of your mother in the morgue?" Mumma's thrice-divorced bridge friend asked as she massaged my neck. I was so angry that I couldn't think of any responses. "Poor, motherless child," another aunty quipped as she adjusted her Burberry handbag and rubbed my shoulders. "If Dev was still around, he could have supported you. We all need a man. Everything is all on you. Tsk. Tsk."

Dev could have supported *me*? When we were married, and attended social gatherings, Dev touching his collarbones was a secret signal that he wanted me right then. No matter the occasion— birthdays, housewarming, or funerals. There were times he would insist I meet him in a secluded corner or the host's bedroom. I wasn't allowed to make conscious decisions to look like less of what I felt Dev would want to see.

I shut down. I was physically in New Delhi, but I wasn't there. I was an only child, that too a daughter, in the city of Delhi. "A woman can't perform last rites," many mentioned in passing when they came home to pay their respects. One of the aunties, while covering her pixie haircut with a designer, white dupatta, whispered to me, "Your Mumma's soul will not be at peace if you put her body on a pyre. Hindu customs demand that a man must cremate for the soul to get reincarnated. If Dev..." She went on to say more insensitive things, but I walked away.

I put my tears on hold until Naina reached New Delhi.

≈ 3 ≈

It was 10 a.m. when a hand shook me. "Ahana, wake up." It was Naina, clad in a *kurta*—the pink-colored, loose, and collarless shirt that Mumma had gifted her a couple of years ago—and denim capris. She ran her short fingers, each knuckle adorned with a ring, through my hair. She slowly got up from my bed and opened the curtains.

I squinted as the sun stared at me. Somehow, I was in my bedroom. I had no recollection of how I got there or why I had slept in a pair of cotton *salwar kameez*. I had a picture frame, with Mumma's photo in it, resting on my pillow. My pillow was damp. Athena was not in her bed. I rubbed my eyes and stared at Naina.

"When did you get in?"

"Last night."

"No one told me." I looked around for Athena and called out to her.

"I asked Lakshmi not to disturb you and to keep Athena in her room."

"Oh. How was your flight?" Not sure why I was making small talk. This was Naina—the one person, aside from Mumma, who knew about my first crush, kiss, and heartbreak. At thirty-two, she was a lot smarter and unapologetic than I was.

"Why don't you clean up and we'll get some fresh air?" She picked up the picture frame and wiped it with her hands. My tearstains were all over it.

"Can't believe Mumma's pictures are all I have left."

Naina sat down next to me.

I held her tight. "I don't want to meet anyone. I don't want to leave my room."

She kissed my forehead. "You don't have to meet anyone. But you don't have to look like a hobo either. Masi would be so upset." Naina smiled.

She opened one of my closets and pulled out a pair of pastel *salwar kameez*.

I looked at her. I could barely remember where I'd been the night before, but Naina could recollect where I kept my clothes and personal items. She knew I had five closets in my bedroom and the one closest to the window was where I kept my informal, wear-at-home Indian outfits.

15

"Everything is the same. Your study, laptop, clothes, five plants, a place for that pint-sized pooch to sleep and relax, your yoga practice spot...nothing has changed." She sat next to me.

I leaned into her. "Mumma is gone. That's changed."

She wrapped me in her arms and rocked me. "Shhh. We'll get through this together."

As soon as Naina said those words today, a dam broke in my eyes. I tugged at her *kurta*.

"I know, kiddo. It's not right." She pulled out tissues from the box of Kleenex on my nightstand.

"I don't understand how this happened," I sobbed. "Mumma was fine in the morning...."

"I am so sorry, Ahana."

I wiped my face with my hand. "She was asking me to take care of myself. Chutney told me that Mumma had heart troubles. She never told us because she didn't want us to worry."

Naina ran her hands through my hair. "Let it all out."

"She was my strength. She helped me leave Dev. I can't live without Mumma. I don't know what to do. Who will make me hot chocolate when I am hurting? Who will practice yoga with me? With Mumma gone, who will protect me?" Snot mixed with my tears flooded my face. I started heaving. "Ask the visitors to leave, Naina. They will dilute Mumma's smell. Ask them not to touch any of the souvenirs—Mumma likes things in order." I rambled on.

At one point, I woke up to my own snoring. "Sorry."

"What are you sorry for? Take as much rest as you need." Naina massaged my forehead.

"Remember how we would hide in this very room when we were kids?" I played with the corner of her *kurta*.

Naina laughed loudly. "Yeah, because, dork, you wanted to avoid all the cute guys and read a book on your recliner."

For the first time since Mumma's death, I smiled too.

"Remember, I wanted to try out all of your chic clothes on our visit, but you had to be a tall, skinny bitch, didn't ya, sis? And a foot taller than me!" She elbowed me with a smile.

Naina called out to Lakshmi in her accented, broken Hindi, "Ahana baby hungry. Hot chai and grilled cheese sandwich, can I get? Umm, as in milegaa?"

"I don't want to eat anything."

"I know. But if you don't eat or drink something, I can't feed my pear-shaped body either. So make a small sacrifice and eat for your little sister." She pulled at my chin.

When we walked to the lower level of the house where the family room and formal sitting room were located, I noticed there were hundreds of people. Incense. Flowers. Religious music. Strangers weeping and moving in circles like dervishes. I couldn't breathe, so I started to crawl to go back up to my room when Naina whispered, "It's okay. I am with you."

"Don't leave me alone."

She held my hands tight every time an aunty mentioned Dev's name in passing. No one from his family showed up or even called to express their condolences.

Naina stayed by my side when we brought Mumma's ashes home, through all the rituals and prayers, my meltdowns, and even after everyone had left. I shook up the urn with Mumma's ashes close to my ear before we released them in the Yamuna River, but I couldn't hear a thing. I looked at Naina—the idea of being motherless on this vast earth was so lonely and strange to me—some things only a sister can understand.

* * *

Even after a few months of Mumma passing away, I couldn't cope. The sofa in the family room and patio furniture no longer carried my mother's scent—J'ADORE mixed with lavender oil blended with jasmine. All of the summer of 2013, I went through life pretending to be a stranger inside my own body. I made myself forget everything about Mumma that I couldn't bear to remember like hiding in her sari as a little girl, twirling in the backyard, gripping her hand and walking together. I tried to bury those memories. I made myself forget, I thought of every meal, vacation, argument, festival, or unimportant time spent together. But by trying not to remember Mumma, I only remembered her more. I pretended not to feel the pain, but the only thing I felt was pain. I was consumed with how suddenly she was taken away from us. I grew dark on the inside. I had no desire or appetite for anything. I became two women—one who pretended to be OK in front of the world, and the other who cried at night because she missed her mother's voice. My life became all about before and after Mumma's death.

I preferred weekdays to weekends because time didn't stand still then. I spent all my time at work and nagged my boss to put me on more projects. Besides that, I was now spearheading the upcoming Annual Women's Conference in New Orleans. The conference had started as a small idea but escalated into a major event over the months. I was grateful that my suggested theme, *No Excuse*, was receiving global recognition from speakers, anthropologists, nonprofits, feminists, activists, authors, leaders, and female survivors of violence refusing to accept any excuse for rape, woman hitting, acid throwing, and bride burning for dowry.

Mumma was so proud I was trying to help other women, standing up for what I believed in.

After her death, I also volunteered to travel for work. Whatever little time I had between coming back home from work and leaving for it, I spent either running or practicing yoga at the studio close to home. Even though Mumma and I often took yoga classes together, I found solace in returning to the studio alone. The space allowed me to escape the mess of my life.

It was September 2013—monsoons were receding, but Delhi was still hot. Scheduled power outages and a water shortage were still crippling the city. I decided to go for an evening run to avoid the seething temperatures. Running allowed me to blend physical pain with the pain in my heart without any suspicion or apprehension.

I was just about to leave when Mumma's younger sister, Chutney, stopped me in the kitchen, "Ahana, I need to tell you something."

"What, Chutney?" I drank a few sips of water.

"Your mother's last words." Chutney sat on the barstool next to the island table in the kitchen. Mumma, though not the best cook in the world, liked beautiful and big kitchens with modern interiors and bright colors. The kitchen was connected to the patio in our backyard. This was the spot where we often got together as a family or for cocktail parties.

"Why didn't you tell me anything sooner?" I sat next to her.

"Because you weren't ready, *beta*."

"What do you mean?" I untied my ponytail and tied it in a bun.

Chutney took a sip of my water. "I am not trying to guilt-trip you. But you are the only one your dad has left."

"What are you saying?" I didn't move.

She bit her lower lip. "You need to get help for yourself."

My eyes filled up, but I didn't cry. I pushed the island table. "Why, did Dad say something?"

She threw her hands in the air. "No, that's the thing with both you and him. You guys like to internalize everything. You bury yourself in your work."

I stood up abruptly. I didn't even realize when I raised my voice. It was loud enough that Lakshmi, who was in the adjoining room—an extension of the kitchen where the big dishes were hand-washed and dried—came running. She asked whether I was OK. I was so upset that I waved at Lakshmi and asked her to continue with her work.

"Are you blaming me for being depressed?" I wiped my tear-stained cheeks with the back of my hand.

Chutney caught me by my wrists. "Ahana, my child." She kissed my forehead. "How can you even think like that?"

"It's because you..." I tried to interrupt.

"You have been through hell this past year." She ran her hands through my hair. "You are stronger than most people I know, *beta*. But it's not fair to you to put so much pressure on your own self. You go for late night runs in a place like Delhi. You either leave for work by 6 a.m. or end up taking late night yoga classes. It seems like you don't care about yourself any longer."

"What kind of help?" I moved her hands.

She hesitated, "Just talk to someone," and looked nervously at me.

I pretended not to understand. "I do talk to you, a few of my friends, and Naina."

Cupping my face in her hands, she whispered, "We all love you, but none of us are truly qualified to help you. We are biased. None of us can see you in pain, so we agree with whatever you say or want to do."

I asked Lakshmi to bring my running shoes. I wanted to get out of the house and pound my stress on the streets of New Delhi.

Chutney followed behind. "This can't be how you live."

I said nothing and tied my shoelaces.

She was stubborn. "It's been a few months since your mother passed away."

I blurted out, "I'll think about it." I am not sure why I said that because I had no concrete intention of seeing a therapist or joining a counseling group. But also, I didn't want to take Chutney for granted. She had left her own house and moved into my parents' place to help us settle into a world without Mumma. She had taken a sabbatical from her high-profile job so she could help us heal from the big mess in our lives.

"Good." She kissed my forehead. "If not for anyone else, do this for your mumma. For your dad, who has already lost his wife and can't see his daughter suffer."

"What were Mumma's last words?" I washed my hands and tugged at Chutney's *dupatta*.

Chutney gently massaged my head, "I worry about Ahana. When will that child of mine be happy again?"

I ran five extra miles that evening and pounded the streets hard. Chutney's words kept playing inside my head. At the seven-mile mark, I stopped. Something inside of me shifted. I told myself that I needed to stop continuously fixing my feelings and my problems. I had to step up and take charge of my life. I had to get out of New Delhi. No, India. In India, people knew my family and my history.

* * *

When I reached my office the next day, I walked straight to my boss, Ms. Shelly Roy. "I know I said I didn't want to go, but I am interested in representing Freedom Movement at the conference next autumn in New Orleans, after all."

Ms. Roy pulled off her glasses. "I am happy to hear that you changed your mind. Let me see what I can do."

"Please," I begged her.

"I will talk to the board of directors at our quarterly meeting next week and get the OK on the budget." Ms. Roy smiled at me. "This conference is important to women all over the world. It was a shame thinking you were the one organizing but not attending the event. The conference is turning out to be bigger than we had anticipated, Ahana."

After Mumma's death, I'd told Ms. Roy that I didn't want to travel to New Orleans. When Ms. Roy had tried to coax me, I remained adamant. "I don't want to leave my father alone in India." Being Indian, she understood my sense of familial responsibility.

But, in truth, a big part of me was scared to be in New Orleans again—Mumma and I had planned to take this journey together. I didn't have the strength to go through with it alone, and open raw wounds. I had such fond memories of spending my summer vacation at Naina's place in the Garden District of New Orleans. The oak tree in the garden: I read the Nancy Drew series in its shade while Naina wrote notes to her boyfriend. There was a long porch from the main gate to the entrance of the house where Naina and I ran endlessly. Because there were tall fences built all around the house, our mothers never had to fear for our safety, so they let us be. There was a swimming pool in the backyard where Mumma served us lemonade right after we got out of the water. I had never seen so many trees in anyone's house. Masi would cook her saffron-layered chicken and rice *biryani, kebabs*, and local NOLA specialties like Jambalaya and shrimp étouffée for us. Mumma would always joke that Masi got the cooking skills while Mumma got the whiskey skills. I loved sitting in horse carriages and taking a tour of the French Quarter when we were kids. Naina and I ran around the sculptures in Jackson Square. Palm readers, artists, musicians, and fortunetellers would line the park outside Jackson Square. Me dragging Naina to the historical and cultural sites as we got older. And Naina conning me into going to clubs and bars in exchange for her time spent at museums.

While I never enjoyed cooking, I did appreciate gourmet food. I fell in love with shrimp po'boys, andouille gumbo, shrimp étouffée, jambalaya, and the Southern hospitality. Mumma, Masi, Naina, and I would participate in walking food tours in the French Quarter. Naina and I would stuff ourselves with beignets and hot chocolate at Cafe Du Monde. Naina once took a picture, with powdered sugar on the tip of her nose, and at the back of the printed copy, she wrote, "Sugar. Gimme sugar."

Another gem in the French Quarter—my literary shrine where I spent many days—was Faulkner House Books on Pirates Alley. Mumma, an avid reader and traveler, had introduced me to it. I remember her dragging me to Faulkner House Books and telling me that it was the former home of William Faulkner, which now served as a shop selling classic and local interest books. Friendly staff, great selection of local authors and historical books; I always found an excuse to spend time in this place where novelist William Faulkner wrote his first novel.

The music, the history, the food, the books, the culture, they all spoke to me. I felt like I belonged in New Orleans.

Mumma and Masi would tease me when I was in high school, "Apply to colleges in New Orleans and find a Louisiana boy, *beta*." But I didn't, and those early memories felt more and more distant, as if they'd happened to someone else. I looked at the old pictures and tried hard to be excited about going back to those old streets, but I couldn't feel any exhilaration. I was an adult with no mother to show her around.

* * *

After talking to Ms. Roy and spending the day at work, I went for a yoga class in the evening. On my way back, as my driver Baburao was pulling the car from the parking lot, my phone rang. It was Naina.

"Howdy!" Naina chirped in a Southern accent.

"Hi, sis." I untied my ponytail.

"Whatchya doing?" Though born and raised in New Orleans, Naina had moved to New York City when she started college, went to medical school, did a four-year residency, got board certified, and eventually started her private practice.

"Just got done with yoga class."

"Whoa! 9:30 p.m. on a Friday? Dude, that's messed up."

"I am too old for late night partying." I readjusted my glasses.

"Sheesh, you are thirty-three, not eighty-two, Grandma. When you are in NOLA, I've got to take you out, girl."

I laughed with a little dishonesty, but it was because I knew where this conversation was headed.

"How are you? How is Masi? And what news of Josh?"

"Mom is busy preparing a menu of all the things she wants to feed you next year when you visit." Naina let out a sinister laugh. "As for Josh Rossi, he's doing well. His friends are busy planning his bachelor party a year ahead of time."

"Are you nervous?"

"No, ma'am. I am hiring a stripper for mine, so how can I be a hypocrite?" She spoke with such ease and honesty. "How are you? Don't give me the shitty version that you tell others, Ahana."

"I am OK. Waiting for Baburao to bring the car. Dad was supposed to pick me up."

"What's going on?"

"Dad and I had dinner plans. But, once again, he forgot."

"Did you call him?"

"What's the point? He'll apologize, but nothing will change. I wonder if he doesn't like to hang out with me."

Speaking with the authority of a psychiatrist, Naina said, "Your dad loves you."

"I know that. But I need him to be a little more present." I thought about my conversation with Chutney and confessed to Naina, "I am worried that my dad doesn't want to hang out with me because I am a reminder of how small our family has suddenly become."

She remained patient with me.

I sighed. "It's like I've lost both my parents after Mumma's death."

"I am listening."

Perhaps it was the clarity post yoga and meditation class that caused my emotions to unfurl. "I want to run away from everything, Naina. From people who know too much about my life and ones who carefully inspect my face in the hope that it'll reveal unshared details of my experiences." Somewhere along the line, in being a wife and a daughter focused on keeping everyone happy, I had forgotten what I liked. I felt as if it was too late for me even to ask myself what I wanted.

"Stop being so responsible all the time." She spoke softly. "This isn't healthy. You are doing yoga too often, not meeting with anyone, and there is a panicked strain in your voice. I am worried about you. And what's with all the crazy running? I've been keeping an eye on your FitBit statistics."

A wave of nausea hit me. I rubbed the empty space on my left hand where my three-carat, princess cut, solitaire diamond, platinum wedding ring used to be. I started to breathe heavily. On some weekends, after brunch, Dev would make me participate in role-playing games. In the very beginning of our marriage, there were times when I had tried to derive pleasure from the attention because I was his wife. But that feeling was short-lived. After forced sex, I would shower and go for long runs without my wedding ring. The open air where I didn't belong to anyone—I liked it. Running made me feel safe even though late nights in New Delhi were risky. On some days, any place felt more sheltered than my own house.

"You must take care of yourself in all of this, Ahana."

"I am trying." I sat on the chaise lounge in the studio's lobby facing a Buddha statue so no one could see me fight my angst.

Naina spoke loudly. "Bullshit! Your marriage with Dev ended because he was an asshole. Masi died suddenly. Why are you hell-bent on denying yourself any iota of kindness?" Naina rarely could keep it together when she was upset.

"You know that I have spoken with my boss. If the board approves the budget, I will be in NOLA for the conference."

"Great, but NOLA doesn't happen until next year. Honey, you still need to see a therapist." Naina never minced her words. They were like an arrow with a purpose.

"I have you."

Naina explained that even though she was a psychiatrist, we were too close for her to remain objective with me. "The conference planning and dealing with violence against women will make your anxiety even worse."

"I can't, Naina." I was hesitant.

"Why not?"

"Remember where I live?" The problem was Dad's position in society and our well-known family, and because I didn't want to expose myself to New Delhi. "It's very likely any therapist here would spread rumors, even if it was completely unprofessional to do so, and the gossip would be so rich that everyone would forgive him or her for it."

Naina didn't push me too hard, but she told me about some online resources I could consider. Her mentor was moderating one of the online counseling websites.

When I got home that night, after we had eaten a dinner of grilled fish, gourd soup with fennel, and cucumber salad, and everyone had gone to bed, I sat in my pajamas with Athena in my lap. *Should I do this?* I asked my sweet-tempered companion. Athena barked, and I took that as a yes.

I surfed a few sites for online counseling until I found the one moderated by Naina's mentor. Something inside me uncramped as I browsed through each page, and I bookmarked the site. I don't know what it was, but I started to feel a tiny bit of relief.

Naina knew me better than anyone else, as usual.

⚡ 4 ⚡

I still wonder how the universe caught two men from Louisiana and sent them into my life around the same time.

The wounded seek out the wounded—that's how I met Jay Dubois, my comrade in the online therapy group when I was at the lowest point in my life.

Before logging in for the first time, I sat down and meditated for a few minutes to calm my nerves. I felt nauseated—the way I'd felt after seeing Mumma's body in the morgue. It hit me, all over again, that I was a motherless woman. I called Lakshmi through the intercom in my room and requested her to make me chamomile tea. "Also, please take Athena out for a walk."

"Wokay *didi*. Pleasing to go," she responded in an eager tone and her adorable broken English.

I found out there were twelve of us in the group: three men and nine women, including the moderator, who was Naina's mentor. She suggested we could use apps for texting, video chatting, voice messaging, and audio messaging to communicate with each other.

We all signed confidentiality agreements. But it felt lonely opening my life to strangers, clad in my pajamas while sipping chamomile tea. When and how did my life turn this way? I was the one with straight A's, who had won a scholarship to the university in London and married the most desirable guy in New Delhi. My life used to be perfect, and then it all turned to ashes.

People in the group had lost boyfriends, babies, parents, and siblings. I didn't want to be around so many sad stories. The tone was intense. It reminded me of the times when I would visit my parents and my dad would be in the middle of some ridiculously noisy project—I wanted to leave, but I couldn't pull myself away. So I would rub the corner of Mumma's shirt or *kurta*.

I realized I was the only Indian in the group. The Americans seemed to be most open about their lives. Interestingly, every single member chose to introduce him- or herself via group texting. No videos, no voices. Once there were only two of us left in the round of introductions, I bit my cuticles. I grew up in a culture where we didn't share our problems with outsiders. How much was OK to share? I wrote something and erased it. Then wrote again. It seemed like Jay Dubois heard my quandary. He typed, "Looks like I am not the only one drunk typing on this Saturday night, so thank you. I'll go next."

25

I started to laugh and brought my palms together, "God, thank you."

"Hi, all. I am Jay Dubois. You all are very brave to be seeking help. Like all of you, I lost a loved one suddenly, mother in my case, and now can't make sense of my life."

I wiped my glasses and reread his post. He didn't share any specific details about himself or his mother. But when our moderator pestered him about his whereabouts, he grudgingly admitted that he was from Louisiana but called NYC home. His mother had passed away a few months before Mumma.

Next was my turn. I looked over my shoulder and then typed. "Hi, I am.... My name is...Ahana." My stomach hurt. I fought a strange sense of suffocation. I looked at Mumma's photograph on my nightstand.

"Hi, Ahana." The other members and moderator typed back. I could feel many eyes virtually stare at me. I didn't know what to write. *Hi, I am here because I lost my mother and divorced my husband the same year and now happiness is unable to find me.* I poured myself a glass of water from the pitcher on my nightstand. The cream-colored crocheted doily covering it—Mumma had bought it for me in Singapore. I rubbed the doily as though it were a lamp and Mumma would appear and help me.

I took a deep breath. Maybe it was the realization of my anonymity in this medium, but I just started to type. "Do you guys feel broken too, lost, and empty on the inside? Like nothing is worth living for? Have you ever wondered why so many terrible people get to live but the one you loved, died? How is any of this fair?!?!"

I let the text sit in the message window, unfinished and unsent, and wiped my tears with the corner of my nightshirt. It felt cathartic to add a voice to my feelings instead of tiptoe around my agony. I started to erase my message. But the chat technology was new to me; I hit *send* by mistake.

My face turned red. I floundered around the website, wanting to delete my post, but I couldn't erase any of it. I screamed softly, *Mumma, help me!* I took off my glasses and threw them on the bed. I started to pace up and down my room. I kept alternating between the chair in the study and the recliner by the bookshelf. Anything to be away from my laptop and the new world where I had started with a mistake.

I heard a series of ping sounds coming from my laptop. I pulled my hair into a bun, put on my glasses, and collapsed on my bed. I didn't know what to do so I blabbered mea culpas. "Sorry. Really sorry. This whole faceless-forum is new to me. I should have just asked about the weather!" After I hit send, I hit my forehead. *I should have asked about the weather. What am I, British? What the hell is wrong with me? People are sharing personal details and I had nothing better to say.* I missed Mumma more than ever. She knew appropriate words for every occasion.

I walked toward the large French windows and drew open the curtains, searching for stars, hoping to get a glimpse of my mother in the sky. I walked back to my bed and covered half of my body. I was ready to call it a night when there was a ping again.

It was like Jay waited to do what needed to be done to make me feel welcomed. *"I'm sick of just liking people. I wish to God I could meet somebody I could respect."* He wrote these lines in his first direct message to me.

I slid out from under my covers and sat up. I introduced myself to a perfect stranger by typing two words real fast. "JD Salinger?"

"Yeah. You a fan too?" There was a grin emoji at the end of his message.

"If reading *The Catcher in the Rye* ten times qualifies me for one," I wrote back promptly. I hadn't felt excitement in a while. I couldn't believe I was talking to someone who lived in the city where writer J. D. Salinger was born. I felt a smile lurk at the corner of my lips.

"I like it when somebody gets excited about something. It's nice," he replied. It was another line from *The Catcher in the Rye.*

Jay ended the message with, "Ahana, we don't know each other. But I do know how difficult it is to open to strangers. I am a misfit in my life and where I come from."

While I didn't know what he was referring to, I could relate to the feeling. I wanted to help Jay. The loneliness in his voice was discernible.

"Thank you."

"I do hope we can become friends one day," he typed back, ending the sentence with a wink.

I didn't even want to know his story. I didn't want to attach myself to him or his life. But I knew one thing: Jay made me feel at ease. I posted a three-line coherent message to the chat group about Mumma and my journey with grief, and then signed off.

* * *

I met New Orleans-based Rohan Brady because of my boss Ms. Shelly Roy. She insisted. "You have to create a social media profile for the upcoming conference. You are the face of our *No Excuse* campaign. You are the voice behind women not accepting violence."

"Me? But...why?" I was still feeling flummoxed by the online exposure. I had overdone it on the therapy forum and was still feeling embarrassed, and now Ms. Roy was telling me to create a social media profile. Me? Someone who was totally inept with online communication. I confessed to Ms. Roy that I had no social media profiles.

She got up from her seat. "Ahana, this is 2013! How can you not have a social media presence? You must know social media is important in today's world. When companies put their money into the kind of event we're organizing, they want a human connection to tell the story. The face behind women's empowerment. The face behind social change. The face behind ending women's violence and not accepting excuses." She slammed a pen on her table. "How could we have not talked about this?"

"You really think so highly of personal social media accounts, Ms. Roy? I think people share their thirty seconds of glorious moments on social media and make it sound like their entire life is flawless." I adjusted my glasses as I presented my case, which didn't even make sense inside my own head. I knew the Arabs had successfully used digital media to exercise freedom of speech and as a space for civic engagement in the 2012 Arab uprisings, but I was scared to put myself out there. Honestly, every step of making myself a public persona was fraught with the terror that Dev would show up and malign it.

She sighed. "This conference brings together the most unlikely people in the best way possible." Ms. Roy sat on the edge of her table with her glasses perched on the tip of her nose. "You know what you have to do if you want to continue to lead this conference."

She made a hell of a threat over something minor. Yes, people called her the dragon-lady boss because at 5' 2", 68 kilos, and with a penchant for shimmering dresses two inches above her knees, Ms. Roy chose to hiss at people across the hallway as opposed to walk up to them and talk. You could barely see her neck and whatever little was visible, she covered it with a thick, yellow golden chain. She had her quirks, but she had always been supportive of me. What was going on? I didn't know and couldn't afford to care. The upcoming conference in NOLA was the only thing I had going for myself in my life. I was intent on keeping it. I sighed, "Fine. I will do so today," and walked out of her office.

I didn't know where to begin, so I set up a meeting with the director of brand and content strategy Peter D'souza.

Peter ran a search and pointed at a picture on his laptop screen of a blue-eyed man with a big smile.

"Who is this?"

"Rohan Brady."

I adjusted my glasses.

"He is important to us, so connect with him over social media."

I sat confused.

Peter continued, "Rohan works in public relations as the vice president of Client Services at Everyman PR Agency based out of New Orleans. He and his team are handling the public relations aspect of the Annual Women's Rights Conference as part of their corporate social responsibility."

"We have Everyman PR doing publicity for a women's event? Are you serious?"

I moved closer to the computer. Rohan's hair was perfect, thick, black and drowned in mousse. He looked about 6' 5" or 6'7". I pointed toward the screen. "Did one of our interns hire him? I mean, look at him—typical frat boy you see in English movies. I can practically smell his body spray transmitting through the computer screen." I took a deep breath and looked closely.

"Don't be fooled by profile pictures on social media, Ahana. People are brands and they have their own strategy for what they share. This guy, Rohan, is considered a genius in his field. Brady became a vice president at his firm before he turned thirty. And he's won like a billion awards."

"What happened to the Chicago-based firm that offered to help us?"

"Their management changed." Peter sighed. "Public relations jobs are like revolving doors."

* * *

I felt wrecked by the time I got home. I was tired from being two women all day. At dinner, Dad didn't say a word and Chutney tried to cut the tension by regurgitating unhumorous details of her bureaucratic workday now that her sabbatical was over. I excused myself and went up to my room. Athena followed behind.

As I changed into my pajamas and sat with a book in my recliner, I saw my laptop peeking out from behind a couch pillow. I dragged it into my lap. There was a message alert—Jay. I remembered my humiliation the night before in the forum and ignored it; instead, I sat at my desk and started researching Rohan.

Thirty-five-year-old, blue-eyed Rohan Brady certainly seemed like a character whom women seemed to love. His outlandishly way-too-confident social media posts and frat uniform—OK, pastel shirts and trousers—made me cringe. "Lakshmi, please mint tea," I ordered over the intercom. I stretched my arms over my head. Rohan handled the alcohol and cigarette clients for his company, which meant many of his pictures posted online were taken at parties and events. *Does he ever sleep?* He paraded his chiseled jaw and the dimple on his chin in every profile picture on social media. "Who dat? Who dat? Who dat say dey gonna beat dem Saints?" he chanted and ranted all over social platforms. Rohan shamelessly attributed his habit of drinking Sazerac, a whiskey-cocktail, to being a New Orleans native and a Saints fan. I didn't grow up in America, but my understanding of the frat culture was that it's associated with hyper-masculinity and the related violence against women. I dreaded interacting with this guy.

I got up from my desk and called out to Lakshmi, "Why is the tea taking so long?"

"Sorry, *didi*. Coming wonly now." Lakshmi entered my room with a nod and big smile.

"Thank you." I gave her a set of multi-colored kohl pencil liners I had picked up at the mall. "Share them with your daughter." I smiled at her. She shook her head like a pendulum and said a billion thank yous.

I sipped on the tea and continued my investigation. Party animal Rohan lived in the Central Business District. I texted Naina and enquired about Rohan's neighborhood. She said, "Dude, I have lots of friends in CBD. Fancy area with bars and restaurants nearby. Why do you ask?" I told her I was doing research for my upcoming conference. She said. "You'd love it there. Most buildings there have art, rooftop hot tubs, a fancy gym, a business center…."

Rohan was a complete Southerner when it came to his charm. None of the women in his social media universe seemed to mind when he flirted with them. If anything, Ms. Pamela, a blonde supermodel from Miami, sent him a tweet with kisses.

Rohan wrote back. "Where ya been, gorgeous?"

She responded with, "I feel so lonely. The world has crushed my 'big' spirit."

Rohan egged her on. "I'm never more than a single tweet away, so tell me what's got you down?"

Ms. Pamela signed off her tweets with "xoxo," but I chose to read it as "I am a ho."

I sank in my chair: Was I really stuck organizing a feminist conference with a seeming womanizer and misogynist? No one at work saw it except me—yet it's what his social media profile said about him, and the message was negative. *No Excuse* was about giving women a voice and fighting violence against them. *Is Freedom Movement even devoted to the cause?*

Perhaps Ms. Roy was pursuing initiatives that *looked* good on paper, but their success was questionable. I, like many others, suspected that Ms. Roy was a social climber, who took the job to rub elbows with socialites and Bollywood celebrities at fundraisers. It was about the status, not about the mission.

There was no way out because Ms. Roy had given me an ultimatum. So I suspected that Everyman PR was simply the lowest bidder for conference publicity. Frankly, I was a tad bit curious to understand the hypocrisy of a sexist pig collecting money to help put together a women's conference, but I guessed I would find out soon enough.

* * *

I spent the rest of the week trying to schedule a meeting with Rohan, but I only managed to speak to his assistant, Crystal. I was annoyed at everyone at work, and perhaps because I was feeling more raw than usual at the end of the day, I sat on the couch and logged in again into our therapy forum.

"Look who is here." Jay posted on the message board after he saw I was online.

I said a hello to the members who were online.

"Somebody has been busy." He sent me a direct message with a grin emoji at the end.

"Haha, no, I am just tired."

"You do know that this therapy group is a safe space where we can all help each other out, right?"

"Thank you, I know. Long day at work. How have you been?"

"Let's see…. I have dealt with my annoying landlady. My dad is getting shit-faced with some neighbors, and I hurt my back. You do the math."

I didn't understand half of Jay's Americanisms, and I didn't want to sound stupid, so I Googled what "shit-faced" meant and wrote back. "Why don't you move to a different locality?"

"Locality? You mean neighborhood?" he wrote back promptly.

"Yes, neighborhood." I rolled my eyes.

"I live in Bushwick, Brooklyn. It's a neighborhood for working class people. Brownstones here are cheap and my father has a good living arrangement with his old landlady. In exchange for lower rents, the woman wants me to do gardening and cook for her three days a week. Money is tight right now."

"Oh, I didn't know." Jay's honesty *seemed* refreshing; in the Indian culture, I didn't know many who shared much personal information.

I exchanged pleasantries with a few women on the message board, tiptoeing around their sorrows. Jay barely commented on any chat threads. I noticed he rarely participated in open group chats, aside from assigned therapy hours. Most of us were connected on social media by now. I observed that, like me, Jay didn't share any profile picture on any of his accounts.

Lakshmi came up to my room to announce that Mom and Dad's friends, the Khuranas, were over to say a hello. *10:30 p.m. on a weeknight without calling first. Only in New Delhi.*

"Sorry, guys; I have to go."

"Everything OK?" He sent me a direct message.

"My parents' friends are over to express their condolences."

"You don't seem thrilled. What's going on?"

I took a deep breath. The group and everybody in it was supposed to be a safe space, right? So, I typed, "While I appreciate the support, I mean, how can anyone heal if you are constantly reminded of what is wrong with your life? All I want to do is hide from all of them."

"I get it. When my mother died, I grew too numb emotionally to even feel any physical pain for days. I just seemed to sleep more, perhaps to fight off the lingering sadness and give myself my energy back. I hated being around people."

He understands. I said a bye to him and changed into a pair of jeans and T-shirt and went into the living room to meet the Khuranas. I hated the way people looked at me—the divorced, motherless woman. Mrs. Khurana, with a glass of gin and tonic in her hands, told me how her widowed nephew in California would be a good guy for me to meet. I looked at Chutney and rolled my eyes. Apparently, I was worth only divorced or widowed men. I wanted to get away from the unpleasant conversations and back to my therapy group where I could talk about Mumma.

After the Khuranas left, I went up to my room to see if anyone was online. Jay had left me a message. "Can we exchange email ids? Our chats will feel less clinical. :)"

"Sure. You can reach me here: ahana@gmail.com," I wrote back.

"Don't worry; I am not some creepy guy who is going to stalk you," he replied right away.

"I never said anything of the sort." I messaged him back via direct messaging on our forum.

"Silence has the deepest voice."

Next morning, after finishing my yoga and shower, when I checked my emails, I saw a message from Jay. "This is the last picture I have of my mom."

His mom had dark hair, green eyes, and olive skin. I replied. "Where is your family from?"

"All over. Greek, French, Italian...we didn't leave much of Europe. He added a smiley at the end.

"Your mother was beautiful."

"The picture was taken two weeks before she passed away."

"I am so sorry. What happened?" I could hear my palpitations.

"My mom was walking home on her way back from work. It was Friday evening; my parents were expecting company. Mom was holding a large cake in her hand and perhaps got distracted and didn't realize that she was in the blind spot of an SUV."

"Did she get hit by the car?" I cringed thinking about it, and then cringed realizing how quickly I was getting comfortable talking about our dead mothers.

"Yeah, the guy ran over her. She died on the spot."

I tried to keep my shock under check, but I started to sob. I threw up in the garbage can next to the couch. My stomach hurt. Athena started to bark, so I picked her up in my arms. I patted her and got up to drink some water, which was five feet away on my nightstand right next to Mumma's picture. I held Mumma's photograph and broke down again.

After I had washed my face and chewed on fennel seeds to get rid of nausea, I wrote to Jay. "I am so sorry. I know what the sudden loss of a parent can do to us."

He didn't write back. I tried to reach out to him several times, but there was no response. I went to his social media profile, but there were no updates there either. Jay never gave out his phone number, so I couldn't call. I wanted to help. I knew what it was like to carry pain in the heart all the time without being able to articulate it.

I figured that, like me, he'd come around again when he felt better.

* * *

After trying and failing on several occasions to connect with Rohan Brady over the phone, I wrote, deleted, rewrote, and finally sent a message to him, introducing myself. It was late Friday evening in India, Friday morning in America. Maybe that's why Rohan wrote back right away. It was a surprisingly nice email, saying he had heard about me and that he was looking forward to working together on the conference. He ended the note with, "Congratulations on being included in the 40 under 40 in the *Women's Herald*."

Yes, *Women's Herald* was considered the equivalent of *The Economist* in the space of women's issues and empowerment. I was amazed Rohan had even heard of it.

"Rohan? That's an Indian name," I wrote to him.

"It's also Irish," he replied immediately.

"I didn't know that."

"I expanded your knowledge-base. You're welcome, :)" he wrote back.

Right when I was thinking that his message was conceited, he sent a note, "I am part Indian, part Irish."

"Your parents have a common enemy," I replied.

"The colonial Brits, you mean?" Rohan responded with a smiley emoticon at the end of his message.

Not everyone understood my sense of humor. Surprisingly, Rohan did in our first interaction.

"Touché."

"I pride my obsession with *paneer* just as much as I pride my thirst for alcohol, loyalty to the New Orleans Saints, and disgust for baseball." There was another happy face at the end of his message.

I rolled my eyes. *Wow, this guy really likes his happy faces. And he is comparing cottage cheese to booze to describe his roots!* "Great! Let me know what's the best place to send you the list of speakers I have so far."

"Take a moment to slow down."

"I am not sure I understand."

"You can send me the deliverables on Monday. It's Friday evening for ya in New Delhi, right? Don't you have plans for tonight?"

"What do you know about Delhi nightlife?"

"My mother was from Mumbai, so I have traveled to plenty of cities in India, madam. I know what clubbing is to Mumbai, house parties with bonfire are to New Delhi. I know there are tons of pretty Indian faces at these parties—that's the reason the social media hashtag, #whatsnottolike, came into existence." There was a wink at the end of his message.

That's it. Total frat boy. I'd pinned him correctly. I loathed that he flirted with me, but we had to work together.

"Let me know where I should send you the list," I wrote, and logged out without saying a bye or fully comprehending what it was about Rohan that irked me. Maybe the charm felt too familiar and reminded me of Dev? When Dev was still pursuing me, he had walked up to me during our annual college dance and said, "Of all the faces on campus, my eyes are fixated on the prettiest one! Dance with me." Next day, the word spread to every college in Delhi University's North Campus that Dev Khanna was turned down by some tall girl. Dev Khanna was someone everyone in New Delhi said a *yes* to.

≉ 5 ≉

Two days after I had connected with Rohan, Jay reached out to me. He was in his garden about 4:30 p.m. Eastern Standard Time, thrilled about some new seeds arriving. "They won't be peonies—Mom's favorite flowers were peonies," he had written. "My mother would say, 'Peonies provide the awe and wonder that only a seasonal flower can—because we wait most of the year just to catch a glimpse of the local crop for a few days.'"

I had come home from work early that day. Lakshmi had given me a hot oil head massage. I was about to turn off my electronic items and take a hot shower to get dressed for the first fundraiser for the conference. But instead, I found myself chatting with Jay and not asking about his sudden disappearance from our chat.

"I can feel the presence of my mother around me. After chatting with you a couple of days ago, that feeling became more intense."

I dissolved on the couch in my room. "You believe that our loved ones hang around after their deaths?"

He wrote, "I think we should trust our senses and heart when it comes to these things. I don't think the big question of life and death is unanswerable. The connection will always be there. If you see signs about your mother's presence, those encounters are a way of saying she will still be around so you needn't worry about that."

"I didn't think most people believe in the beyond." I pulled out a purple evening gown from my wardrobe and paired it with the diamond hoop earrings Mumma had gifted me when I joined Freedom Movement. With Mumma gone, every time I needed to feel closer to her, I wore something that she had bought for me, or used one of her accessories.

"I am not most people." He made a smiley.

I didn't know what to write.

He wrote, "You there?"

I played with the earrings. Jay was the only person who believed that I could feel my mumma and that the experience overwhelmed me. He was the only man I knew who was so open about his feelings.

"Stop doubting yourself just because a lot of people want to tell you that you're imagining things or whatever. I feel this is completely natural and part of our human senses to figure out the universe."

"Thanks for saying that. How did you know I needed to hear those exact words today?" I replied and started to fuss over Athena.

"It's our connection."

I was aware that while I was decorating one woman for the fundraiser, the other one wanted to curl up and listen to Jay. "My mom could do more tequila shots than Dad and I combined, Ahana. She taught me to smell spices and taste flavors. When I was a little boy, my mom took me grocery shopping with her every Friday. We would bake cakes together every Sunday. There was nothing my mother wouldn't add bacon and butter to. Even the greens in our house were sinfully delicious. I get my love of hot peppers from my mother. The more I cook, the closer I feel to her."

Ahh, no wonder he shares mostly pictures of food and flowers on social media, I thought to myself.

Jay, like me, was an only child. "As Salinger says, 'Mothers are all slightly insane.'" I ended with a smiley and picked up my handbag.

I felt the universe had opened the door to a new friend in my life. I was sharing personal details with a man I didn't know well when I was depressed, and wanting to keep my emotional struggles a secret from those close to me.

* * *

At the fundraiser at Hyatt Regency, one of Delhi's leading hotels, many socialites showed up in their designer outfits and luxurious, chauffeur-driven cars. We had picked this venue to raise funds for *No Excuse* because it was in Delhi's central business district, a twenty-minute drive from Indira Gandhi International airport and ten minutes from the embassies, corporations, and shopping hubs.

Ms. Roy schmoozed all the bigwigs of New Delhi in her sequined, backless gown. She complimented my strapless gown and open-toed heels. "Classy and conservative, Ahana. Like your diamond hoop earrings."

Champagne. Diamonds. Gourmet finger foods—some imported from New Zealand and Japan—served by waiters in white gloves and red turbans. Conversations about shopping in Milan and summer homes in Tuscany felt like a noose around my neck. She introduced me as the face of *No Excuse*.

The press had a busy night, but I loathed the limelight. "Violence against women and girls is a grave violation of human rights." I looked at the two dozen reporters taking notes. "Its impact ranges from immediate to long-term multiple physical, sexual, and mental consequences for women and girls, including death. It negatively affects women's general wellbeing and prevents women from fully participating in society."

The conference was expanding—the scope was constantly being pushed wider and wider, reaching for higher targets and more organizations. And that was Ms. Roy's fault, because she was a "status-seeker," and I kept acquiescing because I am a woman who can't say no. I couldn't say no to Dev. I couldn't say no to Mumma.

I finished the interview only to find at least a dozen women with plunging necklines and Cartier wedding rings trying to probe my personal life. None of them asked about *No Excuse*. A few, in their drunken stupor, enquired about Mardi Gras in NOLA and whether I was going to attend it while I was there for the conference. Mrs. Singh of *House of Silk* with her breast implants and poorly executed rhinoplasty had asked me in a hoarse voice, "What's your story? How did you get involved in fighting violence against women?" Another woman whispered, "She is Dev Khanna's ex-wife."

I suspected that Ms. Roy was letting me lead the growing conference because my name—and even the hint of scandal around it—had some attention-getting cachet. It hurt a lot. While I knew there were other women out there in a similar boat, New Delhi didn't allow me the freedom to speak up, which added to my brokenness. Nothing in New Delhi was safe or private. My past wouldn't let me move forward.

I was relieved to be going to America because it meant I would be putting half of the planet between myself and Dev. I was afraid of my worst fears and handling them without Mumma. Lo and behold, they came true: Dev was drinking whiskey, surrounded by a group of older women, all paying attention to every single word that came out of his mouth. The hair at the back of my neck stood up. I remembered when I had decided to switch careers—go from investment banking to work for Freedom Movement, Dev had ridiculed my decision. Mumma stood by me. "Change is the only constant, *beta*. Do what feels right in your heart."

She even told Dev to shut up. Indian moms-in-law are extremely accommodating and respectful of their sons-in-law, but when he mocked me at a party for quitting my cushy job in finance, she stepped in. I quietly walked out of the get-together and sat in the gazebo.

Mumma showed up. "If your compassion doesn't include you, then it's not true compassion, *beta*."

I hugged her and wailed until my bones ached. I didn't hold back my tears or words.

While Mumma was the reason I fought for my dignity and asked Dev for a divorce, I wish she had taught me to stand up for myself instead of becoming my voice.

When we love someone, the memories we make with them are treasures. But when someone hurts us and breaks our heart, all the memories about them become nightmares.

Dev started to walk in my direction. I froze. He tapped his collarbones with his thumb and let out a sinister smile. I almost threw up. Seeing Dev and not having Mumma around made me feel powerless. Seeing Dev and finding my body respond to his signal, even if unwillingly, made me feel hopeless. *What are you, Pavlov's dog, Ahana?* I clenched my left fist.

Dev must have been less than a foot away when my phone pinged and broke the spell. It was a message from Jay. "I spent last Saturday at a nursery in Coney Island. Want to see what I did?"

"I am so happy to hear from you!!!" I wrote back with tears in my eyes and a smile on my face. I preferred talking to Jay rather than to the whole group because he was good at keeping track of my schedule. Plus, it helped that he was always available to chat when I needed to talk to someone. He had remembered I would be at the fundraiser and probably bored.

"Glad I could make your day. :)" Jay wrote back.

That was the first time I ended my message with three hearts.

Dev suddenly showed up from behind and whispered, "You're making it all up, Ahana. You enjoyed it." Even before I could turn around, he walked away. I was so rattled that I stood behind a large plant, hoping nobody would notice me. Wishful thinking. Ms. Roy spotted me and waved. "Ahana, I need you to come and meet Mr. and Mrs. Diwan." Once I was closer, she whispered, "They own several hotels in the South Extension area and Faridabad. They like to support faces like yours. Let's get you in front of them."

I couldn't believe Ms. Roy.

She rolled her eyes. "You are intelligent and capable, but it doesn't hurt that you are good-looking. It brings us money." She sipped her champagne and introduced me to the Diwans. Mrs. Asha Diwan must have worn a five-carat solitaire diamond pendant. I assumed that she would only talk about their yacht trips in the Mediterranean. But it turned out that she had survived an abusive marriage and met her second husband, Mr. Diwan, when she was helping build homes in Nepal. She shared a fierce passion for supporting women. She was a graduate of the London School of Economics; we discussed in depth our respective London days.

By the end of the night, the couple had donated $100,000, and I had learned not to label people by their appearances. Mrs. Diwan offered to connect me to three other organizations that helped female survivors of domestic violence by rehabilitating, educating, and giving them creative training.

I apologized to Jay about leaving the conversation midway.

"I wish I were this busy," he replied with a smiley.

It occurred to me that I had never asked Jay what he did for a living. He alluded to money troubles and not being employed. But I didn't know any of the specifics about Jay's life, and I quite liked it. I felt a connection to him based not just on the Salinger quotes or the grief we carried about our dead mothers, but also on the feeling of being alone in a city: bound to it yet different from it.

He wrote back, "You are doing important work, Ahana. I am so proud of you."

"I met a very important socialite in Delhi. You'd think she has everything. But her ex-husband used to lock her up in their house before leaving for work. She escaped because their housekeeper helped her." I looked around to make sure Dev was nowhere in sight. "How can one human being hurt and try to control another human being?" I ran my tongue over my lips.

"Some men can be fucking animals. I see wife-beaters and women-abusers and wonder how these fuckers or anyone who hurts women is still alive, but my mother is dead."

"Sometimes, when I see mean people alive, I wish I could trade their beating heart for my mumma's." I grabbed a glass of champagne that the servers were walking around with and took a big sip. I had a dark side that became enhanced while communicating with Jay. The chats felt like a great emotional release—the way a recovering cigarette addict sneaks in a smoke secretly—that was the level of relaxation I felt.

I didn't care about Jay's gender, age, color, sexual orientation, or marital status. A part of me was grateful for this connection because it was nice to talk about my life with someone I didn't have to meet and knew only as much as I wanted to share.

⚞ 6 ⚟

I didn't want Rohan to know much about me. He was a smart chap with a razor-sharp tongue and dangerously good looks. Rohan had a way with words that made people believe in him, just like my ex-husband, so I stayed cautious.

Rohan was a coworker. I didn't tell him that my mom used to be the leading liver transplant specialist in South Asia, and Dad was the owner of the largest construction company in New Delhi. I didn't tell Rohan about my mansion in South Delhi. I didn't share any information about the four servants, two chefs, two gardeners, three chauffeurs, or two errand boys. I didn't tell him about the rose garden in the front yard or the Balinese furniture in the patio where my family and I sipped chilled wine on summer evenings and relaxed on cold winter nights with a glass of whiskey or red wine while our non-vegetarian chef made different kinds of fresh *kebabs* and *roomali rotis*—the Indian paperthin flatbreads—for us, which we ate wrapped in Cashmere shawls and under the stars and candlelight. I didn't say a word about the lanai decorated with Indonesian furniture where my parents threw fancy dinner parties where people ate gourmet food, bragged about their expensive vacations, flaunted their new diamonds acquired at Cartier, drank a lot of imported wine, and danced until wee hours in the morning. Some of these guests even pretended to care about world problems and offered solutions after downing a few shots of Glenlivet and warming their hands over the bonfire.

I maintained strong boundaries with Rohan in the beginning.

* * *

Rohan spent many hours brainstorming ideas with me. I wanted the conference to be more than just a place where speakers gave their talk about women's safety and empowerment. "Envision it; I'll help you implement it," he had told me right at the very beginning. Pulling up statistics, doing research, working on presentations, rethinking collaborations, Rohan was always there. I found myself feeling grateful, even if my guard was still up.

"If we raise enough money, we can start sponsoring yoga classes for trauma survivors at domestic violence and sexual assault shelters/NGOs around the world. I ran the idea by my boss and she is willing to speak to the board about it."

"Hell, yes!"

Rohan came up with creative ideas like organizing mobile cafes where speakers could have an informal chat with the attendees. He was forming partnerships with different organizations. That said, Rohan and I argued plenty. We were both invested in the conference but came from different backgrounds. We had different ideas for *No Excuse,* especially when it came to PR and social media marketing.

"According to a recent survey of North American journalists and media professionals, 80 percent of journalists believe photos and videos are key ingredients of effective content," he reiterated when we were on a conference call at 10 p.m. New Delhi time.

"I don't want to be in any videos," I screamed. "Why can't we hire professionals?" I was alone in the office and my skepticism was echoing in my corner office as well as the large hallways.

"For two reasons," he emphasized. "You are the face of this conference. We sound more credible and authentic if you talk about it. Secondly, we lower our total costs by not hiring a model."

"Fine."

"Ahana, the video will be powerful. We will broadcast your message to over a million-and-a-half women."

"You mean one-and-a-half million?" I rolled my eyes. I wasn't bold enough to speak up in front of Dev. I refused to make the same mistake with Rohan.

He laughed. "Haha, always so matronly."

I changed the topic. "Brady, I still need that help with my social media presence."

"Let's work on it tomorrow. It's Thursday night. Don't you have a date?"

There was an awkward silence.

He changed his tone. "How about you play a little with your profiles? And we do a video call your Friday morning, so I can walk you through a few steps. Say about 9 a.m. your time?"

"Sure, but won't that affect your Thursday night party plans?" I asked Rohan in a sarcastic voice. I imagined Rohan as this guy who owned a harem: a redhead, a brunette, and a blonde serving him his favorite drink, Sazerac, every evening.

"Well, it will. I'll have to let the ladies down easy. But I don't want you scolding me either, Matron!" He let out a laugh.

"Idiot!" I said out loud as I hung up.

* * *

I asked the driver to pull out the car. On the drive back, I downloaded several social media apps on my phone and played around with them. Once home, I messaged Rohan. Then I took a shower and poured Chutney and myself a glass of pinot noir and posted the picture of the two glasses on Instagram with the caption, "Happy Hour in New Delhi."

I could barely sleep that night. I shared quotes on healthy living and women's rights. Pacing up and down my room, I pondered over ideas for *No Excuse*. I have no recollection of when I passed out. But I didn't wake up until Athena licked my face in the morning.

I looked at my watch; it was 8:30 a.m. "Oh no, I am late." I called up the kitchen via the intercom, "Lakshmi, chai please."

I messaged Rohan. "Sorry; I am running late. Can we defer the video chat by an hour?"

"Hiya, Matron." Rohan wrote back promptly with a smiley face at the end. "Partied too much last night?"

Idiot! "What do you mean?" I pressed my temples.

"I saw you took my happy hour suggestion. Hot date?"

"Yuck!" I rubbed my eyes. "How can you even see that picture? I took it at home with my aunt and posted it for myself. Was playing around."

"Good thing we are doing the tutorial today." Rohan ended the note with a wink.

* * *

After doing a twenty-minute yoga sequence in my orange lululemon yoga pants and gray tank top, I took a shower and headed to work. The traffic was unusually bad for a Friday morning, so I messaged Rohan, "I am terribly sorry to keep you waiting. I might get further delayed. There has been an accident."

"It's not a problem whatsoever. If you'd like, I can give you a brief introduction over the phone."

"Sure."

Rohan called. "I browsed through all your social media links."

"And?" I brought my eyebrows together.

"How do I say this? You come across as too matronly."

The word stuck in my craw. "What do you mean?" I looked at my sleeveless, loose, polka dot print, knee-length tunic dress and wondered whether it looked too matronly.

"I mean, I see your attempts to be personal—posting about yoga, tea, and good wine. It's a great first attempt. But you have shared photos that include no faces, which fails to convey the kind of warmth and intimacy that a good profile uses."

I got defensive and fussed with my pearl hoop earrings. "That is why I didn't want to handle all this social media nonsense."

"C'mon; I'll help you out. In a few weeks, you'll be the queen of social media." Rohan spoke with such confidence that I started to believe him too.

"You were the one who encouraged me about happy hour."

"I am flattered that you took my advice." He paused for a second and continued. "But with your posts about Earl Grey tea and French pinot noir and women's rights and healthy living, it can make people think that you'll end up an angry spinster."

"Whatever. How do you manage to flirt via social media, Brady, and have these women drool over you?"

"What women?"

"Oh, please. I saw your profiles on different platforms."

He responded with a wink. "Why? Need help finding a guy?"

What an asshole! "Really? That's what you think?"

He laughed out loud. "Success! You are so fucking Zen all the time that I need to rile you up every now and then to see you are alive."

"Sure." I sat up straight.

"You shouldn't believe everything you see or read or hear. Don't take everything literally. How about I leave you with that?" His tone was serious.

Just then, a guy started pounding at my car window. We were barely crawling at 12 mph.

"What was that?" Rohan asked.

"I will call you back." I hung up.

A man on a two-wheeler had unzipped his pants and was touching himself with one hand. With the other, he was pounding at the window to catch my attention. I froze. My driver screamed at the guy, but he was undeterred. The traffic police eventually showed up and took the chap away, but I couldn't get the image out of my head. Filthy men at every corner.

I wanted to take a hot shower. I wanted to hide. I told my driver, Baburao, to turn the car around. I messaged Ms. Roy that I was feeling unwell and was going to work from home.

Dad had left for work. Chutney had gone out to attend a meeting. Lakshmi asked whether I was OK. I gave her my lunchbox with a smile and ran to my room. I threw up. I scrubbed my eyes and washed myself under the hot shower.

What had happened to New Delhi? This was not the Delhi where I grew up. With friends and family, eating ice cream in Connaught Place. Attending loud summer weddings. My mumma sitting with masis on summer evenings and gossiping about everyone in the family, exchanging stories about their neighbors, in-laws, colleagues, and maidservants. My dad teaching us all how to play cricket. This wasn't the Delhi where Naina spent her vacations when we were kids. This was no longer the Delhi where I went to college. This couldn't be the Delhi my parents left London for because they missed it so terribly. I missed the Delhi I wanted to remember.

* * *

I sat cross-legged on the couch in my room and tried alternate nostril breathing. "It calms the nervous system, *beta*." Mumma would ask me to practice it every time I was triggered.

In all of this, I forgot to message or call Rohan. It was around 10:30 a.m. New Delhi time when he sent me a text, "Matron, everything OK?"

I clicked my tongue and hit my forehead. I texted him back and apologized. The minute I told Rohan what had happened, he called me right away. He was extremely nice to me. He made sure I was safe. Rohan's sudden serious tone made me wonder whether he too was "two men" just like I was "two women," even if I was just projecting.

I was really surprised and started to warm up to him, but a few seconds later, he spoke with a grin in his voice, "Matron, glad you're OK. You're too classy for some street thug to think he can mess with you."

It took me some time to accept that Rohan could be a good man. Yet every now and then he would slip in a sneaky comment, "whatchya up to, Matron?" or "Matron is back," and that would slam the door on whatever tolerance I felt toward him. But for the most part, he became my sounding board for the conference. He had the right contacts and attitude; people listened to him. In the few months of knowing Rohan, I started to wonder: *Is he actually a sexist pig or is everything a projection?*

It was January 1, 2014. My birthday had passed, and I was coming upon the one-year anniversary of my divorce from Dev. It was also the first day of the New Year and the day of J. D. Salinger's birth. Every New Year, Mumma would organize an elaborate brunch at home for close friends and family. We would drink mimosas until early afternoon and then play cards on the patio. "If you live correctly, one life is enough, *beta*," she would say.

January 1 was also what Dev called National Sex Day. Before going to my parents for brunch, no matter what time we had returned home from a New Year's Eve party the night before, Dev insisted I dress up as a sexy nurse. My body didn't handle alcohol well, or Delhi winters, and for ten years in a row, I pleaded with Dev to let me be. "I am still hung over from the night before, Dev."

"That's what makes it more fun." He licked my face. "Even when exhausted, you enjoy it, Ahana. I can tell from the way you come alive." He ran his tongue on my hips.

I didn't want to think about Dev. And I couldn't deal with the emptiness of our house or the pity of Mumma's friends calling us over for a meal. It was my mother's tradition, and if I couldn't stop others from starting a new tradition to welcome the New Year, I would at least not participate in it. So, on January 1, after an in-house yoga practice in the patio, the place where I'd last chatted with Mumma, I got dressed in four layers and left for work at 6 a.m.

The temperature had dropped to below freezing in the morning. The dense fog had descended upon the city and reduced visibility to fifty-five yards. I drove slowly because there were several accidents on the road. Mumma would often crib about Delhi winters. "You cannot even escape the city easily in these ridiculous temperatures with all the cancelled trains and delayed flights."

There was no one in the office when I got in around 6:55 a.m. I ordered chai and a grilled vegetable cheese sandwich from a health food store across the street. The beauty of Delhi—delicious food was never too far away, no matter what time or day of the year it was.

* * *

After about thirty minutes, I played some Frank Sinatra and reworked the internal newsletter for our organization. I also needed to work on a report updating the board members about the conference in New Orleans. Even though many aspects of the conference needed to be dealt with, we now had over a dozen confirmed speakers for the event from North America, Asia, Africa, Australia, and South America. Rohan had managed to get us sponsors and 100 percent funding for the speakers. It was a big deal. This conference was unique and important because it would not just create awareness about violence against women but would help fight it, teach women how to defend themselves, and help relocate female survivors of violence. I didn't know how to fight or defend myself in my marriage, but I was determined to help other women not stay stuck in abusive relationships. It would mobilize women and connect them to a global community. The conference would create an accessible platform for the victims and survivors. Sure, there was a lot of work ahead of us, but things were shaping up. The prospects and potential were incredible. They kept me awake at night and hopeful during the day.

I must have been in the office for an hour or two when the phone rang.

"Happy New Year, sis. Get onto FaceTime." Naina must have called home and found out that I was in the office.

"Isn't it a little too early for you to be drunk?" I looked at my watch as I dialed into FaceTime.

"Oh shush, morality police." Naina waved at me while clad in her chic, short sequined dress. "I am calling to tell you that I have made an observation about your Rohan Brady after following his social media posts."

"Why would you look up Rohan? Also, eew!" I cringed as I put my phone on the table and held the iPad with both hands. "He is not *my* anything."

"Shut it. Rohan has great sex hair."

I had no clue what that meant.

She rolled her eyes at me. "It's that messy and tousled kinda hair. You look at Rohan's hair and it feels like he just had sex."

"That's probably because he *always* has sex. All the time." I put my papers in an organized pile.

"What is your issue with him?" Naina asked. "The man has fun and isn't lying about it. He gets my respect as long as he respects you."

"He is probably a horny pig."

"Nun Ahana, he is a guy who likes women. Just because you aren't getting any, don't be a hater."

"UGH."

She interrupted me. "Seriously, though, he works in PR. Did it ever occur to you that he has this online persona as a strategy?"

46

"But…"

"Many of my clients are PR people, and they have this pressure to be a certain way. They have loud, outgoing, exaggerated personalities but can be lonely on the inside."

I tried to get in a word, but she wouldn't let me.

"Rohan has never misbehaved with you. You're the one who told me that women love to flirt with him. What he does in his personal life is not for you to judge. Also, your morality standards might be different from his. He is American and you have Indian roots. There are cultural differences."

"Naina, men like Rohan assume women are all the same—they drool over him and envy his almond-shaped eyes."

"What women? What men?"

I ignored part of her question. "It's mostly those perverse kinds of women who are thrilled to get focused yet detached attention from a good-looking guy."

"You are kidding, right?"

"I cannot even begin to tell you how much mollycoddling a guy like Rohan needs, Naina." Dev enjoyed being the object of female attention on every occasion. The more women flirted with him, the higher was his sex drive and the rougher he was with me in bed.

"How does it matter to you? You do your job." Naina broke my reverie.

"His charm feels familiar. I am not sure." Naina knew about Dev but not the invasive and pertinent details. She never did like him.

"You don't need to personalize Rohan's actions." Naina paused. "He is not—"

I interrupted her. "Can you believe that some of these women leave him comments like, 'Hey, sexy, just give me a chance to work you so I can make everything better! Just feel free to encourage me, baby.'"

"Log into your social media accounts, Ahana."

"Why?"

"Because this is fun and a great case study for me. Let's read through Rohan and his female fan club's posts."

I grumbled. Naina paid no heed.

She spoke excitedly. "Do you notice how Rohan backs down the minute women start suggesting an actual meeting?"

"That could well be because he has an army of women in his backyard and all the dirt happens there."

"You are hilarious, Ahana. What you see isn't always the truth. What you don't see is also important."

"I feel like you always take up for the men in my life."

"Not at all. I was the first person to tear into Dev. I am always on your side. Honey, I am a shrink. I can't help but see people a certain way. Rohan seems more like the all-talk guy. Yes, a typical PR guy with his slick demeanor, which can be a bit exhausting, but nothing more. My therapist gut tells me that he is protecting himself from something by creating this annoying macho shield."

"Puhlease."

Naina interrupted, "If Rohan ever misbehaves with you, I'll kick him in his nuts. He is from my city, after all."

"OK, enough of a sermon for the New Year. Now go and enjoy yourself."

"I wish you would learn to live a little from this Rohan guy."

"I am really not impressed by charming men and flirtatious behavior."

"Every man is not Dev. Love you." Naina hung up.

I picked up the pen and pressed it against my lower lip until it hurt.

The phone rang again.

I answered, assuming it was Naina. "I said I'll think about it."

"Oooh, think about what? Am I calling at a bad moment?"

It was Rohan. He sounded slightly drunk.

"I thought it was my cousin."

"Sorry to disappoint you. Happy New Year, Matron!" he shouted over the phone.

"Isn't it still the thirty-first eve for you, Brady?" I pulled the phone away from my ear.

"Details, details."

"I am sorry. I was taken by surprise to hear from you."

"Why?"

"C'mon; it's New Year's Eve. A chap like you is probably partying up in the French Quarter and doing shots—"

Rohan interrupted me. "Who says I am not doing any of that?"

"Was I right, or was I right?" I hit the tip of the pen on my third eye.

"I wish you were here in New Orleans. It's magical on New Year's Eve. You can smell festivities and happiness." Rohan took a selfie and sent it to me.

"That's very nice of you to say, but I don't like to party." I readjusted my glasses as I looked through the pictures of him and his buddies and very few women. Everyone was formally dressed and sipping on some drink.

"I am on a private yacht on the Mississippi with a few friends."

"Showoff."

"Haha, hear me out. The fireworks will start later, but there is an incredible jazz singer onboard whom you would have loved. His music ranges from Sinatra to that weird dude you like, Michael Bubbly."

"It's Bublé." I changed the topic. "Did you hear back from the printers for the giveaways?"

"Yes, ma'am. That's another reason why I called you. We now have sponsors and printers ready to print tees and tote bags that read *No Excuse*. You need to finalize the tagline and confirm the total number and we are good to go."

"Oh, my God! That's the best news I have heard all day. Thanks, Brady." The smallest of things that I thought would add to the whole experience of *No Excuse*, Rohan got me sponsors for them. I was cognizant that the conference and *No Excuse* would still be a dream had he not stepped in.

"How was your New Year's Eve, Matron?" Rohan asked in the same tone as when he called after the harassment.

"Spent a quiet evening at home with the family." The air in the house felt different without Mumma. There was no longer even a faint waft of her in any room.

"The first year is always the roughest. The first set of holidays without the people you love are cruel. But things get better." He hiccupped.

I realized I didn't want to know, or to share any more. Running my hands through my hair, I said, "I don't want to keep you any longer. Enjoy your party and have a safe start to the New Year, Brady!"

"Find me on television near Jackson Square, eagerly counting down the time until New Year arrives." He paused for a second. "You are the reason behind this conference. You must share your voice with those attending. Every person present at the conference will have a stake in the discussion that takes place, if it comes from you, the creator of this event."

As we both hung up, I muddled over the idea of needing to give a speech, but I felt stymied because of my own marital experience as well as divorce.

⚎ 8 ⚎

On my way back home from a late night meeting, the car broke down. While Baburao, our driver, waited for the mechanic, I decided to head back home. Ten-year-high April temperature, in New Delhi, at 44.9-degrees Celsius or as Naina would describe it, "112 degrees fucking Fahrenheit," the heat wave was making me nauseous. Plus, I had a severe headache from possible dehydration. Metro seemed like the safest and fastest choice at the time compared to an auto rickshaw or taxi.

When I entered the women's compartment in the New Delhi metro, it was virtually empty. Despite the air conditioning in the train, it felt hot, and I had trouble breathing. By the time winter ended in Delhi, my lungs would forget what clean air used to be like. I pulled away my scarf and started to fan myself. Suddenly, three men barged in. They started singing songs and making obscene gestures. I cowered at the sight of them. They sat beside me. I had sample jute gift bags in hand for the conference along with my handbag. I tried to cover my chest with them. Every time I got up from my seat, they too would stand up. I could hear my palpitations. Finally, I decided to get off the train; one of the men slapped my breasts and the other pinched my buttocks. I was disgusted and angry to my bones, but my screams dissolved in my mouth. The four women in the compartment said nothing to the men harassing me.

Once I got home, I scrubbed myself with sandalwood soap and cried in the shower. Men at home—my ex-husband—and men outside had treated me with such disrespect, I couldn't handle it. "You are a cunt who enjoys the touching, so don't fucking pretend," Dev had told me right before our family *Diwali puja* where we prayed to Lakshmi—the goddess of wealth, fortune, power, luxury, beauty, fertility, and auspiciousness. How obediently he bowed his head in front of an idol but mistreated *me*, his wife, referred to as *Lakshmi* in Hindu homes.

I sat in a corner and meditated to calm myself down. There were messages from Jay and Rohan.

Rohan wrote, "Hey, just tried to call. When you have a moment, look at the draft of the invite for the standing advisory groups made up of gender experts from government, NGOs, women's groups, and academia. Once I have your OK, my team can start reaching out. We have a rich list of experts from across the globe. I'll share that list in a separate email."

Jay's email said that he was feeling low and in need of a friend.

I sent them both a message apologizing about the delay and explaining the abbreviated version of the Delhi Metro happenings.

Jay wrote back instantly. "You need someone to make sure you are safe. I wish I were there with you, babe."

I had told Jay several times not to address me as 'babe.' "I said, it makes me uncomfortable."

Jay didn't pay heed. "You needn't worry. I'm the kind of man who will fight to the death for but never lay a hand on his close female friends because I think the friendship is too precious."

Rohan called me up a couple of hours later when I was eating dinner with Dad and Chutney.

"I'm glad you're not still exploring the wonders of the Delhi train system," he teased.

"Whatever!" I shouted at Rohan over the phone.

Dad and Chutney looked at me. I quietly excused myself from the dining table.

"Sorry I couldn't call sooner." Rohan was kind.

I shrugged. "I don't care about your shitty excuses, Brady. Why did you call?"

"Honestly, to make sure you are OK, Matron."

"Oh yeah?" I was tongue-tied.

"You would be better off if you could ignore it all, but I know you cannot. But you can't engage these creepy guys in the Delhi metro or anywhere. That will just make them even worse. You need to make sure you are safe. Don't empower these assholes. Next time, kick the man in his nuts and let him know about the infamous wrath of the Matron."

I pulled my glasses off and left them on the buffet in the dining room. I knew what Rohan was saying was nothing that other men hadn't explained to me before—but the energy of Rohan's conversation was what disarmed me. He didn't make the harassment my fault; he arrived at a punchline that empowered me.

"Or better yet...we can call you 'The Lady Nutcracker.'"

I burst out laughing. "Thanks for the laugh, Brady. And for checking in."

"Thanks for treating me as your very personal joker."

"*Paagal.*"

Rohan repeated the word '*paagal*' in a strong American accent, which made it sound like 'Paygal.'

"What does that mean? Is that a PayPal service for exotic dancers? And why would you ever think I had any business with such a thing?" Rohan sounded offended.

"*Paagal* means mad in Hindi."

"Oh, all right. I learned a new Hindi word today. You take good care of yourself, Matron."

"Sure, Grandpa," I blurted out.

"So, she *does* have a sense of humor!" Rohan laughed. "Game on, Nutcracker."

* * *

I was at the Asia Pacific Women's Conference in Sydney, and with the time difference, I was unable to speak with Rohan or exchange emails with Jay during those seven days. The trip was hectic, and whatever free time I had, I spent catching up on all the paperwork for the NOLA conference and with my dad's sister's family.

My new, bigger goal was to partner with governments, UN agencies, civil society organizations, and other institutions to advocate for ending violence, increasing awareness of the causes and consequences of violence, and building the capacity of partners to prevent and respond to violence. I just had to convince the other organizations that my nonprofit in India was ready for the big league. Sydney was where *No Excuse* could go from a big deal to a huge deal, thanks to participation by a few global women's initiatives with political connections. The conference was covered by all the leading print magazines and television channels. I silently worried about my exposure to Dev, but I stayed focused because Rohan's boss, Michael Hedick, was present at the conference. "Watch out for Hedick; he is a backseat driver," Rohan warned me.

Dracula was an ego-centric man with sexist ideals. Michael had no qualms taking credit for the work he hadn't done, especially if a woman was in charge. No wonder Rohan and his team nicknamed him "Dracula."

I'd met Hedick on a few occasions when he had traveled to New Delhi. He was intense and unpredictable, and his intensity made everyone around him feel guilty of something they weren't responsible for. Michael loved eating *garlic naan* with butter chicken. And he would sweat, like a hosepipe burst in his body, after eating raw green chilis with onions with all his Indian meals. Yeah, that was the other thing that I remembered about Michael: Didn't matter the season, he constantly wiped his forehead. His shirt was soaking wet around the armpits.

I thought these things about Hedick while feeling the need to be articulate. The pressure was double because Dracula was hovering...at meetings, in the cafeteria, at the time I was rehearsing my presentation on victim advocacy, or even sipping a cup of Earl Grey. His constant presence brought on added pressure; his motives were never clear.

Safe Voice, a powerful, feminist organization in the United States that helped rape survivors with rapid access to health clinics, decided to support Freedom Movement after my presentation. "Good morning, ladies and gentleman. I am here today to speak about one of the most pervasive violations of human rights in the world: violence against women. Seventy percent of women in some countries still face physical and/or sexual violence in their lifetime. Sexual offences take away a woman's worth." I swallowed air. Over three dozen pairs of eyes were on me. I took a sip of water. "Sexual violence is an extreme manifestation of gender inequality and systemic gender-based discrimination—it can have tremendous costs to communities, nations, and societies. Survivors of sexual violence need to have access to medical treatment, forensic services, crisis counseling, and longer-term psychotherapy. Not all countries offer this option. Research shows that over 85 percent of victims don't know about the options. *No Excuse* intends to raise awareness and start a dialogue across the globe and share information about rights and options to help victims make informed choices, no matter where they live.

I thought of Mumma and missed her so much. I was ecstatic, so I called up Ms. Roy. "We will throw a party once you are back, Ahana. Good job." But on the last day of the conference, I found out that the executive director at *Safe Voice*, Anna Smith, whom I had negotiated with, was considering passing the project to Rohan's unlikeable boss Michael Hedick. This meant effectively I had to plan a feminist conference under the advice of a mansplaining pig. I was angry and disappointed. Ms. Roy tried to placate me. "*No Excuse* is getting international support because of your efforts, Ahana," but that wasn't enough for me.

Before checking out of the hotel in Sydney, I looked at my personal messages and listened to the answering service on the mobile phone. There was a voicemail and a couple of emails from Rohan saying, "Hope you are out partying like a rock star, stoned and smashed. Just wanted to make sure the young studs you are partying with in Sydney are doing OK. :)"

I shook my head.

As I sat in the cab and headed to the airport, my phone rang. It was Rohan. "One of the largest modeling agencies has decided to showcase their models at a fundraiser in NOLA, which means we can raise more money for the conference. This is good news, Matron. You have worked for this event and it's amazing how it's all shaping up."

While he gave me credit, I knew Rohan had contacts in the modeling world, and we couldn't have landed this opportunity without his help. But he never said, "I got us…" It was always a team thing with him. He stayed with "we."

"Turned on your charm, Brady, and got one of your harem models to walk the ramp?" I teased him.

"Do you really enjoy turning every discussion we have into a tease about my character?"

"I was joking." I felt it hit too hard, too carelessly. But before I could fix it, Rohan shot back.

"You make me sound like a bad person. I hope I'm not half as terrible as some harem-keeping weirdo you imagine I am. Do you really see me in that terrible light?"

"Sorry; I was teasing you. We wouldn't have this opportunity had it not been for you. It's all you, Rohan." I tried to sweet-talk him, and not very tactfully, I think.

"Mwahahaha." He let out an evil laugh. "You think you are the only one who can joke?"

"That's not fair, Brady. I really thought—"

"What? That I was heartbroken with your opinion of me? I'm a stud and I know it."

"You are such a pig! I am hanging up now."

"Don't go, Matron from Scoldingsville."

"I am *still* in Sydney. Listening to your jibes on this international call is going to cost me a lot."

"Sorry; I'll hang up. Enjoy your stay and party up. If you have the time, meet with my buddy Steve and his wife Melanie. They moved there a few years ago from NOLA. They'll be great company. Melanie, too, like you, carries her yoga mat everywhere. You guys can go OM-ing together. Hahaha."

"You talk so much nonsense, Brady. Bye."

"Bye, Matron. Going to Cafe Du Monde later today. Will eat a beignet or two for you. Also, hope Hedick hasn't been a complete dick."

I didn't tell Rohan about Michael Hedick's slimy move. I wanted to talk about it when I was slightly less emotional about the news. I did notice how my humor got sharp when I was feeling emotional, and maybe it was the same for Rohan. Rohan respected that we both needed space. But he, maybe, needed to know that the lag in communication wasn't because he had been abandoned.

* * *

As I relaxed in Singapore Airline's lounge in Sydney, I logged into the therapy message chat room. One of the members, Anita, who was the wife of a diplomat and joined the therapy group after she lost her newborn, had gotten drunk and asked all her expectant friends on social media to share pictures of their pregnant bellies. Her husband got upset and accused her of jeopardizing his career by sharing such posts. Los Angeles-based Tanya, who was grieving her dead boyfriend Paul, said that she had begun to believe in love and second chances again. I privately congratulated Tanya and asked Anita whether I could be of any help. Jay noticed that I was on the chat group so he sent me a note: "Stop ignoring me and start checking your emails. :)"

The minute I logged into my emails, I noticed there were six messages from him. "I miss my buddy. Where are you? Got bored of my friendship? Did you see what Tanya the crazy cat lady posted? Stay away from her, babe. She is a bit of a psycho. :)"

It was a gut-dropping moment.

Jay was immature and needy—and attached to me.

"Sorry," I wrote back to him. "Work has been very hectic, hence haven't been able to write back. I am in Sydney waiting to board my flight back to New Delhi."

He wrote back inside of thirty seconds. "Still? I envy your lifestyle. Man, I wish I could travel. It's so maddening to be stuck at home all the time."

"But you live in the greatest city on the planet: NYC. I wish I could live in that city."

"Cool. Let's trade lives because I hate that it's April and it's still snowing. The cold is so deep that I can't get warm."

I didn't know what to say. I was also partially distracted by the announcements being made at the airport at the same time as the server in the lounge showed up to take my order.

"You doing OK today? Are you angry with me? Something I did?" Jay sent me a note.

I took a sip of my wine and looked over the paperwork. "I have to finish a lot of work, so sorting out everything."

"You seem very not Ahana-like at all."

"Aww, I am sorry if I haven't been able to help you this past week."

"Just missing my regular chitchat with you. :) When do you get back home?"

"Give or take thirty hours."

"Let's chat over the weekend at length. I will be watching the Jets kick some Patriot ass! But will be around if you are bored."

I pressed my palms together and let out a sigh. "I am working this Saturday. My boss wants an update on this trip before Monday. And my friend has thrown a brunch at a club on Sunday. How about Monday evening? I'll be back home from work and yoga on time. I would absolutely love to hear what you have been up to."

Jay didn't write back.

* * *

Once I landed in Delhi, I called Dad. "I am on my way home. Yes. Yes. Don't worry. I understand. You probably got busy. Yeah, Baburao showed up to the airport on time to pick me up. I'll see you soon." I was too tired to react to Dad's forgetfulness.

As I settled in the car and drank some water, I decided to message Jay and make sure he was doing OK. I understood very well what loneliness could turn us into. Jay had mentioned several times that he had nobody else.

"Had an exciting time?" he promptly wrote back.

I rolled my eyes. And it would seem Jay, magically, despite being thousands of miles away, saw it.

"You really don't get it, do you? You went to Australia! You forgot me amid all of your new friends, Ahana!"

I really didn't have the patience for whining right now. "The first thing I do after getting out of the airport is message you, and you still want assurance from me?"

"Wow. Someone tells you they are depressed and that they miss you and you lecture them on how they should not need reassurance about friendship? That's just disappointing."

I lost it. "WE AREN'T DATING! We are friends dealing with losing our mothers and getting to know each other. Frankly, there is only so much you can know of a person you meet online. Calm down. I have work to do." I logged out.

I arrived home, took a shower, changed into my comfy pajamas, which the washer man had cleaned and ironed, updated my family on my trip, ate a simple Indian meal, and got back up to my room. The jetlag had messed up my sleep cycle, but I felt that the MF Husain original paintings on the walls leading up the staircase—ones Mumma had bought at an auction—nudged me to stay strong. I played jazz and sat down to read Sheryl Sandberg's *Lean In: Women, Work, and the Will to Lead* on my fire-colored couch, nestled among its familiar hand-embroidered cushions.

When we were married, I had told Dev, "I am looking forward to reading *Lean In*. Apparently, she offers practical advice to help women achieve their goals."

"Your goal should be to keep your husband happy."

At first, as I sometimes did, I thought he was teasing, so I continued reading my book. He didn't have a sense of humor with me, but sometimes I took whatever I could get—usually sexist jokes that his male friends probably thought were genuinely hilarious. But an hour later, he was climbing on top of me with more ferocity than usual, and that night, he tied my hands with wire. I never volunteered to be tied down or spanked but Dev never asked what I wanted.

* * *

My laptop was on charge on my desk. I heard a ping. I closed the book and walked over to see who was messaging me at this late hour. Jay wrote. "I get that we aren't dating. It's tough to explain so I generally don't bother trying anymore. I just feel like most of my friendships are conditional and even after so many years of life, I don't really know who I can count on as a true friend anymore. I try to do kind things for people because it's my nature, but I just get abused and eventually dropped when I am no longer of use. I have no doubt it's my fault for courting such people into my circle, but I don't do it on purpose, nor do I know how to undo it so I do feel a bit stuck. My mother understood my battles, but with her gone, I feel lonely. I have no one to talk to without the fear of being judged. You are the one friend who understands me, Ahana. I guess sometimes I get too used to chatting with you and miss it when we can't for a while. That's about it. I fear losing you…my friend, that is."

I felt bad for my meltdown with Jay as I had done with Rohan. Was Jay hurtful because he was hurting? I sat at my desk and typed, "What happened, Jay?"

He disappeared again.

I ended the chat with J. D. Salinger's words, "That's the whole trouble. When you're feeling very depressed, you can't even think."

He replied, "I see you're stewing on something I can't grasp. You are making assumptions that I am depressed. You are searching for reasons to be disappointed."

I was stunned by Jay's tone. Dev used to take that tone with me. It made my head spin. "Why the hell are you screaming at me?" I wrote back.

"Screaming? Fuck, what is wrong with you?" He sent me another message right away. "Problem is you can't accept that you're ever wrong. It's all feelings for you—you felt I was depressed. Fuck, you could feel I was a seventy-five-year-old transvestite and never be convinced otherwise. OK, fine. But I will never just accept such feelings, so if I'm not allowed to question your feelings that are simply at odds with my reality, then we really need to stop this and just put the friendship to rest."

"Are you on something?" I could feel my fingers burn. Jay kept bringing up images of my dark past with Dev; it irked me. He was disruptive like my ex-husband.

"I will never understand the depth of your disappointment in nearly every action I take, Ahana. I won't be by email for a while. I have some knitting to do."

I sat perplexed. Even though Jay was condescending, I could deeply identify with him lashing out, and saw similarities to myself. He sent a one-line email the following morning. "I miss the hell out of being your friend. I am afraid you are going to terminate our friendship."

≈ 9 ≈

Mumma would say, "You cannot always control what goes on outside. But you can always control what goes on inside." The realization that I was pathologically dependent on my mother started to hit me with each passing day. I was lucky to have Mumma as a strong role model in my life, but her strength also made me weak because I never learned to wean off and make my own decisions. My marriage, my divorce, my career…Mumma remained a strong influence.

I focused on my work all day Saturday. On Sunday morning, I went for a yoga class to de-stress. After getting dressed, I headed to the brunch organized by my friend Maya at the club in South Delhi, to blend in with New Delhi's socialites.

Across the street from the club, there were families sleeping on the pavement in the seething heat. There was a little girl baking *rotis* on the side of the street, feeding her toddler brothers, and shooing away street dogs. The contrasts in New Delhi! In the cloistered, privileged world that I grew up in—where your value was determined by your wealth, foreign vacations, education abroad, and how well you spoke English—no one wanted to discuss the economic disparities. "Don't ruin the party and people's mood, Ahana," Dev would warn me if I tried to bring up social issues.

I gave the little girl a hundred rupees and entered the club. Maya had warned me about the crowd she was expecting—her colleagues from both the advertising agency and law school days. The women pouted their lips and took a lot of selfies. They posted our pictures on social media. How did I know this? They asked for my social media handle and said, "We have tagged you in the photos. You have such pretty hair, Ahana. And such big boobs!" I wondered whether they, too, thought I looked like a matron. I had had difficulty implementing Rohan's advice about social media posts. None of the pics I'd shared from the Sydney trip had anything to do with the conference. In my efforts to sign up with big-name organizations and the special work moments of forging partnerships, I'd forgotten to capture them.

I felt amused listening to these women's stories of sex, cigarettes, men, cheating, and one-night stands. Every now and then, Maya and I exchanged a look—a sly smile lingering at the corner of our lips. One of them found her brother-in-law attractive when, ironically, she found the same qualities attractive in her husband. One of the women asserted after a big gulp of her single malt, "I am so good at what I do. I am the best fucking lawyer in my entire law firm. But I don't have a dick and that's why I can't get to the next level." Another woman in the group didn't eat or drink; her brunch was a pack of cigarettes. It felt as if her bones were pressed against her flesh and they would all crumble. Maya's boss swallowed her gin and tonic. "My mother still doesn't get it. She keeps getting priests over to pray for me. Men and their private parts, they make me want to vomit." She threw the olive pit in the ashtray.

I was silent for most of the brunch. Maya mouthed to ask whether I was OK with the crowd. I texted her, "Sweetie, never been better." I sipped some prosecco.

One of the ladies elbowed me. "Hope you got bumped by one of the hot Aussie hunks."

"Those Aussie men know how to fuck hard and good." Another woman winked, holding a knife seductively in her mouth. When Dev wanted me to go down on him, he would put the butt of the knife inside his mouth with the tip pointing toward me and pull it out and push it back in continuous motion. That was it: my tipping point.

"I am so stuffed; I need to move things around my stomach." I wiped my glasses and went for a walk in the heat.

After a thirty-minute stroll, I checked my phone. There was a message from Rohan.

"Yo, Matron. You added new life to the crisp Connecticut housewife look. Nice work!" There was a wink at the end of the sentence.

"Oh gosh, those pictures are all over social media, aren't they?"

"Hell, yeah! Haha. You couldn't look unhappier in your pictures of pouts and pastels," he replied.

In my inebriated state, I wrote, "These women are strange."

"How so?"

"All of them want to talk about the intimate details of their lives."

"The balls on them." Rohan ended his message with a smile.

"Fine, I get it. I am not like the harem women you are used to."

"Geez, I am kidding. Walk away, Matron. Tell them you want to go for a stroll."

"That's exactly what I'm doing, genius." I rolled my eyes at the phone as I wrote back. "Why are you still awake, Brady?" I perched my sunglasses on my head.

"I got invited to a fashion show—"

I interrupted Rohan and typed fast. "Lucky guy! Christmas came early for you, right?"

"You choose to be cruel to me, Matron." After a few seconds, Rohan wrote again, "I know you are at brunch. But can we, sorry *may* we, speak for just a few minutes? It's important."

I sat down on a bench and extended my legs, "Yes, you *may* speak," not knowing what I would hear.

Rohan called. "I heard about Anna Smith changing her mind while you guys were in Sydney. Dracula messaged me today."

I stared at the sky so no tears would fall. "I wanted to tell you, but Michael is your boss. I didn't want it to be awkward." A tear fell on my dress.

"Hedick might pay my salary, but you are my friend. I know it seems like it's above our paygrade, but we'll figure something out. I am sure Anna Smith changed her mind because Hedick *did something* about it."

"I am really disappointed, Rohan. I worked so hard for it."

Rohan heard me patiently. "I am sorry you have to put up with Hedick's bad behavior. You totally deserve the lead on the partnership with *Safe Voice*. This conference is your brainchild and nobody can change that."

"That means a lot. Thank you, Brady."

Rohan hung up, and I took a nap with the desert cooler blowing in my face. Soft jazz played in the background and the leaves on the tree shook with ecstasy.

* * *

When I woke up, it was 3:30 p.m. There was a message from Maya to check on me and to let me know that the party was still going on. I stretched my arms over my head. I wrote back, "See you in a few."

There was a ping: It was Jay.

"Hey, just sending mid-day hugs."

What's with the greeting? I thought to myself. After I connected with Rohan and Jay, I checked with Naina whether it was part of American culture to address all women as "babe" and "hon" and send out "virtual hugs." She'd said, "Fuck, no!"

It was 5:00 a.m. in NYC. Jay wasn't a morning person from what he had told me. I wondered how he could spend so much time online, when he said he was trying to turn things around with his career.

I didn't respond. But that didn't stop Jay. "I have gone out of my way for friends, but they use and cast me aside. I have only seen betrayals by those whom I held close to me."

How often in an argument with Dev I would stay quiet because I found him exhausting; Jay was repeating Dev's behavioral patterns, not mine, by alternating between abusing and emotionally blackmailing me. I had no desire to communicate with him in that moment.

* * *

Once I got home, Dad and Chutney could tell something was not OK. They asked, but I refused to say anything. I went up to my room and changed into pajamas and a T-shirt, and then joined them in the family room. Dad was watching the news on a loud volume while Chutney was reading a book.

I asked them both about their day and then followed Lakshmi into the kitchen and pointed at her protruding belly. "Lakshmi, did you go for a walk after eating rice and chicken curry?"

Lakshmi covered her face with the corner of her sari and spoke in broken English, "Now what age to becoming thin, *didi*. You looking beautiful, meeting boy handsome. I no use, so I eating, working, and sleeping." She smiled and her missing front tooth only made her look adorable. Her *sari* barely covered her midriff and her breasts reached the middle of her belly. She pointed at them, "All this gone southwards, *didi*."

"Silly." I smiled at Lakshmi and helped her arrange the teacups on the tray.

There was a ping, again, from Jay about him feeling deflated and depressed. I thought my eye-rolling was obvious only to the ceiling fan above my head, but clearly, I was wrong. Chutney asked, again, "*Beta*, is everything ok?"

"Yup." I pressed the back of the dining chair and walked toward the patio. I was in denial about Jay's erratic behavior. I knew Dad and Chutney wouldn't understand. And that was why I didn't tell them anything.

An hour later, as I put my phone away, Chutney joined me on the swing on the patio with two mugs of savory *lassi*, a perfect yoghurt drink for the heat. I was full from brunch and hadn't eaten anything for dinner; *lassi* garnished with ginger, cilantro, and cumin was exactly what I needed to calm my stomach and mind. She set down each mug on a coaster, and ran her hands affectionately on my forehead, gently tucking my hair behind my ears.

"Ahana, you are one of the wisest people I know."

"Thank you." I hugged her.

"Not so fast." She pulled me away and smiled. "You are also one of the most gullible people I know, who believes sob stories and wants to help everyone."

"Chutney...."

"Ahana, while it's great that you are doing online therapy, there have to be boundaries."

"What do you mean?"

"I don't know this Jay guy, but I do know that you take on too much. Why are your stakes so high in this friendship?"

"Jay is alone in his grieving."

"You have never met him. You live in different worlds. I am not attacking you, kiddo. But I do notice that you look low after interacting with Jay."

For the first time, I confessed to Chutney. "Jay is temperamental."

She interrupted me. "I love you and your sense of loyalty, *beta*. We Indians are always taught the importance of relationships and to take care of those battling hard times. But you have to take care of yourself, too."

"I have Dad, you, Naina, and my close friends. I couldn't have survived a broken marriage and Mumma's death had it not been for all of you."

"Do you like Jay?"

I took a sip of the *lassi*. "I can't even think of any man, or relationships, in my life." I thought about how Jay and I created our respective online presences for different reasons.

"Fair enough. Then even more be protective of whom you allow into your life. Dev took away your smile, Ahana. Don't allow another man to do that."

I put both the mugs on the coffee table and hugged her tightly. She put my head on her lap. I pointed at the stars. "You think Mumma is among one of these?"

"I don't think so."

"What do you mean?" I sat up in surprise.

"Your mumma is probably haunting dirty restaurant kitchens and florists selling poor quality flowers."

We both laughed loudly.

⸗ 10 ⸗

Naina visited Delhi in the hot month of June to attend Mumma's first death anniversary, and to shop for her wedding. "I didn't want my mom or Josh or anyone on this trip. This is my time with you, Ahana."

Naina was shoulder-height to me, and we often joked that half her body was brains, and the other half was belly. Forever dressed in denim jeans, tank top, and a light shirt or jacket, she loved food, and food loved her back. Every time I asked her to exercise, she would say, "I'm an all-American girl, Ahana. I love my food, and I love me some beer."

I took the week off to spend time with Naina. We went all over the city—from *kebabs* in Old Delhi to ice cream in Connaught Place to *papri chaat* in Khan Market. Naina would first eat a bowl of the plain, crisp fried dough wafers, *papri*, even before the chef had blended it with boiled potatoes, tamarind and cilantro chutney, chick peas, and yoghurt. While I ate only three meals a day, Naina was a compulsive snacker. It was fun driving her to authentic foodie joints in India's capital. She rolled down her windows at one point, "Holy fuck! Cars, buses, trucks, three-wheelers, two-wheelers, animal-driven carts and pedestrians on Delhi roads all merge into the traffic."

"Yup, New Delhi changes its character through the day and night. By the way, the pollution will kill you if you don't stop inhaling fumes coming from the automobiles."

"Fine, Ms. Audrey Hepburn of New Delhi." Naina rolled up the windows. But when she saw the truck drivers sipping tea and eating fried Indian flatbread and eggs at roadside restaurants, she started to crave typical Delhi food: homemade *butter chicken* and *pudina paratha*.

Lakshmi looked at Naina as she prepared the mildly spiced chicken curry with a tomato and cream sauce and crispy flatbread with mint. "I like to cook when Naina *didi* visits. Ahana *didi* no eat. She only exercises."

Naina sat on the kitchen counter and spoke in broken Hindi. "You don't know any handsome men for your Ahana *didi*?"

"Sheeeh." Lakshmi hid her face with her *sari* and turned red. "Naina *didi*, anything you say!"

Naina smiled at me. Lakshmi was quiet, or perhaps tongue-tied. She was fascinated by Naina's accent and free-spirited behavior.

Naina said to her, "Put a proper bandage on that cut in your finger. OK? Good night."

Naina filled our home with happiness.

* * *

Naina and I were out for a long drive one evening when we got caught in traffic—three tractors were hauling fodder for mules and a bullock cart blocked their path. People were honking mercilessly. There was never a calm moment in New Delhi.

I honked. "I am worried Rohan's boss Michael Hedick is trying to take over the conference." The traffic policeman blew his whistle, and suddenly we were moving. "Rohan is helping me navigate the political waters." I pressed the brake as we reached India Gate.

With a twinkle in her eye, Naina unbuckled her seat belt and lifted her left eyebrow. "Have you told your guy that you're going to be visiting the States soon?"

"Eew! Rohan is just a friend." I took my hands off the steering wheel.

"If you're so mad, why does your voice sound all sparkly when you talk about him?"

"But…" I couldn't find any words.

"Also, I didn't mention his name." Naina winked. "So, what did your *friend* Rohan Brady say?"

"He is really excited to show me around." Dogs were foraging in the rubbish at the roadside. "Still don't know the exact dates of my US travel since I'm trying to negotiate working from the NYC office."

"Me likey this man."

"Calm down, Naina. He is a playboy." I turned up the air conditioner.

"Sure." Naina elbowed me. "What about fuck face Dubois? What did he say? I can't afford it. I am too broke. The airline can't manage my sorrows. My truck might break down. My garden might perish. My pets won't do well without me. Blah blah blah." Naina made a face that she normally would when her mom asked her to eat bitter gourd when we were kids.

I looked at her. When Naina's nose frowned at me, I didn't know how to respond. "Actually, he said nothing much aside from *wonderful.*"

"Fucker! Calls himself your best friend." Bringing her shoulders to her ears, Naina sighed. "You are traveling all the way from India and he couldn't be any less excited about making plans. Rohan tells you where he lives, what he does, where he works, where he hangs out and so forth. Jay is so secretive—like he doesn't want anything traced back to him—I don't like that."

"You are being unnecessarily paranoid." I tried to maneuver the car so I could park. I glared at the auto-rickshaw driver puttering straight down the no entry zone. *No one follows rules here!*

Naina pressed her palms together and brought them to her third eye. "Has Jay ever told you anything about his personal life aside from his mom's death?"

"*Arrey*, what sort of question is that?" I hit the horn hard.

"Do we know what's tying him down?"

I thought hard as I turned to look at Naina. "Don't know." I shrugged my shoulders. "Aside from the basic information of him moving in with his father in Brooklyn and his mom dying, he never talks about much."

"What does he post then?"

I tapped the steering wheel with my index finger. "I don't know." I swallowed unease as I actually didn't know. "I have cut down on my communication with him."

We entered Naina's favorite coffee shop and ordered two cold coffees. Naina asked me to log into my social media accounts so she could see what Jay had posted recently. She browsed through his various profiles. "For someone who is so smart, sometimes you surprise me, Ahana." Her pupils dilated. "You don't think it's odd that this guy doesn't post a profile picture or anything about a partner or friends or family or his home or office or surroundings? For a man who is always happy to share bizarre captions like 'When life gives you lemons, make margarita,' or, 'It was a $2 castaway on a discount shelf at a nursery but thanks to my green thumb, this girl is blooming,' you honestly don't find it strange that he is so guarded about his life?"

"I think he's gay. He probably just wants to be careful." I slurped through the straw the way Naina and I would drink when we were kids.

"People aren't that careful anymore in the US."

"Stop being so suspicious."

"I will if you stop being over-accommodating." Naina took a sip of her cold coffee. "From everything you have told me, Jay sounds forever irritable and aggressive, so no man or woman would want a jackass like him. But you never know."

"What does that have to do with Jay dating anyone?"

She squeezed her eyes. "It matters because something is amiss." She poked my forehead. I wiped my face. "I have no proof, but I have a feeling he is not who he makes himself out to be."

"C'mon."

"I've been a psychiatrist for a long time now, Ahana. We better find out what's going on before you travel to the United States."

"Jay says—"

Naina put her hand in front of my face. "What he says and what his real situation is, don't confuse the two until you know for sure." She took a deep breath. "You are not his mother, therapist, or girlfriend. Stop being a martyr." She hit me gently at the back of my head as if to shake me out of my hypnotized state.

* * *

As soon as we entered the house, Naina shouted, "Ahana, I have a massage appointment and will drop off the cloth piece for my sexy, backless blouse at the tailor's first thing tomorrow morning. I am hoping you would have spoken...sorry, he doesn't come to the phone because he is in a bad place in life." Naina paused for a few seconds. "Yeah, so chat with him and figure out what's going on before I return home."

I asked Naina to be kinder.

"I've seen what kindness got you. I will not allow another man to fuck around with my sister." She started to investigate the bar.

"But...." I tried to explain and pulled out a bottle of tequila.

"Ya, I know." She put her arm around my shoulder. "Jay is probably gay, and even if he isn't, you have no desire to date him. I don't give a shit about any of that! All I care about is you and your safety."

"I know." I didn't make eye contact.

Naina pulled away. "I am going to say something, and you won't like it, but it's time."

"What is it?" I started to fix drinks for us.

"For some fucking reason, you carry shame about your marriage turning out the way it did."

I was cutting a lime, and as soon as those words left Naina's mouth, my hands stopped above the cutting board. The knife. Dev. The past clawed its way out. I froze.

"Dev was manipulative, and it took you a while to understand his motives. Don't let Jay play you. Unless you deal with Jay and put an end to this stagnant chapter, I feel nothing good can happen in your life."

I stayed quiet.

"Talk to me, Ahana."

I sat on the barstool. "How did Dev turn into someone I didn't recognize? How did I allow myself to become so powerless in my own marriage?"

Naina cupped my face in her palms. "You and Dev didn't work out because he didn't understand the meaning of love or relationships or respect. Dev didn't respect himself or you, and he wanted you to become someone you couldn't relate to, much like Jay. In your heart, you know what's wrong, but you are so deeply trained, even if subconsciously, to 'please' these fuckers."

I sighed. "I have no confidence, Naina. I am terrified. I have to give a speech at the conference and must *show up* as myself. I need practice being honest to let go of my shame."

"What shame? You are a divorced woman? I don't see the big deal."

I looked away. I wasn't ready yet to share the sordidness of my dark past with Dev.

In the morning, after Naina left, I went for a run and played with Athena on the patio. A part of me was nervous, asking Jay about his personal life. Jay had a curt, hurtful tone when he felt cornered. I kept tiring myself out physically to stay distracted. I felt wiped out from thinking about Jay, so I took a nap. When I woke up in the evening, I figured I'd check what was happening in the online world. By now it was Saturday morning in the States.

I washed my face and came down to the family room. "Lakshmi, can I get a cup of green tea, please?"

"I am making fresh *pakodas* for Naina, *didi*. You also eating, please?" She pleaded with me.

"Too hot for vegetable fritters, Lakshmi. But thank you."

She wiped her forehead with the corner of her *sari*. "No point. Never eating."

* * *

There was a message from Rohan.

"Yo, Matron. I sent you a document with the list of vendors for the tea sponsorship at the conference. Can you check your LinkedIn account and see if you have any contacts in these organizations?"

"Sure. I feel we need more women of color and immigrant speakers for a diverse range of sponsors to take interest," I wrote to him.

"That's a good point. I can also look up the lists I have of women speakers from the domestic violence event we sponsored last year, and maybe we can find someone soon?"

"Good plan, Brady."

There was a follow-up message.

"Oh, how is your cousin's stay been? Hope you have been showing her fun sights around Delhi. And not being a temple-going Matron." He ended the note with a smiley emoticon.

"Nah, we are going to party tonight," I wrote back without putting much thought into my response.

"Lock up the boys," Rohan typed back immediately.

"Whhaaaat?"

"I wish I was with you guys in Delhi."

"Is the New Orleans club scene so bad that you want to party in Delhi?"

"Nah, but I want to connect with my roots."

"Oh, so sleeping around with Indian women is how you connect with your roots?" I inserted an emoji of someone rolling their eyes in disgust.

"Jesus!!! Why would you say that?"

I stayed quiet.

Rohan sounded serious, "I reached out to make sure that you are OK. It's the week of your mother's first death anniversary. You somehow turn most of our chats into offhanded comments about my prurient lifestyle, which is something that doesn't exist but you have created in your head."

Maybe I was perpetuating the stereotype of Rohan as a jerk?

I sent Rohan a message, "I am sorry for what I said earlier. In your words, 'It was my bad.'"

"It's OK. Americanisms suit you." Rohan forgave so easily.

I felt guilty and called him. "I am sorry, Brady. That really was unfair of me."

Rohan and I talked about Naina's visit. I told him Naina had insisted on going boating in the Yamuna River, which was massively polluted.

"I get it. I am a Louisiana boy—still remember going fishing in one of the few protected/unpolluted bayous left in the state with my dad, when I was young. Every Sunday, Dad and I would pack sandwiches, chips, and soda and throw them in our boat and explore Louisiana's roots. From dark swamps thick with cypress trees to sun-kissed marshes playing host to herons and egrets, it is a watery but photogenic wonderland."

Rohan didn't mention his mother.

* * *

I tied my hair into a ponytail and focused on what I was going to say to Jay. I sat in the patio and took a deep breath.

69

"Hi!"

"Hello, my best buddy," Jay replied right away. "I have missed you."

"Are you seeing someone?" I couldn't mince my words.

Jay didn't write back.

I waited for five minutes. "Did I lose you?"

"Don't be so insecure. You will never lose me." He ended his reply with a wink. He didn't ask about my reduced communications. He didn't ask how I was coping with Mumma's death anniversary. He had nothing to say about Naina's visit.

"Eew!"

"What's so disgusting about me?"

"I didn't say you were disgusting, but the idea of you flirting with a friend helping you through a bad patch is repulsive."

There was an awkward silence in our communication. Out of nowhere, Jay gave me unsolicited advice about giving out friendship bands knitted by him to all attendees at the conference. *This man just changed the topic.* It made me wonder whether Jay had ever had a serious job outside of high school. Leaders of the world, women in powerful positions, survivors of violence, this was our audience. And he thought gifts that teenagers exchanged with each other would work for adults?

I rolled me eyes but didn't respond.

After about ten minutes, Jay wrote again. "OK. Fine. Yes, I am seeing someone."

"Are you guys serious?"

"It's on and off."

"Aaah."

I closed my laptop and put my phone aside. Naina was right. There was more to Jay than he let on. Why had he never brought up his relationship status? Was Jay worried that I would judge him for being gay? Because I was an Indian woman from a different culture and a Third World country? Did he think I would not understand or have an opinion one way or another?

I walked to the patio and turned on the desert cooler with the blast hitting my face. Right then, Chutney walked in with some salted chickpeas in a bowl.

"Want some, *beta*?"

I waved my hands. "No, thank you."

"You are missing out." She sat in the chair.

"Haha, I'll live."

I picked up my phone. There was a message from both Rohan and Jay. I figured I'd see and answer them in the order I had received the messages.

"*Paagal*." I smiled and rolled my eyes.

"You look happy. Some boy?" The one thing that excited Chutney the most, especially after Dev and my marriage collapsed, was the prospect of me dating.

"Haha, not a boy; a mad man."

I showed her Rohan's picture. He was grinning in the photograph. His face was beaming and covered with dry colors. The caption read, "5K Color Run, or as I like to call it, penalty for traveling to New Jersey."

"Such a handsome boy!" Chutney winked at me.

"Ah, he's OK."

"What OK? Blue eyes. Indian name. Head full of hair. And the dimple on his chin. What is not good-looking about him?"

"Want to go out with him, Chutney?" I put my hands on my hips.

I looked at Rohan's pictures, again—the ones he had emailed me from his run. Chutney was right; he was good-looking. In that photo, he was surrounded by a group of men and women. I saw a few of the T-shirts read, "Play with colors. Fight cancer."

"Scroll down. There is another picture." Chutney excitedly pointed at my phone.

"All right. All right. Why are you so eager?" I sat on the swing.

"Because this friend of yours looks happy and brings a smile to your face." She walked toward the kitchen.

I smiled.

There was a long email from Jay. I was at first shocked and then teary-eyed as I scrolled through the dense, insipid note he had written.

What stood out to me was, "Because I don't share my relationship status with you, you walk out on our conversation. Despicable. FINE. I am in a strange space in my relationship with her. And why do you care? It's not like you and I are dating, Ahana. We are barely friends. I don't need to inform you or seek your permission about whom I can date. You need to understand that friends need boundaries and you don't have any. I am not interested in any romantic entanglements. You have upset me so much. FUCK! FUCK! FUCK! Why do you test my patience? We have a good, unique friendship. I am your support. Why did you have to make it personal? WHY?? I won't be by my phone so don't bother messaging me."

I was so overcome by shock that I typed up, without thinking, a response to Jay's accusatory email.

Lakshmi walked into the patio with my green tea. She shouted upon seeing me, "Chutney madam, Ahana *didi* crying. Coming quickly."

Chutney ran back to the patio. "Lakshmi, get a glass of water for Ahana."

"What's wrong?" She hugged me.

I didn't say a word. I had never felt so insulted. Chutney gave me a tissue. I wasn't sure whether it was pain, hurt, embarrassment, or anger I blew into the tissue.

Naina walked in right at that moment with her wedding shopping bags in her hands. "Guess who is back?" She couldn't see my face.

"Naina." Chutney pointed at me.

"I am going to kill that son of a bitch." Naina dumped all her shopping bags on the ground. "Ahana, give me your phone." Naina widened her eyes. "Now."

I didn't move.

"Will someone tell me what's happened?" Chutney persisted.

"I am about to find out." Naina started to pace up and down as she read Jay's messages.

"I'll leave you two alone." Chutney gave me a kiss on my forehead.

Naina wiped my tears as she ran her hands over mine. "Is he off his meds? Piece of shit! I hope you didn't write back, Ahana."

I couldn't look Naina in the eye.

"What did you do, Ahana?"

I went to my sent folder and showed Naina what I had written, "I thought you were gay."

Suddenly, Naina burst into laughter. "I am still fucking mad at him, but you are adorable. That was the best response, ever!"

Naina kneeled so that her arms were on my legs. "Ahana, I love you. But you have got to start valuing yourself. Jay is micromanaging your emotions. He criticizes your beliefs and opinions. He knows the quick and easy way to put you down, hurt you, and insult your intelligence."

I looked at Naina with pleading eyes. I couldn't believe Jay would deliberately hurt me. I had done so much for him.

"Ahana, don't make me say something we'll both regret. How can you not see that Jay changes the subject to evade accountability? He tests your boundaries."

I got up quietly and saw another message from Jay, "Awww, honey. What made you think I am gay? I am sorry you got confused and made me upset."

72

I didn't respond. That was the first time I realized that I had let someone toxic into my life again. My sheltered upbringing had, once again, left me vulnerable and eager-to-please. The phone continued to ping, but I ignored it. Naina snatched the phone. She read the new messages from Jay—ones even I hadn't seen—and, finally made a forward flicking gesture with her chin. I gathered the willpower to turn off the phone and put it away. It made me extremely uncomfortable.

That night at the party, Naina stayed with me throughout. My phone was turned off and in Naina's purse. On the way back home, we picked up Chutney. She sat up front next to the driver and complained about the smog-filled skies of New Delhi—Mumma would have probably done the same thing. Naina asked me to turn on my mobile. "Let's see what the douchebag has to say."

She peered over my shoulder and read Jay's messages. With her hand on her forehead, she screamed, "He doesn't apologize for being a jerk. He blames you for making him upset. He deflects responsibility. He deliberately misrepresents your thoughts and feelings to the point of absurdity. I am going to squeeze his testicles so hard until his eyes pop out!"

Naina breathed hard. "Jay is a malignant narcissist. You need to break off this friendship, Ahana."

I started to sweat and feel queasy. I normally never get carsick. But I asked Baburao to pull over so I could puke on the side of the road. Chutney got out of the car and offered me a bottle of water while Naina held my hair. Chutney offered me tissues. "Naina is right, *beta*. Stay away from Jay."

I blew air out of my mouth and drew my arms above my head as soon as I sat in the car.

"I bet he'll come back with gaslighting." Naina shook her foot.

Both Chutney and I gave Naina a puzzled look at the same time.

"Meaning, he will try to erode your sense of reality. Jay will probably say things like 'That didn't happen,' 'You imagined it,' and 'Are you crazy?'" Naina sighed loudly. "Or he'll plead and come up with a sob story. I know his type." She looked out the window as Baburao started to drive. "This fucking therapy group; I wish I could ask you to quit, Ahana. Because, for better or worse, he comes with the group. But I also know it helps you."

There was a ping.

I hated that Jay could tell from my settings whether I had read his messages.

Naina took the phone from my hands and started to read aloud. "C'mon, babe. You are imagining things and getting all riled up.

Don't be crazy! I didn't tell you about the relationship because it almost doesn't exist any longer. After over seven years together, the bitch walked out, saying we weren't compatible. It's that aspect of my life that I don't like to mention because it reminds me what a failure I am. But you are my best friend and I feel this is a safe space for me to be vulnerable."

The email went on, but Naina stopped to read it. She looked at me. "Fucker still hasn't admitted whether he was married or not and he still defines it as 'on and off.'"

* * *

When we got home that night, I logged onto my therapy group. I wanted to tell someone, *I am so confused about why I let Jay into my life and refuse to cut him out*. When I didn't engage with Jay, he wrote me another message. "You have a pattern, Ahana. No one can tell you anything that you don't like. You turn around and insinuate they hurt you. You walk away from them."

That was my *first* real realization that Jay sounded caustic, just like Dev. It was exhausting, even thinking about the two men.

≈ 11 ≈

We all tried to fill the spaces between silence after Naina left for the United States. She stood by me for Mumma's first death anniversary rituals, and she stayed until I had a lot more clarity about Jay.

Jay had missed checking-in on me on Mumma's first death anniversary, despite my conversation with others on the therapy board about how hard the day was for me. Naina was right; Jay was self-involved and cared for no one. He never wanted to know anything about my life or work. He chose when he would walk away from conversations. It was almost comical how randomly he was offended. I was angry at Mumma for letting me grow up so shielded that I literally had no defenses against the world except a rigid, laughable modesty.

In the summer of 2014, we ran an artwork competition for the T-shirts we were going to give away to conference attendees. I happened to mention this on our chat therapy board. "Babe, maybe you can take my work," Jay had messaged me privately.

"I didn't know you painted."

"Our friendship has changed, Ahana. You no longer take any interest in what I can do. I miss us."

There we go again! "Jay, the competition is open to anyone above the age of eighteen. You should definitely consider submitting your work."

Jay sent his artwork—it was a moustache. A long moustache curling up at each end. The left tip he had painted *hers* and the right tip of the moustache had *his* painted on it.

"Babe, what do you think of my artwork? The *his* and *hers* stands for equality."

"It reminded me of a Roald Dahl character." I couldn't think of anything better to say. I had seen signs like these outside restrooms in Mexico.

We wanted an artwork that would speak of women, safety, and protection without the need to have the name *No Excuse*. We wanted the severity of violence against women highlighted. Understandably, the team didn't pick Jay's ridiculous submission. His competitors had sent in artwork focusing on women's empowerment, VAW, equal pay, and gender equality. We selected the logo of a woman, a caricature, saying NO to violence against women by extending her right arm, with her palm facing forward. It was red in color, as red demands attention, and makes us feel a variety of feelings tied to primitive needs.

Jay got upset when he received the formal rejection email. "I thought you were my friend and you would help me with my business."

"I am your friend, and that's why I told you that we were holding a competition. The final selection, it's not up to me, Jay."

Predictably, he didn't write back. His social media update read, "One of the worst days of my life."

Sore loser! It made me respect him even less.

* * *

Between preparing for the conference and Naina's wedding, and coordinating travel dates with all the relatives, I had very little time to agonize over Jay. I couldn't force him to respect me, but I did make a choice not to be disrespected.

I was buying *laddoos* from Mumma's favorite sweet shop for Rohan when he called on Skype video. "I can't believe you will be in NOLA while I am away in Los Angeles. There are so many places I would have taken you to. Crappy planning, Matron." He made a sad face.

"I am sorry—the dates weren't under my control. I do want to taste Sazeracs with you." I paid for the *laddoos* and walked out of the store.

"Really?"

"Of course! What are they made from?" I sat in the car and asked Baburao to head toward the pickle store. Masi loved mango pickle from a shop in Old Delhi.

"Sazerac is a rye whiskey based drink with Herbsaint, bitters, lemon juice, and a sugar cube. It's pinkish brown because the bitters redden the bourbon. Truly original Sazeracs are made with rye whiskey, though. The Herbsaint adds a very distinct licorice flavor like absinthe, and the lemon makes it tart. If you use bourbon, then it is sweeter so even more complex."

"Can you use wheat bourbon instead?"

"And you call *me* an alcoholic?" Rohan grinned.

"Shut up, ya."

"Nah, no self-respecting Southerner would bastardize their Sazerac with an overly sweet wheat-based bourbon." He smiled.

"Aaah."

"How do you know so much about whiskeys?"

"My mom was a whiskey connoisseur."

* * *

In the third week of September, over three months after Naina had left for the United States, it was time for me to travel westward, and divide my stay between New Orleans and New York.

I was going to fly into New Orleans by the end of September, and spend a few days with Naina's parents, then head over to New York in early October to work with Rohan on the conference. Eventually, I'd fly back to NOLA in November 2014 for the conference and Naina's wedding.

Naina had screamed with joy. "Josh and I can't wait to show you around the Big Apple. Love you. Can't believe you are going to stay with me in NYC! Yay!"

Jay knew I was going to be in NOLA-NYC-NOLA. But since he had never expressed any interest in meeting, at the last minute I decided not to tell him the dates of my stay or travel. I was quite exhausted from the one-sided friendship and his temper tantrums.

* * *

I flew into New Orleans on a Tuesday. Naina often teased me, "Yo, you're the only woman I know who doesn't wear sweatpants on fourteen-hour flights. How can you wear boots and fitted skirts on a trans-Atlantic journey?"

I poked her dimples, "Just the way you can wear track pants with 'glamor' embroidered across your buttocks."

It felt good, thinking about Naina, as I checked in my luggage. I was at Terminal 3 of the Indira Gandhi International airport in New Delhi, purchasing Ayurvedic foot lotion for Masi, when someone touched my shoulders. I turned around. Clad in a red shirt and black designer jeans, my past had caught up with me.

"You are leaving India now? Our marriage wasn't enough?"

I took a few steps back. How did Dev know to find me here?

He walked closer. I could smell his Giorgio Armani Eau De Toilette. "You didn't want to pose for me. But you post pictures on social media for the world to see. You have male friends who comment on everything you post and address you as 'babe.'" He added air quotes.

I held my bag to my chest. Dev has been stalking me online!

Dev didn't raise his voice; others in the store couldn't tell I was being harassed. "You are the biggest hypocrite." He walked an inch or two closer. "You like all the male attention, but you hid inside your Mumma's sari to keep up the pretense of being a *good girl*. Your Mumma is the reason you made up those accusations about rape."

77

Something inside of me shifted; I pushed him. "Don't you dare!" I didn't care if I was making a scene. "You hurt me." I prodded his chest. "Thank God for my mother because I was able to walk away from a monster like you!" The tears blurred my vision. A few store clerks asked whether I was OK. Dev looked stunned. "This isn't over, Ahana."

"No, it is over. Stay away from me." For the first time, I wagged my index finger at him. He stepped back. Whether my words would stop Dev or not, it didn't matter in the moment. I dared to set boundaries. I dared to speak for myself. I boarded the flight with my head held high.

The airplane ride felt longer than usual. This was my first trip to NOLA without Mumma. This was the first time I was going to see Masi after Mumma's funeral. I was cold, and I could barely keep anything down during the flight. I tried to meditate, and then read a book. But my mind kept going to memories of my trips to NOLA with my family. Mumma, the bravest woman I knew, feared flying. She would always sit in the middle, Dad toward the aisle, and me in the window seat. She would press both our palms tightly both before and after takeoff. Even single malts and fine French red wines couldn't calm her nerves.

I looked out the airplane window and realized how much had changed in my life in the past year and a half. Divorced Dev. Moved in with my parents. Lost Mumma. Spearheaded the conference. Got introduced to Jay and Rohan.

I looked for Mumma's face amid the stars. For the first time in my life, I openly admitted to myself that I was slightly upset with her for enabling me. *I wish you had taught me to protect myself instead of overprotecting me, Mumma. If only you had allowed me to stand up for myself instead of becoming my voice.*

* * *

Louis Armstrong New Orleans International Airport felt so strange without Mumma. I felt a sudden emptiness inside of me. I almost thought of turning around and going back to India, when I suddenly saw a fellow traveler's T-shirt with the quote, "What cannot be endured must be cured." I sat on a chair with my bags to my side, and palms cupping my face. What and who would I return to in Delhi? Yes, there was Dad, Chutney, Athena, and a few of my friends. But that was about it. The universe was giving me a fresh start. I had to learn to move on.

Masi and Mausa picked me up at the airport. "You look just like your mother, *beta*." Masi cupped my face in her palms. Her eyes looked empty. I hugged her tightly. Masi pulled out a cigarette or two. We drove home in quietude.

Masi had cooked my favorite *kebabs* and *chicken biryani* with *raita*, a cucumber yogurt salad garnished with crushed mint. "After a long flight, Indian food works best." She patted my palm.

"Good thing you aren't a doctor." Mausa nudged Masi.

We all smiled.

Masi and I sat late into the night, talking. "My mother was a health nut but a terrible cook." Masi and I laughed, thinking about Mumma frying samosas and cringing at the smell of oil. "I get my lack of culinary skills from Mumma, Masi." I leaned into her.

She massaged my head with hot oil, and asked about Dad. I told her how aloof he had become. "I am going to visit him after Naina's wedding, and give an earful. Problem is, after your Mumma, there is no one around to scold your dad. You pamper him too much." Masi kissed my forehead. Mumma, Masi, Chutney, and Naina—they were all just outspoken women. I was the only one who was happier when not using words.

I spent the next few days with Masi. She lived in the Garden District, which was an easy cab ride to downtown New Orleans as well as the convention center. The weather was warm, and passion flower and cosmos flower were in bloom. I strolled through Jackson Square in my summer dress. Two children ran around with airplane arms, just like Naina and I used to.

I was happy to take time off from the conference, therapy group, and chats with Rohan and Jay. Masi met up with me for lunch every day. The bank she worked for was in downtown New Orleans. She took me to Mumma's favorite restaurants. I binged on jambalaya, blackened catfish, and crawfish étouffée. We visited Cafe Du Monde and shared a plate of beignets along with cafe au lait. Mausa, being the leading cardiologist in New Orleans, was able to join us only for drinks and dinner in the evening. He bought Mumma's favorite whiskey and raised a toast to her. He had mapped out the best running trails close to their home for my morning runs. In Delhi, because of pollution, I could almost never go for morning runs. "Going out earlier, before the smog settles, could be injurious to your health," Mumma had warned me.

"How do you know these routes, Mausa?"

He smiled. "These are my secret routes for running away from your Masi when she asks me to unload the dishwasher." Masi threw a cushion at him. Naina got her sense of humor from her father.

On my fourth day in NOLA, Masi got stuck at work; we canceled our lunch plans. I changed into pajamas and got comfortable in the family room and got much needed rest. Running into Dev had unraveled raw wounds, and I hadn't had any time to process our altercation.

I called up Ms. Roy to inform her I had arrived. She said, "On the day you caught your flight to America, Dev showed up at work and demanded to see you." Apparently, our team's newly hired assistant got nervous and blurted out my plans—I knew how Dev worked his charm and intimidation. And Dev knew I only flew Virgin Atlantic or Emirates. There were no Virgin Atlantic flights to NOLA from New Delhi that night and only one Emirates flight that evening. I sighed with relief; it meant Dev and Jay weren't in contact.

I browsed through my phone; there were no messages from Rohan. He was on the West Coast for some work, and then to attend a friend's wedding.

I tied my hair in a bun and wiped my glasses with the corner of my T-shirt. I missed chatting with Rohan. "Aloha, Brady," I texted him and folded my legs up on the sofa. I was such a different person without Dev around.

"Welcome to America!! How was your flight? By the way, I am in California, not Hawaii, :)" he wrote back.

"Ya-ya, very funny. :) Been having a great time in your city." I flipped over so my stomach was pressing against the sofa.

"You are mean!!! You are not even missing me."

"Then why did I reach out?" I ended the message with a smiley.

Rohan sent me an emoji of a man doing the disco.

Paagal." I got up and went into the kitchen to warm up leftover rice and crawfish étouffée.

"You can't have too much fun without me, Matron. Also, given the party animal that you are, thought I should warn you," there was a wink at the end, "much like Delhi, New Orleans is a city of extremes, especially at night. The city is not only known for its rich history and culture, but also for its notoriously high crime rate. The less you stand out as a tourist, the safer you will be. Be careful!"

"Thanks for the tip, Brady!"

"I look forward to seeing you in NYC in three days."

"Bye." I gently tapped the phone against my chin. I wondered what Mumma would have thought about my online friendship with Rohan.

* * *

My first week in NYC was about establishing personal rapport with Rohan's team and as many participants/sponsors as possible in the tristate area. Since Rohan and I worked closely on the conference, both our bosses were thrilled when Rohan suggested he could rearrange his travel schedule to mirror my stay in the United States and work out of New York City for the weeks when I was going to be around.

Five beautiful days in NOLA with Masi and Mausa, and I flew to NYC over the weekend where my adorably mad "sister," Naina, awaited my arrival at JFK airport. When we got to the lobby of her high-rise on the upper east side in Manhattan, Naina hugged her doorman, who was probably seven inches taller and fifty pounds lighter than her. "Haven't seen you in a while, Carl. Where ya been?" She introduced me to Carl. We shook hands. In New Delhi, I couldn't imagine any of us hugging the peon at my dad's office or our driver Baburao. Lakshmi was like family to us, but she too lived in the outhouse and ate after we were done. At Dev's house, the staff wasn't allowed to cook in the same utensils as their bosses.

There were no memories attached to Mumma in NYC. Naina and Josh were the most perfect hosts. We watched a musical at the Lincoln Center, grabbed Thai food in midtown Manhattan, and ate dessert all the way downtown at Rice to Riches. Cool temperatures and a fresh breeze were refreshing after the October heat in New Delhi. We laughed, ate, explored NYC, and shopped as I continued to battle my jet lag.

Sunday night, I debated whether to log into my therapy group and whether to check my emails or not. But given the interaction with Dev and the prospect of having to battle with Hedick, I decided to log in and chat with the group but ignore Jay. Of course, Jay was online, but I didn't initiate a conversation. I had a long, personal chat with Tanya. We came to the realization that I was an over-protected single child. My dependence on my mother was paralyzing. I told her about Dev showing up at the airport. She was shocked my assistant had shared my travel details with my ex. I ended the conversation with "That's Delhi for you, Tanya."

Before I logged out, Jay sent me a note, "What, you come to America and don't even say a hello?"

"How did you know?" I replied immediately and then hit my forehead. I was so mad at myself for writing to Jay. It was out of habit.

"A little birdie told me." He ended the message with a grin.

I stood up and double-locked the main door.

* * *

On Monday morning, I got into work early, which was Rohan's PR Agency's NYC office. Fortunately, Naina's apartment was twenty blocks from it, so I decided to walk.

Rohan and I were supposed to meet directly on Monday evening after I finished speaking with an organization that supported the end of acid throwing on women in Asia. We were to meet at a coffee shop near the entrance to Brooklyn Bridge in downtown Manhattan.

The breeze slightly cut through my skin as I stepped out of the six-train subway stop near the bridge. Autumn in New York was crisp and fresh. It made me nervous. I took my time to readjust my attire, a peacock blue, straight, knee-length skirt with brown-colored knee boots, a crème silk top with a deep neck and orange scarf, brushing away any creases that had sneaked up on me in the train.

I saw gingko leaves scattered on the streets, and I debated picking them up. I didn't like showing cleavage, but thanks to Naina's insistence, my big breasts were nestled comfortably in a Victoria Secret push-up bra that she made me buy. I thought of my cleavage, but I bent over anyway because the leaves were distractingly beautiful. As I did, I noticed a pair of oxblood cordovans a yard from my nose, and I stood halfway up, hair stuck across my face, to see Rohan Brady looking down at me. I stood up immediately, realizing that my cleavage was the first thing in the line of vision.

I tucked my hair behind my ears, revealing the Mikimoto pearl earrings Mumma had bought for me a few years ago for Diwali. I buttoned my earth-colored jacket and pushed my glasses on the bridge of my nose with my index finger.

I had expected Rohan to run late. He had told me. "Matron, it's not that I try to keep everyone waiting. But greatness takes time."

Rohan Brady had shown up before me. He was dressed in a pair of dark blue denim jeans, burgundy and beige striped full-sleeved shirt, and a brown-colored fall jacket. He wore too much mousse in his hair. He was wearing his glasses, not contact lenses.

He stared at me for a few seconds, which made me feel conscious. Rohan wasn't lecherous, but he was gaping.

"Ahana? Is that you, Matron?"

We walked up toward each other. Rohan moved his body forward to give me a hug, but I moved away, gently, not to offend him but to make my stance clear that a handshake was all he was getting that evening. No hugs. No kiss on the cheek. It was as if Rohan were expecting me to be that way. We exchanged a few pleasantries.

Just when I was feeling relieved that Rohan didn't try his playboy charm on me, he said, "Did you never consider modeling?"

"Why do you ask?"

"You have the perfect face. And attitude. Definitely the attitude."
He laughed at his own joke, as I stood cold.

"Brady!"

"What? I was just...."

I was annoyed at myself for getting agitated. Why did Rohan get under my skin?

It was getting nippy and the sun had begun to hide behind the New York City skyline. He blew warm air between his hands and rubbed them together. Being a Delhi girl, I was used to much colder temperatures than Rohan.

"Grab a coffee?"

I suggested we walk around with our drinks.

Just as soon as I ordered my hot chocolate, Rohan said, "Swoon!" He looked faintly bemused, trying to find our old playful groove and forcing it. "One of *those* women, huh? I'm a café au lait guy myself."

I clicked my tongue and told the lady behind the counter that I wanted extra marshmallows.

"Extra marshmallows? Whoa, a woman after my own heart!"

I gave him a dirty look.

Rohan didn't let me pay. He held the door for me as I walked out of the coffee shop.

We started to walk toward Brooklyn Bridge. I carefully scooped out a big piece of marshmallow with a spoon, so it wouldn't stain my clothes, and put it inside my mouth. It was seething hot. It didn't take Rohan more than thirty seconds to say, "Whoa, Matron. You devoured that marshmallow with utter disregard for decency or propriety."

I didn't think it was funny. Or appropriate—no one was allowed to comment on my appetite except for our help, Lakshmi.

Rohan seemed jarred by whatever he read in my lack of a response. He quickly dialed it back and retrenched in a different mode of being with me. He pointed to the different buildings and views and explained the history of New York City. He asked whether I was cold and offered his jacket.

"I am good, thanks." I smiled.

But he couldn't resist. "Are you turning down my chivalry?"

"Stop it, Brady." Rohan tried to get a few words in, but I was relentless. "I know you are trying to be nice, but we'll enjoy the evening more if you can just be yourself, not a PR guy. OK?"

"Sorry." He bit his lower lip.

Practicing yoga for over a decade had taught me to introspect when at unease, and get to the core of the problem. I realized that Rohan's personality, to a degree, reminded me of Dev—the right words, the suave moves, the bright eyes, the endless charm. The feeling of dark familiarity in an unfamiliar place rattled me.

We quietly crossed Brooklyn Bridge, discussing the upcoming conference, when a cyclist, headed from Manhattan toward Brooklyn, rode up close to us on purpose. The suddenness of the cyclist in an unknown place—I thought he was going to grab my breasts or squeeze my buttocks. That's what an incident like this would mean in Delhi. I lost my balance and clung to Rohan. I turned around to make sure it was just a cyclist and not a mugger. Rohan asked if I was OK. Skeins of hair covered part of my face as I grasped for my bearings.

No denying it, there was a spark when I touched Rohan's arms. We both looked at each other and then we didn't. I had spilled my hot chocolate on the bridge. And as soon as I regained my balance, I apologized to Rohan and let go of his arm. We stood surrounded by a few seconds of silence, and then I tried to break the awkwardness of the moment with a few apologies.

"You're basically a sweet girl hidden inside the body of a brave woman trying to make the world a better place—all so selflessly—freaked out like a five-year-old child by a man riding a bike."

"I thought he was a mugger." I lightly hit his arm and checked to make sure my glasses had no scratch.

He took a sip of his drink. "India isn't a place for women. But this is New York."

The hair at the back of my neck stood up. I pulled myself away. "And you know this because?"

"My opinions come from a place of experience. I have traveled to India on several occasions."

I swallowed as much air as I could because the pressure of unstoppable words gnawed at me. I sat on the bench and stared at the open waters. The sun was spreading its orange branches in the sky. The horizon looked beautiful. I wanted to remember the beautiful sight.

I rubbed the pendant I was wearing.

"Is that your mom's necklace?" Rohan asked.

I nodded. "How did you know?"

He smiled. "You were a lucky family that cared about each other."

I smiled but didn't say anything. Before I could ask anything, Rohan turned to me. "Tell me what's really on your mind."

I took a deep breath. "Is India perfect? Not at all. Is it dirty? Yes. Is there poverty? Sure is. Do women get harassed and assaulted?" I bit my lower lip, "Yes, Brady. But no country or culture is perfect. I am not overlooking India's painful truths. All I am saying is that there is a lot of India to go around; one generalization or description or experience or assumption does disservice to any nation or culture. It's like me saying that because statistics show that the United States has the most number of serial killers, all American men are violence-seeking, psychotic assholes."

Rohan moved up closer. "You are absolutely right."

For the remainder of the evening, Rohan and I spoke about the conference. "The theme *No Excuse* was garnering lots of positive attention. All the media powerhouses were going to be present in New Orleans during the three-day conference. Rohan ran a few ideas for another series of press releases his team was going to send out. We had a leading Hollywood celebrity endorsing our conference and the CEO of a Fortune 500 willing to share her story of surviving an abusive marriage, putting herself through school, and attaining all her success. I touched my earrings, hoping Mumma could hear how far along I had come since she last saw me—I was feeling challenged by my own story, but Dev showing up to the airport had pushed me in the direction of needing to not stay quiet any longer.

Rohan and I also talked about our dogs, Socrates and Athena, as well as our hobbies. He was a lot calmer. I tried to be a lot more patient with him. I conceded that over the past few months, Rohan had never given me an opportunity to distrust him. Sure, he annoyed me and I had to fight hard the desire to smack him because he teased constantly. But he always remained kind toward me.

Rohan said, "Despite your tough and strict personality, you care about the small things. You remembered the toys Socrates likes to play with. Like, wow!"

"What's the big deal?"

"I am not used to people caring for me. And definitely not without wanting anything in return. But you are so generous." He spoke in a serious tone.

I knew Rohan meant something deep about his life, but I chose not to let my guard down around his innate abilities. This was our first meeting.

Before we said a goodbye to each other, I handed him a packet.

"What's this?" Rohan asked.

"*Laddoos* from Delhi." I smiled at him.

Unwrapping the box and biting into the decadent, round dessert made with chickpea flour, sugar, ghee, and nuts, Rohan said, "This is heaven. Thank you so much." The solemnness in his eyes stood out.

There was a comfortable silence for a few seconds.

He dusted his hands and said, "Wait, I forgot. I got something for you too."

"You didn't need to."

He pulled a box out of his laptop bag. "Oh, I know. But I wanted to. Since beignets would have gotten spoilt between NOLA, LA, and NYC, I got you this authentic beignet mix."

"But—"

"I know you hate to cook. Maybe your cousin can make it for ya? She is a NOLA girl too, right?"

"That's incredibly sweet of you to bring me this. Thanks, Brady."

Right before we parted ways, I turned to him: "You don't have to pretend with me. You don't have to try hard. I am comfortable with the Rohan Brady I've gotten to know over this past year."

≈ 12 ≈

I sat in the chair and opened my purse. I ate two Altoids and looked around Rohan's temporary office. It was spotless. There was a small basketball net and a bookshelf with books on management, travel, and photography. I got up and picked out a few books without any intention of reading them. I walked back to my seat, put my purse on the empty chair next to me, and busied myself with the folder in hand. The convention center at the hotel in New Orleans where the conference was scheduled had sent over more paperwork.

Rohan walked in and sat in his chair.

I kept pulling my fingers. "I see that you've lined up six radio interviews for me over the next four days. I don't like being on television and radio. I don't like talking to strangers about why this conference means the world to me." I paced up and down. "Why do you throw all this media stuff my way?"

"Because you're the face of the conference. These news outlets help with scalability. Trust me. Just a few more weeks."

"But why do I have to talk about my personal life to others?" I tried not to get angry. "Then have them judge me."

He looked at me, confused. "No one is judging you, Matron. Truth is, people wonder why women work for these organizations and how common abuse really is."

Was Rohan asking me about my life story? The collar of my blouse felt tight.

Rohan walked closer to me. "You have the right to share only as much as you want. Don't say anything that makes you uncomfortable. I'll have Crystal run the latest statistics and give you a spreadsheet so you can talk about numbers. Deflect any unwanted attention. OK?"

I closed the door behind me.

* * *

The next few days were full of meetings with the in-house team. Rohan shared the detailed social media strategy for the three-day conference. We were using hashtags across all social networks for consistency. "I want the conference to trend and the attendees to talk about it weeks before the actual event. Earned media can be powerful." Rohan recommended doing an inspirational post once a week on those working in the space of women's empowerment. "Building a community is vital."

Ads were running; promos and press releases were starting to surface. Rohan had also organized for me to appear on some of the big, feminist, and humanitarian talk shows to promote the conference.

First radio, then television. I was annoyed with Rohan for pushing me out of my comfort zone. On our way to the first out-of-town meeting in Hartford, Connecticut, we got into an argument.

The plan was for Rohan and me to meet at Grand Central Station, go over the presentation, and then take Metro North to meet with the owner of a food company, a big sponsor for the afternoon vegan and gluten-free snacks during the conference. I was supposed to appear on a local radio show in Connecticut, along with the sponsor.

It was raining outside, and despite my light, long jacket, a few sprinkles didn't spare me. I assumed Rohan would be late, so I didn't look to my right or left and basically took off my coat and wiped myself with pocket tissues. The lacy, black bra underneath my beige, silk blouse was visible now. In all this mayhem, as I bent forward to straighten my skirt and wipe any spots on my blouse, the top button fell off. There I was, standing in one of the most picturesque locations in NYC, with my cleavage protruding again.

I cursed Rohan under my breath. Something untoward happened every time I had a meeting with him. I looked for a restroom. As I turned my head to the right, I noticed Rohan standing five feet away with an evil grin on his face. He stood with his wet hair and blue eyes, witnessing my every move. His burgundy tie echoed the color my cheeks were about to turn.

With a tilted, side smile, he walked toward me. "You look beautiful."

I didn't want to encourage him, so I replied with two syllables, "Uh-huh."

He pulled out a handkerchief from his pocket and said, "Take it."

I waved my hand. "No, thanks. I have tissues."

"I am sure you do. But that's not why I was offering."

"What do you mean?"

"I figured you could wear this as a sarong."

"Stop it!" I am sure I growled at him.

"Matron, we both know you are modest. Wouldn't want the world to see your...immodest aura!" Rohan had a wicked twinkle in his eyes.

"What's your problem?" There was no patience left in me for Rohan's sassiness that day.

Rohan laughed unabashedly. "Quite a few."

"I mean, what's your problem with my modesty?"

"*Nothing*. Your modesty rocks." There were no expressions on Rohan's face.

"Listen, Rohan Brady. I admire your brains, and all the work that you do. I love that you want to help a great cause. I recognize that you have put your life on hold for the conference to be a success."

"Why thank you, Matron. Does it hurt to be always nice? You look pretty when you are...."

"I do not care for your ridiculous persona. I don't fall for it like your bimbettes and harem girls." I stuttered to keep up with the speed of angry words sputtering out of my mouth. Grand Central was a busy terminal. Unlike Delhi, where two dozen grimy faces would huddle around those arguing, people in New York walked past us, and no one interfered.

"What persona? You mean my indomitable charm?"

My heart rate increased. "Charm, my foot."

"Ahana..." Rohan tried to get a word in and offer comfort, but I jerked away. I was like a cargo train with failed brakes headed for an accident.

"Don't try your stunts with me." I wagged my index finger at him. "Don't make me lose any respect I have for you."

He looked shocked—probably that I had any respect for him to begin with. We both sat quietly and far away from each other in the train as we rode up to Hartford. My legs were crossed, eyes closed, with hands resting on my knee.

Aside from the necessary conversations with the sponsor in Hartford, Rohan and I didn't talk to each other. I did the interview and disliked every second of being on air, though I acted professionally. "We also promote the need for changing norms and the behaviors of men and boys, and advocate for gender equality and women's rights."

The interviewer wanted to know why I quit my cushy job in banking and started to work for a nonprofit. Dev's face appeared in front of me. My hands handcuffed on my birthday—because he wanted it to be "special." He never once asked what I wanted, which was an intimate brunch with my family. Mumma was supportive of my decision to work toward empowering women, but she too never asked why I changed my career. And here a stranger in a foreign land wanted to know about my inspiration and reasons for supporting women's rights when my own people hadn't asked me *the* why. First Ms. Roy, and then Rohan too, didn't ask if I wanted to be the face of *No Excuse*; he informed me that I was expected to do the interview.

"*No Excuse* will help women stand against violence and educate them to find their voices." I delivered answers to the interview questions with all the verve of a person reading a menu.

The train ride back into Manhattan was scenic; I stared out the window. As soon as we reached Grand Central, I walked out on Rohan and took a cab back to Naina's apartment.

I felt like a foreigner in my own body.

* * *

When I returned to work the next morning, Rohan didn't say anything. I acknowledged that I'd overreacted at Grand Central. I could have told Rohan what I felt without being obnoxious about it. Rohan could have said a lot that afternoon. I am not exactly a saint. But he stayed quiet.

We went about the day as if nothing had transpired the day before. There were more in-house meetings, and brainstorming sessions, which Rohan spearheaded, but not once did he make me feel like I was going to be reprimanded for having rebuked him.

At the end of the day, I asked Rohan whether I could speak with him. He opened the door to his office and asked me to wait inside a few minutes. He had to assign his assistant, Crystal, a few tasks and send a report to his boss, Michael Hedick, who was in London for a big meeting.

Ten minutes later, Rohan walked inside his office and closed the door behind him. "Sorry; I got held up."

"That's OK." I tugged my hair behind my glasses.

"How can I help you, Ahana?"

Rohan addressed me by my first name. It sounded strange in his mouth.

"I am sorry about screaming my head off at you last evening." I got up from my seat and spoke with my hands intertwined with each other. "You must be upset?" I could feel sweat beading on my forehead as I walked around his office. "I'm not saying what you did was acceptable." I kept pulling my fingers apart and bringing them together.

Rohan sat down in his seat. There was an eerie silence in the room for a few seconds. I sat down too.

"I am sorry too. Even if it was not in any way meant to hurt you, I crossed a line." Rohan spoke in an apologetic tone. "You seemed so intense that I was trying to defuse the situation by being funny. That's how I handle stressful situations. Humor. On one hand, because we have communicated over the phone all these months, it feels like we know each other; on the other hand, there are so many nuances that

90

we don't understand until we meet in person. I think we both need to be patient with each other."

I started to walk around his office, again. I paused in my steps and looked at him. "Thing is Rohan, when you joke with me that way, I feel like you are disrespecting me. You are...." I pulled my skirt down.

Rohan got up from his chair and sat on the edge of his table so he was facing me. "I what, Ahana?"

"I take a lot of pride in who I am as a person. I respect you and expect the same in return."

"You respect me?" Rohan sounded surprised.

"Of course I do. Why is that a surprise to you?" I brought my eyebrows together. "I talk to you and seek out your advice often enough—and you've seen that I am not exactly the social and chatty type."

Rohan started to count. "Let's see. You rarely speak and mostly scold. You always refer to my fictitious harem members in our conversations." He stared at the ceiling as if attempting to recall something. "I never bother to correct you because, from whatever little I know of you, once you make up your mind about someone, I have rarely seen you change your opinion." Rohan shrugged his shoulders.

"You are the one who started the joke about women and all the flirting."

"Ahana, I like to joke. You can't take everything so literally." He ran his hands through his hair. "I am not some philanderer who jumps from one woman to another. I am not some fucking sadistic psycho who lies and does things behind anyone's back."

"That's a fair point." I spoke without hesitation.

"Did none of your guy friends ever talk about women?" Rohan looked inquisitive.

"I've never had close male friends." I said it as a matter of fact. "They were friends in college, but they never talked about...."

"What? Women? Boobs? Who they were going to hook up with?"

I looked shocked at the revelation and Rohan's sense of ease with who he was.

"Maybe not to your face, Ahana." He shook his head and continued. "Boys will be boys—doesn't matter where they grow up."

I looked away. That's the justification Dev's mother gave me when I filed for divorce. She used similar words to excuse Dev's sexual violence toward me. She had even gone on to confess that her husband did the same to her, and that we women should accept that as a positive part of our lives—husbands were giving their wives, not mistresses, attention.

"Are you all right?" Rohan asked in a kind voice.

I spoke abruptly. "I have an American friend, Jay Dubois, and he never talks about women and their bodies. He mostly talks about feelings, knitting, gardening, and cooking."

"Gay?" Rohan folded his lips.

"You have an answer for everything, right?" I stared at the floor and rubbed my sandals against the carpet.

"All I am saying is that we have one life to live. Don't make it so hard." There was genuine affection in his voice. Mumma too would often remind me to be kinder to myself.

"You swear to always treat me with respect?" An intense situation was defused, all thanks to Rohan.

He asked with a smile, "Do you want me to give it to you in writing? By the way, I already respect you more than I respect most people."

"No, I trust you. Don't try so hard."

"I'll give it an honest shot. But you also need to relax a little." He looked out his office window and stared at the East River. "I tease you because we are friends, but I don't mean anything by it."

I stood next to him. "But when you make remarks about my looks, and so on."

"Ahana, you are beautiful!"

I felt my face flush.

Rohan took a deep breath and ran his hands over his face. "It's hard not to appreciate that sometimes. But I will work on it. I adore our friendship. I'll never do anything to jeopardize what we have here."

He paused dramatically. "We both need to at least try to believe that the other person only has our best interest at heart. How we respond and communicate might differ because of how and where we have been brought up."

"Valid point." I shook my head.

I knew I wasn't perfect. I was judgmental and had rarely done anything vicarious, as Jay often reminded me. From my therapy group, I had learned that my opinions were mostly rock solid and rarely was I flexible about them. This attitude of mine was unfair.

"You shook your head like a pendulum," Rohan smiled and offered me his hand. "Are we cool, Matron?"

"Yup!" I smiled and gave Rohan a thumbs-up. He was back to addressing me as Matron. It felt comfortable.

As I started to leave, he called out, "Matron, smiling looks good on you. Whatever shit is bogging you down, I'd say give it a rethink. It's not worth losing your happiness over."

I walked out with the folder clutched to my chest.

* * *

I went back to Naina's apartment in the evening, and after a short meditation session, thought about what Rohan had said. He was right. How long would I hang onto memories and nightmares of my past? How long would I chase perfection? How long would I punish myself for a mistake I didn't commit—be it my inability to predict that Dev would change after marriage, or to see that Mumma had heart troubles. I had assumed responsibility and started to feel guilty about things that had nothing to do with me. I had been this good kid and perfect daughter while growing up. I was organized and predictable. I was overprotected. Perhaps that's why I couldn't make peace with my reality: my life was imperfect and I couldn't control any of it.

I played some jazz and read in the living room of Naina's two-bedroom 1,400 sq. ft apartment. After a little, I got up from the sofa and made herbal tea—for a change, it wasn't chamomile. I sent the picture to Rohan.

"Rebel! Don't drink too many of those," he replied right away with three smiley faces at the end.

꞊ 13 ꞊

A few mornings later, I called Rohan. "Can you meet me now?" I spoke fast, but stuttered. "I am sorry to bother you." I couldn't believe that inside of ten days of spending time with Rohan and getting to know him, I had started trusting him.

"You OK?" He sounded groggy.

I paced up and down my bedroom. My face was burning.

He yawned, "Give me twenty minutes and I'll see you at the French coffee shop near Time Warner Center."

I took a cab to the Time Warner Center. The sun was just about coming up. The air was cold and crisp, but the streets of New York were busy. There were runners out for their morning jog like the morning walk devotees in New Delhi. Unlike Delhi, there was no garbage littering the streets. There were no rich, drunk guys driving on the sidewalk and taunting traffic policemen at the crack of dawn. No milkman, with his face wrapped up in a woolen muffler, making home deliveries in steel cans on his bicycle. Even amid the crowd and chaos in New York, I found rhythm.

I shivered as soon as I got out of the taxi and quickly buttoned up my autumn jacket. Rohan was standing outside the coffee shop, dressed in work clothes. I ran to him in panic. "Since his return from London last evening, Michael Hedick has contacted a number of the major speakers to introduce himself, making it look like he's as or more important than you or me!" I shouted.

"Are you sure? Dracula is a dick, but this is really low, even for a sleazeball like him."

"Haven't you seen your emails? One of the speakers, Nancy Gomez, who doesn't want to work with Hedick, reached out to me last night. She copied you on the email."

"Sorry; I haven't checked my emails since last evening—didn't get home until 3 a.m. The meeting with Manchester Distillery, the company sponsoring our cocktail reception, ran over."

I showed him the note from Nancy Gomez.

Rohan's face grew red and intense. "What the fuck?"

I rubbed the tip of my nose. "I can't believe it, Rohan."

"I am so sorry, Ahana. This conference is all because of you. No one should be allowed to take it away from you. We'll figure this one out."

"How?" I felt embarrassed and tried to wipe the tears with my hands, but my eyes betrayed me.

"Nancy Gomez cannot be the only one who doesn't want a sexist pig like Hedick organizing a conference that empowers women." Rohan rubbed his chin. He turned toward me. "How about, in the press release due later this week, we specify that it's an event spearheaded by a woman for the women? Dracula will never put in any hard work if there is no scope for him to get credit."

"No, we can't do that. You are a part of the conference too, Rohan."

"If we want to keep Dracula from stealing the limelight, we have to do this, Ahana. I am not working on this conference for credit. I truly believe in it and you."

I silently cried into his unbuttoned jacket. Rohan cradled me in his arms. "Shhhhhh."

"How can Hedick take over substantive control of the conference? He has never had to visit a colleague in the hospital because she was gang-raped in broad daylight in the middle of Delhi; Hedick has never been groped every day of the week he steps on public transportation in Delhi; Hedick has never had a motorbike rider start masturbating in traffic right next to his window, and have it be an obscene but everyday occurrence. What the hell does he know about women and violence? What does he know about feeling violated every single day in your life?" I whispered into his sleeve.

Rohan pulled me away from himself. He stared into my eyes and asked whether I wanted some water.

I nodded.

He handed me his handkerchief. "Not a sarong substitute before you scold me, Matron."

I smiled a little.

He bought a bottle of cold water from the breakfast cart nearby and urged me to sit down at the tables outside the cafe.

"Ahana, I'm going to ask you something. If you don't want to talk about it, then that's fine. But..." He sucked his lower lip, "what happened with you in Delhi?"

I blew my nose into the tissue. I took a sip of water. I could hear my heart beat. I scratched my forehead and slowly looked at Rohan. "Remember, you asked me if I ever loved someone?"

"Yes."

"His name is Dev."

"You guys dated?"

"We were married."

There was an awkward silence.

"What, you don't talk to divorced women, is it?"

"C'mon, Ahana. I am trying to process everything."

"Such a good, Indian woman, I am. Right? Right, Rohan?" I stood up with my hands across my chest. "Divorced in my early thirties. Don't even look Indian. Don't like to cook. Tall and thin like a palm tree."

"What are you talking about?" Rohan got up.

"I get taunted all the time for not fitting the Indian standards." I came closer to him.

"Whoever says such stuff is fucking ignorant." Rohan paused. "What happened with your ex?"

"I became the biggest cliché in my life. That's what happened."

"He hit you?" Rohan clenched his jaw.

"No...." I gulped some water.

Rohan didn't push me for clarification.

"Dev pursued me throughout college. He was charming and handsome and successful. He had a line of women waiting to date him. He didn't stop chasing me until I eventually said yes. It was familiarity that I liked. Dev and I were from similar families and shared similar tastes. It was easy. But love isn't supposed to be easy."

"You lost me."

"Dad and Naina disapproved of Dev. They always felt he was too influenced by his mother and there was something untrustworthy about him. Mumma was impressed by his charm, and, perhaps fooled by it for several years. She was one of the big reasons why I accepted Dev's proposal." I remembered when Dev raped me, I couldn't fight him off. My body, sometimes, responded to his aggression even though I didn't want any of it. But it was still rape, and I had nothing to be ashamed of; I still had to learn to accept.

"I am sorry, Ahana." Rohan looked at me earnestly.

"He was the only guy I ever dated. He wanted me to turn into a posh socialite who discussed diamonds and European vacations. I was his personal...." I couldn't complete the sentence.

Rohan sensed my discomfort. "You refused the opportunity to be Princess Kate of New Delhi?" He nudged me. "Well, I'll be damned."

I smiled, and it felt good. My insides felt refreshed. I no longer carried the shame of being a divorcée or a sexual assault survivor. New York allowed me to be what New Delhi never did.

"You don't judge me?"

"I always do," Rohan grinned. "But what about specifically?"

"You know," I kicked a pebble, "because of my past."

"That would make me a douchebag. C'mon; you know me better than that."

"It's just that where I come from, a divorced woman is a free-for-all. That was another reason I screamed at you the other day at Grand Central. I felt like you too were…"

Rohan completed my sentence. "Taking advantage of you?" He shook his head. "I flirt and tease because I like you as a friend and we understand each other. At least I thought we did. I respect your devotion to your work and your commitment to making the world a better place." He took a sip of water. "I'm from the South. We'll tell it like it is. None of us has a thin skin, either. Seems to be working out well enough for me in a place like New York."

We walked to the fountain at Columbus Circle. Dog walkers were fussing over their pets.

Central Park was a block away. I stared at the fall colors and thought of the last time I had felt so alive.

"Look at me." Rohan turned me so I faced him. "You're a lot more together than you think or know." He stared into my eyes. "Yes, it kills me to admit that you are nicer, kinder, and a more reliable human being compared to a lot of people I know." He smiled.

I drank some more water. "Have you ever loved and lost anyone, Rohan?"

He looked hesitant.

"What was her name—the one because of whom you pretend to be a playboy just so you can shield yourself from a heartache?"

Rohan ran his palms over his face. "Is it that obvious?"

"Well."

"It's a long story." He tried to discourage the conversation, but I was determined.

"And I have nowhere to go." I started to walk toward the entrance of the park. The newsstands were opening and people were buying newspapers and lotto tickets. I passed a man selling fresh fruits and juices. Horse carriage rides and horse poop welcomed us along with the morning sun. I didn't see many elderly people. Commuters in business formals were rushing toward the subway or entering yellow taxis. Young moms with babies in strollers and lululemon fitness wear were out for a run inside the park. There were patrol cars making the rounds as street vendors started to line up their food carts at different intersections. They were selling inexpensive coffee and bagels and pastry and donuts and the like. There were at least two dozen pigeons fearlessly attacking people holding breakfast bagels in their hands. They were too lazy to fly and too fearless to abandon bread even when shooed away. A few young boys were on skateboards chasing the birds. Homeless men were digging food out of trashcans.

Rohan crossed the street with me. "Rita. Her name was Rita. But this can't go anywhere." He touched my shoulder.

I patted his hand. "I promise."

"We were high school sweethearts. Studied at Tulane University together. It was going perfectly well until I found her in bed with my roommate my sophomore year."

"I am so sorry, Rohan."

"I confronted her. She denied it. Asked for a second chance. I gave it to her like a fool. We dated through college and even after that. I proposed to her and she said a yes." Rohan's eyes looked empty. "We had planned our wedding and honeymoon. But she had plans of her own." He kicked an empty soda can.

"What happened?"

"Oh, I became a cliché in my life, Ahana. While I was in graduate school, working two jobs so I could buy her the house of her dreams, Rita continued with her affairs."

"I am...."

"It is what it is. I'm glad all that shit happened before we got married and decided to raise a family. But betrayal from someone you love eats at your confidence and ability to judge people, doesn't it?" Rohan stared at the ground and let out a sigh.

I knew exactly what Rohan meant.

"Bloody bitch!"

"Thank you, Ahana Chopra, for siding with me." Rohan stared brazenly into my eyes.

"I shouldn't have said that. But it's her loss."

"You think I'm a good catch?" Rohan pulled out a smile from somewhere as we walked toward the Bethesda Fountain.

I laughed. "Oh, God, dumbo! Be serious."

In New Delhi, I couldn't imagine a morning like this. The only place Dev wanted to accompany me to was parties or our bedroom. And almost every time I went for a walk or run alone, there was a scene—the abuse and intimidation in the middle of a road, zero support from passersby who crowded and watched women get harassed like zombies, the auto-drivers rushing to pacify the perpetrator— nothing was pleasant.

"I met her too early in life. Got too serious too soon. Learnt my lesson never to make the same mistake again."

"Meaning you'll never fall in love and settle down?"

Before Rohan could answer, a female tourist stopped to ask Rohan for directions.

I didn't repeat my question. Figured I didn't want to put him in an awkward position.

After talking to Rohan, I felt much lighter. I hoped he felt the same way. It amazed me how Rohan and I could talk about the most dark, painful, and serious matters yet always find space for light humor.

* * *

Rohan and I arrived at work. It was still early, so there was no one around. Before we both went into our respective offices and closed the door behind us, he said, "Matron, I didn't get the chance to respond to your question about falling in love."

"Yeah?"

He flaunted his dimple. "Never say never."

"Good. I'll be on the lookout for a hottie for you." I smiled.

He tapped on the door of his office and smiled. "Don't be picky, Matron—even if there's a pole and an audience involved, don't rule her out."

I looked for an object to throw at Rohan.

"Heehee." He closed his door.

The day progressed. I hadn't been exaggerating when I told Rohan that a colleague had been raped in broad daylight. Word had gone around the company a few days ago, and now, my boss in New Delhi was updating me on my colleague Rakhi's deteriorating status and the political bureaucracy. I worked harder to channelize my disappointment with Delhi, where men preyed upon women and did not allow them to breathe with dignity or safety.

After his 4:00 p.m. meeting, Rohan followed me into the pantry area. As I made a cup of tea, he poured himself a cup of coffee in his patent Saints mug with "Who Dat Nation" printed in giant gold and black. "How are you holding up?"

"It's been an awful day. I am very upset about Hedick. How can he be so conniving?"

Rohan heard me patiently. Somehow, his silence calmed me down so much more than anyone's words ever would have. "I have the draft of the press release ready. Come take a look, and we'll send it out to media outlets bright and early tomorrow, OK? I promise, this countermove will shut up Dracula."

I told Rohan about Rakhi and the email from Ms. Roy with the update. "I am disgusted with New Delhi right now. I never want to see it. But it is also where my family lives and where Mumma's ashes reside. It's her birthday tomorrow and I just...."

"If there is anyone who can take on these fuckers, it's you, Ahana. I know it. Never stop believing in yourself." He gently pressed my shoulders.

I marveled at Rohan's ability to say the most tedious things but somehow manage to comfort me.

* * *

That evening after work, I went to the Ganesha Temple in Flushing, Queens, with some relatives visiting from Connecticut. Naina didn't like them, so she went away to Pennsylvania to hear a psychiatrist speak. I didn't want to go to the temple, but I didn't want to hurt Mom's cousins. More importantly, it was Mumma's birthday the next day, and I knew it would mean a lot to her. We always went to the temple on birthdays. My online therapy friends had suggested I do the things Mumma enjoyed for her birthday and celebrate her. I borrowed Naina's *salwar kameez*, a brocade red, sleeveless, heavily embroidered piece of work, which was rather short and very loose for me. I often teased Naina that she had Bollywood tastes in Indian clothes. On my therapy forum, I posted a selfie of me at the Hindu Temple with the title, "Desi Girl," after the temple visit.

I didn't check my messages until I got back home later that evening. Everyone but Jay had posted comments about how they liked the outfit and my "Indian look."

"I didn't recognize you in your Indian outfit." Jay sent me a message the second I got online. *Stalker?*

I wore my glasses and tied my hair up in a knot and wrote back. "Is that a bad thing?"

"Nah, I am your favorite friend, so I will always recognize you." He added a wink at the end. "I meant you looked beautiful."

"Haha, thank you. But how many women do you pay these empty compliments to?" I added a smiley at the end of my message.

"The only woman I see is my cleaning lady. Trust me, you are not like those fat Mexicans."

I remembered why I'd been out of touch with Jay for a while. I was bloody annoyed at myself for replying so breezily to his message. "How can you make such racist, cruel, and sexist remarks, Jay?"

"Fuck, I feel I am always walking on eggshells, Ahana. We can go from fun to serious so fast when you misinterpret a single little thing. I talk to my other friends, and they all understand that I am funny. Yes, it feels like you are looking for a reason to be disappointed with me sometimes."

I threw my arms in the air. "I misinterpret because we communicate via emails and messages, Jay. You never come to the phone or Skype."

"There we go, again. I told you I am depressed and don't want to pull you down by getting onto the phone, but you won't let it go."

100

I collapsed on the chair as I heard my heart beat loudly. I was angry at myself for engaging with Jay. He knew what buttons to press; I reacted. Mumma would say that my empathy was my strength, but it only made me prey for men who knew what weaknesses to look for.

* * *

Next morning, October 14, I didn't want to get out of bed. I had woken up every hour after midnight. I had gazed at the stars, hoping to catch a glimpse of Mumma. *Is she celebrating up there? Did people wish her a happy birthday at midnight?* I called up Dad, Chutney, and Lakshmi. I tried not to cry when I spoke with them. They had said a small prayer at home and planned to go out to dinner to Mumma's favorite Greek restaurant. The last time we took her there, Mumma had picked up pieces of her favorite feta cheese and repeated a few lines from William Carlos Williams' poem "This is Just to Say":

> "Forgive me
> they were delicious
> so sweet
> and so cold."

When Dad raised a toast to her, she said, "Darling, gastronomy and poetry are a natural pairing."

It felt cruel to wake up in a world where I couldn't celebrate the woman who meant everything to me. I composed myself when I spoke with Naina and Masi in Pennsylvania and New Orleans respectively, but it was hard. My family was big into celebrations. We would cut the cake at midnight. Give our gifts. Plan the birthday dinner a month ahead of time. Being completely alone on Mumma's birthday was another reminder of the solitude in my life.

After finishing the phone calls and freshening up, I did a few sun salutations in the living room to calm myself down. I went to work but didn't see Rohan. When I asked Crystal, she said he was busy with a client. I didn't expect him to remember the importance of the date, anyway.

But Jay was a part of the online therapy group where I had shared that it was Mumma's birthday. There were no "Hope you are OK" messages from him, yet our entire friendship was based on helping each other heal through our maternal losses.

I had mailed him a card from Delhi for his mother's birthday at a P.O. Box number Jay had shared for Baton Rouge. I had checked up on him several times that day to make sure he wasn't depressed. He'd written back, "If you weren't around, I'd probably be someplace way the hell in the middle of nowhere. In the woods or some goddamn place. You're the only reason I'm around, practically."

It did seem odd Jay saying this as though I were a major presence in his life. But what did we really share? My voice had only been a stream of bytes in the global data network. That wasn't a real friendship, was it?

I finished some more paperwork, and right before shutting down my laptop, looked at the time. It was 6 p.m. Not a word from Jay. I didn't want to talk to him; however, I expected a note. A part of me wondered whether Dev and Jay had connected over social media—all the hints that Jay had been dropping about my past made me nervous. Dev hadn't made any contact since the airport incident. I needed to stay connected with Jay to find out what he knew and whether he was in communication with my ex-husband.

⚡ 14 ⚡

Rohan was sitting in the lobby of Naina's building when I entered. I was so lost in my thoughts that I jumped when he cleared his throat.

I held my laptop close to my chest. "What, are you a stalker now?"

Rohan pointed at his phone. "Or a good friend who is worried about you not answering your text messages."

I pulled out my phone from the handbag. "Oh shit, I am so sorry! I put it on mute while I was working on estimating breakfast costs for the conference."

"I bet you thought I was an inconsiderate jerk not to call and check on you." He pressed the elevator button and held the door for me.

I was overwhelmed to see Rohan. Today was one day when I didn't want to be alone. And without me uttering a word, he had shown up.

As we reached the eighteenth floor and the entrance to Naina's apartment, I stepped around him and slid my key in the lock. "Seriously, why are you doing this?"

Rohan set my bag, his laptop, and a bag of groceries down on the cubby by the door. "I am cooking you dinner. This is a major friendship step. Now, remember my awesomeness whenever you get mad at me." He laughed in an exaggerated tone.

"*Paagal.*"

He stretched his arms over his head. "Since I wasn't in NOLA when you visited, I am bringing New Orleans to you tonight."

"I am not hungry."

"You look like you haven't eaten all day, Matron!"

"But...."

He pushed me onto the sofa. "I am sorry I couldn't call you earlier. I was at a client off-site in New Jersey. Fucking, moronic drivers in the Garden State. I tried to text you several times to ask what you were in the mood for." He rubbed his hands together. "But I am here now, and I'm going to make us some Southern comfort food."

Rohan looked around for something. "Do you not have any wine, Matron? Shame on you. And here you keep bragging about Indian hospitality. Tsk. Tsk." He grinned.

I was so tired; I didn't rise to the bait. He continued, "See, my Irish genes come in handy in moments like these." Rohan pulled out a

French pinot noir, my favorite, from the grocery bag, and set it down on the table. He hummed and fumbled around in the kitchen, looking for a corkscrew. He looked so comfortable in a strange kitchen, happy to cook, while I ran away from the mere mention of cooking. Rohan poured me a glass of wine and served some olives stuffed with bleu cheese along with it.

"This is too much, Rohan." I had spent the day feeling lonely and exhausted with no one to talk to. The outpouring of his generosity overwhelmed me, especially today.

"No, it isn't. I am a Southerner. And you know what they say about Southern hospitality?" He busied himself in the kitchen.

I crossed my legs and sank deeper into the sofa. "No, I don't."

Rohan covered my feet with a throw. "Relax and enjoy yourself."

It felt good to be taken care of for a change.

We discussed my own thirty-minute talk scheduled right toward the end of the conference. We had argued plenty, and he was aware of my reservations, so Rohan asked me gently what I was willing to do for my job, how I would approach my responsibilities, and what I was willing to risk for the conference so it would truly be a truth-to-power event. With the conference less than three weeks away, I needed to decide. This had to be a speech and closing remarks to remember.

Rohan poured me my third glass of wine.

"Can I ask you something, Rohan?"

"Are we turning this evening into let's-grill-Rohan night?"

"No. No." I waved my hands as if trying to dismiss a bad smell.

"Then sure." Rohan smiled and sat back on the sofa.

I wiped my mouth and collapsed deeper into the sofa. "Why do you like New Orleans so much?"

"New Orleans is the perfect place for romance." Rohan took a sip of his wine.

"You know what intrigues me the most about New Orleans? Women sit on their guys' shoulders and flash the world? I know using the word logic defeats the purpose of Mardi Gras. But, c'mon; everyone but the guy sees her *thing*. That's awful!"

"Verbalize *thing*? What does *thing* mean?" Rohan teased.

"Her tits. Boobs. Breasts. Happy?" I stared at the floor as my face heated up.

"I'm assuming the guy sees them later when the girl is totally drunk and they are in the hotel."

"Excuse me? What are you hinting at?" My hands were on my hips.

"Haha, don't flatter yourself, Matron; I said hotel."

I tried to hit him, but he was too quick for me and got up from the sofa.

"All right, let's get some food into you before you get sick." Rohan hummed and behaved like the perfect friend and host.

He played Frank Sinatra in the background and made a big Cajun meal: blackened catfish, red beans and rice with Andouille sausages, corn in a special sauce, and a big salad.

Dinner was delicious.

I raised a toast to him. How well Rohan and I fit, despite our opposite worlds; it scared me. I was learning to trust and take risks again. How he helped me open the lonelier parts of myself that I shared with no one confused me. Our friendship had started to feel so old and comfortable; I was grateful.

I ate like I had never eaten before. "That's my third helping," I said coyly.

"How are you not as big as a house?" He laughed loudly.

"You caught me on a day I hadn't eaten anything at all," I mumbled softly with tears in my eyes. I didn't tell him I hadn't eaten this well since Mumma's death or my divorce.

There was a pause for a few seconds. I have no idea what that meant.

Rohan cleared up the dishes and didn't allow me to get up from the table. He served us some New Orleans style bread pudding with whiskey sauce that he'd brought with him. "To your mom. Happy birthday!"

I stared at him with tears in my eyes.

"It was your mom's favorite dessert, right?"

When we were married, Dev didn't even remember Mumma's birthday. I had to remind him every year to wish her.

"Any tea or coffee, Matron?"

"No, thank you." I looked at him. "I won't be able to sleep."

Rohan picked up his laptop bag and walked toward the front door. "I better get out of your hair. We both have an early start tomorrow."

We were facing each other.

"Thank you for celebrating Mumma tonight," I said with my voice cracking. A dam broke in my eyes, but I didn't allow the tears to fall outside my eyes. "I will always remember it."

Rohan pouted. "I never get any lap dances from you. I am beginning to not trust you any longer." He smiled and offered me the box of tissue next to the shoe rack.

I punched him lightly.

"Your mom sounds like an amazing lady. I am honored to have celebrated her birthday with you." He opened the main door.

I closed the door and stood between the door and Rohan. "What happened with your mom?"

"Well, that came out of nowhere." Rohan arched his eyebrows.

"I am sorry. It's just...." I ran my fingers through my hair and looked for the right words.

"Nah, I am OK talking to you about it."

He sat on the cubby close to the door. "I didn't know my mother really well."

I sat next to him on the floor in *Virasana,* also known as Hero Pose—kneeling on the floor, with my thighs perpendicular to each other and my knees touching. I slid my feet apart with the tops of the feet flat on the floor. This asana made me feel rooted, and I had to be strong to support a friend and listen to another story of loss. This pose also aided with digestion, and after all the wine and food, I knew I could use help.

Rohan didn't comment on my seating choice. He looked lost in the corridors of his past. "My father was born and raised in New Orleans. He met my mother when they were both in graduate school. She was the teacher's assistant, and he always needed help—at least pretended to just so he could hang out with her." Rohan sighed. "The year Mom left, everything felt confusing. I didn't understand what was happening."

"Did she say anything?" I handed him a tissue.

"Not really. She had started to keep silent. My dad, like a typical Irish man, wallowed in guilt after Mom walked out, and he somehow decided to blame himself for the wreckage in our home. He turned into a recluse and I had nowhere to go." Rohan stroked his chin. "I kept wondering if I had done something wrong. My mind went to places no eleven-year-old boy's mind should go. I wondered what had made Mom leave. I even waited on the front porch of our house, many nights, until it was dark, but she didn't return. I didn't know of any other Indian kid whose mother had walked out on him. I didn't know any Indian kids in foster homes. I didn't know of any broken, Indian homes. All Indian moms I knew were like your mom, Ahana."

I couldn't comprehend how any mother could be so callous. Naina and I were the epicenter of our mothers' worlds.

He wiped his face with his long fingers in a downward motion. "Ahana, you are lucky to be surrounded by attentive family members who seem to have given you reinforcing, empowering messages throughout your life. After Mom left, my dad taught me never to cry. 'Because crying makes us weak and vulnerable,' he said. He didn't want people at school to pity me. He didn't want us talking about Mom. I was stupid to think that my mother would come back. After being abandoned by both my parents, in their own way, good thing I don't believe in waiting for anyone any longer."

"My dad, like your father, doesn't like to talk about Mumma or his pain. We can't evade the truth that Mumma is gone. Instead of tiptoeing around the subject and avoiding spending time with me, it would be nice if I had his support."

Rohan looked at me, "I didn't know."

I shrugged my shoulders. "Like you say, 'It is what it is.' It's like I lost both my parents at the same time." I stood up. "I am sorry about your mother, Rohan. No child should have to grow up without a mother." My head felt heavy.

"I am sorry about yours, Ahana." He gave me his hand as I fumbled for my steps and stretched my eyes.

I hugged him tight. It was comforting, being around Rohan. I could feel his unspoken words: *I hear you, and I am here for you.*

Rohan patted my back softly and gently pulled away.

Our eyes met.

He cleared his throat. "I better leave."

* * *

After Rohan left, I made some mint tea and sat on the sofa. I couldn't tell whether he hated his mother or felt confused by her behavior.

I took a sip of the tea and mindlessly scrolled through my phone. There was a note from Jay. "I guess that is the true definition of being broken, though. Not knowing where even to begin after being heartbroken and betrayed. It's brutal, isn't it? Good thing I am there for you. I know others have broken your trust."

I sat up straight and ran my tongue over my lips. I poured myself a glass of water and reread Jay's message. My throat suddenly felt dry. What did he mean by "heartbroken" or "betrayed?" I pressed my temples.

Was my privacy at stake? Jay made me feel a little afraid. For the first time, I used the door chain lock to secure the main door.

≈ 15 ≈

My head hurt from all the wine the night before. But being a running addict, I woke up before sunrise, drank hot water with lemon, and changed into my running pants, a long-sleeved shirt, and light workout jacket in case the morning chill was damp. I looked at my Garmin right as I stood up from tying my shoes. It was 5:45 a.m.

My cell phone rang.

"Brady? Everything OK?"

"Sorry to wake you up. I was worried whether your family is all right."

I pressed the phone between my left ear and shoulder as I rubbed hand sanitizer on my hands. "Wait, what?

"There was an earthquake in Delhi."

I sank into the cubby next to Naina's shoe rack. "How did I not know about this?"

"It happened in the middle of the night for us." Rohan sounded a bit congested.

"Thanks for letting me know. I'll call Dad right away." I always stay calm under crisis—a trait I get from my father.

A little later, I showered, dressed, and left for work. I walked into the office and literally ran into Rohan's room.

"You all right?" He got up from his chair.

I threw my arms in the air. "I can't get through to my dad. I have been trying all morning. Naina tried, too."

"Did you try your aunt or anybody else who would know about his whereabouts? Or even your dad's work number?"

"It's after work hours there." I scratched my eyebrow. "I keep getting a message that he is out of area. My aunt isn't answering her phone either." I rubbed my pendant and tried to breathe. "Maya, my friend in Delhi, is vacationing in London." My eyes were welling up. "I shouldn't have made this trip to the US. I shouldn't have left him alone in Delhi. I should have stayed with Dad."

I opened Rohan's office door and started to walk out.

Rohan quickly followed behind and stood in front of me. He closed the door and asked me to sit on the red couch in his office. He sat on the edge of his office table and spoke sympathetically. "Ahana, none of us can control what's going to happen in our lives. You could have been in India but traveling when the earthquake happened. You can't lock your father up in a room and punish him because you fear something will happen to him. You can't become a prisoner in your own life. If not today, you'll resent him for it a few years from now. And he'll resent you for it."

Mumma was gone. I couldn't lose my father too. I started to cry. "He's all I have left."

"He'll be fine. I promise." Rohan's voice dropped.

"You don't know that so don't make promises you can't keep."

"I am sorry." Rohan handed me a tissue and spoke in a tone that mothers use to pacify their five-year-olds' temper tantrums.

"No, I am sorry for being edgy." I felt tightness in my chest. "Ever since Mumma died, I have never once stopped to worry about my dad. Yes, his work and golf keep him busy, but I also have a feeling that he buries himself under an insane schedule so he doesn't have to deal with Mumma's absence. He forgets to meet me when we have dinner dates. A few times, he forgot to pick me up at the airport. How many times am I supposed to let it go?" My face was burning.

Rohan poured me a glass of water. "You're the one who says that we must think positive because that impacts the outcome of everything. Why have you made up your mind that anything bad will happen to him?"

"You listen to what I have to say?"

"I know, right?" He smiled and brought me a piece of pen and paper. "Write down your dad's contact information. We have offices in Delhi. I'll have someone check up on him."

"That's so generous. Are you sure?"

"Who is being formal now?" Rohan put his hands on his hips, emulating my style. "Didn't the Doña of Matronsville, as in you, once tell me that friends help each other without keeping scores?"

As I started to wipe my tears, he asked, "Do you need a few minutes alone?"

I breathed heavily. "Yes, that would be nice." I didn't need the rest of the office to see what a wreck I was in the morning. I was a terrible crier. Somehow, in front of Rohan, I cried so easily.

I gave Rohan my dad and Chutney's mobile phone numbers as well as their office and our home addresses. Rohan dialed a number as he walked out of his office and closed the door behind him.

I looked over my shoulder, and once he was gone, I blew my nose into the tissue and threw it in the garbage. I pulled out the small mirror from my makeup pouch and noticed that the kohl underneath my eyes had spread to my cheekbones. I pulled out another tissue from the box on Rohan's table and cleaned my face. I stood up and looked at the boats in the East River. The waters looked calm.

A few minutes later, there was a knock at the door.

"Is it OK to come in?" Rohan asked.

I turned around. "Please. Don't embarrass me."

Rohan closed the door. "I have some media contacts in Delhi who have special access to telephone lines in times of crisis. They'll patch you through to your dad."

I wet my lips and throat. "Is he fine?"

"Yes, he is, Ahana. You might not be able to talk to him for long because these guys need to keep the line free for emergency reasons. But you can hear your dad's voice."

I walked to where Rohan was standing, "I don't know how I'll repay you."

"I am pretty creative; I'll come up with a way." He grinned.

The phone rang. A familiar voice said, "Hello, Ahana."

"Dad!" I spoke in an authoritative voice. "You OK? And Chutney and Athena? And the rest of the gang? Why didn't you call me?" My voice cracked.

"I didn't want to bother you in the middle of the night," Dad said in response.

"Seriously? It didn't occur to you that I might be worried."

"I am sorry, *beta*. Come back to Delhi now. I need you here." For the first time since Mumma's death, Dad asked me for something.

"No golfing until all this settles down." I hung up without acknowledging his demand. I didn't want to leave the US without finishing what I had come here for: the conference.

As I said a bye to my father and handed the phone back to Rohan, he said, "Wow, you are a dictator even with your dad."

"Of course! Aren't you with yours?"

Rohan ignored the question.

"Sorry…. Didn't mean anything by it. I should be nicer to you, Brady."

"I can teach you new ways to be nicer." He winked at me.

I picked up my handbag. "You are an ass."

Rohan smiled. "Matron, hope you remember about the planning meeting with national officials, representatives of NGOs, and grassroots women's groups? Hedick won't be there now that the press release is making its rounds."

I high-fived Rohan. "Yes, of course! I have printed out twenty-five copies of our presentation."

"Awesome! I have to see Megan Black before our big meeting this afternoon. How about I meet you in the lobby of the building fifteen minutes before the big meeting? You have the address, right? It's right across from Bryant Park."

"Coffee date, Mr. Brady?"

"You've been keeping me so busy; I've been ignoring all the women in the Big Apple." Rohan pouted.

I rolled my eyes.

"Matron, Megan Black is the PR Head for Shine On, the bath products company sponsoring the gift baskets for the speakers."

"I know!" I winked at him. "I was teasing you, Brady." I tapped on his door. "I am wondering whether we can ask Megan to host the segment on acid attacks at the conference."

"What does that have to do with Megan? If we want to pitch it to her, we need to be sure of the angle we are going to use."

I moved closer to him and showed Rohan a video on YouTube. "You don't remember this one?" I pointed at his laptop. "This campaign where a young girl teaches high-school girls and their moms to boost their self-confidence and expand their views of what beauty means by taking makeup-free selfies with their smartphones and posting them on social media? Brady, even in India everyone was talking about the five-minute documentary film."

"Oh fuck, now I remember. Megan's documentary director, Anisha Blackwood, made this piece. Fuck, I had completely forgotten about this connection!"

I touched Rohan's arm. "If you get her to say yes for handling the segment involving female survivors of acid attack, it will be brilliant. She'd be such a positive role model for it."

We thought of names for the segment and finally agreed on "Shadow." Rohan covered my hand with his. "I've worked on a project with Megan in the past, so I think I can make this work." He smiled at me as I closed his office door. "She is a powerhouse with a big ego, but will be pivotal to the conference. Keep your phone near you—in case we need to join forces to win her over. Megan needs winning over."

* * *

The preparation to detach myself, so I could speak with a steady voice at the meeting, started in the women's bathroom. I practiced *pranayama*, a few breathing techniques, and told myself over and over again: *you are not your past.*

The meeting and my presentation went well. I wanted to include a special reach initiative that was often ignored: marital rape. Inspired by Hillary Rodham Clinton's remarks at the U.N. 4th World Conference on Women Plenary Session in Beijing in 1995, I gave my presentation.

I emphasized that the only way for a society to flourish was if women were free from violence. The only way families could grow was if women were free from violence.

I breathed deeply. "In many countries, exemptions are given to husbands from rape prosecution. People do not understand the extent of trauma suffered by rape and sexual assault victims, especially when the offender is a loved one. Opinion polls show that people still believe that wife rape is less harmful than stranger rape." I cleared my throat and took a deep breath. "These women battle depression." I paused and pressed the sides of the podium. "Umm, they have trouble forming trusting relationships, blame themselves for the mess, and often develop poor body image issues." I thought I would break down in the middle of the room.

Rohan stared at me with a crease in his eyebrows, but eyes filled with pride.

I took a sip of water. "Women raped by a partner is sacrilege, because in addition to the violation of their bodies, they are faced with a betrayal of trust and intimacy. They are violated by someone with whom they share their lives, homes, and possibly children. Often, victims of wife rape are not likely to see what is being done to them as a violation of their rights, because of lack of awareness as well as support. Society has only recently legally recognized wife rape as a crime in some countries."

I saw heads nod in agreement. My confidence grew. "Cities and nations and schools and offices and streets need to be made safer. People of all genders need to be taught the importance of *No Excuse*. Not accepting any form of violence could help communities and nations do well. That is why every woman, man, child, every family, every community, and every country could only gain from supporting ending violence against women."

My face was burning and turned the color of a tomato by the time I finished my presentation. Many of the people present spoke with me personally about the initiative. Given the number of executives present, I was surprised we didn't have any ego battles at the table. They understood why we needed to come together as a coalition and create awareness about freeing women from violence, especially intimate partner rape.

"Dude, you were a rock star!" Rohan shook hands with me just as soon as we got inside the elevator.

"You think so? I was so nervous." I wiped my sweaty palms.

"You nailed it." He pointed toward the building's entrance. "What you did in there, that was fucking amazing! Even if it's not this year because of logistics and what have you, I have a feeling we'll have more partners and supporters next year for the event."

"What makes you think this event will become an annual thing, Brady?" I just wanted to get through the next week and not think about Dad's insistence that I return to New Delhi.

* * *

It was a quiet evening in Bryant Park. I wanted to know whether Rohan had guessed what transpired between Dev and me. The way he had looked at me in the middle of the presentation told me a lot. But Rohan didn't say much.

I spotted a team of little girls ganging up against one boy. "This reminds me of when Naina and I were kids. We would always become a team. And Naina would make all the boys run errands for us. If anyone objected, she would ostracize them from the game."

"Is any woman in your family not a tyrant?" Rohan asked teasingly.

"Haha. I don't think so. Naina and I, we even slept in the same bed, curled up against each other, holding hands. We all spent the summer vacation at our house in Delhi or at her house in New Orleans. My grandparents too would join us."

"Such fun memories."

"During my Christmas break, and sometimes summer holidays too, Mumma, Dad, Chutney, and I traveled to New Orleans to be with Naina and her family. And just like these girls you see, we would ignore all our boy cousins and other guys in the neighborhood. We were so happy to count stars and chase butterflies. Mumma and both my masis kept *mango lassi or* lemonade ready for us after we had been out in the sun. Naina and I even shared our drinks."

"The pair of you, such tormenters. How come I never saw you in New Orleans? Your aunt lives in the Garden District, right? That's where I grew up."

"Because you were probably chasing cute girls when I was playing in the rain."

"What makes you think you aren't cute, Matron?"

I blushed. "Rohan, *kuch bhi boltaa hai.*"

"What did you say in Indian?" He prodded my elbow as I looked at the floor.

"In Hindi, *ullu*. I didn't speak in Indian."

"Say that again. What does it mean?"

"I said, 'This owl says anything that comes to his mind.'"

"This *ullu* made you blush." The word sounded hilarious in Rohan's mouth.

113

To avoid further embarrassment, I changed the topic. "I love the St. Louis Cathedral in New Orleans."

"What about it?" Rohan looked at me.

"The architecture is gorgeous. But there is this peace I get from attending the Mass. I feel like everything will fall into place."

"When you are in NOLA, I'll take you to a cafe that makes the best bread pudding. It's right next to the cathedral. As a kid, I went there, well my parents prayed there, only so I could eat that darn bread pudding." He smacked his lips.

Before I could say anything, Rohan stood up. "I'm going to get us some coffee." He hit his forehead with his right palm. "Oops, tea for the British Matron here."

"Very funny." I shook my head. "But it's my turn, *yaar.*"

He interrupted me. "*Yaar.*" He repeated after me in a heavy American accent.

"It means 'friend' in Hindi."

"You keep talking to me in Hindi. You must like me."

"Such an ass." I rolled my eyes and pretended to look annoyed.

"I know. Stop obsessing about it in public." Rohan grinned.

"*Paagal.*"

Rohan paid for two beverages and added a few bills to the tip jar. The server looked like a young boy who was probably a student. He flashed a big smile in Rohan's direction. It was these small things about Rohan that I appreciated.

"Here you go, Matron." He spoke with an English accent.

"Thank you." I took a sip. "May I say something, Rohan?" I held his hand. He looked at me.

"Don't worry. I am not proposing." I laughed.

He smiled.

"You have a safe space with me—if you ever want to talk." I offered him a fist bump.

He returned my fist bump. "You are a good friend, Ahana. I'm on your side."

I got up and dusted my dress. I finally knew what I wanted to focus on for my speech for *No Excuse.* I had worked too hard on this conference for someone like Dev or Jay to tarnish my reputation.

I exhaled loudly. "It's OK to trust people. Not everyone is looking to hurt you." I suppose I was also preaching to myself.

16

A few days after Rohan and I hung out in Bryant Park and shared a little bit more about our personal lives, we were scheduled to meet with one of the sponsors in Midtown west.

"I'm glad Doug is only one of our sponsors. I could have run around the reservoir twice in the time you guys spent talking about sports."

"A runner, eh? Seeing as we only talked about sports for maybe ten minutes, you must be an Olympic medalist."

I dusted my hands. "Maybe I am. We've never talked about running."

"Why do we need to talk about it? Meet me at the South Park entrance at 5:30 p.m., and we'll see how fast you are, Matron. If you win, I'll stop calling you Matron."

"Let's make this interesting, Brady."

"I am listening."

"If I win, which I will, you'll have to take a yoga class with me."

"At the studio near Naina's place?"

I held Rohan's wrists. "How do you know?" I ran my tongue on my lips.

"Chill out and stop thinking so much, Matron!" Rohan smiled with the authority of a mind-reader. "You post quite a few pics of the yoga studio and your hot teacher Sheila on social media."

"Oh." I sighed loudly.

Rohan smiled and brought his shoulders to his earlobes. "Back to our bet. If I win, which I will, you'll hang out with me at my favorite dive bar in NOLA. Keep your cocktail dress ready."

It was fun being competitive around Rohan. "Fine, and how about loser buys winner dinner?"

"Ooh, look at you trying to wiggle out a date with me." Rohan's tone changed.

I hit him lightly on his arm.

"I am teasing, Matron. I'm not that desperate."

I half-snorted.

Rohan gave me an amused look and joined in the laughter.

I felt something in that moment. *Did he feel something too?* I wondered. Rohan read my mind it would seem. "All your New Delhi boys in the metro will be happy to see this smile."

"I don't take the metro, mister." I spoke without thinking.

"Princess Ahana has a Mercedes and a chauffeur. She fancy." He double-stressed *fancy*.

"I didn't mean it like that."

He put his hands in his jacket pocket and bit his lower lip. "I'll see you in the evening."

We said our goodbyes, walked in different directions, and went about the rest of the afternoon.

* * *

It was Friday; I left work early so I could get back to Naina's and relax a little. Be it the bureaucracy or dealing with cultural misunderstandings or getting reminded how much evil exists in this world, the conference preparation had exhausted me. I put on the kettle and listened to Ella Fitzgerald. I noticed I was humming, for the first time in years.

I changed into my running clothes and walked to the park. Over a dozen horses were tied to carriages, ready to give people a tour of midtown Manhattan. Tourists were bargaining with coachmen. The Middle-Eastern street vendor was making fresh falafels, while street performers were prepping up for their next act. The rush of traffic, meandering tourists with their shopping bags...it was nice to leave them behind and enter Central Park. The big rocks, birds chirping, array of fall colors, small pond, crisp air, the temptation of quiet and peace inside the park. I didn't think of work or therapy or Jay. I was grateful to be here.

Rohan showed up, fifteen minutes early and ready to go. He had his Garmin. He stretched his quads and then his arms. I knew Rohan ran everything from 5Ks to marathons. But the calves on him told me I was going to grab a drink with him in NOLA and buy him dinner later that evening. *Shit!*

We both switched on our Garmins.

"OK, so I have the route mapped out." I pointed toward a map of the six-mile loop on my phone.

"Got it, Matron!"

We ran. We looked happy. We competed. We didn't have to make eye contact with the other runners we crossed. Rohan, every now and then, tried to run in front of me, so I would slow down. Such a *paagal*. We ran to run away from whatever each of was running away from. It would seem running gave us both an out. In Delhi, I often had to wear a mask because of the polluted air in the mornings. At night, if I decided to go for a run, I had to worry about my safety. I clenched my jaw thinking about New Delhi. In New York, people and the weather let me be.

While I was lost in my thoughts, I saw Rohan speed up. My average run speed is 8:23 a mile. Yes, I am that into details. But Rohan was way ahead of me. I sped up. I ran like I was running away from my attacker or chasing a mugger. But Rohan won.

"Cheater." I was panting.

"Hey!" Rohan hit me lightly on my elbow. "I won fair and square."

"Is it really fair and square," I imitated his American accent, "if you don't tell people you are a seasoned marathoner and entice them to compete with you...." I waited to catch my breath.

"Oooh, sore loser!" Rohan folded the fingers in his right hand such that it looked like a microphone and coughed, "loser" into it.

"Shut up, *yaar*." I smacked him.

"All right. All right. Let me show you something."

"What? Where?" I squinted my eyes.

"Sheesh, you difficult Indian aunty." Rohan smiled at me. "Trust me. I think you'll really like this place."

We started to walk in quietude. No specific reason, mostly because we were exhausted. After a few moments, we arrived at a castle in the middle of the city. My eyes couldn't believe it.

"Pretty neat, eh?" Rohan looked at me. "It's the Belvedere Castle."

"I love castles." I spoke excitedly as we climbed the stairs.

Once we reached the upper observation deck, I saw a 360-degree view of the park. Buildings on one side and the reservoir on the other, I had never seen anything more calming in my life. I felt free.

I took out my phone to capture some pictures.

Rohan snatched my phone. "Let's take a selfie."

"Give it back." I tried to reach Rohan's right hand.

"I will if you take a picture together first. And the caption will read: 'Team *No Excuse* reports from NYC.'"

"Thank you for all your support, Brady."

Rohan put his arms around my shoulders. There was a beautiful blue pond in the background. The sun was shining in our eyes. "Say, 'Who Dat?'" Rohan yelled in my ears.

The picture turned out to be hilarious. Rohan with his lips twisted and me with my eyes rolling.

Rohan started to laugh hysterically.

"Laughter comes so easily to you, Rohan." I focused on an empty space in the air between us. Yes, I envied him.

"It's important for all of us to surround ourselves with positive people who lift us up." Rohan gave me his hand. I grabbed it; he pulled me up.

He and I walked to the park entrance.

"I am going to head back to New York Road Runners. You wanna come?"

"What's that?"

"It's a non-profit running organization based in New York City. They have free lockers where I left my stuff."

We were at the fountain at Columbus Circle, waiting for the walk light to turn white, when Rohan said, "Did you know that the New York Marathon is the world's biggest and most popular marathon?" He pointed at the park. "A lot of people we saw running in there might have been prepping for it."

I stretched my arms over my head. "I wish we had things like these in Delhi."

"Fitness stores? Or marathons?"

"Locker rooms and public places in the middle of the city where you feel safe. In New Delhi, women have two choices—one, to retaliate and make it clear that lack of safety is unacceptable; two, to cower down, look for the shortest route home and make a mental note to avoid that particular road or store or locality whenever possible. I feel suffocated. And there is also the case of monkeys."

"Monkeys? I don't get it."

"I have a wild story for you."

"You're giving me goosebumps, Matron."

Rohan grinned; I hit his arm.

"In New Delhi, a few times, monkeys have chased me." I started to laugh thinking about the time when I was out for a run near the parliament and the monkeys came running after me. "I was screeching like a mad woman and the monkeys kept chasing me until they had a run-in with a fruit vendor. Then they went after him and the bananas displayed on his cart."

"You are making shit up." Rohan tried to stifle a laugh.

I touched the lump in my throat. "I swear. I am not kidding." I started giggling. "Once our help, Lakshmi, was attacked by monkeys because she refused to let go of the bag with fresh bread in it. I kept telling her to put it down, but she was adamant."

Rohan asked intently, "What happened?"

"They bit her bum." Despite my efforts to hold in my laughter, I sputtered like an old water faucet and snorted loudly. "I am sorry."

"God, this is the funniest and weirdest story I've ever heard." Rohan erupted in laughter. "Move to the United States." There was a certain look in Rohan's eyes that I hadn't seen before. "I mean it, Matron. Move here. New Orleans, much like New Delhi, is notoriously famous for its sweltering hot summers, cuisine that makes

118

your taste buds sing, and legendary musicians. And you can tell me more of your monkey stories." He elbowed me.

I looked at him. "Brady, before I can even think about moving, we have to get through this conference." I didn't want to tell Rohan about my father's request without determining whether my dad really wanted me to return to India or he had just blurted those words in a vulnerable moment.

"At least make it an annual thing."

I shrugged, "One thing at a time, OK?" We were at the mall entrance.

Rohan laughed, "Really? What crazy life are you leading outside of work? So far, I've seen mugs of chamomile tea, a book, and a lot of very late e-mails from you. Sounds like a rocking social life."

I laughed. "Are you saying I couldn't go out on a date if I wanted to?"

"I *know* you can't pick a guy."

Our argument continued as we crossed the streets and entered the Shops at Columbus Circle and took the escalator up to the New York Road Runners' store.

"How about I prove you wrong?" I stood in front of his face as he opened his locker.

"Pick you up, at 7:30 p.m.?" He slammed the locker.

"Where are we going?"

"You owe me dinner, Matron."

"I know! I mean where?"

"That's a surprise."

"Fine. I'll pick up a guy afterward."

Rohan shook hands with me. "We have a deal."

* * *

When I reached Naina's, I took off my running shoes and socks. Naina's luggage was in the living room and dirty dishes were piled in the sink. *Piglet!* I cleaned up the kitchen floor and wiped the counter with anti-bacterial wipes. After making myself a glass of green smoothie, I pulled out a colorful glass from the cupboard and poured the healthy drink into it. I folded my legs and sank on the sofa. The quiet time was so sacred. I liked living in a city where I was unknown.

I noticed an arch of a rainbow outside the living room windows fading quickly. NYC was full of magic indeed. I texted Naina, "Welcome back!!" and told her about my dinner plans with Rohan. She was in a meeting, so she sent me a quick response with three heart emojis and one of fire emoji.

I browsed through my work emails. There were pictures of jute tote bags, which we had ordered as gifts for our plenary speakers. I'd hired a nonprofit in rural India to make these handmade bags, and they had done an incredible job.

I logged into my online therapy group to share the success and recent developments related to the conference, because the moderator said it was important to share positive improvements with the group in order to reinforce positivity. I was delighted to read the message from Nina, the lady who'd lost her son in a car accident, that she had brought home a puppy. She finally felt ready to care for another living being. I left her a congratulatory note on the therapy group's message thread.

There were several notes from Jay.

"Hey, what's up?" That was the first message.

"Guess what? I bought another cat. I saw her and I had to help. I have a weakness for those in need."

"She is a Persian cat. I have named her Diana...you know, like the princess? She is a beauty and I had to have her."

"She looks into my eyes and purrs. Looks like she was betrayed just like you. You would love her. Beautiful things like each other. :)"

What did Jay mean by *betrayed like you*? I took off my tank top and fanned myself with it. I knew we were no longer talking the death of my mother. Jay sounded unhinged. How I wish he'd just log off and go feed his cat.

I looked at my phone again. There was a photo of Diana the cat. I read further.

"Nothing from you, Ahana. Sorry; didn't mean to disturb you on your busy day."

I wrote back, "Hey, I was out for a run. Congratulations on Diana. I had no idea you were planning to adopt a cat."

Once again, it felt as if Jay was waiting by the phone. In less than ten seconds, I heard from him, "I didn't adopt. Paid big bucks for it. $1,500."

That's a weird comment.

He sent me a picture of Diana perched over his head. This was probably the first time Jay had sent me a close-up picture. Maybe he was starting to build trust? In all his selfies he shared on social media, you could see mostly his silhouette, not his face clearly. I took out my glasses and wiped them with a tissue before putting them on again. I looked closely. Jay had small green eyes, wide eyebrows, angular features, a long chin, and a narrow mouth—the expressions on his face made him look untrustworthy. I tried not to be harsh, but having worked with female victims and survivors of violence, I could get a good sense of people's personalities by just looking at their faces. With Jay, even his smile seemed fake—it only involved his mouth. There was no emotion in his eyes or face. I couldn't tell what his hair looked like because the cat strategically covered his head.

But I was relieved about one thing: Jay's picture proved beyond any reasonable doubt that Dev wasn't behind Jay's online personality. They were two different men. But I still had to find out whether they had connected over social media.

The first time I'd seen Rohan's photograph, right before he and I connected over social media, I never felt anxious or fearful. Rohan looked cheeky, handsome, and a bit of a cad. But there was something warm about his face. There was coldness in Jay's eyes.

"You there?" Jay interrupted my thoughts with his note.

"Nice cat hat. :)" I wrote back.

"I wish the universe would show me kindness the way it has shown you. You are so lucky to have everything you do."

I didn't write back. Seriously? Could we for once not discuss how "lucky" I was?

Suddenly, my phone rang. I was startled, thinking maybe it was Jay.

"Whatchya doing, sis?" Naina sounded excited.

"Jay...."

"What did the fucker do this time?" Her voice was stern. "Cough it up."

"He got a cat."

"Sooo?" Naina had this drawl in her accent whenever she was taken by surprise.

I wanted to tell Naina about my suspicions about the Jay-Dev connection, but she was so critical, I shut down. "He got a Persian cat and sent me the photos."

"That Jay is turning into a real loser. Hope you didn't write back."

"How could I not, Naina?"

"Yeah, because the good Indian woman is trained to take shit from all."

"Naina...." I tried to interrupt. I wanted to tell her that I was slightly scared.

"Ahana, stop being so fucking available all the time!"

I tried saying something, again, but Naina yelled, "I am not done yet. When was the last time Jay asked about *you*?" She continued, "He bought a Persian cat? They don't come cheap. Every trip to the vet costs upward of $200. I know because my fiancé has one. If a guy is so broke that he can't visit you, his 'friend' in NYC, how can he spend over a grand on a cat?"

"I don't know." I had wanted to tell her that I shared similar concerns, but I couldn't tell Naina anything because we never did have a normal conversation when it came to Jay.

"He got busted, pal. He is a liar...that much we know for sure. I need you to ask yourself what *positive* although dysfunctional purpose Jay serves in your life."

I couldn't take Naina's harshness any longer. "I've got to go, Naina. Rohan is picking me up at 7:30 p.m."

"Yeah, you just don't want to hear anything against that fuck face. I don't know why you can't see that Jay is manipulating you."

"Love you too!" I hung up abruptly. Seriously, Naina! If only you'd hear me out once.

I was uncomfortable with the vibe I was getting from Jay, but a hunch about Jay wasn't enough to come to any conclusion. I had to know more.

Even as I stumbled from the sofa and hopped into the shower, I felt a little tired. The run had felt so good to my body and mind, but I just wanted to crawl into bed and sleep.

That said, I didn't want to cancel on Rohan, maybe because I worried he would tease me to death: "Yo, Matron! You ditched coz you are avoiding treating me!" Or maybe because I was starting to enjoy his company. After my divorce and Mumma's death, I had not cared for anything social or myself. I met with my friends in Delhi occasionally because they were old relationships and could get away with dragging me to places. But the emptiness inside my heart grew an inch bigger every day.

I scrubbed my body in the shower, but I couldn't wash away Naina's opinion of Jay. She was right; how did he find the money to bring home a Persian cat when he had repeatedly told me, "Money is tight, babe"?

He never so much as even sent me a card. I mailed him a first-edition J. D. Salinger for his birthday from Delhi. He sent me a picture of a flower the day after my birthday. I sent him a gardening set for Christmas, again from New Delhi. He sent me an ignorant note, "Merry X'mas! Or is it offensive to wish you since you are Hindi?"

I massaged my head with conditioner and thought clearly for a moment—I had to mail the gifts to an address in Baton Rouge because Jay always had an excuse. "Not NYC, hon. I like to go to the place my mom liked for me to visit over the holidays or my birthday."

Wrapping my body in a towel, I stepped out of the shower. Maybe Jay doesn't live in NYC at all. If he lied about his whereabouts, he could be lying about anything. I felt ants crawl all over my body.

A little while later, I checked my phone. It was 7:15 p.m. *Shit*, I muttered to my reflection in the mirror.

"Running a little late. Sorry. Fifteen extra minutes, please?" I texted Rohan.

"Are you trying to wiggle out of that dinner you owe me?" he wrote back.

"No, I swear."

"Chill, Matron. Now that I know you are running late but still coming, it's totally fine. I know greatness takes time." He ended with a smiley.

I put my phone on the dresser and pulled out clothes, jewelry, and shoes from the closet in my room. I changed into a fitting, spaghetti strap blue dress slightly above the knees. I wore pink lipstick and pearls and left my hair loose. With a pink jacket, brown Christian Louboutin heels, and a clutch, I walked to the elevator around 7:42 p.m.

There he was, clad in a sports jacket and denim jeans, sitting on the sofa in the lobby of Naina's building, furiously typing away.

"Hello, there." I waved.

"You look like a million bucks, Matron." He gave me a gentle hug.

I smiled at him. "Thank you. You clean up pretty well yourself, Brady."

"Shall we, Madame?" He offered me his elbow. I took it.

Despite being a loyal NOLA boy, like a seasoned New Yorker, Rohan whistled and called for a cab. He gave the cabbie the address, but I didn't pay attention.

I checked my phone. There was a message from Jay: "You must be out. Enjoy time with the family. Shimmies and hugs sent your way."

"Boyfriend trouble?" Rohan tapped my shoulder.

"Please." I rolled my eyes and hid my phone.

"All OK at home with Dad and Naina?"

"Yes, it is, Brady."

"You seem distracted. What's going on?"

"Sorry; I have some bloody crap on my mind. A glass of wine and I promise to be better company."

Rohan pointed toward the entrance to a tiny bistro hidden in the corner. We were in uptown Manhattan on the west side. This little gem of a place, called Mom's Recipes, had Turkish lanterns, Mardi Gras beads and Indian copper cooking utensils as part of the décor.

"Table for two." He smiled at the female maître d' who looked extremely young.

"Did you make a reservation, sir?"

"Yes, I did. It's under Brady."

"Like Tom Brady." She fluttered her eyes. "Your table will be ready in five minutes, Mr. and Mrs. Brady."

"It's not Mrs. Brady. We are friends." He grinned at the maître d'.

"Oh, in that case, I get off work at 11 p.m." She bit her lower lip.

What a bimbette! I muttered to myself. I took off my jacket. "Gosh, it's hot in here."

Rohan stared at me. "Wow, you look fucking amazing."

"Thank you." My plan misfired. I was trying to be sarcastic about the sexual undertone in the chat between Rohan and the maître d'.

Rohan whispered into my ear. "Hah, I scored a date before you did, Matron. Shame on you." I could feel his breath and grin on me. And that made me feel something I had never felt before.

I walked an inch closer. "The night has only just begun, Brady."

Rohan looked at his shoes, closed his eyes, and let out a sigh.

As we sat at the table, I looked Rohan up and down. "I bet you're one of those guys who has never heard 'No' from a woman before and dated gorgeous girls through school and college."

"School? Pfft. I started in kindergarten." He grinned.

"*Paagal.*" I arched an eyebrow.

Rohan leaned forward. "You like me!"

"Shush, I am finally beginning to find you borderline tolerable. Don't push it."

He leaned in. "We can work with that."

Our server got us the menu. Rohan turned to him. "I had pre-ordered a few items before we got here. The last name is Brady. Could you bring those out first? Thank you."

"Certainly, sir."

"What did you do, Brady?"

"Nothing. Just made sure the foods I like were in stock."

"You're a terrible liar."

There was a bottle of French pinot noir and good Delhi-style food—*paneer* and almond *kebabs, seekh kebabs* made out of chicken mince, *butter chicken, naan*—leavened Indian bread, *saag*, and a green salad inside of ten minutes of us sitting at the restaurant.

"This is such a nice gesture, Rohan." I tried not to let words choke in my mouth. "Some of these items remind me of food at my mom's, especially this *saag* dish made from mustard greens and spices. In Delhi winters, this is a staple at my parents." Mumma, though not the best cook in the world, made the most delicious *seekh kebab*.

Rohan looked pleased. "Don't get emotional. I brought you here so you could finally start to think of me as a good guy."

"And that helps me how?"

"Not you, silly. Once you approve, I can show some Rohan-love to your friends and cousins."

"Aaaah. Now I know your motives." I ate a big spoonful of the *kebabs*. I felt famished and insatiable that evening.

Rohan noticed. "Easy, tiger. That *kebab* ain't going anywhere."

"Very funny. This isn't an Indian restaurant. How did you get them to make these dishes?

"Mom's Recipes has a cool concept. The owner is from back home. They have a fixed, international menu, but you can order ahead of time and ask them to cook homely dishes too."

"Doesn't matter what cuisine?"

"Nope, it doesn't. They guarantee the taste of grandma's cooking."

"The food is mind-blowing."

"I am glad you like it." Rohan wiped his lips with a napkin.

He gave me undivided attention that evening. I didn't think about Jay or Dev. Rohan had also ordered a traditional Indian chai made with spices and one of my favorite desserts: *gulab jamuns*. Naina referred to them as "heaven disguised as fried cottage cheese dipped in sugar syrup flavored with rose."

Suddenly, my phone rang.

I looked at the screen. "Hey, Nainz, everything OK?" I said with food in my mouth.

Rohan frowned with worry. I wiped my mouth and put my hand on the receiver. "Sorry to be rude, but I'll be a second."

"Please, by all means."

"Ahana, the photographer rescheduled our meeting to Saturday afternoon. Did you wanna hang?"

"I am out to dinner with Rohan."

"I know. What are you guys doing after?"

"I am not sure."

"Give the phone to him."

I looked at Rohan.

"What?" He looked puzzled.

I covered the phone with my hand, again. "Naina wants to talk to you."

"Sure," he took the phone. "This is Rohan."

The two chatted like long lost friends. I looked confused when Rohan snapped his finger. "Preach it, sister." He laughed. "Nice talking to you too, Naina. See you guys in a few." Rohan hung up.

"What just happened? Did Naina actually like someone, one of my friends, enough to make plans?"

"Yes, ma'am. We are meeting Naina and Josh at a club in Chelsea."

"This late?"

"Don't worry; we'll get you a senior citizen drink."

"Such a meanie."

"What? You asked for it."

"But, seriously, you are very lucky."

"How so?" Rohan dropped his fork on his dinner plate.

"Naina has rarely liked anyone new in my life." My mind went to Jay. I sighed and took a sip of water.

"Looks like you talked me up in front of her." Rohan let out a grin.

"High hopes."

"Always." Rohan smiled.

While we were talking, the maître d' stopped by. "May I help you with anything else?"

"I think we are good for now. Thank you." Rohan wiped his mouth and set the napkin on the table.

She spoke in a husky tone, "Was everything satisfactory?"

She sounds desperate! I took a bite of the *gulab jamuns* and tapped my bowl.

Rohan stole a quick glance at me. "I am in extraordinary company tonight, so yes." He looked at the maître d'. "Thanks for your fabulous service."

The maître d' walked away.

Before I could say anything, he looked at me. "Don't gloat. I said all that so she'd leave."

"Here I thought I was amazing." I dabbed my lips with the napkin and smiled at him.

"Oh, you very much are. But tonight is about you picking up a dude, not me."

I put my hands on his wrist. "I haven't felt this happy in a long time. Thank you so much for everything."

While we were chatting, the server brought the check. I tried to snatch the bill from Rohan's hands, but he didn't let me pay.

"But I lost the bet."

"You are a guest. I insist." Rohan ran his eyes over the total and gave his credit card to the server.

"But it's not fair, *yaar*."

"You can show me around Delhi when I visit." Our eyes met, but I broke it off.

"Who knows when that'll happen!" I took a big sip of my chai.

Rohan looked confused.

I put my cup down. "I'm sorry. I'm misdirecting my annoyance."

Rohan held my right hand, pausing me in the way. "What's on your mind, Matron?"

"I know I'm an idealist. But I have a hard time believing that a friend could ever be jealous of their friend."

"Where is this coming from?"

I liked how Rohan immediately didn't assume I was referring to him the way Jay always did.

I sighed loudly. "I've told you about my friend Jay, right? He wrote to me today and said that he thinks I'm very lucky and blessed."

Rohan stayed quiet while I ran through the quick version of the past year.

"It hurts because he knows everything I have been through with Mumma. Nothing comes easily to me."

I couldn't read Rohan's face. It frustrated me. I wanted him to say something. Take my side. Bash Jay. But that wasn't Rohan.

Rohan wiped his hands in the napkin. "I am between a rock and a hard place. You tell me; you want my suggestion, or do you want me to hear you out?"

"Both."

Rohan took a deep breath.

I had no idea where our conversation was headed.

"You expect people to be a certain way and attach a mental note to their abilities."

"That's not true." I sunk into my chair with the cup of chai in my hand.

"You take things too personally." Rohan lowered his head.

I felt slightly attacked. "What do you mean?"

"Take your friend who has been bothering you. Whatever he does, you think he's personally attacking you." He put his cup on the table. "Are you two a thing?" His face changed expressions.

"God, Rohan. No! Can you ever think a man and a woman can just be friends?" I said in my most annoyed voice.

"For the most part, no. Because one of them eventually falls in love and the friendship gets messed up. But there are always exceptions."

"Typical American."

Rohan's face settled into a grave expression. "See, this is what I mean. Stop personalizing everything."

I was about to respond, but the server brought back Rohan's credit card and the customer copy of the receipt. He looked up. "I am not talking about you and Jay. I am making a universal statement based on my observations."

"Well, your observations are inaccurate. I have no feelings for Jay."

"Then why does he get under your skin?"

"It's fine. I can manage this on my own."

"I can't help you unless you tell me what's going on."

I had tears in my eyes. I blurted out, "I am in therapy.

"Yeah, OK, so?" He signed the receipt. "I see one sometimes, too, along with everyone else in New York."

"When Mumma died, I couldn't deal with it. My marriage had ended not too long before. I reached a place I never thought existed. I joined an online therapy group and that's where I met Jay." Tears rolled down my cheeks.

Rohan offered me his handkerchief. "Where is the problem?"

"Jay gets upset when I'm happy. Like he wants me to stay depressed, you know? Isn't that what we want for someone we call a friend?"

"A word of advice: a true friend might sometimes get jealous, but they will always be happy for you."

"You don't think I'm being judgmental in thinking Jay doesn't always have the best thoughts?"

"You have strong instincts. If they tell you something, believe them."

I scratched the tip of my nose.

Rohan spoke with a straight face. "Maybe Jay likes you?"

"No, ya, Rohan. For the longest time, I thought he was gay. That's why I got so comfortable opening up to him. He's straight, but there is nothing going on between us. We chat about our moms." I stopped for a second and ran my fingers through my hair. "We used to discuss our mothers, food, books, gardening, and yoga. But lately, it's gotten a little bit weird."

"Have you tried talking to him?"

"We have only ever chatted over the message board or email. He says he's too depressed to talk over the phone."

"You have never spoken with him?" Rohan scratched his forehead with his right hand. "How long have you known him?"

"Pretty much as long as I've known you." It felt cathartic talking to Rohan. Naina was so biased against Jay that I no longer wanted to talk to her about my suspicions about him.

"Are you for real?" Rohan exhaled loudly. "Where does your friend Jay live? What's his full name, again?"

"Jay Dubois. He shuttles between NYC and Baton Rouge."

Rohan typed something on his phone and then looked up at me. "When will you guys hang out?"

"It's not important for him that we meet in person." I didn't look Rohan in the eye.

"And you are OK with whatever terms Jay chooses." Rohan poked his tongue into his right cheek.

I got defensive and pushed the chai away. "Jay and I are each other's support structure. That's what part of our online therapy is about. I mean, who takes the time these days?"

Rohan shook his head. "Your cousin Naina, who you said got back into town today, is taking you out to a club because she wants you to have a good time. I am in NYC so we get to know each other as friends."

"I'm sorry. I didn't mean...." I tugged at his arm.

"Ahana," Rohan interrupted me in a firm voice. "Everyone is busy. We make time for the people we care about."

"I know," I said with a little embarrassment.

"I don't know Jay Dubois. I understand he fulfills a certain side to you. All that is great. But you feeling obligated to take care of him is ridiculous." Rohan got up from his chair and slipped his jacket on.

"Uh-huh." What more could I say? As I buttoned my coat, I understood that Rohan was just being a friend. He wasn't making a martyr out of me.

I walked up to him on the sidewalk as we prepared to go to the club. "Rohan, you care about me?"

He looked at me intensely. "Sometimes, you are so oblivious to everything."

"Like what?"

He walked a few inches closer to me and stared into my eyes. "Everything can't be spelled out, Ahana."

His deep blue piercing eyes had mischief in them, but they also made me feel safe. I looked at him. "Thank you for spending time with me and showing me around the city. It means a lot to me, *yaar*."

Ten minutes later, Naina and Josh emerged out of the subway, holding hands. The two of them had something I never did with Dev—perhaps, most people searched their whole lives only never to find it. Naina kissed me on the cheek. "Damn, girl! Looking smokin' hot."

I could feel my face flush; Rohan smiled.

Naina looked at Rohan. "I am so sorry. The subway broke down and there was no signal—couldn't call you guys."

"Not a problem. New York subways are unpredictable."

"Hey, man, they are better than public transport in other cities." Josh spoke in a heavy Italian accent in defense of the Big Apple. "By the way, I'm Josh Rossi." He extended his hand to Rohan. Josh, at 6' 6", with a crew cut and brutish good looks, believed in firm handshakes and keeping relatively consistent eye contact while communicating. He looked away only when the other person was thinking.

"Nice to meet you, Josh. I'm Rohan Brady. I work with Ahana." The men shook hands.

"You are the Southerner to whom Ahana lost the running bet?" Naina gave Rohan a gentle hug. "I've been wanting to meet you."

"And I have been wanting to meet you." Rohan smiled at Naina.

"You're from Louisiana, Ahana tells me."

"Yes, ma'am. Nawlins."

"I'm a NOLA girl myself. Josh here is a Yankee policeman who refuses to move down South and learn what life means." Naina covered her mouth with a gasp and said "Yankee" with a drawl. Dramatic flair was a part of Naina's personality.

I hugged Josh. "Now there are two mental people from New Orleans adding drama to this evening."

"I heard that," Naina growled.

Josh said, "Unless you guys want to reenact the Civil War on the streets of New York, I suggest we move our conversation inside."

"Hold on; do you have something against us Southerners?" Naina hit Josh with her multi-colored, beaded clutch.

"I'm on Josh's side." I high-fived Josh. He never crossed his arms on his chest or slouched, so I had to jump to reach his hand.

"Is that so, Matron?" Rohan moved up closer. He was no longer acting distant.

"Don't mind my sister. She's a New Delhi snob," Naina said to Rohan.

We all walked toward the club entrance. Our names were on the list. One of Naina's colleagues' husbands worked there.

Surprisingly, the club was not loud. One section was the bar and dance floor. Several smaller sections for small groups were divided off by chiffon curtains. I guess I must have looked surprised when Naina turned to me. "What? You didn't think I'd bring you to a loud place filled with harassers?"

"When you said club, I thought...."

"See, she doesn't even trust her sister." Naina looked at Rohan and pointed at me.

The two had ganged up against me. It was both endearing and annoying.

"How is New York treating you, Ahana?" Josh asked as we went through the process of checking in our coats. I'd first met Josh seven years ago in NOLA, and I had immediately liked his sincerity. He was the only guy I knew who was as involved in the wedding planning as his fiancée. Josh was level-headed, and it occurred to me that I could probably discuss my suspicions about Jay with him. But I didn't want to talk about Jay in front of Naina because she would get judgmental.

"Not bad. But I am ready to go back home to Delhi after the conference. I miss my dog, and Dad said he wants me back." I spoke loudly so Rohan could hear me. I saw his face drop. What did he expect?

"Naina and I will visit you once she knows how many more *saris* she needs after the wedding." Josh put his arms around Naina's shoulders.

"I am going to be a new bride once, Josh. And I need at least as many *saris* as my age."

"What logic is that?" Both Josh and I spoke at the same time.

"Am I wrong, Rohan?" Naina asked.

"A beautiful lady is never wrong." He smiled. "What can I get you guys to drink?"

"I'll come with you, man," Josh said.

"I'll have a Bourbon. Neat." Naina put her arms around Josh's neck and pulled him toward her. She gave him a short kiss on the lips. The two belonged together.

I looked away, but not before stealing a glance at Rohan. I'd thought he would roll his eyes and make faces at romantic gestures. But he looked mellow.

"Bourbon for Naina. French pinot noir for you, Matron?"

"Nope, a spicy vodka martini, please." I didn't want Rohan to think he knew me.

Rohan gave me a look of surprise before he and Josh walked toward the bar.

Naina settled into the comfy sofa and took off her shoes. "Oooh, you're having a crush on Rohan right now!"

"I am not! We're just friends!" I crossed my legs.

"Liar! I can tell you like him."

I told Naina about the dinner but not the conversations with Rohan about Jay.

"Do you know how difficult it is to get a table at Mom's Recipes, Ahana? Three months minimum. How did he pull that off?"

"I don't know. But he had arranged authentic Delhi food. Everything was extraordinary."

"Rohan is a good guy. His intentions seem genuine and important. He pays attention to your needs—the dinner tonight he organized for you, that's sincere. He's here hanging out with Josh and me on a Friday night when, if he wanted, he could have any choice of women. He's a fucking hottie!" Naina looked around to make sure Rohan and Josh weren't around.

"I don't know what to tell you. He's a great person; just not someone I want to date."

"All I'm saying is, keep an open mind." She stretched her arms over her head. "What news of fuck face?"

"His mood swings baffle me." I was cautious with how much I shared.

"I know that look. What did he say, Ahana?"

"A lot of things." I stared at Naina's bright pink stilettos.

Naina pointed at my phone, "Show me." When I didn't, she snatched it from my hands and unlocked it. She read Jay's messages in silence. I saw her face change color as she scrolled up and down the screen.

Naina clenched her teeth. "Ahana, Jay is a fucking psychopath. He's manipulating you. He is unwilling to see his own shortcomings and uses everything in his power to avoid being held accountable for them. He guilt trips you, knowing fully well how you'll respond."

"I agree there is something creepy and exhausting about Jay, but I can't walk away from a friend when he needs me."

"What friend? A friend is someone who shows up. And that person in your life right now is Rohan." Naina pointed in the direction of the bar where the two men were. "Jay only knows how to take from you."

I brought my eyebrows together.

"You aren't a part of Alcoholic Anonymous, Ahana. You aren't his fucking sponsor."

Naina raised her voice. "That dipshit has never ever sent you so much as a thank you card. Jay is playing you and you don't wanna see it!"

Naina got up from the table after handing my mobile to me.

"Where are you going?"

"You are being exceptionally stupid right now, and I can't see you hurt yourself. I'm going to smoke a cigarette."

"Naina…." I wanted to put my head on the table and rest.

Before Naina could leave, Josh and Rohan returned with our drinks.

"Hey, babe. Is everything all right?" Josh handed Naina her bourbon.

"Just dandy." Naina sat with a loud thud. "Catching up on business at Ahana's House of Charity."

I closed my eyes. Josh was about to say something, but I cut him off. "What is that you're drinking?"

"It's a Sazerac," Josh replied.

Naina's eyes popped. "They make Sazeracs here?"

"No, they don't. Rohan told the bartender how to make it. Like a boss!" Josh folded his palms together and moved like a wave, as if honoring Rohan.

"You mind if I steal a sip?" Naina had still not buttoned up her coat.

"Honey, you don't have to ask," Josh replied. He looked at Naina so dotingly. I had never once seen him look at another woman. He was one of those guys: one woman, one life, one love, and one marriage.

"Rohan, this is good shit! I'm so impressed you got the bartender to make a Sazerac."

"I got one for myself too. I'll trade it for your bourbon," Rohan suggested.

"Are you sure?"

"It's just a drink." He smiled.

"I'll take me a Sazerac, please." Naina happily switched her drink with Rohan's.

"Are you not going out for a smoke?" I asked.

"Is it a problem if I sit here?" Naina glared at me.

"Naina...." I ate three olives from my martini and gulped my drink. It was delicious but slightly bitter and spicy. But I liked it. It tasted better than Naina's words.

Naina took another sip of her drink and turned to Rohan. "We're throwing a party next week for our engagement in NOLA. Do you want to come, Rohan?"

I stared at Naina with disbelief.

"Sure; I'd love to! If it's all right with Josh too," Rohan replied.

"Awesome!" Josh chimed in. "JetBlue still has tickets available, so you might wanna get on it, bro."

"Thanks, man!" Rohan pulled out his phone and went to the JetBlue website. "And there'll be a tea bar for the Matron, right?" Rohan asked Naina jokingly.

Naina brought her palms together and placed them between her eyebrows. "And a fucking charity corner too where people will be given ten minutes per person to share their problem with Ahana Devi." Naina, when angry, could be mean.

I felt alone in that crowd. I felt a part of nothing. All I wanted from Naina was a little empathy, but what I got was harsh criticism and judgment. It felt like I didn't matter to anyone. The more I cared, the more it all hurt. I felt like a prisoner in my own body. I wanted to go away from these familiar faces and memories.

I picked up my embroidered clutch and walked heavy-legged toward the bar without saying a word to anyone.

The line was long. In Delhi, sons of politicians or goons never waited their turns at any clubs or pubs. If you tried questioning them for breaking rules, you'd hear one common threat: "Do you know who my father is?" But in New York, some people looked as if they were born to stand in a line.

With bodies rubbing against my neighbors, I tried to cover my chest by folding my arms across them—the agony of being big-breasted.

"Miss, can I buy you a drink?" A blonde guy, who looked like he was in his mid-thirties, asked.

"Who me?"

"Of course. I'm talking to the prettiest girl in the club."

It was a tacky pickup line. And I almost said no. But I turned around to see Rohan standing at the bar, looking straight at me. *What the hell is he doing here?* I was tired of being the strict Matron. I was fed up with people thinking I was one-dimensional. I was feeling humiliated by having Naina reinforce the image of me as a weak, matronly person, so I decided to flirt a little.

"Hi, I'm Ahana." I hiccupped. "Sorry."

"Beautiful name, just like you." He extended his hand. "Mike."

"Thank you." I tucked my hair behind my right ear. My balance felt a bit weakened.

"Where are you from?"

"Umm, India." I felt mentally confused.

"Indian girls and their accent. Something you can never have enough of."

"Hahaha." I threw my head back and my walk staggered a little. I caught Rohan staring at me and making a so-so gesture behind Mike's back. I ignored him.

"What can I get you to drink?"

My gut said not to accept the drink, but I decided to anyway. "I'll have a dirty martini," I whispered into Mike's ear. My lowered inhibitions surprised me.

"Good taste and good looks. Hard to come by," he whispered back and winked at me. His index fingers pointed at me like they were a pistol and he was firing at me.

Just as soon as Mike used his elbows to break through the line and reach the front of the bar, Rohan showed up behind me. "Lose the guy. He's a creep."

I turned around and stared directly into Rohan's face. My speech was slurry. "And this is coming from a guy who had no problems flirting with a young server at the restaurant?"

Before Rohan could say anything, Mike showed up with the drinks. "All cool?"

"Oh, yeah. My colleague was just leaving."

Rohan walked away. I sipped on the martini. It was potent. Something felt light in my head. My steps faltered further; my breathing slowed.

"Don't you worry; I'm here." Mike held me by my waist. I tried to be OK with it.

The music blared. I hated dancing. My body didn't know rhythm, and I kept losing my balance. But that night, I did the steps others were doing in the club. After a while, women turned their backs toward their dance partners on the dance floor. With the beats, first the women gyrated their hips and went low, closer to the floor. And then it was the men. That was my out. I started to leave, but Mike pulled me closer to himself. I shrugged. He leaned in close and touched my hair. I pushed him away, but he got progressively grosser. He moved closer, so close that I could feel the bulge in his pants. Dev, at a friend's farmhouse in the outskirts of Delhi, had done the exact thing to me on the dance floor. He was drunk and literally dragged me to one of the bedrooms. I was on my stomach; he was on top of me being all aggressive. Suddenly, I realized he had passed out—with his man parts in my buttocks. Because he was drunk, he was a dead weight and I couldn't get him off or out of me. I had to lie there, crying, waiting for him to go flaccid. Feeling Mike so close to me, I couldn't stop the flashbacks. I tasted anger and vomit in my mouth. I tried to free myself from Mike and was about to elbow him in his stomach, when Rohan, in less than a minute, came to separate me from Mike.

"You again?" Mike moved his hands from my body.

"A boyfriend won't let his angry girlfriend make a mistake, now will he, bro?"

"Dude, I had no idea!" Mike put his hands up in the air and walked away.

Even in my slightly intoxicated state, I remembered Naina's words. "Southern men will always protect you. They won't punch a guy for you, but they will use charm and intelligence to make sure you're always safe."

Music. Booze. People. Hungry bodies. Rohan and I stood on the dance floor, staring at each other.

"Are you all right?" Rohan looked concerned.

I didn't say a word.

"Let's go, Ahana." Rohan held my right wrist.

"No, I'm not going anywhere." I released my hand from Rohan's grip.

"If you don't leave, I'll carry you out." Rohan pulled me closer.

"You're the reason I'm here."

"What are you talking about?"

"You're the one who said I couldn't pick up a guy. I picked a guy and danced with him." I was two inches away from Rohan's face.

"Fine. I get it. You win." Rohan shook his head.

"It's not about winning, Rohan. I don't like any of this stuff...a stranger touching me or nonsensical drinking. I wasn't brought up like this. To binge date or sleep around or have a random man touch me."

"Then why are you doing something that clearly makes you so uncomfortable?" He held me closer.

"Where do you get off asking me these questions when you insisted I couldn't find a date? I'm tired of everyone thinking I'm stupid and incapable."

"I was teasing you." Rohan spoke loudly so I could hear him.

"Well, it wasn't funny!" I shouted.

"I'm sorry." Rohan spoke gently.

Tears started to roll down my eyes. I couldn't control them. A few minutes later, Naina and Josh showed up. Josh intervened without alarming me. As a cop, he had his professional crowd-control face on and took me home.

We entered Naina's building; I spoke softly. "Sorry I made a scene."

"You have nothing to be sorry about." Josh pressed the elevator button. He had a key to Naina's apartment. He opened the door and went directly into the kitchen and emerged with a glass of water. He pulled out a few tissues from the Kleenex box next to the side table and handed them both to me.

"Thanks!" I swallowed.

"I know Naina loves you more than she loves me." Josh could say the truth and feel so easy around it.

I sniffled and stared at my dress. My head was bent—my chin touched my throat, subconsciously blocking my throat chakra.

Josh sat down next to me. "But sometimes you have to let people who love you know what's acceptable and what's not."

I stared at Josh.

"To me, Naina is the most amazing woman I've ever known. Rohan, from what Naina tells me, has been a good friend. Their intentions seem to be in the right place."

I nodded.

Josh had always treated me like a sister. I appreciated his strength and presence so much more today. How he showed me both sides to Naina and Rohan.

Josh said a good night and closed the door behind him.

I put the glass in the kitchen sink and walked to my room. Ever since Mumma's death, I'd searched the sky at nights to feel comforted. Some days, the stars brightened up my life and gave me the space I craved; on other nights, I found the stars and they allowed me to hide. I didn't close the blinds in my room, so I could see "Mumma Star"—the brightest star in the sky—or whatever ones I could make out, given the ambient light in NYC.

◦ 17 ◦

Next morning when I woke up, it was still dark outside. I looked at my phone: 5:05 a.m. My body was sore, as if I had climbed a hill five times the night before. The sound of my own breathing hurt my head. I tied my hair into a knot and quietly went into the bathroom.

Looking at my face in the mirror, I noticed my eyes were swollen. "Crying doesn't look good on you, *beta*," Mumma would always tell me and wipe my tears with her hands. How I wish she had let me fight my battles and wipe my own tears instead of turning me into an overprotected, oversheltered weakling who felt clueless at every difficult juncture in life.

I brushed my teeth and tried to relax my entire body as I sat on the toilet. Thinking about my meltdown at the club, I felt embarrassed. I looked at the clock: 5:20 a.m. I jumped into the shower and got dressed for a 6:30 a.m. yoga class. The past week had been a lot, and I needed deep inhales and exhales to jumpstart my weekend. I pined for Mumma and wished more than anything she could join me on the mat. Two years before Mumma died, for Mother's Day, I had ordered a Manduka yoga mat for her. She had yelled at me when she found out I had spent close to $200 on the colorful, eco-friendly, top-quality yoga mat, a few accessories, and shipping. But Mumma took that mat with her everywhere. Every conference. Every trip. Every vacation. "It's music to my knees, *beta*," she would say.

I changed into my purple yoga pants and a black halter tee, and wore a hoodie on top of it. Tiptoeing around the apartment, so as not to wake up Naina and Josh in case he had spent the night, I put my keys and money in my jacket pocket.

I went into the kitchen to fill up my water bottle. Carefully moving through memories and the dark living room, I wore my sneakers and quietly opened the main door so it wouldn't squeak.

"Good morning," I greeted the doorman on duty in the lobby.

When I stepped out into the streets, my bare legs felt cold. But my lungs and heart filled with gratitude—there was no one staring, throwing insults, wolf-whistling, stalking, or groping me. How often women in New Delhi were reminded that public spaces were not for them. How effortlessly I asserted my claim of public spaces in New York.

I liked reaching the studio early in the morning and sitting on the stairs of the brownstone, watching the world not move. I checked my phone: 5:45 a.m.

I heard someone call my name. I didn't pay any heed. There was no one in New York who would look for me at this hour. I heard my name again. I finally looked up and saw the last person I had expected to see: Rohan Brady.

He was crossing the street and simultaneously calling out to me.

"Getting old and losing your hearing?" He bent down, his hands on his knees, and breathed loudly.

I stared at him hard. I checked the time. It was 5:51 a.m.

"Aah. You are giving me the cold shoulder?" Rohan stood up straight. He was in his workout clothes.

I stood up, dusted my buttocks, and walked toward the end of the street. I didn't want to disturb those asleep.

He followed behind.

"What are you doing here, Brady?" I turned around and asked him.

"What do people do at a yoga studio?"

"Neither do you practice yoga nor do you wake up this early." The words glided out of my mouth.

He stretched his arm over his head and stood in front of me. "I came here this morning because I felt bad about last night."

I crossed my arms across my chest.

Rohan sucked in his lips. "Sorry to have wasted your morning."

I dragged my feet. Breathing deeply, I said, "I am tired of going unseen. I am sick of not mattering to people."

Rohan made meaningful eye contact. "What are you talking about? You matter to me, Ahana."

I stared at him with a million thoughts running through my head. *I have faulty instincts. Yes, I have attracted jerks like Dev and Jay into my life. But it's not like I want to hurt myself. They were both nice men in the beginning. Sure, they both eventually exploited my kindness. And it's changed my ability to trust men. But I have led a bloody protected life; I can't identify deceit.*

"I've been thinking all morning. For a few weeks now, actually." I shook my head.

Rohan patiently waited for me to complete my thoughts.

I paced up and down the street. It was cold out; I covered my hands with the sleeves of my jacket. "Mumma never trusted me to make my own decisions. Maybe that's why I could never tell my mother the truth about my marriage. I feared she'd be disappointed. I

139

wondered if she would accept me in all my strengths and weaknesses."

"I don't know what to say, Ahana." Rohan tried to hold my shoulders, but I pushed him away.

"I am sick of walking around on eggshells with people. If I ever bring up my suspicions about Jay, Naina starts with her criticism. I tried discussing him with you last night, and you called me stupid."

"Sorry—"

I interrupted him, "I am *done*. I am so done with people not respecting me and hearing my side. I string Jay along because I fear he knows about my past, and he might use it to emotionally blackmail or hurt me." I wrapped my arms around myself. "I have worked way too hard on this conference and myself for anyone to tarnish my reputation." I pressed my temples.

He offered me his handkerchief. I blew my nose into it.

He looked at me with kindness. "I'm sorry for everything you have been through. And if I hurt you. I am and will always be on your side." Rohan walked toward me. "Let's bury the hatchet."

I abruptly caught him by both his wrists. "You didn't think I acted stupid and slutty last night?"

Rohan looked shocked. "You have way too much intelligence and class to ever be 'slutty.'" He used air quotes. "I was there, as were Naina and Josh. We wouldn't have let anything happen to you. Allow yourself mistakes and fun, Ahana."

He gave me a hug. "You're the most amazing person I know. You make me a better person, Ahana."

I leaned into him and held him tightly. I didn't care that we were in public. I needed Rohan to remind me that all men weren't jerks. I needed Rohan to remind me that even though sometimes I was immature in my reactions, it was OK. That's what made me human.

* * *

In yoga class, I picked up two mats and put them side-by-side. Rohan confessed that he had never done yoga before.

I unzipped my hoodie and readjusted my halter neck tank top. Rohan glanced at me but didn't say anything. I noticed that Sheila adjusted Rohan plenty during the class. He left the more difficult poses quickly and went back to child's pose and corpse pose.

As Sheila instructed us to get into Warrior I followed by Warrior II after a dozen sun salutations, just like that, the heaviness in my heart went away. Just like that, the tightness in my chest dissipated. It was in that moment I understood the difference between good and bad friends. Good friends fight in a relationship to fight for the relationship. Good friends never abandon you. Good friends help you deal with the darkness enveloping you.

As we got into *Savasana*, corpse pose, after seventy-five minutes, I felt at peace. That was the magic of yoga. It allowed me to pause and gave me the opportunity to introspect. When we sat up and chorused three "Oms," we all bent our heads down and brought our palms together. The class echoed: "Namaste." Mumma was not on a mat next to me, but the universe had sent Rohan. He made me feel safe and calm.

"When did you learn to move like this?" Rohan asked as he rolled his mat.

"I've been practicing yoga for as long as I can remember." I picked up my mat and put it in the bin marked "dirty mats."

Sheila interrupted us. "Your boyfriend is cute. Chatty but cute."

"Noooo. Nooo. No. No. Nooooo." I took a deep breath and that turned into an absurd smile as I said, "No! He is not my boyfriend. We are colleagues."

"Nice to meet you, Sheila." He extended his hand. "I'm Rohan, by the way, and getting the idea that I'm not her boyfriend."

Rohan's joke elicited a laugh from Sheila where it was awkward just a second ago.

I thanked her for the class. Sheila excused herself to speak with other students.

Rohan turned to me. "I am your colleague, eh? Not even a friend."

"I got flustered, *yaar*. I'm sorry." I spoke tentatively.

I think we were both surprised at how honestly we told each other how we felt. Being around Rohan made me less defensive—he quickly forgave and moved on. Neither Dev nor Jay were that way. They both held onto grudges and sharpened them into weapons for when I was at my weakest.

I switched on my phone as we stepped outside the studio. There was a text from Naina. "I'm sorry about last night. We need to talk. I'm home until noon. Can you see me before I head out? Love you loads, Nainz!" There was another message from work. I started to type but Rohan interrupted me.

"I am standing right here and you are ignoring me now." Rohan spread his arms and then brought them dramatically to his chest.

"You should have been an actor!"

"Why, thank you." He bowed down.

"Sorry; this is an important message." I looked at the screen and thought of the best way to respond to Jen from work.

"Text from an admirer?" Rohan lifted his left eyebrow and gave me a cheeky smile.

"If Jen falls under that category." I smiled back at him.

"Jen texted you? Is everything all right, Ahana?"

"Nope. Hedick made another, even more aggressive move to steal credit for the conference. Jen is at work today and found his email printouts."

Rohan came to my defense. "I know from freelance writers that we can start a murmur about the irony of a guy trying to stifle the female organizer of a women's empowerment conference." He stared into my eyes. "But for it to work, you need to have a sharp sound bite, even an aggressively sarcastic one. Can you do that, Ahana? It's a gamble, but if it works, he'll fall all over himself getting out of your way."

"Ugh. Let me sleep on it. I'm going to go home and work on the details of the poster—the one for the entrance at the conference."

"You are gonna work on this gorgeous day?"

"Why not?"

"We are going to a bar in NOHO. Hang out with me; you'll get to meet some of my friends, too."

"That's really sweet. But I'd much rather stay in tonight."

Rohan's face changed expression. "Don't be an Indian aunty. One of my friends just returned from Delhi. You guys can talk about the Qutab Minar or something."

"Haha; look who's stereotyping now?" I arched my left eyebrow.

"You said last night that you were missing Delhi." Rohan sucked his lower lip.

"Can I think about it?"

"Text me if you change your mind."

Rohan whistled and a cab stopped. He had this unique charm where people stopped in their steps for him.

I waved at Rohan and started to walk but not before pulling out my phone from my jacket to check whether there were any messages from Jay.

Naina would say, "Ahana, you know how to sabotage your happiness."

She was right.

Jay had posted a picture of a wilted rose on social media. And the caption read, "Emotionally raped."

I never did learn to take the word "rape" lightly. I instantly sent him a private message.

"Hey, everything OK?"

"You are my true friend. You always know when I am low and depressed." Jay knew what parts of me would get triggered and respond.

"What happened?"

"I was insulted by someone I trusted a lot."

"I'm sorry to hear that." I felt my throat closing—I had been in the same place the night before with Naina. "Who is this person?"

Jay went silent. *Typical.*

"I guess you don't want to talk. Take care of yourself." I wrote to him.

"You are the only friend I have and you too are leaving me," he replied right away.

"I didn't abandon you. You didn't write back."

A few minutes later, he sent a note. "It's Amanda from our therapy group."

"I didn't realize you guys were friends."

"We were close."

OK, this was news to me. Not that Jay needed to announce names of people he was friends with, but Amanda, he, and I were part of the same therapy group. It felt like he had purposefully hidden that information.

I was lost in my own thoughts when the sound of several incoming messages broke my reverie.

"Now you have abandoned me too?"

Oh, my God! I took a deep breath. "Jay, I am trying to understand your situation."

"What is there to understand? History repeated itself, Ahana. I go out of my way to accommodate people and they kick me to the curb when they are done with me," he replied.

"Were you guys dating?"

"We live thousands of miles apart. How could we date?"

"OK. Did you love her?" I was angry at Jay for throwing his problems at me without even having mentioned he had a personal life or problems to begin with.

"If I didn't meet her, how could I love her?"

"We have all had friendships die and friends move on. But the way you are reacting, it seems like more than a friendship, Jay."

"I helped her cope with a heartbreak. Amanda's last boyfriend dumped her when she was least expecting it. I tried to show her that there are good men like me out there."

"That is nice of you." It wasn't easy for me to fake anything, but I did my best.

"She's had a rough life. Her father abused her. Her mother witnessed everything but did nothing about it. I was the sweet, lovable friend in her life she could be goofy with. We had the same interests in food and music. That bitch...."

Wow! Jay not only revealed all of Amanda's secrets because he was angry with her, but he didn't think twice before calling her names. Is this how he speaks about me to others when we argue?

I have no idea why I asked Jay what I did next. "What does Amanda do for a living?"

"She's an investment banker."

"Nice!"

"We were supposed to meet and start a business together."

"In New York?" I wanted to see what he would say.

"If I could afford New York, wouldn't I come to visit you?"

I ignored his flattery. "Where does Amanda live?"

"In Ohio. She was going to come visit me in Louisiana."

I wondered why an investment banker lived in Ohio instead of New York or Silicon Valley. "I didn't realize you guys were such good friends."

"Awww, don't be jealous, Ahana. No one can be cuter than you."

All my Zen bubble broke and I wanted to reach across the phone and punch Jay. Who did he think he was, and where did he think he got the authority to talk to me the way he did?

"Why did she cancel?"

"I have no idea. She said I was too exhausting. Fuck her! I helped that bitch all this time and when it's her turn to repay, she said NO!"

"I am so sorry, Jay."

"Yeah. She insulted me repeatedly over email. She has done this in the past and I forgave her."

I tried asking in a different way. "Did she give a reason?"

"Nope. The bitch probably has fucking PMS. Who cares about her? I have you, Ahana. My best friend!"

"Sure."

"I wish we could hang. And throw stones at ugly, mean, fat people."

"Or we could grab a chai? Another option." I was repulsed by Jay, but I didn't want him to know that, so I ended the sentence with a smiley. "Do you miss her a lot?" Jay was opening up; I needed to know what was going on.

"We were friends for ages. There were feelings involved."

How could they have been 'friends for ages'? Our online therapy group was slightly over a year old. Jay had never even met Amanda.

I squinted because the sun was high enough to glare off of my phone.

He quickly added. "But Amanda has changed. She isn't the same person I met."

Met? Asshole, you've never seen her!

"I feel bad, Jay." I played along. "How about picking up the phone?"

"I am not going after someone who doesn't see the value in my friendship."

Wow, Jay was selfish, abusive, and narcissistic. When he'd lied to me about his partner, I let it go because I knew how belittling it was for me to admit to anyone I was a divorcée and a survivor of sexual assault. Who was I to judge what kind of shame Jay carried around. But lying to me about Amanda made me squirm.

I needed to figure out the level of danger I was in—was it just an emotional threat? Or could I finally listen to my gut and feel that Jay was maneuvering me into position for something? Could it be physical danger, too? The heavy silence of the moment made me breathe harder.

The only way to find answers was by keeping my lines of communication open with Jay.

≈ 18 ≈

When I reached Naina's apartment, she was clad in her pajamas, drinking coffee. Always strong. Always black. Always fresh. Her taste in coffee spoke so much about the person she was: unabashedly bold.

I put my keys on the keychain holder and took off my shoes. I reorganized the stack of newspapers on one of the side tables. Naina had all the space and intention to stay organized, but structure just wasn't her.

"Morning! Did you go for yoga?" She waved at me.

She wasn't in a bad mood. But I didn't want any of my words flung back at me, so I responded, "Yup."

"Did Rohan join you there?" She smiled at me.

"How did you know?" I looked up as I rolled my socks.

"Last night, when Josh came to drop you off home, Rohan asked me for the address to your yoga studio and we looked up your class schedule online."

"Oh, no wonder." I pulled out a cleansing wipe and wiped my neck and armpits.

Naina ecstatically got up from the sofa. "I can finally hear it in your voice that you like someone."

"I thought you wanted me to come home because you wanted to apologize. Where is that sorry?" I looked at Naina with no expression as I threw the wipe in the trashcan.

She stopped and stared at the floor. "I feel awful about last night, Ahana. Josh gave me a huge talk." She dragged her feet. "I know you'd have never spoken to me the way I spoke to you. I am truly sorry."

I washed my hands in the kitchen sink. "Thank you for reminding me what a true apology looks like."

Naina rushed toward me. "Sorry, babes. It's just that I don't want Jay to hurt you. Dev has already done that."

"I do not like Jay romantically."

"I know that, Ahana. Even more, why waste time on that loser?" she whispered into my hair. "You get carried away by people whining about their pain."

I untied my ponytail and ran my fingers through my hair to disentangle any knots. "I have something to confess, but I need you not to be cruel, Naina."

Naina examined my face. I walked toward the living room. My face burned. I could feel the heat rise through my neck.

Naina ran her fingers along the handle of her coffee mug. "What's going on, Ahana?"

"I don't know how to explain. If you have a few minutes, read Jay's messages from this morning." I collapsed on the sofa.

"Wait...from this morning? I thought you were at breakfast with Rohan."

"No, I saw the messages right after class."

"You mean, you sat in the park on a beautiful morning like this and devoted almost an hour to this toxic son of a bitch?"

I glared at her. Naina bit her lip as soon as the words left her mouth. She read through the message exchange between Jay and me. "What's with all this name-calling? Sheesh, the guy has an awful high sense of himself. It's appalling!"

I went into my room to change into a pair of crop pants and tank top. Naina spoke loudly from the living room. "He's playing martyr and labeling Amanda the toxic one, fucking jerk. And making sure she doesn't have a support network to fall back on. He is good at being sick."

My hands shook as I pushed my lululemon yoga pants and yoga underwear down my thighs. I placed my contacts in their case and put on my glasses.

Naina walked toward my room. I was folding up my dirty clothes to put in the clothes hamper. She gave me a kiss on my forehead. "I am so proud of you."

"What?"

"You handled Jay really well. I bet it bothered you when he called Amanda names and didn't tell you that he was in love with someone else. But you stayed classy, not surprising, but sensible in your interaction."

I became quiet.

Naina rubbed my shoulders. "What's on your mind?"

I shifted in my feet.

"You are thinking about something too hard."

As Naina was reacting, I forestalled her and asked, "Do you think I deserve it?" I sank to the floor. My body felt worn-out.

Naina sat next to me. "What are you talking about?"

"It haunts me. I thought I would be over it by now," I mumbled.

Naina shook me. "Ahana, you are worrying me."

"Dev... Our marriage... I...." I paused and took a deep breath. "I asked for a divorce because...." I kept swallowing my words.

"Ahana?"

"Dev raped me, Naina." I spoke softly, but there was a tsunami of pressure behind my eyes. I was surprised at my forthrightness. This was a secret I had held close to my heart for a decade. But I couldn't deal with the burden alone any longer.

"He did *what*?" Naina pounded her fist into the wall. "When? Did your mom know?"

I was still struggling with everything, so I lied a little. "It only happened a few times," and looked away when it happened a few times *a week*.

"Why didn't you say anything, sweetie?"

"Dev made sure I stayed silent. He took pictures and threatened to share them with Mumma and Dad." I started to sob.

Naina cupped my face. "Ahana, look at me." She wiped my tears. "You have *nothing* to be ashamed about. Dev is a rapist."

"But sometimes," I said, "my physical body.... He said it was proof that I liked it. I had to live with a crippling sense of corruption and his attack on my credibility. I couldn't talk to anyone, Naina. Not you. Not Mumma. Dev made sure. I felt embarrassed and so dirty." I buried my face in Naina's arms.

"You never *asked* to be raped. Biology works differently. So what if your body responded; your mind didn't! He violated you, and I'm going to chop off his dick and feed it to the mongrels near India Gate."

"I didn't enjoy it, Naina. He made me feel really small." My tears were mixed with my snot. Naina hugged me tight.

"He is an abusive narcissist who hurt his own wife and deflected any responsibility for his actions." She was crying, too.

After a little while, I pulled myself away. "Do I need to be actively disrespected to feel seen?"

"What makes you think that?" Naina stroked my forehead.

"Because Dev broke my heart and my trust, and I stayed quiet. Jay seemed like a reasonable guy when we started to interact, but he changed, too."

I looked up at Naina. "It is me, right? Somewhere people think it's OK to treat me like shit because I look weak? Because deep down I think I deserve it? Because I was never taught to fight my battles!"

"That's exactly why I like Rohan in your life. Dev and Jay ate at your ability to trust yourself, and inevitably, you were disabled from calling out abuse. But Rohan empowers you."

"We can't be anything but friends, Naina."

"Stop fighting yourself." Naina sat next to me.

I put my head on her shoulder. "I can't leave Dad alone. He demanded I come back home after the earthquake in New Delhi a few weeks ago."

She patted my hands. "We live in a globalized world. If, only if, you guys really liked each other, one of you could move."

"Dad being needier will make it harder for me to be with Rohan for any real period of time. I can't deal with additional stress."

"Your dad will love Rohan."

"How much do you know Rohan to side so blindly with him?"

"He is sincere. Rohan makes you more confident. When I'm not around, I feel like I can trust him to show up for you." Naina got up.

"I don't need a babysitter." I stood up so quickly that I felt dizzy.

"Of course, you don't. That's not what I meant."

"Sometimes I feel you think I am incapable of taking care of myself after Mumma's death."

"I feel you're still vulnerable. It's understandable why. You lost your mom and marriage inside of a year. I mean, listen to what you just told me about Dev. Of course you're still healing. Weirdos of all types will try to exploit that."

"You mean Jay?" My arms were crossed across my chest.

"I mean most people. I have no proof, but I am convinced that Jay has made it his business to know you. He has figured you out and is already ahead in the game."

Naina got up and looked out the windows of my bedroom. "Remember when my high school boyfriend died in a bus accident on his way from a football game?"

"Of course."

"I opened myself up to trouble because I wasn't careful about whom I let into my life. I was hurt, angry, broken, and so lonely. You'll be surprised how many vultures out there wait for victims."

"I am sorry, Naina." I gently pressed her shoulders.

"Meh, it's an old story. I am with Josh and I love him more than I can handle. All I am saying is that Rohan has principles, and he would never take advantage of you. Jay, on the other hand, I don't trust one bit. It took him less than a day to badmouth and abuse the woman he didn't love but did love but didn't date but is heartbroken over."

There was silence for a few seconds. Naina picked up Mumma's picture from my nightstand. She dusted it with her bare hands. "Have you told Jay and Rohan about Dev?"

I felt fear rise from my *root chakra*—which represents our foundation and feeling of being grounded—to my *crown chakra*—the highest chakra, which represents our ability to be fully connected

149

spiritually. I noticed my heart rate was faster and my palpitations increased.

"Ahana."

With my index finger tapping my lips, I took the photo frame from her hands. "I've told Rohan a little, not Jay."

"Has Rohan ever used that information in an inappropriate way?"

"God, no. Not at all. He has been kind and caring."

"Why do you think you told Rohan but not Jay, even though Jay and you connected over loss and suffering, as you say?"

I lifted my shoulders and brought them to my ears.

"It's because your instincts told you to safeguard yourself against Jay. The same instincts also told you to be authentic around Rohan. Always listen to your gut, Ahana."

"You make Jay sound like a criminal." I walked to my dresser to pick up a hair clip.

"Isn't he, Ahana?" Naina walked up to me. "He is a smart dude; I'll give you that. He scoped out the emptiness inside of you and moved into that space."

I felt the need to say something but stood wordlessly.

Naina excused herself and went for a shower. She and Josh had a meeting with the photographer.

Naina's words made my skin crawl. I walked into the living room and sat on the floor with my legs stretched out in front of me. I drew my heel toward my abdomen and placed my right foot on the top of my left thigh. Then I pulled my other heel up toward my navel and rested my left foot on the top of my right thigh. I closed my eyes and started to breathe deeply. I must have meditated for over thirty minutes because when I opened my eyes, Naina was sitting on the sofa and staring at me.

"You look pretty." I stretched my arms over my head and smiled at Naina. She was clad in a light green dress.

"Ms. Yoga Queen, would you like some bagels?"

"Nah, I'm OK."

"Let me rephrase my sentence. I am ordering some bagels from the deli below and you must eat some breakfast, too. Which one would you like?"

"Such a bossy lady." I hit her lightly on her shoulder. "Whole wheat with low fat vegetable cream cheese slightly toasted and layered with avocado, tomato, and sprouts."

"Such a diva," Naina rolled her eyes at me.

In less than ten minutes, we had bagels and freshly squeezed vegetable-fruit combination juices delivered to the apartment. After all the dancing and drinking the night before, clean food felt good in my stomach.

"You better deal with him before we leave for my engagement party."

"What do you mean?" I wiped cream cheese from the corner of my mouth.

"I can talk to my mentor and have him kicked out or whatever. She's the moderator and always has the final say."

"No, don't do that." I was firm mainly because I was afraid of Jay retaliating.

While Naina was still talking, I made my own secret plan to turn into Detective Ahana and get to the bottom of Jay's identity. I knew I had to be casual, but not too affectionate or empathetic.

"What's going on inside that head of yours?" Naina prodded me.

"Not much." I looked away.

Both Naina and I rinsed the dirty dishes and placed them in the dishwasher.

Naina leaned into the passageway. "Promise me that you won't waste another minute of your life on this guy."

"Go." I pushed Naina from behind. "Josh must be waiting for you. It's already 11:45 a.m."

"Fuck!!" She perched her sunglasses over her head.

As Naina stepped out of the apartment, I closed the doors and brought my mobile phone outside. There were no messages from Jay or Rohan. I was determined to find out what he wanted from me.

I tapped my phone impatiently against my chin.

"Hey, just a note to see how you are doing?" I didn't write nonchalant notes. This was difficult for me. I stretched my legs and shifted my weight from foot to foot.

"You know I am still feeling lonesome," Jay wrote back right away. "I wish I could be like you. You have shit in your life yet you manage to stay focused and do what you got to do. Much respect!" He sent me a selfie with a sad expression.

Jay's words today sounded empty, much like our friendship. Like he pulled from a list of manipulative things to say. It was alarming, the realization that Jay might not be feeling depressed at all. *He's coldly, boredly, and steadily using a script to wear me down.*

"Have you eaten anything?" I wrote and then deleted. I was getting too empathetic. "Did you hear from Amanda?"

"Nah, she is a cold bitch."

My stomach cramped.

"Can't beat a dead friendship with a stick, ya know?"

I walked into the kitchen to get myself a glass of water. My phone made a sound.

"What are you doing today?" Jay asked.

"Just relaxing. A bit tired, Jay."

"You care too much about people, Ahana."

"The universe keeps a tab, I am sure." I rolled my eyes as I wrote back to him.

"The universe doesn't give a fuck."

He was back to being angry. Naina was right; Jay was emotionally unstable and he had the ability to turn me into a yo-yo too. I had to take control of the situation.

"Are you feeling depressed about Amanda ending the friendship?"

"Not depressed but definitely disappointed. "I wasn't going to marry her or knock her up, if that's what you are trying to ask."

I can't believe he said that!

Before I could reply, the battery ran low. It took me a few minutes to find a socket and put the phone on charge.

In the interim, there were several messages from Jay.

"I guess you got bored and left. I am a burden to those around me. I am going out of my fucking mind."

I ignored him on purpose. I saw a coldness in myself that I didn't like. For the first time, I understood what it felt like to be a manipulator. I felt a discomforting chill in my bones.

Ping. Another message from Jay. There it was, just as I had suspected. "Maybe we can talk on the phone one of these days? Maybe you can drill some sense into my head?"

I took this as a possible sign of success. I was hunting Jay in this emotional warfare game instead of the other way around. I got him to suggest a phone call. I drank an entire pitcher of water. With my phone on charge in the living room, I went into my bedroom. My runner's quadriceps and yoga hamstrings failed me, so I sat on the bed. With a cushion between my legs, I placed my laptop on it.

There was a Salinger quote from Jay. "I'm just sick of ego, ego, ego. My own and everybody else's. I'm sick of everybody that wants to get somewhere, do something distinguished and all, be somebody interesting. It's disgusting."

It occurred to me that Jay, while sharing pertinent Salinger's dialogues to describe his feelings, rarely recognized Salinger's works when I sent them to him.

And for that matter, how had he known that I liked Salinger in the first place?

* * *

152

It was time to check Amanda's social media accounts to figure out what was truly going on. Amanda, during the online therapy session, was so conservative with her interactions that even I barely remembered her, and I almost never miss a thing. She was so disconnected with most of us that it didn't even occur to me to connect with her on social media. I hoped her settings were such that anyone could see her posts.

Amanda posted a lot of scantily clad selfies, and Jay engaged with every one of them. There was a picture of a plate of bacon from a few weeks ago. And the caption read, "The cure-all drug for impotence."

I almost closed my laptop. *Who posts things like these?* Rohan's training combined with the increase in my social media followers told me I was good enough now to see how others do such a poor job of it. Amanda was an investment banker; how did she manage a public profile with heavy sexual undertones in all her interactions?

Jay had left a comment. "Hahaha."

"Bacon gives me lady boner," Amanda had responded.

"What a classy image. No wonder I love you."

There was no way I could ascertain whether Jay's "I love you" meant something platonic or more.

My fingers found their way toward each other, and my palms pressed together at my heart. But what really confirmed my doubts that Jay and Amanda were involved in a romantic relationship, even though he denied it, or at least that Amanda really liked him more than a friend, was when I saw that she had dressed her cat in a forest green football jersey with white ribbons. The caption read: "My cat got the Jets colors on for mah man today. Buckeyes next time, people!!" There was a comment from Jay below the picture, "You have impeccable taste."

I shut my laptop and got up from the bed. Jets! JETS. JETS! That was the team Jay supported. Anyone who knew Jay probably knew that he swore by the New York Jets. I thought it was weird because Jay was from Louisiana and its football team was the Saints. Rohan was a Saints devotee.

I had caught Jay L Y I N G about his relationship with Amanda. He said they were just friends, but there was more to it. There was so much I didn't know about Jay. Our intimacy was all about our dead mothers. But he and Amanda shared intimacy like a couple that was dating. I was getting sucked into the mystery, and the thrill of hunting down clues.

⚡ 19 ⚡

On Monday evening, Rohan and I were scheduled to meet with Manchester Distillery, an alcoholic beverage company, downtown. There was a kerfuffle over the drinks ad. Manchester Distillery was one of the largest sponsors of the cocktail reception for the first night of the conference. They were willing to back food and beverage for all the speakers, nonprofit representatives, and any attendee who had bought the pass to the three-day event. We mentioned them in all our media promotions. Their logo was on the invite and agenda. But one of the largest women's organizations from California threatened to pull out of the conference because Manchester Distillery had used sexist images and messaging in its latest marketing campaigns.

Rohan and I were supposed to make everything go away. We were both stressed—there was a lot riding on this meeting. How could we bring people of two extreme viewpoints to meet in the middle? The executive director for the nonprofit had flown down from California, and the senior vice president for corporate social responsibility at Manchester Distillery had reached NYC earlier that morning from London.

Earlier that afternoon, Rohan had shown me the draft of a one-page story by his freelancer friend, who'd gotten the OK to run the piece in *Salon*. It was bold—"Dick Move: CEO Michael Hedick Hijacks Women's Conference." I had chuckled, but the piece didn't feel right—it wasn't quite news. When I looked at Rohan, I saw that he too shared my squeamishness about stirring up a nest of snakes so close to the conference.

I said to him, "I think I have a better idea," and called Ms. Roy late. But Ms. Roy picked up and I told her the problem. What was once annoying was now an asset: social-climbing Ms. Roy promised to pull some high-level social strings, and that in a few days, a week tops, she'd make sure that a half-dozen of the conference's celebs and diplomats would ask some pointed questions over who was in charge of the conference, and express displeasure over participating in an event hijacked by a bully. In other words, her strategy would quietly embarrass Hedick into stepping back. Sure, this was a softer solution, but one that was likely to succeed. More importantly, it would detonate far enough from Rohan and me that Hedick couldn't blame us for the situation.

"We are leveraging Ms. Roy to use social pressure, Brady, just as the California organizations pressured the conference over their sponsor."

After Rohan high-fived me and left, I picked up my bag and went home. While making myself tea and processing all the escalating tension the week had brought into my life, I picked out my clothes—figured French chic ensemble might be apt for drinks and talks at a Champagne club. I pulled out a one-shoulder, black georgette jumpsuit and held it against my torso in the bedroom mirror. I had picked it up on my friend Maya's insistence when she and I had traveled to Mauritius together. I figured I'd wear ankle-strap heels and pear-drop earrings. Red nail polish, red lipstick, and a silver clutch would complete the look.

My laptop was set up in the living room, so I could review our presentation. Even in my office in New Delhi, Ms. Roy always asked me to go over the presentations just a little before we shared them with a sponsor. "Nothing misses your eye," she would insist. I scrolled through the decks and decided to take a break after a little while.

* * *

My head was on the armrest of the sofa in the living room when I heard a ping. It was Tanya from my online therapy group.

I put more water into the kettle, pulled out some chamomile tea bags, and looked over Tanya's message.

"Hi, Ahana. Tanya from London. :)"

"What a pleasant surprise, Tanya," I wrote back fervently. "But isn't it rather late in the night for you?"

"I'm all right. Not been able to sleep the past few weeks. Downing some wine."

"What's going on?" I pulled my glasses away from my face and wiped them with the corner of my T-shirt.

"I have a habit of allowing myself to be attracted to liars—men who flirt and are emotionally unavailable. Or they control and manipulate you but make it seem harmless. I hold onto hope that I won't be falling for any liars. But there you go."

"I am so sorry. How did you find out the truth?"

"Deductive instincts. All our interactions were only over social media or email. He never came to the phone. This guy is charming, intelligent, attractive, and made me laugh when we interacted online."

I kept seeing confirmations of my suspicion at every step that the guy was J A Y. While the concept of people becoming intimate, without meeting each other in person or knowing them, was still alien

155

to me, I too had grown emotionally close to Jay without ever speaking or meeting with him. Loss and aches, it brings out a side in us, which we don't know exists.

Tanya continued, "But I met him once in NYC. Truly thought there was something there because we liked the same foods, shared similar hobbies, we were both geology nerds exchanging pictures of rocks and shells we found. When he asked for help with his business, I agreed to it blindly. I flew to NYC all the way from Los Angeles just to see him because he made it sound like we had something going on. But in person, he just whined about betrayals and the world being bad and suggested I invest in his business."

Yes! It is Jay. My heart both hurt and filled with pride at the same time. I wasn't crazy in thinking Jay was not who he pretended to be.

"I wear my heart on my sleeve, Ahana, and after nearly 47 years you'd think I would've learned by now. Yet I haven't. Maybe I am supposed to be the crazy cat lady after all. :)"

Crazy cat lady? Damn! That's what Jay called Tanya when I was in Sydney.

"I am so sorry," I wrote with sincerity, "such men, they are a special breed."

"I never sleep on first dates, but I fell for his crocodile tears and ended up in bed at my friend's house where I was staying. After he had shoved his tongue down my throat like a horny teenager and fucked me like I was a slut, I lent him $20,000 for his business idea to start a coffee shop. He said he needed to meet with an investor that evening. Later, we were supposed to get dinner. I waited for him at Pershing Square, the restaurant opposite Grand Central Terminal, but he never showed up. When I tried calling him, he didn't answer the phone."

"Did he give a reason?"

"His apology was half-assed and his excuse was that his landlady was sick and that's why he had to rush home from the meeting. I tried calling him again and again. I sent him an email explaining my feelings and asking what the afternoon together had meant. He texted me back saying that he got my voicemail and appreciated the time spent with me. I mean, what the fuck?! He seduced me, took my money, and made it sound like we had played volleyball at the beach."

I wanted to feel shocked, but at this point, I believed the man was Jay, and I put nothing past him. "What about the money you loaned him?"

"I was so blindly in love that I gave him a check but asked for no guarantee or any formal paperwork. UGH!! That's why I am here in

London to spend a few weeks with my best friend and start from scratch."

My heart was pounding. "What an asshole!!" I typed furiously.

"Look at you using swear words. :)" Tanya wrote back.

"Sorry. I can't believe this guy."

"No worries on cursing. :) I actually like you now."

"What do you mean?" My suspicion was correct; Jay had made up stories about me too.

"C'mon, Ahana. You want me to spell everything out?"

I quickly threw the teabag in the garbage and pulled out some honey from the kitchen cabinet. "Hey, if it helps, I am going to get bloody wasted. :)"

"You go girl!!!!!!" Tanya wrote back.

I added a teaspoon of honey to my tea. "I am sorry to pry, but who is this guy, Tanya?" I walked to the dining table. I knew it was Jay. I knew it. But I needed to hear it from Tanya.

"It's Jay from our online therapy group."

There was a pause.

My face tightened. I closed the blinds. I didn't want to be seen. I didn't want to see. I didn't want to be surrounded by fear.

"Tanya, I am sorry for everything you've been through. I want to talk more, but I must log off now. Have a big meeting with a sponsor this evening; can we chat a little later? I need to look over the presentation for the evening, shower, and get dressed."

More women needed protection from men like Jay. I was going to put every ounce of my energy in the conference—my conference. Plus, I didn't want Rohan to wait for me.

"Of course! You know where to find me." Tanya ended her message with a heart emoji.

* * *

Rohan met me in the lobby of Naina's apartment. I had asked him if he wanted to come up. He'd said, "You never know what kind of traffic we'll hit. Let's leave a little early."

When I got out of the elevator, I noticed how strikingly handsome he looked in his white fitted shirt, mousse in his hair, designer jeans, loafers, and a Brooks Brothers jacket with a snazzy fit. "Looking good, Mr. Brady."

"Look at you, Ms. Paris." Rohan cleared his throat. "All the guys are going to hit on you tonight. I don't think we need to do any presentation."

"Is it looking vulgar, Brady? My outfit?" I tried to cover my one bare shoulder with a shawl. I couldn't believe I had come to a point in my friendship with Rohan where I was OK taking wardrobe advice from him.

He smiled. "You are high-strung."

I frowned.

"But never indecent."

"Oh...." I held my clutch tighter as we sat in the black limousine Manchester Distillery had sent for us.

"Fancy." I ran my hands over the interior.

"I know, right?" Rohan followed suit.

There was champagne chilling right by where we were sitting. The driver pointed us in the direction of chocolates, fruit, and a cheese platter accompanying the champagne. I held the elegant flute glasses. Rohan popped open the bottle and poured champagne into them. "To the conference and your NYC trip!"

I smiled at him and slowly drank a little—didn't want to repeat the recent club scene in front of him. I didn't want to fill the empty spaces that Jay had created inside me with champagne. I tried so hard not to think about my conversation with Tanya. Rohan too drank cautiously. I guess neither of us wanted to get tipsy before our big negotiation.

"You look breathtakingly beautiful. At a party like tonight, I can only imagine how many men will want your number and want to hook up with you." His face hardened in concentration. "Be firm...."

"Eew! I am not that kind of a woman." I pulled my shawl away to wrap myself completely, but one of my shoulders was bare—the side toward Rohan.

"I know that." He turned toward me. Our eyes met. "It's just that you'll be drawing every eye in the room tonight."

My throat felt parched. "Rohan, why is it you say that I look nice and warn me that others will hit on me, but you don't say anything nice?" I have no idea why I asked that. I guess, learning the truth about Jay had made me wonder what was it about Rohan that I didn't know.

He asked me to hold his glass. He pulled my shawl and wrapped my shoulders in them.

"Do you want me to hit on you, Ahana?" He ran his fingers on my arm draped in the shawl.

I shuddered. He tucked the hair behind my left ear.

"That's not what I meant." I spoke weakly as I looked up at him.

"I know, silly." Rohan gently touched my hands. He was about to say something when my phone buzzed.

It was Tanya. "Ahana, I know you're busy, but can I take ten more minutes of your time? It's important. You need to hear what I have to tell you."

I gulped air.

I turned to Rohan. "I'm sorry; it's Tanya from my therapy group. She says it's urgent."

"Of course." He smiled and looked out the window.

"Tanya, log out of the therapy chat group. Let's chat on Messenger. This way Jay can't tell we're both online."

After a few minutes, Tanya wrote to me, "Jay is playing you like he played me."

"How do you mean?"

"I recently noticed that he started to leave needy and over-friendly comments on your social media posts. I figured I should warn you that's how it started with me. Has he met up with you in NYC? Has he made excuses about money being tight and personal failures putting him in depression? Does he call you his *best friend* and then complete your sentences?"

I felt angry to my bones, but I faked calmness.

"Thanks. I don't know what to say." What is his final game plan with me? How dangerous is he?

"This is what he does best, Ahana. Jay looks for his prey online."

My head ached dully. Jay caught us all at our lowest—me after Mumma's death and my divorce and Tanya after her boyfriend Paul's death.

"I saw another person fall for him the exact same way I did. And then he broke her heart. I just wanted to make sure he didn't do the same to you."

"Do you mean Amanda?" Wow, Jay moved on at least three of us from the therapy group.

"Yes, how did you know?"

"He told me that Amanda used him and walked away when he needed her."

"Son of a bitch! Amanda was willing to invest $45,000 in his business. Amanda is obsessed with *When Harry Met Sally*. Jay quoted from it all the time to move into that trustworthy space of '*I get you*.'"

J. D. Salinger. Is that what Jay did with me? It seemed Jay created a fake sense of familiarity and intimacy by claiming he liked the same stuff as Tanya, Amanda, and me. It felt good, admitting my suspicions.

I continued to read Tanya's message. "Amanda is in her early twenties, so she uses less discretion in her relationships and what she shares on social media. He is hanging on to the salacious pictures she sent him of herself and is blackmailing her."

I pressed the veins popping on the side of my forehead and stretched my neck. Rohan smiled at me but didn't say anything.

"I had no idea. Have you told the moderator of our therapy group?"

"No, I haven't. I am too embarrassed. And Amanda is hooked in and messed up. Please don't utter a word to our moderator. I want to forget and move on. But you better watch out, Ahana."

"Why me?" I checked the lock on my car door.

"Jay is a sociopath. It was easier with us because we fell for his fake romance. But since you have no romantic feelings toward him, he has to come up with better ways to make you vulnerable."

"But—"

Tanya didn't let me finish. "Given that you live in a different country and will be in the US for a defined period, he has to up his game. Stay safe and strong, Ahana."

"I will. Thank you, Tanya."

All my doubts and hunches about Jay had come true. He didn't even belong in the online therapy group. I had to let Naina's mentor know or file a lawsuit or get someone to slap the shit out of Jay. Ugh. I ran my hands over my face. But I needed more proof to make a case or take any action against Jay.

Rohan touched my shoulders to make sure I was OK. I looked at him and my fears turned to strength. My anger morphed into resolution. No man was ever going to hurt me, again. I made up my mind; I would do whatever it took to find out the truth about Jay. I was better than the woman Jay thought I was.

I was still agitated when we reached Manchester Distillery. I went into the women's restroom and meditated for five minutes. This was a last-minute confusion we were hurrying to solve before Naina and Josh's engagement. *Tonight is extremely important. Concentrate, Ahana. Jay doesn't get to ruin it.*

I focused on abdominal breathing, which lowered my heart rate and calmed my mind. I took a deep breath and joined Rohan.

The meeting involved ego-petting, promising, showing different viewpoints, and mollycoddling. Rohan was good at keeping people happy and bringing up tactful objection. Everyone listened to him. We all came to an agreement that Manchester Distillery would not run its new ads until the conference was over. This way, it didn't have to waste all the money and time that had gone into creating the new ad and marketing campaign. And the women's organization from

California wouldn't interfere with the alcohol company's campaigns once the event was over.

Many pointed to Rohan as "The man of the hour." Rohan shone the spotlight on me instead and introduced me as "The reason we were all in the room together." Everyone raised their glasses. Alcohol poured, but I barely drank.

On the way out, Rohan whispered softly, "You all right?"

"Yeah." I gave him a big smile. I rested my head on his shoulders as we waited for our car. "Thank you."

"What for?"

"A resolution to the sponsorship kerfuffle tonight means that we can go to Naina's engagement party with a clear conscience!"

Rohan put his arms around my shoulder and leaned into me.

≈ 20 ≈

The morning after the meeting and cocktail reception at Manchester Distillery's downtown location, I left for New Orleans to attend Naina's engagement. I figured I'd reach NOLA a day or two early and help Naina and Masi with the last-minute arrangements.

Naina, Masi, Josh, Mausa, and twelve other cousins were at the airport to receive me with *dhol*—a large, barrel-shaped, cylindrical, two-headed Indian drum and garlands. For a minute, I felt like I had been transported to New Delhi. Naina lifted me up. "And now that my sister is here, the celebrations truly begin."

It was nice being in NOLA with everyone. Eating. Chatting. Listening to family gossip. Trying out Indian clothes. The arrangement was fantastic. Even though most of the family was staying at either the Hilton or Hyatt in downtown New Orleans, Naina insisted I stay with her.

I missed Mumma—but so did Naina and Masi. Mumma was the organizer and strength of the family. She would have comforted Masi, thrown away her cigarettes, pampered Naina and Josh, gone over the expenses with Mausa, helped me plan my outfit for the engagement ceremony, and politely handled Mausa's traditional family visiting from Punjab. Everyone loved Mumma, for she did a lot of ordinary things with extraordinary affection. I pointed at the sky, "Mumma is looking at all of us and disapproving of your smoking, Masi." Naina smiled and Masi cupped my face in her palms.

Next morning, I woke up early and went for a long run. NOLA was much warmer than NYC. Being close to nature and smelling the history and stories of NOLA made me think of Rohan. A part of me missed the crispness of autumn in New York. Running reminded me of New York and my bet that I had lost to Rohan. *Why haven't I heard from him after the party at Manchester Distillery?*

When I got home, Naina looked upset. She was walking away from her dad's side of the family. Masi was trying to placate her. Naina turned to Masi, "Mom, ask them to stop."

"I know they drive you crazy, *beta*," Masi whispered. She was referring to her in-laws. "Why don't you and Ahana get out of the house on the pretext of last minute shopping and get some time away from them?"

"I didn't want to invite them to the wedding." With her sunglasses in her hand, Naina pointed in the direction of her paternal family.

"That's not how Indian culture works, Naina. A little tolerance, *beta*."

Naina rolled her eyes.

* * *

Wanting to avoid tourists, we went to an out-of-way neighborhood place that did beignets equal to those of Cafe Du Monde. We also ordered two hot chocolates. Surprisingly, Naina didn't bring up Jay or Rohan, and I quite appreciated this refreshing change in our dynamic.

"Ahana, how do you deal with the asinine questions aunties in Delhi throw at you?"

"How do you mean?"

"The women in the park who stuff their faces with Tibetan dumplings and talk crap."

"You mean *momos*?" It was one of New Delhi's favorite street foods all-year round.

"Yup! The type who stop and badger you when you are out for a run. How do you not argue with them?"

"I used to get upset. But Mumma once sat me down and told me, 'You can't change the aunties, so change your attitude. Don't explain yourself to them.'" I took a sip of the hot chocolate. "Why do you ask?"

"I am losing it with my dad's family. So judgmental. They slyly keep asking me about my living arrangement with Josh. What religion our kids will be! What the fuck?"

"Ignore them."

"How, dude? A bunch of Dad's family peeps surrounded me this morning when you were out for a run. 'A Waldorf Astoria Hotel for the engagement. It's a five-star luxury hotel.' They nodded their heads like robotic mannequins." Naina took a decadent bite of her beignet. Wiping her mouth, she imitated her paternal aunt's traditional Patiala gesture of throwing her hair back and moving her hands as if the wind were blowing them away. "'*Haan. Haan.* Lot of money you all must have spent. Did Josh's family pay for anything?'"

I started to laugh. "I am sorry."

"Shut up!" Naina hit the back of my head. She dusted her hands and shook her legs. "Maybe I need to try yoga?"

"Might not be the worst thing." I smiled.

It was mid-day, yet there was no message from Rohan. I sent him a picture of the bookstore on our way out.

He wrote back, "Cousins wreaking havoc in NOLA? ;-)"

I responded with a smiley.

I turned to Naina. "How does Rohan know you and I are hanging out?"

"Some of us post personal updates on social media." Naina poked the space between my eyebrows with her index finger. "You haven't said a word about fuck face Dubois since you got here. I am waiting."

We started to walk to Naina's favorite bar.

I couldn't tell Naina that I was doing my own detective work. "I need you to trust me, Naina. Don't ask me to explain anything about Jay. I need a break from him and any conversations about him. Please."

Surprisingly, Naina didn't argue with me. "But you know I nag only because I care about you?" She sat on the barstool and looked at the drinks menu.

"Never doubted that for a moment." I hugged her.

Naina ordered a Sazerac and I ordered a glass of wine. There was live music, Cajun food, and an afternoon away from work. I didn't bother logging into my online therapy group or emails to see whether there were any messages from Jay. I had finally told myself what Mumma would have said: *This is your time with the people you love. Take care of yourself.*

* * *

On the evening of the engagement, Naina, Josh, and I showed up early at The Roosevelt New Orleans to welcome the party guests. Rohan had texted me before catching his flight to NOLA. "Matron, see you in my city soon!!!" After an exchange of multiple messages, I knew his flight details, what time he would arrive at the party, right down to the kind of drink and peanuts he planned to order on the airplane.

The party room was abuzz. The hotel had played host to Ray Charles, Frank Sinatra, and Louis Armstrong at one point. It was lavish and the view of the city from the hotel was stunning. Large windows faced city lights. All of Naina and Josh's cousins and friends were present. Josh, coming from Italian ancestry, had a big family too. His cop friends had flown down from New York.

Champagne flowing. People swirling. Music. Booze. Indian, Italian, and Cajun food. Laughter. Designer gowns and Indian outfits mingled. The room had Naina's energy and Josh's personality. A perfect treat for friends and family. It was an intimate party. Naina looked gorgeous in a backless green gown, and Josh in his tuxedo.

My eyes kept turning toward the entrance. Rohan should have been here by now! Of all the days, why is he late today?

My mind was on Rohan when Naina's little cousin on her dad's side, Mindy, walked up to me. "Ahana *didi*, I need your help with my dress, please."

As soon as I returned after disentangling Mindy's zipper, I saw several heads turn toward the entrance. Rohan walked in with a gift in hand. He looked charming in his all-black Armani suit, with a pink Burberry tie. I walked toward him.

"Looking pretty, ladies."

"Thank you, Rohan." Naina kissed him on his cheek. "When did you get in?"

"This afternoon actually."

"Brady. Why are you late?" I pretended to make a stern face.

Naina glared at me and walked away. I knew she had purposefully left me alone with Rohan. I stared at the ground. I could feel Rohan stare at me. "What?" I spoke in a pretentious annoyed tone.

"Nothing. Never seen you with your hair tied up, though." Rohan paid attention. "You look beautiful in this dress." He noticed the small things and the big things.

I felt conscious of my ensemble—a short, beige, strapless, tight-fitting dress with heavy embroidery. Big heels, bright red lipstick, and hair tied in a bun, and Mumma's diamond chandelier earrings.

"You can't expect me to talk to you just because you compliment me." I touched my hair on both sides.

"Hahaha. So much, ego." Rohan walked an inch closer.

I could feel my breathing change. I could feel the fine fabric of his tailor-made suit on my skin.

He stared into my eyes. "I'm not the kind of guy who'll tell you what to do…. So, I'll just *strongly suggest* you go stand over there by that window where the light will make your earrings lovely, and let me bring you a drink."

"Fine." I stomped my foot and dug into the carpeted floor of the hotel.

"Ahana *didi*, come here. I'll show you a new step." Mindy tugged at my dress.

"I don't dance, Mindy."

"That's totes crazy, Ahana *didi*." Mindy pushed her right hip out and played with the locks in her hair.

"What?" I burst out laughing, watching the diva emerge from inside a pre-teen.

"You look so cute when you laugh." She continued to play with her hair.

"Thanks, Minds!" I kissed her on the cheek. "But I truly don't know how to dance."

Mindy put her right hand on her head with her palm facing down and pressing the crown of her head. Her left hand was on her left hip. "It's simple, Ahana *didi*. Push your left hip up and down."

I casually scanned the room and adjusted my hands and dress. A few years ago, Mindy had insisted that I dance with her at her cousin's wedding she'd attended in Delhi. We had danced with abandon to the beat of a *dhol* at the henna ceremony.

"OMG! Since when did you become lame, Ahana *didi*?"

The little brat.

"OK. OK. I'll try. Don't be such a grownup with me." I pulled her cheeks.

Mindy showed me again how it was done. "Now you try."

"Shouldn't I wait for some music to play first?"

"Fine." Mindy, clad in her braces and two-piece traditional Indian clothing ran toward the DJ.

I looked around the room. I couldn't see Rohan anywhere.

"Boo," someone said in my ears from behind. I turned around to find Rohan holding a Sazerac in each hand. "It's Naina and Josh's big day. Let's drink to peace."

I waved a "No" at the drink. "I'm involved in a much more important engagement with her." I pointed toward Mindy.

Rohan laughed and put both the drinks down.

I whispered. "She wants me to dance with her...and you know how 'good' I am at it."

"I have seen you dance in NYC. Remember?" Rohan whispered back.

"*Brady!*" I elbowed him.

"I am teasing." Rohan swirled his drink. "So, why don't you tell her that?"

"And disappoint her? That'd be mean."

"I like how you never get tired of doing small things for people. Sometimes, that's what occupies the largest part of their hearts." He smiled. "I'll bring you a glass of red to calm your nerves."

"Yes, please."

Suddenly, the music blared. By the time Rohan returned with a glass of pinot noir, Mindy too was back. She tugged at my dress, "You are totes late, Ahana *didi*."

"I am sorry." I gulped down the wine.

"Easy there, tiger." Rohan smiled as he took the glass from me. I noticed his drink still looked untouched.

I looked at him. "Trust me. I need this right now."

"You remember the steps?" Mindy sounded like a strict headmistress of an all-girls convent school.

Lightheaded, I spoke with uncertainty.

Suddenly the dance floor was occupied. The DJ played Indian techno music. Mindy started to do the step: one hand on the head, another on the hips. And she moved her hips up and down.

Not sure whether it was the glass of wine on an empty stomach or Mindy's company. Soon, I started to move too. It felt liberating not to care about what anybody thought. I took off my Louboutins and put them next to the DJ station. "Watch them for me, please, will ya?" I said to the DJ's assistant.

I returned to the floor. Shaking my head from side-to-side, I jumped along with the others. Mindy taught me to close my right hand into a fist and throw a punch into the air. I twirled her.

Naina pulled me into the center of the room. To the beat of upbeat music, I swiveled my hips. Naina mirrored my steps. Who was this person? The old Ahana would have never moved this way. She would have never allowed herself this freedom. The crowd whistled and cheered us on.

I waved to Rohan, gesturing him to join. He raised his drink but didn't move.

I walked up to him. "I thought you'd be on fire out there tonight." My arms were folded across my chest.

"I also know how to burn myself. Staying out here and out of trouble, Matron." He grinned.

"So unfair." I threw my arms up in the air.

"All right, Matron. Only for you." Rohan had joined the rest of us on the dance floor for a few minutes when Naina's boy cousins joined in. Before anyone could say anything, they lifted Josh on their shoulders and sang, "*Balle. Balle.*" Josh's friends chimed in, and suddenly, there was a big circle and a lot of *Bhangra* dancing.

Once the engagement party was over, which was after 1 a.m., and most guests had left, Rohan said a bye, but Naina insisted, "No way. Join the fun part."

Masi, Mausa, Naina, Josh, his family, Rohan, and I sat down for a little bit. Naina and Josh organized cappuccino and herbal teas for the small group. The cozy room and warm conversations, how Mumma would have loved this moment.

"You braved the Indian madness, dude!" Naina gave Rohan a fist-bump.

He smiled. "What a fabulous party! Thank you for having me."

"Tomorrow afternoon, we have organized a small get-together for Josh and my side of the family and a few of our close friends. It's at my parents.' You should totally come." Naina looked at Rohan and then turned to Josh. "Right, honey?"

"I concur." Josh gently ran his hands over Naina's shoulders.

"Unfortunately, I fly back to New York tomorrow morning."

I took off my shoes and rubbed my feet. "Oh, I thought we were taking the same flight back on Sunday evening. No?"

"Sorry, didn't get to tell you before." Rohan pressed his temples. "Hedick wants some analytics delivered to Sarah Goldstein—one of the professors at Columbia University."

"Sarah Goldstein. Oh! The director of the UN women's initiative whose support and participation would raise the event's profile and make it a true resource for high-level diplomats and NGO directors?"

"Exactly! Since it's sensitive information about women in Latin America, Hedick wants me to deliver the flash drive with the analytics personally before our Monday meeting. More importantly, Sarah is available to meet tomorrow; I will stop by the UN headquarters to have her introduce me to the government media liaisons."

"Do you need me to join you?"

"No, you spend time with your family. I'll take care of stuff and see you on Monday at the meeting with Dracula."

"Dracula?" Naina asked in a singsong way.

"My boss, Michael Hedick." Rohan smiled. "You don't wanna know."

* * *

I waited with Rohan as the valet brought out his car. Something about Rohan felt distant and quiet.

"Thank you for making the trip. For just a day?"

"Don't be formal, Matron. I had a really nice time and loved your family."

We both stood in silence for about five minutes. The wait for the car was long, since it was Friday night.

"Are you OK?"

"Yeah, why do you ask?" Rohan brought his eyebrows together.

"You seem unusually quiet."

"You are probably going to hate me for saying this...."

"Try me, Brady."

He ran his hands over his face. "Your family is so great! They made me feel so welcomed. But a part of me also realizes that I will never have a sense of completeness. A complete family picture." Rohan looked at the sky. "Everything changed after my mother left. Every time I visit my father, I feel invisible in front of him. I love your stories of India and your family."

I saw sadness in his eyes.

I held his hand. "I know the feeling, Rohan. Trust me. I have missed Mumma every single hour these past couple of days. I feel abandoned, despite everyone being so loving."

He pressed my hand. I looked in his eyes. They were moist. I said, "Maybe one day, when you have your own little world, with your wife and kids or whoever makes you happy...it'll help fill up the empty spaces." I rested my head upon Rohan's shoulders. "You're a good man, Brady. Good things happen to good people."

"Thanks, *yaar*." Rohan smiled.

"See, you already look slightly happier than you were before." I pulled out my mobile phone from inside my clutch. "*Chalo, chalo*, let's take a selfie and capture this moment."

With one arm around my waist and camera in another hand, Rohan pulled me closer for a photo. He whispered into my hair. "Maybe we are beginning to make a happy picture."

I gently ran my thumb on the dimple on his chin.

꞊ 21 ꞊

On Monday morning at 6:50 a.m., I was in the office. I had returned to NYC the night before. I figured I'd reach work before the others and settle in before the day began.

"Hope you meditated this morning," Crystal, Rohan's assistant, whispered.

I stared blankly at Crystal's red hair since her glasses were too thick and I could never tell where she was looking. "Yes, I did. But why do you ask?" I was surprised to see Crystal in the office this early.

"*Dracula* is here." Crystal put her right index finger on her glasses to press them back to her face.

"Michael Hedick? Already?" I looked at my watch. He'd set up the meeting for 7 a.m., but I didn't think he'd be in the office until 7:45. That's what happened when he visited our Delhi office. He was habitually 45-50 minutes late. But Hedick had been under pressure from Ms. Roy's contacts lately. Maybe he showed up early because he was feeling trapped and annoyed?

"I feel it's not for a good reason." Using her eyebrows, Crystal pointed in the direction of where Michael was standing, which was next to the coffee pot.

I peered into the hallway to catch a glimpse of Michael. "Where is Rohan?"

"He's not here." Crystal pulled her short skirt down her meaty thighs and buttocks. "I tried calling him, but his phone keeps going to voicemail."

"When did you last speak with him?" I whispered softly.

"When he left for the WestTry meeting on Friday morning."

"I saw Rohan on Friday evening at my cousin's engagement party in New Orleans. He was supposed to fly back to NYC on Saturday for his meeting with Ms. Goldstein." I hadn't checked in with Rohan the rest of the weekend, which wasn't unusual. We were very good with giving each other space and taking time off from work when we could.

"Rohan was running a high fever on Friday. But he flew to NOLA to attend your cousin's engagement party?"

I held Crystal's hands in my palms. "I had no idea."

Before Crystal and I could complete our conversation, I heard someone call my name. It was Hedick.

"I'll catch you later."

* * *

"Good morning, Michael." I straightened my clothes and tried to remain calm as I offered to shake his hand. Michael had a heavy aura. Maybe it was his height; he towered over everyone, which made people feel smaller. In his company, everything, including my body, felt tensed.

"Morning. New York treat you OK?" Michael took a sip of his coffee and wiped his bald head with his other hand. He was so pale that his white shirt looked like the color of his skin. He was in his late fifties, but he had one of those faces where you couldn't gauge his age correctly. He called out to Crystal and then swept his arms in the direction of the conference room.

Crystal and I exchanged hurried looks on the way in, and Michael slammed the door behind us. With his hands on his hips, he paced up and down the room. If he was trying to watch his temper, then he was failing completely, because his each step got angrier and he pressed his foot into the floor. Crystal's face tensed as I continued to maintain my poker face.

He finally paused. "We are fucked!" He slammed the table—the space between the projector and Crystal and me. I was glad the room had no glass windows because Michael would have probably put his fists through them.

I couldn't take another tantrum. "What happened, Michael?"

Michael wiped his forehead. "Rohan was supposed to meet with Sarah Goldstein on Saturday at the UN headquarters. That was thirty-six fucking hours ago." He punched the desk. "Sarah had set up meetings with government media liaisons."

"Is she available another day?" I asked with a straight face as I tried to maintain the upper-hand vibe.

Michael adjusted his glasses. "She travels out to Ecuador tomorrow for the Annual South American Women's Empowerment Summit. That's why we needed the analytics delivered on Saturday when Rohan was scheduled to meet with her. *Fuck*, this meeting has already been rescheduled a few times." Michael prodded the furniture with his fingertips. "It was all fucking Rohan's idea and now he's missing!"

Rohan had returned to NYC early because of his meeting. Why didn't he say a word to Crystal or me about not being able to make it? Was he seriously sick or in trouble? There was no doubting Rohan's commitment to the conference. My mind went in directions I didn't want it to. My feelings ranged from concern to irritation, but I

171

continued to stay calm in the face of Michael's anger. I would deal with Rohan later, but right now, I had to do something. There was also the possibility that Hedick was overreacting to punish us.

I started to rub the gold and diamond pendant Mumma had gifted me on my eighteenth birthday. It was the first piece of white gold jewelry I had ever owned. *Yellow gold is so loud and déclassé, Mumma.* But now, it worked as a mnemonic device. Yellow gold reminded me of Sarah Goldstein. Sarah was Jewish. And I had learned while working with organizations in the United States that many Jewish people didn't work from Friday sundown to Sunday morning. That was it: I had found the perfect excuse. "Rohan asked me to cover the meeting for him because he got sick, and I was supposed to deliver the analytics."

"YOU?!" Hedick was angry and shocked at the same time.

From nowhere, I made myself sound very confident in my reasoning for not delivering the thumb drive—I was in charge, it was my call. "Yes, me." I sounded more convincing the second time around. "I thought Ms. Goldstein shouldn't be disturbed over the weekend because she is Jewish. I wanted to respect her faith." I said it with a straight face, shocked at how smoothly I had lied.

Crystal just looked at me. Michael was gargling the insides of his mouth with coffee and then swallowed it in a loud, deliberate gulp.

"That is awfully nice of you to be considerate of Sarah's religious faith. But nobody really cares." His tone was harsh. Or maybe it was sarcastic. "I still don't understand why Rohan wouldn't tell you that Sarah is anything but religious. That woman eats bacon like other people eat chewing gum." He was loud and crass and sweaty. And his comments sounded more insulting because Sarah was a large woman. Rohan was right; Michael Hedick was a dick.

I fake-laughed at his cruel comments and apologized for my lack of cultural understanding. I thanked Michael—my colleague, or was it my subordinate or my superior—for correcting me.

"You think too much." Michael tucked his shirt into the waist of his pants and stared at me with cold eyes.

I tried to breathe. "Don't worry about it, Michael. I will go now and deliver the analytics. We might have lost the opportunity to meet at the UN headquarters, but we can always Skype with Goldstein. I will reach out to her."

Michael didn't say a word. He wiped his forehead and smiled. "Crystal, figure out how sick that son of a bitch Brady is."

I smiled back, but my mind was elsewhere: yes, Rohan had looked quieter than usual at the engagement party. He had held a drink but hadn't sipped it. His body had felt a little warm when he hugged me to say a bye, but Rohan had shrugged. "It's the exhaustion catching up or maybe I am just that hot." Typical Rohan. Where was he? Gosh, Michael was right. I thought too much.

Crystal and I walked out of the conference room together. "Rohan says you are rare and exceptional." Crystal pressed my hand gently. "Now I understand why."

Since I didn't handle compliments well, I withdrew my hand and changed the topic. "OK, we've got to figure out how to reach Rohan. Michael thinks I have the analytics and wants me to deliver them." I spoke faster than usual.

"I'll try to call him."

I thought of what I needed to do next. How much time would it take to go see Ms. Goldstein? And, if she was angry about Rohan missing the meeting as well as the delayed delivery, would that impact her level of involvement in the conference?

"Got Rohan's voicemail, again." Crystal hung up.

I picked up my cellphone and readjusted my handbag on the shoulder.

"Where are you going?'

"Damage control. I'm going to Rohan's service apartment to find out what happened."

"Don't leave me alone with Dracula."

"You'll be fine." I squeezed her shoulders. "Call me if you need anything." I pointed toward my phone. "Can I get the address to Rohan's apartment, please?" I knew Rohan stayed in an apartment on the upper west side in Manhattan.

Crystal tore a sheet of paper and wrote down Rohan's address.

≈ 22 ≈

Sometimes, we need a random person to show us a fresh perspective on old abscesses and issues.

As I sat in the cab, I browsed through the posts and messages of my online therapy group. Amanda and Tanya were unusually quiet. How violated they must feel, sharing their vulnerabilities, knowing their perpetrator was still reading everything and they could do nothing about it. Or had they made the choice not to act on it? I was familiar with that stance.

There was an email from Jay. Oh no, there were multiple. He had replied to his own emails where he sounded like a broken record.

"Sorry if you thought I was a jerk." That was the first email.

"Here is the thing: I'll just say it. I am not at my best these days."

"Maybe you are sick of this whiny friend and don't want to be friends anymore. I get it."

"See, I knitted a new blanket for Cat. Awesome, right?" There was a picture of Jay holding the blanket.

Why did Jay insist on continuously messaging me and making everything more complicated and annoying? Because Jay was a pathological narcissist. He had no sense of obligation to people in his life. It was always about him and his problems or his hobbies. Not once did he ask about Naina's engagement or the conference or me or anything else. *Not surprised!*

I couldn't even bring myself to read all his emails. "Ugh, whiny, hormonal high schooler."

The cab driver looked at me in the rearview mirror. "You all right, miss?"

"I don't understand people." I hated talking to strangers and here I was venting to a taxi driver.

"Some boy troubling you?" he said in an accent I hadn't heard before. It was singsong, and so relaxed. "Life is too short to give another minute to anyone or anything that doesn't make you happy."

I hesitated.

The cabbie pressed the brake and pointed to the entrance of a fancy building on the upper west side in Manhattan. "Here is your address." He printed the receipt.

I don't know what it was about the stranger's words, but they made sense to me. I handed him a twenty-dollar bill. "Keep the change."

"That's too much."

"Consider it your fee for the wisdom you just shared."

We both smiled.

I walked to the lobby and asked the doorman to buzz Rohan's apartment, which was on the eighteenth floor.

"Your name?" He dialed 1802 on the building intercom.

"Good evening, sir. A-hannah is here." He spoke into the phone nervously looking at me for pronunciation assurance.

My phone pinged. It was Jay with his abrupt message, "I am so afraid we are losing our connection."

I knew what he meant, but I pretended not to. I noticed how urgently he felt the need to reel me back in. "The signal seems fine at my end. And unless one was speaking over the phone, the signal strength doesn't make a difference. Wi-fi works." I made a smiley.

"Wow! You won't stop harping about us not talking on the phone and keep mentioning it passive-aggressively. Yes, I am a fuckup. But I own my mistakes. You pretend to be this perfect thing, Ahana, with no faults. You call yourself empathetic when you are anything but that. Do you even have a heart?"

Jay was chronically unwilling to see his shortcomings. He wasn't going to break me. Instead of taking Jay's tirade personally, I distanced myself and observed what set him off and what the pattern was. I had to make a more calculating approach to our correspondence. I just had to tell him what he wanted to hear. "Jay, I'm really sorry. I didn't mean to come across like that. I get crazy sometimes. Are you mad?"

I was disgusted by him, but I knew I had to do this if I wanted to find out why he wouldn't leave me alone and whether he was dangerous.

The doorman pointed me in the direction of the elevator banks. "Please make a left at the water fountain and any of the elevators on the right will take you to the eighteenth floor. Mr. Brady's apartment is the third one to the left of the elevator banks."

Before I put my phone inside the bag, I wrote to Jay, purposely playing along with the emotional charade. "Clearly, you are disappointed in our friendship. I have been there for you whenever you needed me—even when others weren't, from what you've said. Looks like that's not enough. I'll let you be."

As I entered the elevator, my phone pinged. Predictably, Jay was all sweet again. "Oh, hon, c'mon. Your friendship is one of the few things I am thankful for. I have lost so much in this life and that's why I lose it when you doubt my integrity."

Jay wasn't getting any more of my time today. I locked my emotions inside.

* * *

I took a deep breath and walked toward Rohan's apartment, unsure what I'd find.

Draped in a housecoat, eyes droopy and puffy, Rohan opened the door. "Sorry you had to wait downstairs." He sounded weak. "Eric, the doorman, he is new."

"You don't look good." I stepped inside the apartment and took off my shoes. I noticed the unfinished brick wall behind the television and home theatre system, with three artworks hung on it.

Rohan showed me inside and walked toward the kitchen. I looked around and quickly scanned the apartment—whatever else I could see. There was a ceiling fan. Classy, modern furniture. Pictures of his dog. There was a picture of Rohan with his dad. An in-built library. Everything was neat and folded up. So much sunlight.

Rohan remembered the first thing I did whenever I entered any office, restaurant, bar, or theatre: he brought me a glass of water.

"Thank you." I settled on the sofa and took a sip.

"I am surprised to see you." He sounded weak.

It would seem I had finished my quota of patience with Jay. "Surprised? You flew down to NOLA for the engagement party despite your fever. You didn't show up to your meeting with Sarah. You didn't deliver the analytics to Ms. Goldstein. You didn't inform me you were unable to make the delivery." I stood up. "You look so pale but won't say a word about what's going on."

"I got sick the day before Naina and Josh's engagement party, but I didn't think it was anything big. But by the time I returned to New York, I was running a fever of 105." Rohan blew his nose into a tissue. "I tried calling Ms. Goldstein a few times, got voicemail, but then felt so sick I went to the ER. Time moved differently there, and then it was already midnight on Sunday."

"You could have at least told one of us to make the delivery and meet with her." I waved my hand as if swatting away his words.

"Don't make it sound like an unforgivable sin, Matron."

"You can't take everything lightly, *yaar*. You know how things have been at work with Hedick. He hounded us this morning because Ms. Goldstein doesn't have the analytics. Apparently, she was upset you didn't show up to the meeting. How will she connect with the women in Latin America?"

"It sucks you had to butt heads with that asshat Hedick! I'm sorry if I made things harder at the office." Rohan grabbed his face with both his palms and sank in the sofa. "I emailed Sarah on Saturday afternoon and mentioned I was sick. I sent her the analytics with the encryption code and told her I would drop off the hard copy by Monday evening—she would still have everything before catching her flight to Ecuador."

I put my hands on my hips. "Well, looks like she didn't get your email."

"Crap!" His face darkened. "The email must be in her spam folder because of the attachment."

"Did you not follow up with her?"

"I could barely think. I completely passed out after that."

I sat next to him. "Why didn't you ask either Crystal or me to drop off the analytics?"

"Crystal's son was in town for a day yesterday to visit her. You were in NOLA; I didn't want to ruin your trip. Sarah had the electronic copy of the document in any case."

"One last thing."

"What?"

"Why didn't you tell me you were sick?"

Rohan's nose was red. His eyes looked weak. He massaged his temples gently in circular motion and rested his head on the backrest of the sofa. "I'm used to being on my own, Ahana. I have never had anyone take care of me ever since I was a kid."

He got up and went into the kitchen. I followed. As Rohan warmed up water to drink, my heart melted. How could any mother abandon their child? How did he grow up without a mother to pamper or dote on him? He read the perplexed look on my face as he took a sip of the water. "Don't worry; it's not a big deal. I shut down and rest until I feel better."

"In India, this would never happen." I shook my head. "People would cook for you and take you for doctor appointments. We all need TLC when sick."

"How about I move to India with you, so you can give me TLC when I fall sick?" Rohan elbowed me.

"*Paagal.*" I looked at the floor. "Have you eaten anything?"

"Nope."

"That's not OK. How about I go down and get you some chicken noodle soup?"

"You really don't need to, Ahana."

"I know, but I want to." I smiled at him. "Mumma would make me chicken noodle soup with loads of vegetables when I was sick. It would always work like magic. The cook did the daily cooking based on what she asked him to make. But when I got sick, no one could touch my food. Mumma made everything with her own hands despite her long hours at the hospital."

"Spoiled brat," Rohan teased me.

"Nah, more like very loved."

"All right, lady love. You are spoiling me. Continue doing so and I won't let you go back to India." He smiled.

I looked at him shyly. "Will you let me leave your apartment, at least?" I started to walk toward the main door.

"If I had my way, never." Rohan let out the biggest grin.

I poked his third eye.

Rohan held my hand. "I'm so sorry you and Crystal had to deal with Dracula."

"No worries. Rest up. I'll bring you something to eat so you have your strength back right away."

"Yes, ma'am."

I touched Rohan's forehead to see whether he had any fever. "Do you have any acetaminophen?"

"English, please." He sat on a chair.

"Fever-reducing-medication." I purposefully stressed every syllable to tease Rohan.

"Haha, yes. Tylenol."

"I need to check the date of expiration."

"All right, Dr. Ahana." He handed me the bottle of Tylenol.

I inspected it and threw it in the dustbin. "I am a doctor's daughter." Before pulling the main door close, I said to Rohan, "Freshen up; you'll feel better. Also, can you bring me the analytics— I will personally go and deliver it to Sarah Goldstein."

He saluted me.

"*Paagal*, I'll see you soon."

* * *

I was wearing stilettos and a fitted dress and didn't realize until now that walking anywhere would take me double the amount of time. From an organic deli, I bought a carton of eggs, fruits, energy drinks, ginger root, cough drops, Tylenol, hot soups, hearty salads, stir fry chicken with vegetables, lamb shawarma, and picked up a copy of the *Economist*.

When I returned forty-five minutes later, Rohan opened the door in a fresh set of clothes. He looked better.

"Did you rob the grocery stores on the Upper West Side?" Rohan took the bags from my hands and walked toward the kitchen.

As I took off my heels and placed them on the shoe rack, I peeped into the hallway. "Aah, you missed me." I winked. The entranceway gave the intimate, welcoming feeling of a historic townhouse, which I hadn't noticed when I visited him earlier that day.

"Well, actually, I did." Rohan's face was serious. I had never seen him this way.

"*Paagal*, fever has made you mental." I gently tapped his forehead and feigned a smile.

He smiled back.

"There is enough food for you for the coming week." I pulled each box carefully out of the bags.

"Thank you." He helped me unload the groceries.

"I am doing all this *only* because I want you up and running before NOLA. Now get me the flash drive, please."

Rohan, very dramatically, put his arms around his chest. "Stop seeing me as a sexual object. It hurts." He pointed toward the coffee table; the USB flash drive was on it.

"Why, only your harem can see you like this?" As soon as the words left my mouth, I bit my tongue. "I am so sorry. Old habits die hard."

He placed his palm on my wrist. "Old Indian aunties have a hard time letting go of old habits."

"Who did you call an Indian aunty?" I opened his freezer, took out ice, and threatened to throw it at him.

"You," he pointed at me.

"I will *always* be younger than you, Grandpa."

"Did you just call me Grandpa?"

I proudly threw two ice cubes in the air and caught them in my palm like a seasoned bowler in cricket. "Yes!"

"That ice touches me and I will return the favor, Matron."

I hated dares. But in Rohan's company, I often did things I didn't think I could do. I put ice down the back of his collar. "Aah! Cricket power." I showed off my biceps and blew air into my fist.

Rohan grabbed both my wrists.

Suddenly, the terror took me. I was locked in a cage in Dev's house getting ready for a cocktail party at his aunt's and he was pressing my body hard. I worried for my safety. Felt the sting of rope around my wrists, the pull of a bed railing or doorknob. I was unable to scream. Even if I did ask for help, no one would listen to me.

I stared at Rohan. "Let me go." His hands were warm.

"I warned you, Matron."

"I will yell."

Rohan took ice cubes out of the freezer and he aimed them at me.

I arched my eyebrow. "DON'T TOUCH ME!" I shouted louder than I knew I could.

Rohan let go. "I'm sorry, Ahana. I didn't mean to.... I was only joking."

"I need to get out of here." I picked up the flash drive with the analytics and put it inside my bag.

"Ahana..."

I slipped on my shoes and pulled the door shut behind me. No amount of me trying to explain anything would do any good. I didn't know what was happening to me.

* * *

Rohan sent out an email to Ms. Goldstein and Michael—he had promised we would stick to my version of the story. He copied Crystal and me on it. The email with the analytics was indeed in Sarah's spam folder and she hadn't bothered checking her office voicemail. Michael took credit for sorting out everything. Crystal sent me a message, "The world needs more people with your kind of heart."

By the time I made the delivery and cleared my head, I realized it was time to explain everything to Rohan—why I had gone from happy to neurotic without an explanation. Rohan gave me no reason to mistrust him. But I was still anchored to the trauma in my past. Even as I grew past it, it sometimes caught up with me again and surprised me.

I figured I'd go to the office, change, and enjoy a long run in Central Park. After reconnecting with my Zen space, I'd check in on Rohan.

When I reached the office, Michael had left for the day. He spent more time playing golf at country clubs and drinking bourbon in fancy bars than he spent doing any kind of real work. Crystal was still there poring over a big chart while a pot of coffee was brewing.

"What are you still doing here?" I peered inside the kitchen.

"Michael said he needed the seating arrangement sorted out for the final VIP dinner."

"But didn't we finish doing all that while I was in India?" I opened the refrigerator and pulled out a bottle of water.

"Yeah. But this is what Michael does. He makes last minute changes."

The screw on the bottled water was so tight that I grunted, "I am sick of these men screwing around with our happiness. Ego-centric, self-centered maniacs who cannot even be human for a day."

"What's going on, Ahana?" Crystal looked up at me in shock.

"You shouldn't be sitting here working while Michael is out living his life."

180

"Well, what can ya do?"

I spoke fast and pounded the coffee table. "You and I are both leaving right now."

"Ahana, I cannot afford to lose this job." She donned her glasses and put a pencil behind her ears as she contemplated.

"You won't." I turned off the lights in the kitchen and walked into my office.

"What are we going to tell him?" She followed behind.

"I am going to think of something." I quickly opened my laptop and sat in my chair.

"Hi, Michael. Thank you for stopping over in NYC and for sorting out all the confusion. I came back to the office after dropping the analytics at Ms. Goldstein's only to find Crystal still working. It would be a shame if she wasted a chance to take the evening off for all of her hard work, and get rested up for our busy week next week. Sorry I missed saying a bye to you. You might already be on your way to New Orleans. My team and I are grateful to you for your support. Thanks, Ahana."

Just like that, I sent the email to Michael. I had hit reply all so Ms. Goldstein, Rohan, and Crystal were all marked a copy. Michael loved looking good in front of others. Thrice divorced, he was always looking for the next best woman and trying to impress others.

He sent a reply all with, "Glad my trip helped you all. Crystal, you call it a day and have a great evening."

I shut my laptop with force.

Crystal was a hugger. She held me tight and shook me up.

I changed into my running tank, lululemon pants, and the remaining running gear. I pulled my hair into a high bun and locked up my day clothes in the office.

"Thank you so much for caring and saving our Southern asses today, Ahana. I'll take you out for some Cajun food when we are in New Orleans," Crystal said as the two of us stepped out of the elevator of our office building. She walked toward the subway stop, and I headed toward the park.

A few quiet moments with your own self is the best way to find any answers, Mumma often said. I rubbed my pendant, gently but fast. Inhale. Exhale. I asked my heart to reveal answers and told my head to stay out of the way.

Rohan didn't take advantage of me. I am not sure what experience made Rohan into a good guy, but if I were to guess, it was early responsibility at a young age. My mind went to Jay. What would Jay have done if he were in Rohan's place? It took him nothing to violate both Tanya and Amanda. To what extent would Jay go to get whatever it is that he wanted from me?

I started to run. Not away from my problems or people; toward what I needed to sort out.

≈ 23 ≈

Rohan opened the door even before I had pressed the bell.

"I don't think my apartment is big enough for you to jog." He tried hard to smile, but his eyes still looked heavy.

"Ya ya ya. So funny." I made a face and took off my shoes.

"How come you're here?"

"Because Crystal wanted me to check on you." I didn't look at him.

"Just Crystal?" He stood with his arms across his chest.

"Yup." I washed my hands in the kitchen and wiped them on the kitchen towel.

"You are a terrible liar, Matron."

"And you are a terrible patient." I looked around. Most of the food I'd brought for Rohan was sitting untouched on the reclaimed kitchen island.

Rohan walked closer to me. "You missed me. C'mon; say it, Ahana."

My knees trembled just a little. "Did you miss me?" I gently pushed him away.

"Of course, I did." Rohan stared into my eyes.

My breathing became heavier. I rested against the barstool arranged near the kitchen island.

Rohan stood unmoved. "You still haven't answered."

"What do you think, Brady?" I smiled weakly.

Rohan rubbed his three-day old stubble.

The evening sun was painting the sky and Rohan's niceness made me feel guilty. I knew it was time to have the talk. I unlocked the door to his private balcony, which led to a beautiful view of the Riverside Park. The splash of fall colors combined with the gush of cold air reminded me of Mumma. On some weekend evenings in December and January, she would drape a Pashmina shawl around her shoulders, drink a few pegs of whiskey, and quote Rabindra Nath Tagore. *You can't cross the sea merely by standing and staring at the water.*

I sat on Rohan's sofa and looked at the light wooden floor, which contrasted beautifully against the gray walls. The door to the master bedroom was open, and I could see the masculine blue walls.

I whispered softly. "I'm sorry I ran out this morning." A bead of sweat flowed from my forehead into the hollow of my collarbone.

Rohan sat next to me and looked at me with sincerity.

"Sometimes, I feel like a fraud for leading this conference." I looked at the floor. "I suppose Hedick knows it too."

Rohan prodded, "We're not here to talk about Michael Hedick. Whatever it is, just say it, Ahana. I'm not stupid. I have my guesses, but you can tell me whatever you need to say."

I heard a *thud* in my heart. I couldn't look at Rohan, but I got up again and walked toward the living room windows—away from him and closer to my memories that had been carved into my flesh as scars. Every part of me hurt. The bruises from the handcuffs Dev used on my wrists in our bedroom were gone, as were the red bangles—signs of a married Hindu woman. I rubbed my wrists. He would pin me down, push me against the wall. Dev would grin at the end of the night.

I felt oppressively hot from the memories, so I cracked open the windows. The crisp autumn air cut through my skin. It was a cool, strikingly clear, nearly cloudless evening. As I explored my heart, my eyes explored the streets of New York. The city was bustling with activity and beauty. I wanted to feel the same lightness. Winter would soon claim these leaves; the way Dev had claimed my happiness. I needed to speak up.

Rohan walked up to me. "Talk to me."

I was going to share the darkness of my marriage and talk about my own "pleasure" with someone for the first time, and a man at that. Mumma had speculated on parts of it. I had opened to Naina recently. But not in entirety.

My eyes were filled to the brim with tears. I closed them and tried sniffing discreetly. Rohan held my shoulders in a sweet way that took the slight chill away from the air. It had taken me years to come to terms with exactly how much damage my ex had caused. "*No* meant nothing to Dev."

Rohan's eyes widened as he ran his hands over my shoulders.

I held my opposite elbows and ran my fingers vigorously over my upper arm. "He made my body his slave."

Rohan clenched his fists.

I turned away from him. "Dev wanted me to cooperate in his sexual sadism, and I did at times so he wouldn't hurt me. Nobody was going to listen to me anyway, I knew." My throat tightened. "But if I was coerced into pleasing my abusive husband and occasionally my body got pleasure out of these assaults, could I still call it rape?" I felt dirty, guilty, and violated all over again.

An involuntary whimper escaped my lips. Once that first tear broke free, a stream of tears escaped my eyes. Rohan moved closer and wiped my tears with his hand. I didn't freak out.

"I became the poster woman for shame, Rohan. That is the kind of shame that really sticks, and it's as strong as the shame over staying in an abusive relationship so long. That is the kind of shame that took away the safety of my small world." I covered my face with my shaking hands.

"Ahana, look at me." He stared into my eyes. "A *No* means nothing but a fucking *No*! It is always the rapist's fault."

I tried to battle the onslaught of tears.

"You didn't cause your rape. You shouldn't feel any shame."

As soon as those words left Rohan's mouth, I hugged him tightly and cried some more.

Rohan ran his hands on my back, "I am so sorry he hurt you. You're incredibly brave, Ahana," he whispered as he ran his hands through my hair. "Is that why you got scared earlier today when I was messing around with ice cubes?"

"Dev has taken away so much of my confidence and ability to trust." I understood that the seeds of shame were planted by Dev. "I was an abused/silent woman in my own marriage, and now I'm expected to be the face of a global campaign to fight violence against women—if this isn't hypocrisy, what is?"

Rohan kept both his hands on my shoulder. "You walked out of a bad situation. And now you are helping other women stand up against violence." Tucking my hair behind my ears, he continued, "You are a lot stronger than you think."

I sighed loudly. "I pretend to be strong, Rohan."

Rohan brought me a glass of water.

"Thank you."

He moved up closer. He covered his face with his palms and moved his hands slowly as if wiping away any obscurity.

"Do you still have any feelings for him?" He asked with a straight face, but I felt him shrink away.

"Dev?"

He nodded.

"He mattered to me a long time ago." I took a sip of water. I looked at my left hand where the wedding ring used to be. I was finally feeling free despite having been divorced for close to two years.

"And Jay?"

"Yuck! No!" I sighed loudly and played with my pendant. I knew I had to come clean and tell Rohan I was trying to do something about my issues in the past by taking control of this thing with Jay. I gave him a hint.

"Are you sure about the way you are handling the situation, Ahana?"

I put the glass down and gently held Rohan's hands. I kissed his left cheek and then his other cheek. Rohan looked at me in awe. "I'm sick," he said, and gently stroked my face.

I shivered. "I don't care."

Rohan pulled me closer to him. I could feel palpitations in my chest. My mouth was dry. For the first time in my life, I didn't think what anyone would think or feel; I listened to my heart. I kissed Rohan on his lips and he kissed me back. The kiss felt so complete that I felt the kiss alone would heal me. I had so many thoughts running through my head. I felt feelings I hadn't felt in a very long time.

Were Rohan and I flirting with each other, or was it something more? It could have been Rohan feeling emotional and getting caught in the moment? It could have been me handling a breakdown. A kiss in India meant something very different from a kiss in the United States. Dev and I kissed, and then the next thing we knew, we were married. In America, relationships worked in stages. People hung out, dated, lived together, and only sometimes got married. Rohan and I not only belonged to two different cultures but also lived in two different countries.

Perhaps Rohan sensed my quandary. As he pulled away, he said, "You deserve only the best in life."

My head hurt but my chest felt lighter. Rohan felt a little warm, so I made him lie down on his king-size bed and gave him a little head massage. I put away his iPad on the nightstand. I warmed up some soup and poured it into a ceramic bowl. Rohan was happy to sit and eat on his bed. He ate well. We watched reruns of *Seinfeld*, one of Rohan's favorite shows. I sat on the recliner next to his bed overlooking high-rises in Manhattan. So much noise outside, so much peace inside his room. I had always secretly wanted care in my relationship with Dev, but I had never found it.

We didn't talk about the kiss. I made him *Tulsi*-ginger tea, and he fussed a little about the taste, but he drank it eventually. "We want you all better for the conference," I told him. I took the mug from his hands and placed it on the coaster on the nightstand. I got up and turned off the study lamp on his work desk.

"No one has ever done so much for me," he said with misty eyes. I planted a kiss on his forehead and closed the blinds so the Manhattan lights wouldn't hinder his sleep.

It was after 10 p.m. "Shit. It's late."

"What happens after 10 p.m.? You turn into a pumpkin?" Rohan pulled the comforter to his chest and smiled. He still looked exhausted.

I touched his forehead. "Oh, good, the fever is coming down. You should sleep."

"Do you have to go?" Rohan whispered weakly into my hair.

I smiled at him. "Keep drinking plenty of fluids, Brady."

Rohan passed out even before I left his bedroom. He looked like a child. I had never felt more awake as I packed away the leftovers in the fridge. Rohan's immunity was low; I didn't want him exposed to germs, so I wiped the kitchen counter with anti-bacterial wipes. I warmed up water and poured it in a carafe. I put it on the nightstand next to Rohan's bed along with a glass and a note, "Drink this water and do not chew on ice, you American boy. :) Do some steam inhalation and salt water gargle in the morning, please." I turned off the lights in the living room and kitchen. As I let myself out and reached the lobby, I felt I had left the heaviness of my past behind.

I got out on the streets of Manhattan. Even as I aimlessly walked around Rohan's neighborhood, wondering whether I wanted to hail a taxi or take a subway back to Naina's, I watched the cozy golden light from a few iconic buildings in just the right way. Cab drivers were honking, pedestrians were jaywalking, food trucks were serving a long line of tourists, local New Yorkers were eating their way through all pumpkin everything in the city—I understood the magic of New York. It's the city where amid all the mess, you find your bliss when you are least expecting it.

* * *

I spent the rest of the evening reading and watching mindless television. It was nice to be alone after all these days. While listening to a little Frank Sinatra and having a hot cup of chamomile tea, I thought about the kiss with Rohan just as much as I thought about what Jay would do next. I had avoided him all day. I had shown him his place in our friendship. None of it Jay would have accepted easily.

I logged into my emails to see if he had sent a note.

There it was. "I know we aren't dating. But where have you been all day? Don't you miss your best buddy? By the way, I don't mind a little chase." There was a grin at the end of his message.

Silence fell at my end. Jay was relentless despite all the insults. That meant he wasn't willing to let go of of me easily. Whatever I had started, I had to find a way to finish it.

24

The next morning, which was a Tuesday, I got into work with a green juice in hand at 7:30 a.m. On the same wrist, I wore one of Mumma's watches. Her watch next to my skin reminded me of the promise I had made to her—never to let any man break me again. "We will bury all the demons from Dev," one of the last few things Mumma had said to me.

I looked at the streets full of runners prepping for the upcoming New York Marathon. *I hope I can participate in it one day,* I thought to myself.

The office was quiet. Walking past Rohan's office brought back memories of the night before. I tried to push aside the memory of his lips on mine—so gentle so full—I didn't want another heartbreak.

Suddenly someone whispered "boo" in my right ear. I dropped my handbag on the floor. I turned around; it was Rohan smiling and apologizing in the same breath. He looked healthy. The kiss the night before.... I thought about it and my face turned red.

"Good morning, Matron." Rohan helped me put the stuff back in my handbag.

"Morning, Brady." I pretended to be blasé.

"How was your Monday evening?"

"I was with you, if you remember?"

"I will always remember." Rohan tucked a tuft of hair behind my right ear.

I lifted my right shoulder and rubbed my right earlobe with it. Rohan moved his hand.

"I am glad to see you're feeling better."

"I was royally pampered yesterday. Woke up feeling a 500 percent."

"Good!"

"Thank you for everything, Ahana." Rohan and I stood up from the floor at the same time.

"Don't be silly. That's what friends do." I smiled weakly at him and tried not to stare from his perfect hair to his powder blue shirt and khakis to his piercing blue eyes matching his shirt.

Rohan bent his knees so he could look me in my eyes. "Let me take you out and show you a few cool, hidden spots in NYC."

"You have already done enough for me."

I walked toward my office. Rohan followed behind. He leaned against the edge of my desk. I could smell his aftershave.

"I need to prepare for a meeting starting in ten minutes." I felt nervous.

"Liar. No one comes into this office before 9 a.m."

My mouth turned dry because of the two syllables in the word *liar*.

"I um..." I was mad at myself for not finding the right words.

Rohan kept staring at me. His smell lingered in the room. His glare pierced through my body.

He walked out. I wet my lips. No one—not even Dev when we were dating—had had this effect on me.

Suddenly, Rohan appeared again at the threshold of my office, "Fine, I'll make this fast. I am not going to pretend."

"Pretend what?"

He stepped inside my office. "I am not asking you to hang out. It's a date. One date. I really like you, Ahana. Just go out with me once."

My pulse throbbed. I liked the certainty of Rohan's words.

"Fine. I'll give you one evening to show me."

Rohan leaned into my face. His breath melted me. "See you at Dionysus at 9 p.m. on Friday night. You won't be sorry."

The minute Rohan went inside his office, I swiveled in my chair and called up Naina. "I agreed to go out on a date only because I didn't want to keep saying no. He's been a good friend." I didn't tell her that Rohan had kissed me the night before.

"What are you so scared of?"

"What if it's a bad date? It'll affect the conference and my friendship with Rohan."

"Rohan can keep his personal and professional life separate. He's not a fucking imbecile like fuck face Dubois." Naina grunted. "Men like Rohan, don't be cold with him. Give him some sugar."

"Naina...."

"What time are you meeting Rohan?"

"At 9 p.m."

"Awesome. Wear something sexy. And don't play hard to get."

"Stop it!"

"No, you stop kidding yourself, Ahana. You guys have a fiery chemistry. I can feel the heat all the way across a room."

My breathing was loud and heavy just from thinking about Rohan. I hung up on Naina.

* * *

When I went home that evening, I pulled out my yoga mat in Naina's living room and did a headstand for ten minutes. I needed clarity and peace. I realized that conference preparations were nearing the end. My list of tasks was mostly crossed off.

I took a shower and burnt some sage after the at-home yoga practice. I logged into my personal messages and the online chat group after eating a salad for dinner. Frank Sinatra's *Fly Me to the Moon* played on loop. I messaged Tanya and asked whether she was doing OK. She hadn't heard from Amanda.

Jay noticed I was online. He sent me a private message. "I'd love to meet you. I am not avoiding you, though I can understand why you might feel that way."

"I didn't say that, Jay. I know you have your reasons." I was getting good at reverse-manipulating Jay.

"I'm planning to come and meet with you in person, Ahana."

"Oh." I took a deep breath and paused for a second. *This is new.* "When are you planning to come down to New Orleans?" Naina and my entire family were in NOLA. Jay couldn't touch a single strand of my hair on their turf.

"Today is Tuesday. I was thinking Thursday. I will come up to New York."

I took a sip of water. "Really? NYC?" I felt my throat close.

"Yes, milady."

Does he know that Naina isn't in town? Does he know I'm alone? How will I manage my first meeting with him? I pushed my thoughts aside and replied.

"OK. Whatever works best for you, Jay."

"You couldn't be more unenthusiastic about my visit. Money is tight. I might have to crash at a friend's."

What did Jay expect—that I would ask him to stay with me? *Asshole!*

I wrote back after a few minutes. "Not true." I ran my tongue over my lips. I couldn't let Jay know that I was onto something. "I'm surprised is all. A beautiful surprise nevertheless." I feigned happiness by ending my message with three purple heart emojis.

"I'm taking all this effort to come see you. You have no idea what I've been through. My own father betrayed me. It's difficult for me to trust anyone. You are the one person who makes me feel sane, Ahana."

"A surprise is not a bad word, Jay. All I asked was about your plan." I couldn't let him suspect that I didn't trust him any longer.

"You have changed, Ahana. Our friendship isn't the same anymore."

Jay was an intuitive man. I knew what I had to do to win back his faith. I cringed as I typed, "I miss our chats, Jay. But it seems that chatting with me upsets you more than it makes you happy. That's why I am cautious about how much I say to you."

I felt victorious when he wrote back. "C'mon, hon. It's not your fault. You have been the best friend I've had in years. Human interaction is not my strength lately, so I am damaging my own abilities."

"We'll work through whatever is bothering you, Jay."

"Yeah. We'll order bottles of wine and throw rocks at fat people."

Jay's weight obsession was harsh.

"You can tell me about your dark secrets, Ahana."

"My secrets?" My face turned into a twisted knot.

"You never tell me about what's really on your mind, Ahana. If I can't help you, my best friend, what's the point of my existence? I feel like you talk to everyone else but me about your life."

What aspect of my life is he referring to? Focus, Ahana. This is all part of the plan. You can't lose him. I stretched out my legs and yawned. "You know me so well." I was grossed out by my fake empathy toward Jay. "Naina's wedding is coming up. And I feel broken. I hate attending weddings because there are complete and happy families there. I'll never have that with Mumma gone." I sent him three sad faces emojis, with one crying.

He wrote back immediately, "I can relate to that. I went to my friend's kid's birthday party last weekend, and the minute they started to pose for family pictures, I felt broken."

And he is back in. Score: Ahana-2, Jay 0. I made a victory sign with both my hands.

"Thank you for caring, Jay."

"I care. A lot. I wish you would trust me. I have been an open book—told you everything about my life. I feel like a failure in this one-sided friendship where you give me advice but I can't help you. I feel like I am burdening you. And for a guy who is depressed, being a burden on others is only doing damage."

"That's not true. You have helped me plenty with Mumma's demise. You showed me how to remain strong. Thank you, Jay." I put a finger inside my mouth to gesture vomiting.

"Don't thank me. I'm glad to be of help to you. You have done so much for me."

A few more email exchanges later, it was settled that early evening on Friday would work well for both of us. Jay said that he would meet me at Naina's apartment.

How does he know where Naina lives? While I deliberated my response, Jay wrote, "What, you don't trust your dear buddy?"

Just when I thought I had everything under control, Jay caught me off guard. I thought of believable reasons. "It's not that. This isn't my place, so I'd much rather not impose on my cousin."

"But isn't your cousin already in New Orleans?"

Jay knew Naina's schedule. I felt spiders crawl all over my body.

"Yeah, but doing the right thing in someone's absence is more important than doing it in their presence, no?"

"I understand." Jay typed fast. "How about I email you a few options?"

"Sounds good. Or I could send you a few too, if that's more convenient?"

"Nah, you are in my city, Ahana. Let me show you around." This time, he ended his sentence with a smiley.

I decided to sleep over the conversation and speak with Naina in the morning. I chose not to share anything with Rohan. He and I were in an interesting, unexplored space in our friendship. I didn't want conversations about Jay to spoil anything.

I was massaging my forehead and processing my conversation with Jay when the phone rang.

"Hello, madame!" Naina spoke in a French accent.

How often the universe conspired to send Naina my way right when I was either at my lowest, or seeking advice.

"You aren't laughing. What's going on?"

I updated Naina on the phone conversation with Jay. She heard me out. It was only after I told her that Jay wanted to meet with me in a place of his choice, she yelled, "You are out of your fucking mind, Ahana!"

"Naina..."

"Sever ties. Block him. Disappear the way Amanda did. Why meet with this bastard?"

"Naina..."

"He is a fucking psycho."

"I need to do this." I spoke from a place of conviction.

"You're being foolish! That asshole knows I'm not in town. He's been keeping tabs on your life. You tell me he's violated two other women we know of. God alone knows what he has in store for you."

"I am done with men scaring me and putting me in a place I don't deserve or want."

"You think he'll walk up to you and confess?"

"Naina, I'm meeting with him in the middle of the afternoon for chai, not alcohol. I'll be safe."

"I am coming back to New York and accompanying you on this date with fuck face Dubois."

I breathed hard. "No! You stay in NOLA." I poured myself a glass of water.

"Fine, then call Rohan."

"Keep him out of this." Some of the water spilled.

"You can't expect me not to do anything, Ahana..." Naina continued to share her opinion on the subject.

I wiped the mess and left the dishrag on the kitchen counter. As I walked up to the living room windows, I looked at the sky and saw a few stars. I tried to touch the stars through the windowpane. *Mumma.* I knew she was watching over me. In that moment, I knew I had my mom's blessings to sort out my life.

"I have a date with Rohan that evening; I don't want to say anything to him about Jay." I spoke firmly.

"Jay is bad news!"

I sighed. "Yes, I might have agreed to meet with a criminal and put myself in danger. But I am tired of hiding. I stayed quiet and accommodated Dev, but what did it get me? I want to walk into the mouth of the lion this time and show myself that he has no power over me."

Naina spoke with patience. "I get it."

"Here is my backup plan: I want you to call me every twenty to forty minutes. This way you know I am safe. There is no phone tracking on my iPhone, but I'll give you my iCloud password if you ever need to find out where I am but can't reach me."

"Are you sure there's no other reason?"

"Yes! I am compelled to see this through to the end and find out what Jay wants from me."

The week went by quickly and slowly. I clocked in late hours to finish the last-minute bit for the conference. And also, so I didn't have the time to obsess about my meeting with Jay or date with Rohan on Friday.

⚡ 25 ⚡

My meeting on Friday afternoon ran over and the subways were running slower than usual. I had no time to go home and change before my meeting with Jay. So, clad in my work clothes—a fire-colored skirt, beige silk blouse, brown jacket, and Prada totes, one of the last handbags Mumma had bought for me—I got off from the 1 train at 110th street and Cathedral Parkway.

The streets were wider and the buildings around had a lot of character in this part of the city. But I didn't see families pushing strollers, walking dogs, or business professionals settling in for coffee meetings at any of the cafes. I was irritated that Jay had picked a spot in an out-of-the-way neighborhood for a 4 p.m. meeting.

The time was 4:20 p.m., and it was still bright out. The trees were a vibrant shade of yellow, orange, and red. Rohan had told me that the fall colors were rarely this intense until October's end. "You brought a splash of Indian vibrancy with you, Matron."

Just thinking about Rohan calmed me down. I took a deep breath and walked toward my rendezvous point.

When I entered Café Angelique, a pretty French café not too far from Columbia University, the bells jangled. I surveyed the room and saw a man with a cap that read JETS. Even though he was facing the main entrance, his head was bent and his gaze was fixed on his phone with his back not straight.

From whatever I had seen in the few selfies Jay had shared, he always had his Jets cap on. Naina maintained, "I think he's bald and conscious of it."

Was the guy Jay? I slowly walked up to him, "Excuse me."

Jay looked up from his phone. He'd always bragged about his good looks, but he seemed so much older and tired in person. He didn't take off his cap. His eyes were sagging and it seemed like he had a receding hairline.

He got up to hug me, but I inched away. I quickly offered to shake his hand and said a few lines from *The Catcher in the Rye*. "I am always saying, 'Glad to've met you,' to somebody I'm not at all glad I met. If you want to stay alive, you have to say that stuff, though.'"

"Are you unhappy to meet me?" He looked above my eyebrows. His voice sounded harsh—like steel wool scraping the bottom of a steel saucepan.

We had barely spoken a sentence or two with each other and arguments were already budding. Because, once again, Jay didn't recognize Salinger's famous words when he had repeatedly told me, "I have every line from *The Catcher in the Rye* memorized."

"Salinger!" I smiled so hard my cheeks started to hurt.

"Ohh." He narrowed his eyes. "You know how distracted I am these days. Didn't realize."

His mendacity came naturally to him. Jay was a formidable adversary; he could think on his feet. Maybe, somewhere I had been hoping that Jay would be a little bit stupid—why else would he hit on three women in the therapy group and never once think that he would eventually get caught?

"C'mon, hon. Give me a hug." Jay held me in a tight embrace for a few minutes. At one point, he lifted me off the ground. I hated his touch. He smelled of nothing.

I disentangled myself from his arms. "I'm sorry for being late. The trains were a mess."

"'If a girl looks swell when she meets you, who gives a damn if she's late? Nobody.'" Jay laughed loudly.

"Ah, Salinger." I put my bag down and unbuttoned my gray autumn jacket. The dialogue he had memorized and come prepared to use, perhaps. I hung my jacket behind the chair I was sitting on.

Jay complimented how I looked, several times, which made me uncomfortable. I brought up work—he didn't say much about what he did. He shifted in his seat as he talked about his latest hobby: coin collecting. This was the tenth or eleventh hobby Jay had shared with me since we became friends online. His intense enthusiasm about a new hobby would begin as abruptly as it would end, all inside of a few months.

I felt awkward sitting in a cafe, using its space and not ordering anything. But Jay seemed unfettered. When I got up to order a chai for myself, I turned to him. "Would you like something?"

He laughed again. I didn't understand why he laughed when nothing funny was being said.

"Sure. A slice of their cheesecake and espresso."

With Rohan, I had to fight to pay. Sometimes, I would let him win because I didn't have the energy to protest. But Jay didn't even pretend to touch his wallet. I didn't mind buying, but his sense of entitlement intrigued me.

He inspected my handbag as I pulled out my wallet. "Prada! Madame, you are loaded."

I brought my eyebrows together. "It was a gift from my mother. I bring it with me when I need to feel her presence more than ever. You know the feeling, right?"

Jay ignored my remark. I peered at the menu behind the counter.

When I put money in the tip jar, Jay said to me, "Oh, you are so nice."

"Thanks! But I didn't do anything special, Jay." I sat back in my chair.

"There we go again. I thought when we met in person you'd understand that this is who I am. I see the good in people. I like to commend others on what they do." He sank into a small couch perpendicular to my seat.

I noticed his ears were clogged with wax and his neck had layers of Play-Doh-like dirt. I couldn't help but silently judge him.

The server brought out our orders. I thanked him and swirled my chai. Jay gave me a kiss on the forehead. It was so sudden and undelightful. This was my cue to go to the bathroom. I noticed Jay clean the dry, crusty deposits in the corners of his eyes and wipe his hands on his jeans. He then took out his phone.

There was nobody there in the women's bathroom. The red door and the blue tiles had graffiti on them. I wiped my forehead—the exact spot where Jay had kissed me. I checked Jay's social media profile as I sat on the toilet. He had posted a picture of the cheesecake and espresso. And the caption read, "Fine foods are my forte." I thought it was interesting that he didn't tag me in any posts or pictures or add any location. There was a comment from two women inquiring whether he had baked the cheesecake and made the espresso himself.

"True genius never speaks of his work :)," Jay replied to their comment.

I called Naina. "I wonder if there are others too aside from Amanda and Tanya whom Jay has betrayed."

"I wouldn't be surprised," Naina sighed loudly. "But what makes you think that?"

"Just noticed some comments on his post—and so quickly. It's like he has a fan club."

"Ahana, you are being careless; Jay could spike your chai while you are in the bathroom. Leave already!"

"No, he won't. He needs something from me, Naina. I'm no good to him passed out."

I looked at my reflection in the bathroom mirror as I scrubbed my hands with soap. I told myself I had no choice but to go through this afternoon if I wanted to know the truth. I wiped off my annoyance in a sheet of paper towel and wore a smile as I walked out almost convinced that Jay would ask about my marriage or Dev or something intimate.

I asked Jay about his marriage and wife. He didn't say much aside from "New York City is filled with grime. It got to us." He didn't bring up my personal life.

"Do you think you guys will get back together?" I took a sip of my chai.

With his forehead creased into a question mark, Jay took a big bite of the cheesecake. "You ask a lot of questions. Hahahaha." He ate with his mouth open.

Something about his lack of commitment to words made me feel as if the walls were closing in.

"Would you mind looking at my business plan?" he asked abruptly out of nowhere. "I could use that MBA brain of yours." He sat with a slouch and adjusted his cap.

I sat up in a shock. I was prepared for Jay to give me surprising information about me. That's what he had hinted at several times in our chat. But how did he even know I had an MBA in finance? When I'd met him online, I was no longer working in finance and never spoke of anything about my past. Was it Internet stalking or was someone else, like Dev, giving him tips? Sweat began to trickle down my lower back. I wiped my mouth with a napkin.

"Always so elegant. Even when you wipe your mouth. So British."

I stayed silent.

"What's the business plan for, Jay?" I maintained a professional demeanor.

Jay opened his knapsack and pulled out a folder. He handed over the fat bundle to me. "I want to open a cafe in New York. A place where we sell flowers. Home-baked goods. Some of my knitted designs."

"No books or art or music or beverage?" I flipped through the pages.

"No; that's why it would be unique. It'll be about bringing my skills in one space."

A part of me wanted to say, "*Go for it,*" and watch the asshole fail. But a bigger part of me knew I had to fake a little and gain more of Jay's trust to find his ulterior motive.

"How will you make money if there is no beverage?" I flipped through his plan. "How will you get people to stick around in the cafe?"

"I'd love to travel to India one day. Wouldn't it be amazing if I could take my business there?" Jay spoke out of nowhere, once again, as he stuffed his face with cheesecake.

"There might be a lot of legalities you'll have to sift through, Jay. You are a foreign national. But...."

"You mentioned that your aunt works for the finance ministry in Delhi." *Nope, I never told him that.* "Do you think she could...you know? The Indian economy is doing so well. I'm sick of fucking living in America."

"Do what?" I took a big gasp of air.

"Don't make me spell everything out, Ahana. I'm a broken man." Jay made a sad face and took his glasses off. He rested his head on the couch.

Bloody drama queen. I tried to swallow the rising bile in my mouth. He wanted my aunt, Chutney, in New Delhi to help him set up the business when I hadn't mentioned Chutney's high profile job. The hair at the back of my neck stood up.

"I have very little pride, Ahana." He looked disappointed.

"I can ask her when I go back. But no promises. She doesn't believe in doing favors for random people, Jay."

"If I'm your best friend, I'm no longer a random man." He gripped the edges of the table and let out a big smile.

I took a sip of my water.

Jay stood up with his right hand on his hip and his left hand stretched out in my direction as if he were going to kiss my hand.

I withdrew my body.

"Shhh. Don't get scared. This is sheer testosterone in the Big Apple, pointing the way to a prosperous future for both of us." Jay went from disappointed to dramatic inside of a minute.

"You are so theatrical." I folded my arms around my chest.

"My mom was dramatic. For her sixtieth birthday, I got her a tiara and she asked if it would be uncomfortable to shower in it. Now you know where I get my diva qualities from...."

"Hahaha." I feigned laughter. "Your mom sounds adorable."

"Like me?" Jay batted his eyelids real fast and sat down.

I pretended to let my guard down. Jay told me more stories about his mother and how she would often say the most inappropriate things in public without realizing how audible she was.

Out of nowhere, Jay put his hand on my right knee. "Would you be interested in investing in a business idea like mine?"

"I will give you my honest answer, Jay." I politely moved his hand away. "I'm not sure if the idea is unique enough to be an international venture. I mean, even in New York, bookshops with cafes are a dime a dozen. Maybe I'm not seeing it, but how will you keep traffic in the store?"

Jay's jaw dropped. "I thought you were supportive of my dreams."

"I'm giving you a realistic picture."

There was an awkward silence.

"I see." Jay put his folder inside his knapsack.

"You know I don't mollycoddle. As your friend, I'd much rather show you the truth than see you crumble under an illusion."

Jay punched his left hand with his right fist. "I am sick of not being anybody." He covered his face with his palms.

I was out of patience; I said nothing. I quickly looked at my phone. Naina had texted emojis of a man wailing. Her note read, "Is fuck face Dubois crying?"

I typed, "And much more," before putting my phone away.

I couldn't help note how different Rohan was compared to Jay. Rohan made me feel special—like I was the center of his universe. Jay was distracted even in the café. He was watching a police car chase show and taking out his frustrations on me. Rohan was always playful but in a light-hearted, silly sort of way. He had never tried to seize an opportunity with me.

My phone rang a few times. The text was from Rohan. "Don't chicken out, Matron. Our table at Dionysus is all booked for 9 p.m. Looking forward to you trying out my favorite drink." His text message had emoticons at the end of it: one of a woman dancing, another of a drunk man, people saying cheers in Hindi, and many others.

"I won't, Brady. :)"

Rohan wrote back right away, "Prepare to be wooed Southern style." There was a thumbs-up emoticon at the end of his message.

I took a sip of my tea and typed back. "*Paagal.*"

"Turn that off already." Jay pointed at my phone.

"Sorry, expecting an important call."

"Boyfriend?

"No." I smiled. "A dear friend." I put the phone inside my handbag.

"But I'm your best friend, right?" Jay searched for answers in my eyes. When I didn't say anything, he stood up abruptly. "I'm sorry, but I need to step out to make an important call."

"Sure." I shrugged.

I needed to manage patience and understanding to get through the evening, that much I had gathered after just a coffee meet-up with Jay.

As soon as Jay stepped outside, I called up Naina. I looked over my shoulder to make sure he wasn't anywhere around. "Listen, I know that Jay wants money from me. Now that I have turned down his offer to invest in his business, he must figure out other ways of monetizing our 'friendship.'"

"Get out now, Ahana. I don't have a good feeling about him."

"For the temper-throwing man Jay is, he has been relatively stable today, which makes me wonder if there's something else he wants from me." I was confronted by my own vulnerabilities.

Jay returned a second later; I hung up abruptly.

"You are so popular." His mood was different. He looked happier.

"Haha." I couldn't think of a more banal response.

"Since you love nature, I figured I'd show you a pretty part of NYC."

"I've seen Central Park, Jay. I should head back."

"Sheesh; you don't have to rub it in that you have other friends who have shown you around." He rolled his eyes.

I spoke in a fake, apologetic tone. "I didn't mean anything by it, Jay."

He pushed an empty chair. "I mean I visit New York for you. I have fucking money problems, and you can't even stay a little bit longer."

Jay had severe anger issues. "You are right." I took a big gulp of water.

"Good." He adjusted his cap. "You haven't been to The Ravine, I know."

How does he know where I have or haven't been? Has Jay been in NYC this whole time?

"What is that?" I stood up and buttoned my coat.

"It's intended to resemble the wilderness of the Adirondacks, but it's all manmade. Central Park. Around 103rd Street."

"Do you come up here often?'

"Of course! People, who can't afford vacations and getaways come to this point to enjoy the magic of nature. The rushing sound of the waterfall drowns the city noise. I often go up there just to get away from everything, especially when I miss my mother. It's hard to fill the emptiness inside my heart sometimes."

His eyes looked sad and cold.

I clutched at my coat. The darkness inside of me started to rise and I couldn't push it down. I was familiar with the feeling Jay described: the haunting loneliness after Mumma died.

I peeped outside the glass doors. "It's getting dark out. I don't think it's safe to be in the park, Jay."

"Maybe not for a woman. But you are with a blue-blooded, athletic American. You will be safe. I have punched muggers in the face."

I didn't think Jay knew how to get rid of the slime in his personality.

* * *

Jay and I started to walk toward the entrance to Central Park. His coat was flapping. I wanted to call Naina, but there was no time or opportunity. I quickly sent her a text with my plan and put my phone inside my bag.

It was slightly nippy outside. Trees bursting with vibrant colors reminded me of *Holi*, the festival of colors, in New Delhi. Mumma would say "*Holi* signifies the victory of good over evil." Thinking of my mother's words gave me an upsurge of confidence that everything was going to be OK. I didn't realize that lost in my thoughts, I had wrapped my arms around my shoulders and was rubbing them subtly.

Jay pointed at his Jets sweatshirt. "Do you want my hoodie?"

"No, thank you." I smiled at him. Now he was faking friendliness and gentlemanly behavior.

"I thought you were a fitness junkie. You're walking slower than my turtle." He brought his palms together and laughed loudly.

"I didn't know that the first time we met, you'd take me out for a walk." I walked as fast as my legs would carry me.

"Where did you think I would take you?" Jay added air quotes as he said the word "take."

"Don't go there." My voice was tight. I didn't care that I was in public or if people on the street were staring at me or if Jay was doing some innocent flirting. "'That's the thing about girls. Every time they do something pretty...you fall half in love with them, and then you never know where the hell you are,'" he quoted J. D. Salinger.

I crossed my hands on my chest but didn't respond. Jay suddenly stopped and spoke softly, "I know there's something eating you alive. I'm here to help you." He held my shoulders.

I stared at him.

He let go. "I'm not some perv who wants to harass you. I'm your friend who cares about you deeply, Ahana."

Before I could say anything, after walking for about twenty or maybe twenty-five minutes, we stopped on a quiet block and entered a world I never knew existed. We made our way toward The Ravine in Central Park's North Woods.

The place was so serene but eerily quiet. I could listen to water cascade over the falls. I squinted as I adjusted my mind and eyes to the new surroundings—a nature lover's heaven.

Jay picked up his pace as I struggled to keep my balance in my stilettos.

"Come over and look at this paradise." Jay sat on one of the rocks where a couple of turtles were sunning themselves before the sun went down completely.

But I couldn't enjoy the place fully. Something didn't feel right. I looked around and saw no one else.

"Let's go back," I pleaded with Jay as I looked for exit points.

"What, you don't trust me?" He smacked his lips.

I spoke confidently. "I never said that."

Jay didn't move. "All I'm trying to do is show you the unique places you have never been to—"

I cut him off. "I know that. And I appreciate it so much. But we can't enjoy much right now in any case—it's dark out here. Maybe we can come back?"

"This isn't Delhi, Ahana. I'd take a bullet for you." Jay tried to placate me.

"Why are you being weird, Jay?" I narrowed my eyes.

Jay grabbed my hand.

"Don't *touch* me." I pulled away.

"What is with you, hon? I'm joking."

It struck me as odd that Jay didn't want to listen to anything I had to say. I exploded. "It's always about you, isn't it? What works for you and what doesn't! The rest of us need to realign our lives according to your mood and schedule." I was mad at myself for reacting to Jay.

"What are you talking about?" He arched an eyebrow and came closer.

I wet my lips and moved away. "I asked you about your mother and Louisiana, but you didn't answer. You are always so moody!" The park was quiet, and I feared walking back alone out of it.

"I have never been the guy who sits and talks. I don't get onto the phone or do video chats." Jay's tone was different. "I'm not the kind of guy who will remember to bring you your favorite tea or cook your favorite meal when you are sad." Was Jay referring to Rohan and my time spent with him? I was terrified.

I stuttered. "I'm sorry, Jay, but I need to leave. I have a date."

He looked provoked. "I'm not good enough because I can't be Mr. Moneybags who introduces you to high society life. We both know the kind of men you like to be with, Ahana." Jay wiped his hands on his jeans.

Nervously, I put my hands on my hips and turned around to see whether anyone else was around. My back toward Jay, I heard a noise. Someone was screaming. I saw Jay's hands were in the air right above his ears as if he were trying to swat a fly. There was an old white woman, with two braids, saying something to him. I couldn't tell what, but he was saying something back to her.

I walked toward him at a pace I couldn't believe my feet knew in a pair of heels.

"Ma'am, what are you doing?" Jay was walking away from the woman trying to claw at him.

The woman mumbled something and wiped her nose.

"You touched my wife?" A six-foot plus black man appeared out of the bushes from behind the petite white woman.

"No, I did not." Jay pulled the sleeve of his jacket down over his hands like he was about to punch someone. "Your wife tried to pick my pocket, so I tried to stop her."

I couldn't believe this was happening. "Let's go, Jay. Let's go." I was holding onto my bag real tight.

A heavy hand grabbed my shoulder from behind. I froze. I could smell cheap cigarettes. I turned around and it was a middle-aged white guy.

"Don't touch me!" I yelled.

The guy let go.

The black guy walked toward me and grabbed my arm. He smelled like mints. He squeezed my shoulders hard. "If he can touch my wife," he pointed toward Jay, "why can't I touch his girlfriend?"

"I am not his girlfriend!" I exclaimed. I didn't want to belong to Jay.

The muggers let out an empty laugh. I stumbled forward and on to the ground as the black guy let go of me. The two men then walked toward Jay.

I kept looking at the park's entrance, hoping someone would walk past and save us. Darkness swallowed the twilight sky. It was hard not to panic. I kept mumbling to myself. *This can't be happening. This can't be happening.*

"You have a problem, boy?" The white guy pushed Jay.

Jay lost his balance. He almost fell, but stood up straight.

"He asked you a question." The black guy stood a few inches away from Jay. "Answer him."

Both the men had a Southern accent. The white woman looked high. Her feet were unstable and the braids in her long hair swayed every time she wobbled. Jay moved toward her but the two men intercepted.

"You motherfucker!" The black guy punched Jay in the face.

Jay fell. His cap and glasses came off.

"Oh, my God, stop it! Stop hurting him." I ran toward Jay. "Are you OK?" I helped Jay to his feet as panic swept through my spine.

Jay quickly picked up his cap. It was only then I noticed he was bald in the middle of the scalp. He wiped the corner of his mouth and adjusted his cap so the logo was facing the front and his bald patch was hidden. His fingers were pulled together in a tight fist. He brought his fists closer to his face.

I picked up his glasses and handed them over to him. "Let's go from here, Jay."

Jay's breathing got harder.

The two men didn't say a word. The woman seemed disinterested.

I ran my eyes over Jay's face. There was no cut. No blood. His eyes were not bruised at all. *Thank God!*

I begged the men. "We're sorry about the miscommunication."

"Ask your man to keep his temper where his balls are." The white guy adjusted his crotch and spat on the side.

"Just give them what you have, Ahana. They won't let us leave." Jay whispered into my ears.

"No! They can kill me if they want, but I will not give them my handbag."

"Are you out of your fucking mind?" Jay raised his voice.

"How can you not understand? You have lost a mother too." I became unafraid in that moment.

I noticed that the men stepped away. They didn't touch me. No one grabbed me by my hair. I wasn't picked up and thrown against the rocks. There was no gun barrel dug into my skin. There were no knives threatening to cut me up. No one tried to hold my head underwater. That's when I realized: these men were not killers. I saw something in their eyes, but I wasn't sure what. But having worked with a women's organization that helped survivors of violence, I knew what danger looked like. These people looked poor and hungry. And they also looked unfit.

"Ma'am. Sir." I turned to all three of them. They were a few feet away from where Jay and I were standing. "We're going to leave now, and I suggest you do the same." I didn't hesitate to use my words forcefully as I backed away.

Jay looked shocked. "What are you doing?"

I rummaged through my wallet and took out two $100 bills. "I'm going to leave this here for your dinner." I put a rock on the two bills.

"We won't call the police if you let us leave." A sudden calm filled me. Who had I become in the face of adversity?

The muggers looked confused, but as soon as they bent down to pick up the $200, I said, "Run, Jay, run," in a low but forceful voice.

In my stilettos and with a heavy handbag, I ran without turning back. From the corner of my eye, I saw that Jay was to my right. We ran until we reached the entrance. The route was a lot shorter than the one we had taken on our way in.

"That was a pretty stupid move." Jay was bent over, breathing heavily.

"Or a gutsy one. But the point is we're safe now." I turned around and there was no sign of the muggers.

He stretched his facial muscles and let out an "ouch."

I was surprisingly calm when I said, "Let's go to the police station and file a report. And get you checked out at the doctor's."

"I don't think that'll be necessary." He placed his right palm on his forehead and let out another, "ouch."

I pulled my phone from my bag, but Jay snatched it from my hands.

"What are you doing, Jay?"

"You've done enough." He held me by my shoulders. "I'm supposed to protect you, not the other way around. Involving the cops would mean admitting I couldn't take care of my friend. Don't make me feel weaker."

"But...."

We argued more, but Jay remained resolved in his decision not to report to the authorities or see a doctor. I was too worn-out and numb to argue.

"What do you want to do?" I took out a wet tissue from my bag to wipe my hands.

"That's the whole trouble. You can't ever find a place that's nice and peaceful because there isn't any. You may think there is, but once you get there, when you're not looking, somebody'll sneak up and write 'Fuck you' right under your nose."

"Are you quoting Salinger right now?" There was a hint of shocked annoyance in my voice. He doesn't recognize Salinger when he hears it, but he's got this apropos quote all queued up and ready to go right after an alarming event!

"You didn't cry when the men punched me or threatened you. I guess we're all full of surprises."

"I don't waste my tears," I blurted out.

Jay brought his fingertips to his chest and pressed them hard. "I see. I am not worthy of your tears."

I had to gain control over the escalating situation. "That is not what I meant, Jay." I looked down.

"What is it that you mean, Ahana, because I'm having a hard time accepting you don't trust me."

I pressed his right palm in my hands. "I never said that."

Jay squeezed my hands. "Then prove it." His green eyes, the stare...it pierced through my bones. "Don't be scared." Jay ran his finger on my chin.

I inched away. I wanted to stand under a hot shower. Scrub my face with antiseptic *neem* and turmeric scrub. Disinfect and recharge.

Jay laughed without any inhibition. "Have dinner with me."

For the first time, I decided to think for myself. "I have dinner plans. I told you earlier."

Jay made a face, "Sure. Whatever."

"I'm sorry I can't reschedule the dinner tonight."

Jay touched the spot where the muggers had punched him. "This really hurts. Can you blow some air so it burns less?"

I looked closer and noticed there were no cuts or swelling on Jay's face. "I still insist you see a doctor. You don't want me blowing my germs into a wound."

"Nah, my hotel is across the park."

How can he afford a hotel by the park when he initially said he'd crash with a friend? I tried to say something, but Jay put his right index finger on my lips. "Shhh."

"Come with me to my hotel for some time." Jay moved uncomfortably close to me.

"After the attack, it's funny how I'm filled with fear and trepidation. I used to walk through the park at 3 a.m." He ran his index finger from my third eye to my lips.

I moved his hand with a jerk. "Let's call you a cab."

"I don't have any cash on me."

"Well, I gave my money away to the muggers." I spoke without any expression. "This is New York City, and cabs accept credit cards."

"I'm not sure I can find a cab at this hour. It's Friday evening." He looked at his watch.

"Sure, you can."

"Boy, you really want me out of your hair." Jay touched his eye this time.

"No, as your friend, I want you to rest well and get better. You've been up since 4 a.m., right?"

"I'll see you tomorrow?"

"You can count on it." I forced a smile.

I said a quiet goodbye to Jay. In turn, he hugged me tightly and then reluctantly hailed a cab.

I stood still for a few seconds before calling for a taxi. The day had been so random.

Once home, I tucked my nose under my blouse. I didn't recognize the smell that came from my body. Before jumping into the shower, I texted Naina, "I'm back."

"You OK? Where is that shithead?"

"Back in his hotel. I'm hopping into the shower. Will chat later."

"Enjoy your date with Rohan."

I tried to memorize everything that had transpired. Surreal. Every part of my body ached. I brushed my teeth and washed my face, carefully, with tea tree oil cleanser and scrubbed every spot Jay had touched me with turmeric and *neem*. I couldn't tell what Jay was about. He was not easy to like, but the guy took a punch to his face to keep me safe. But how was it that Jay seemed uninjured after being attacked by three muggers? How was it that he knew pertinent details of my life?

When I stepped out of the shower, I noticed he had already updated his social media profiles. There was a picture of his broken glasses and the caption read, "When Batman gets hurt saving Gotham." I laughed humorlessly.

Both Amanda and Tanya had commented on Jay's picture. Wait, what? Tanya and Amanda were back in his life? What did Jay have on them? Did he know I was onto him? Suddenly, Jay seemed even more mysterious and dangerous than I had imagined.

I stretched my arms out in front and exhaled all the memories Jay had built up inside me. I went into the kitchen and got a big drink of water. I folded my legs in lotus position and tried to meditate, but nothing. I closed my eyes, but all I saw was the big guy punching Jay. The darkness outside reminded me how vulnerable I had been today.

It was 7:45 p.m. I didn't know what to do—not after a headstand, not after a long shower, not even after meditation. I knew I needed to talk to someone before heading out to meet with Rohan.

My hands shook as I picked up the phone. Maybe they understood dialing this number would lead to the beginning of a new journey.

"Hi, Josh?" I stuttered.

"My favorite sister-in-law. How are ya?" Josh replied happily.

I could hear people in the background. "Is this a good time?"

"What's going on?" Josh's voice grew serious. "Do you want me to call Naina?"

"No. No. I actually need to talk to you."

"Give me a second." I heard Josh tell someone he had to take an urgent call.

"Are you in trouble?"

I could hear him better now. It would seem Josh had walked to a quieter space.

I squeezed my eyes shut. "No. Not that I know of..." I pressed my right temple. "I met with Jay today."

"Jay Dubois? Naina talks about him a lot."

I understood what he meant.

I narrated the events of the evening to Josh. Josh heard me patiently and interjected a "huh" or "really?" or "okayyyy" or "interesting" every now and then. His tone was sometimes skeptical, other times intrigued. But when I started to tell him about the mugging incident, he asked whether I could do a FaceTime or Skype call with him.

I walked to my bedside to pick up the iPad and then threw on a sweatshirt over my casual T-shirt.

I dialed Josh.

"Hey, sorry to make you do this, Ahana."

"Please don't embarrass me." I looked at the bright lights in the background. "You are at a party. I should be the one apologizing." I readjusted my glasses and saw a few bodies dance far in the background.

"We're at a friend's weekend home outside NOLA. It's like Mardi Gras in there."

"Oh, shit, Naina had told me about it. Sorry."

Josh pointed over his left shoulder in the back. "You're fine. Just overlook the noise in the backdrop."

"Done deal." I smiled.

"I'm a cop. You might not like the questions I ask. But this is what I'm trained to do. Got it?"

"Yes."

"I want you to close your eyes and go back to The Ravine. I know it's not easy. But do this once. Does anything stand out?"

I poked my third eye with my right index finger. I sat on the floor with my legs crossed over each other. I tried hard to think about specific details. I pressed my lips together and closed my eyes. Just when I thought I didn't remember anything, I surprised myself. "The mugger punched Jay, but it all happened so fast." Suddenly, I was moving around the room, demonstrating the angle of the attacker.

"Jay fell down. I helped him stand up. But what did surprise me was that Jay had no bruises or cuts on his face. He kept touching the place where he got hit, but there wasn't even a scratch mark." I took a deep, meditative breath. "Something didn't feel right, so I thought I'd ask for your professional opinion."

"Not even a black eye or a swelling?" Josh brought his index fingers and thumbs to the corner of his lips and rubbed those points as if in deep contemplation. "How was Jay after the attack? Did he seem antsy? Incoherent? Freaked out? Angry? Scared?"

"He quoted goddamn Salinger."

"Hmmm." Josh paused. "And the muggers?"

"They didn't even chase us!"

"Did you call the cops and file a report?"

"Jay was adamant about not seeing a doctor or filing a police report."

Josh scratched his forehead vigorously.

"I feel responsible—had Jay not made the trip to NYC, none of this would have happened."

Josh tried to cut straight to the truth. "Stop feeling *responsible* for something that's not on you. Tell me, did he misbehave with you at all?"

I went into the kitchen and filled a glass with water. "He hit on me." I stiffened and stared at my bare feet. I felt like I was running down an unfamiliar street where shards of broken glass were scattered everywhere.

"I'm glad you're safe. But I don't see how any of what transpired makes any sense." Josh spoke kindly.

I shifted uncomfortably and tried to breathe. That was the feeling I had tried to battle all evening.

"I have to go now." He pointed to a woman and a few men behind him. "They're calling me."

"Of course!"

Josh spoke in a stern voice. "Send me Jay's first and last name, date of birth, and mailing address." He also asked for Jay's picture. "Don't meet with him until you hear back from me."

After sending all the information to Josh, I looked at the clock. It was 8:30 p.m. *Shit, I'm late for my date with Rohan.*

I pulled out a simple, orange dress from my wardrobe. It was strapless and just below the knees—nothing fancy. I wore my contact lenses, but I barely had the time to put on any makeup or even blow-dry my hair. I put on some lipstick and eyeliner in the cab as the driver battled through Friday night traffic. Every now and then, I looked over my shoulders. In every passing face, every baseball hat that I saw in the crowd on the sidewalk when we stopped at the lights, I feared I was seeing Jay. I hated being this rattled.

"You are coming, right?" Rohan texted.

"Of course! Why would you ask that?"

"It's unlike you to run late and not inform. I wasn't sure if you changed your mind."

I looked at my watch. It was 9:30 p.m. *Oh damn! Rohan thinks I'm abandoning him. Crap! Crap! Crap!* "I'm on my way. Sorry, got caught up with something."

"Are you all right?"

"I can't wait to see you in a few." I ended the conversation abruptly. *I need to focus on our date and stop acting like a heroin addict.*

My phone rang again. It was a text from Josh. "Rohan messaged Naina and me if we'd heard from you."

"What did you tell him?" I asked right away.

"I gave him a guarded reply," Josh replied.

My heart sank. I was ridiculously late. I hoped Rohan didn't assume the worst—that I didn't want to meet him.

≈ 27 ≈

It was closer to 10 p.m. by the time I reached Dionysus—Rohan's favorite bar on the lower east side in downtown Manhattan, named after the Greek god of wine and ecstasy. I ran out of the cab in my three-inch, transparent heels with my autumn coat resting on my arm. I noticed Dionysus was a quaint, personable, and cozy space.

Rohan had told me, "I treat it as a hidden gem for when I want to go for a drink by myself. Be it the mahogany furniture, art deco architecture, tasteful menu, funky music, and friendly staff, I love it all."

"What do you do there by yourself?"

"I sit at a corner table, listen to Bob Marley, and enjoy the time alone with a perfect Sazerac."

"Is that where you meet your dates?" I had asked sheepishly.

"You are the only person I've ever invited to Dionysus," Rohan had answered with a straight face.

I looked for Rohan as I entered. My heart paced for a reason I didn't fully understand. Everyone around, mostly well-dressed men, stared at me unabashedly. I felt eyes pierce through my bones; I pulled down my skin-hugging dress.

I was relieved to see Rohan and waved at him. He was clad in a pair of dark blue jeans, a light pink cotton button-down shirt, and brown loafers.

He swirled the drink in his glass and got up from his seat.

"Hi, Brady!" I held him tightly. I liked how his stubble felt against my skin. I wanted the moment to linger on. I felt safe in Rohan's arms. Jay couldn't touch me here.

Rohan gave me a light kiss on the cheek. "You showed up, Matron...even if an hour late." He looked like he was primed for bad news.

I withdrew myself. "I am so so sorry, I am late. I truly am." I pointed at myself. "I left in such a rush that I've shown up as a mess. I feel really bad, Rohan."

"Mess? Look around the room." He took a sip of his drink. "All these men. Their fucking jaws are dropping, looking at you."

I pulled out my silk scarf from around my neck. "You should be proud; I might actually pick up a man tonight." I meant my words as a joke, but heard them fall flat.

Rohan gave me a concerned look and covered my bare shoulders with his arm. "Let's get a table toward the inside."

"But don't you have a favorite corner?"

"I do. But let's sit somewhere you're a little inconspicuous."

I folded my arms and looked to the right. "How about that table?" It was midway between where Rohan wanted us to sit and where he was originally seated.

"Okayyyy." Rohan led me to the table I'd picked out. Even though he was holding his drink in one hand, he pulled the chair for me. He gently ran his hands on my back. Jay hadn't extended the same courtesy, I remembered. My face tightened, thinking about Jay and the incredulousness of the afternoon.

"You all right?" Rohan patted my shoulder.

I moved my body away. "Yeah. I...um...." I didn't know how to explain my day. And I remembered Rohan got irked when I brought up Jay when we were eating dinner at Mom's Recipes.

He moved his hand, but I saw a tinge of sadness.

Am I totally ruining the date? My first date with Rohan? I need to stop. My cagey behavior is making matters worse.

As soon as we sat down, Rohan asked, "What will you drink?"

I touched his hands. "I'll have whatever you are having, Mr. Brady."

"I am glad to hear that." He ran his fingers over my lips.

I twitched and moved a few inches away. Jay had run his finger from my third eye to the top of my lips right before he got inside the cab. The memory was still fresh.

"What happened?" Rohan asked.

"No. Nothing." My voice became slightly shaky.

"You pulled away, Ahana."

I sat wordlessly.

Rohan got up and walked up to the bar. From the corner of my eye, I saw him observe me. I tried to organize my thoughts—what do people on a date talk about? But I also checked the entrance to see whether Jay was lurking.

Rohan quietly walked back to the table, "You look beautiful, Ahana. I mean it." There was sincerity in Rohan's eyes, which I noticed. My name sounded different in his mouth this evening, more personable.

"Wow, a straight-faced compliment from Rohan Brady. Am I dying?" I checked his forehead to see whether he was warm. "Or maybe you? Haha. How do you say it, Rohan? 'I crack myself up.'"

"Somebody is a little too animated this evening." Rohan took a sip of his drink.

I so wished I could talk to him about why I was such a wreck. I so badly wanted him to know I hadn't abandoned him. But I couldn't do it; Rohan had advised me to avoid Jay.

"What did you order for me?"

"Sazerac."

"They know how to make Sazerac here? Pretty impressive."

"Honestly, the bar didn't make the drink originally, but thanks to my patronage, my favorite bartender, Anthony, has now learned it. I can get a taste of New Orleans inside a glass."

Before either of us could say anything further, the server brought out two drinks.

Rohan looked at the cocktail in the martini glass. "I didn't order that."

"I know, sir." The server paused. "It's from the gentleman at the bar for...." He pointed at me.

"Whaaaat?" Rohan and I spoke at the same time. His face became stern.

My face tightened—was my behavior with Rohan so erratic this evening that even a stranger had found an entry point to mess things up? Was the chemistry between us so irrelevant that even people didn't see us together? Was my vulnerability and internal chaos so visible that a random guy at the bar thought he could buy me a drink despite another man around? Or was it that Jay had followed me to the bar? I had to know.

I bent my head at an angle to get a good look at the guy from the bar. It wasn't Jay. I smiled out of relief. But my timing was bad. Raising his drink to me, the guy at the bar smiled back.

Rohan gritted his teeth. "Looks like your Prince Charming came early? Or the guy you are going to take home tonight."

I sensed sarcasm in Rohan's voice.

"But I want to drink the Sazerac, Rohan."

"I couldn't care less." He looked detached. I touched his hand. He moved it away.

In my head, Rohan was being cruel. I refused to let any tears flow. I took a sip of his Sazerac.

He didn't say anything.

I took a few big gulps, the way one would drink *mango lassi*. My eyes widened as the alcohol aggressively traversed from my mouth to my insides. It tasted like nothing I had ever tasted before, but it heated me up like a furnace. I took another sip or two in quick succession. I started to fan myself. I rubbed my throat, but finished his drink.

Rohan held my right hand.

"Tell me, Rohan, what do you care?"

He didn't say anything.

"I thought as much." I pulled my hand away and then drank the cocktail.

I slowly stood up from the table. I wanted to let go of everything that was holding me down. But I could barely move with two potent drinks inside of me.

A bit wobbly in my steps, I slowly started to sway my hips to *"Get Up, Stand Up."* Then it was my arms in the air, running through my hair. I shut my eyes and rocked my entire body. It was cathartic.

"Fuck." Rohan realized I was about to trip. He stood up and stared at me. I had never seen that look in his eyes. His eyes followed my hips, my chest, my hair as I danced to the music.

I came slightly closer to him and tugged at his arm. And in doing so, I lost my balance. He was swift and caught me by my waist. I clung to him. He smelled nice. I wanted to run my hands through his hair. I wanted to be in his arms all night, swaying to Bob Marley's music. We were so close—the space between us was inconsequential now.

I put my scarf around his neck.

"All right. I think we're done for the night." Rohan cleared his throat and asked Anthony to bring him the check.

"You wuss!" I gently played with his collar.

He tilted his head to one side. "I'm dropping you off home." He draped my scarf around my shoulders and handed me my purse. He held my coat.

I kissed him on his lips. A long, wet kiss. Rohan pulled himself away and stood in disbelief, it would seem. I pinned him against the wall.

He caught me by my wrists. "Ahana, why are you acting this way?"

I stopped moving. I knew I couldn't carry on the pretense—the way I had for Dev for so many years. I didn't want to pretend with Rohan.

Before going to the restroom to splash water on my face, I asked the server to bring me a cup of coffee. When I returned, I slowly sipped on the coffee and told Rohan everything that had transpired with Jay. My face was still flushed.

"You dodged a bullet today, Ahana!"

Before I could say anything in response, Rohan slammed the table. "I warned you about Jay. But you fucking didn't believe me." I saw a hardness on his face. There was anger radiating from it. He curled his fists. "Every finger in his hands with which he ever hurt you, I am going to break them. Period!"

My heart felt very out of place. "Jay was nice when we first met online."

Rohan rolled his eyes. His nostrils started to flare. "Why do you think he was nice to you? Why was he always available to chat? Men don't just make friends with women in their thirties so they can discuss their wardrobe problems or heartbreaks. Sex. Yes, that's what they want."

"Is that what you want too, Rohan?" I searched for answers in his eyes where I had once seen respect for myself; today, all I saw was anger.

"Really?" He turned toward me. "Is that what you think?" He pushed his drink away. "You are comparing me to Jay?"

I tried to breathe.

He covered his face with his hands. "Sometimes you can be so naïve, Ahana." Rohan brought his index finger to his lips. He sighed loudly, "He fucking researched you and read up on you. He did his homework—found out about your likes and dislikes. What you do, where your family lives, the story of your life. He pretended to be in the same place as you just so he could have an in. And when he realized you weren't going to fall for him or part with your wealth or play along and act like an emotional slave, he understood the best way to damage a woman of your morality: get you into bed sneakily because he couldn't get into your pants using his I-am-a-fucking-victim-whining-shit." He finished his entire drink in one gulp.

The confidence in Rohan's voice irked me.

"He didn't count on his plans failing. Jay doesn't know you, so he miscalculated his moves. I'm going to find that son of a bitch and kill him. And, you..." He pointed at me. "You need to be a little less clueless."

"Rohan." I spoke softly. I had never known him to speak roughly with me. The shift in our friendship dynamic baffled me. My eyes welled up. I played with my pendant and readjusted my clothes. I got up unsteadily.

He grabbed my hand.

I narrowed my eyes at him and pulled away.

"Fine. As always, walk away. Leave important conversations incomplete, Ahana." He got up from the table.

I picked up my coat and started to walk with a slight stagger.

"I will call for car service."

"No, thank you; I can manage."

"We have all seen how good you are at taking care of yourself."
He took his phone out.

He put me in the car and made sure he tipped the guy extra. I saw him from the rear window as the cabbie waited for the lights to change. Rohan ran his fingers through his hair and pulled his palms over his face. He angrily kicked a pebble on the street.

I felt guilty for having repelled Rohan.

≈ 28 ≈

The next morning, I woke up with a throbbing pain in my head, grasping at the air in front of me. I moved my slightly entangled hair from my face and squinted at the sunlight hitting my eyes. I stretched my right arm to check the time. It was 9 a.m. "Fuck." The first word out of my mouth in the morning, for the first time in my life.

I ran my eyes over my body. *Shit. I didn't change out of my clothes after getting home. Or wash my face. Or take out my contacts.* My feet were jammed inside the high heels I'd worn the night before. I picked up the wood butterfly hair claw from my nightstand and sorted my hair.

I threw the covers off and slowly sat up, leaning against the headboard. As I started to get up, my body felt in knots. It was as if the Sazerac, the cocktail, and Bob Marley's music had never left my system. My every cell felt sore. I tried to make sense of everything that had transpired.

The harder I tried to repress the memories from the night before, the more alive they became. Rohan's handsome looks and his sensual lips. The maddening scent of his body. And our fight because of Jay. I closed my eyes and let out a soft grunt. Rohan had cut the night short.

I leaned on the doorframe. So many more thoughts raced through my tired and emotionally charged mind. What did I know about men? Was it something in me that made men resort to their worst instincts?

I will avoid Rohan to make things less awkward. But wait, I need to work with him on the conference. I began to sweat profusely from underneath my arms and along my spine. I felt humiliated and angry with myself for having let my guard down. I somewhere knew that I had hurt Rohan. But I had no idea how to handle the day, so I took a hot shower. I curled up my legs and sat in the corner, crying. *Where am I to go from here?*

Rohan had become a big part of my life, and the thought of avoiding him made me feel like a wounded animal. Aside from the conference, where I had to work with him, there was Naina's wedding in New Orleans. Rohan Brady wouldn't be the reason I would miss a family function. *But how will I look him in the eye?*

Suddenly, New York felt like a city full of sorrows.

* * *

I wiped my tears and rubbed my pendant. Mumma, what kind of a mess have I put myself in?

The phone rang right around the same time and I jumped out of fright. I put on my glasses and looked at the screen. It was Josh. There were several missed calls and texts from Naina, and a few text messages from Jay.

I picked myself up. My body and heart still ached, but I brushed my teeth and combed my hair and started to read the messages in the order received.

Josh's text said, "Call me as soon as you get this message, Ahana."

I felt nauseous.

Next, I looked at the message from Jay. "Hey, babe! Trust you slept well last night and too many dreams didn't keep you awake." There was a wink at the end of his sentence. I rolled my eyes. Jay sounded so perky in his texts yet so low-energy in real life.

There was another message from Jay. "See ya at noon today for brunch." *But we never made plans for brunch.* The last message read. "I will swing by your apartment at 11:45 a.m. and we can go vroom vroom vroom from there." *How does he have Naina's address?* I called the doorman and left him with explicit instructions not to let any man up to the apartment.

As I put the kettle on the stovetop, I read through Naina's messages and listened to her voicemail. It didn't sound like Josh had told her anything. She was anxious to know about my date with Rohan.

I brewed my Earl Grey and looked at the bright sunshine burning up the sky. I messaged Naina. "Sorry; just woke up. I'll call you in a few."

There was no response from her; figured she was busy.

I wanted a breath of fresh air, so I opened the living room windows and dialed Josh's number.

I didn't know at the time I would be opening doors to the biggest scare of my life.

Josh answered the phone on the first ring. He asked whether I was OK and whether Jay had made contact again.

When I told Josh that Jay wanted to meet me for brunch, he said, "NO WAY!"

Before I could say anything, he continued, "What if I were to tell you that Jay Dubois isn't who he says he is?"

My legs felt heavy.

"I had his records pulled." Josh sounded grave. "Jay spent time in jail for aggravated assault."

"How do you know any of this is true?" I spoke so loudly that I startled myself.

"For cops, there is a central database we have access to. But I have friends at the FBI who have higher security clearances. I had them delve into Jay's life—where he lives, who is a part of his life, where he works. You know."

I stood up so suddenly I felt dizzy. Jay had hurt many of us, but to think we had shared our most emotional moments with a criminal without any prior knowledge of his background. What else did we not know about him?

"How can this be happening?" I clutched at my chest. I looked outside the window. *Is Jay lurking around the corner?* I even walked to the main door and peered through the peephole. *What if Jay sneaked into the building last night?*

"I get that you're in a state of shock, Ahana. But Jay is a sociopath."

"But he looks like a regular guy."

Josh interrupted me. "We have a perception of what a sociopath does or how he or she behaves. We think sociopaths...we assume sociopaths are serial killers and rapists and monsters." He spoke kindly. "I know it's not easy to accept, but that's the truth. I need to ask you a few questions."

"Sure."

"Has he had any anger management issues while interacting with you?"

"Yeah." I collapsed on a barstool. "He has an erratic temper and a cruel tone." I paused and looked out the living room windows. "He never takes any responsibility for his actions, and he has a habit of making others feel guilty...but what has that got to do with his criminal record?"

"I just forwarded you something from a colleague. Read through it, but I want you to stay on the line." Josh spoke with a sense of urgency.

I browsed through my inbox. "Attached is a comprehensive background report on Jay Dubois that I pulled up from Lexis. The DOB and address appear correct. I checked to see if he had any criminal records on the Pacer website and found sufficient information on him. By the way, records show this man never lived in New York, worked there, or filed for any taxes. His wife is the one earning and paying taxes in Baton Rouge for them. What a slick fucker!"

I read and reread the email. My feet turned cold but my face was on fire.

Jay had shown me pictures of Brooklyn, New York, where he lived. He had shown me pictures of the garden and the flowers that he cared after. He whined that he was all by himself in NYC.

"Are you there?" Josh enquired in a caring tone.

"Yeah...I mean...how did he fabricate all these details when he never lived in NYC?" I went into the kitchen and filled up a glass of water.

"He probably stole other people's pictures online and mailed them to you as his own. Or clicked the pictures during one of his visits."

"I've mailed him gifts." Pacing up and down the living room, I took a sip of water. I spoke coarsely so I would get some strength in my spine.

"Was it a P.O. Box number or a full mailing address?" Josh asked me in a very cop-voice.

"A P.O. Box number for Baton Rouge. And another time, it was an address, also for Baton Rouge."

"Can you send me the address where you mailed him the gift?"

"Sure."

"I am sorry, Ahana. Jay is not only married, but he lives in Baton Rouge in a house owned by his mother-in-law."

My heart sank as Josh and I compared the address where I had sent mailed gifts to Jay to the one on file. They weren't the same. I buried my face between my palms. "What about his father, Josh? Does he live in Brooklyn? Or was that a lie too?" I let out air.

"I need you to sit down for this, Ahana."

"What is going on, Josh? Please. Just tell me." I put the phone on speaker and placed it on the kitchen counter as I refilled my glass.

"Jay's mother is alive and still married to Jay's father. They both live in Baton Rouge."

A vacuum of silence threatened to pull me into it. The glass of water slipped from my hands. Pieces of glass spread across the floor. There was water everywhere...on the floor, on my shins. I couldn't feel a thing. I could hear a faint voice call out to me, but I couldn't hear anything. My body pressed against the refrigerator as I dragged it down. I collapsed on the floor without realizing that a small piece of glass was underneath my right foot. Blood. My heart broke into a million pieces as my foot started to bleed.

Shock stemming from betrayal can make a person feel so small; I'd had no idea. The ground started to feel like it was moving away. I pulled out a shard of glass from my heel. I kneeled on the floor down on my knees in Hero Pose. I rocked my body forward and backward as if trying to remember and forget everything Jay had told me about his mother. "*I know pain, Ahana. I understand what losing a mother*

221

can do to you. I hate that I will never feel complete. I hate that we will never have a family picture for Christmas postcards. On some days, I feel so broken without my mother, Ahana; I wonder if I would be so lucky as to never wake up from my sleep."

I would give anything in the world to talk to Mumma just one more time. I would trade everything just to be able to hold her tight for even a few minutes. I had told Jay the smallest of things I missed about Mumma and he'd said, *"I know, babe. If there is anyone who can understand, it's me."*

Jay had a wife at home, but he hit on me and exploited Amanda and Tanya. Jay had touched me with his lying, dirty hands. He had spoken to me with his filthy mouth.

Josh broke my reverie. "Ahana, are you OK?" He had so much compassion in his voice. "AHANA. AHANA. This isn't your fault." It made me feel irresponsible for not trying hard enough to remember.

"What does Jay want from me?" My breath was burning the phone. My head had been emptied of thoughts and filled with pockets of shock.

"We'll find out soon. Did he ever ask you for financial help or a business investment?"

I sighed and shared further details of everything that had transpired when Josh said, "I have been doing this for a long time, Ahana. I don't yet have any proof, but I am willing to bet my next paycheck that Jay planned it all out. I bet there are others, but victims tend to blame themselves and often don't come forward."

I felt bile rush into my mouth and corrode everything. "The mugging was a setup? But they punched...I saw."

"I don't know for sure. It could be a mere coincidence. But what the muggers did was a fake punch." He spoke confidently. "The recipient of the fake punch—Jay in this case—acts dramatically as though he was really punched. It's an old trick we used in college all the time."

That was the last proof I needed to be reminded that Jay had played me. He had lied about his life, his mother, his career, where he lived...everything.

There was an intake of breath at Josh's end. "Don't beat yourself up. Jay earned your sympathy. He made you feel bad for him."

I shook my head. "Two women. Apparently, Jay faked romance with two women from my online therapy group. He even cheated and stole money from one of them." I tried to sound audible as I told Josh about Amanda and Tanya.

"Aah, so the fucking sociopath is a catfish!"

"Catfish?"

"A catfish is someone who pretends to be someone they are not online to create false identities, particularly to pursue deceptive online romances." Josh continued to be patient.

What romances? Jay and I are ONLY friends. I wanted to scream. "What tripped you up about Jay?"

"The same things that made you wonder," Josh cleared his throat, "when you didn't fall for his final bait of spending the evening with him, he invites you to brunch." He paused. "Jay picked up that you had no interest in him, so he might need to exploit your vulnerabilities."

A fresh wave of shock and panic arose inside of me. "Exploit how?"

"I am speculating here, but he could have assaulted you last night or tricked you into being more intimate with him had you guys gone out to dinner. There are a million ways. I would put nothing past a sociopath like Jay."

I had a flashback about the number of times Jay had touched me despite my disapproval.

I have never known how to accept my own blunders or live with them. I sat stupefied with my back resting against the wall and legs stretched out.

"Jay sent a text that he will be here at 11:45 a.m. to pick me up."

"What's the area code of the number?"

I looked it up. "It starts with 917."

"He has access to a New York phone. I don't know if others are involved. I don't want you seeing him or speaking with him."

"He never comes to the phone, Josh."

"He'll call if he feels he's losing you. He's desperate. Under no circumstances let him know you are on to him. I think you should talk to the police. I can give you my buddy Ramon's number."

"One step a time."

"We are going to get this guy, Ahana. I'm sorry about everything."

It was 11:15 a.m. by now. I looked at my reflection in the mirror near the hallway. My eyes looked dreadfully puffy. All I wanted to do was crawl into fetal position on the sofa and cut myself off from the world. I gripped the kitchen sink, loudly crying.

I closed my eyes and thought about the time Jay had sent me a message, "There remains a pang, a tug and an emptiness in my life. Till I rejoin with my mom again."

A bad person, once again, was able to make me feel bad about my life.

It hurt to breathe, but I washed my face and texted Jay. I told him something had come up at work and brunch would be difficult.

Josh was right. Jay called right away. "Hi, hon!"

I answered without thinking. "Sorry, I can't make it."

"You sound pensive. Are you OK?"

"Yes. Yes. How is your wound?" As I faked kindness toward Jay, I lost a little respect for myself.

"Oh, it's swollen and it hurts. But I'm so glad I could take that punch and keep you out of harm's way."

I wanted to punch Jay so hard right now. "I hope you'll take good care of it." He was no longer a friend. He wasn't even a stranger.

He made a whiny sound. "Is there no way we can hang out for even a couple of hours? You won't make time for your best friend?"

"I wish I could. You know how much is at stake with the conference. Last night our server crashed and we lost a bit of data."

"It sucks that I can't see you. Your presence would have been therapy for my bruise. Your support is like my morphine."

"You certainly sound delirious." I sounded insipid, feigning laughter.

"Ahana, you mean the world to me."

"Thanks, Jay. I can't even tell you how helpful your visit has been."

"Don't be formal, hon."

I wanted to pull his tongue out.

"I've got to get back to work."

"I fly back tonight."

"I guess this is it."

"You never know how I might surprise you, babe."

After Jay hung up, I held the phone against my ear. I conceded: his stories never added up. And if you are friends with someone whose story doesn't seem to make sense, it might be because he is being dishonest. In the age of technology, it has become increasingly easier to reinvent yourself, and that's what Jay did. I felt like I knew Jay already, and this was a danger I hadn't known to protect myself from.

224

≠ 29 ≠

I considered sitting at home, but my pride wouldn't allow Jay to cage me like a prey. I refused to mourn my broken heart because Rohan was upset.

I am sick of men controlling my life. I am done with being an emotional yo-yo. Starting today, I am putting up better boundaries. I am going to find strength inside me, I repeated to myself as I tied my hair into a low ponytail and changed into running clothes. I put on a headband to catch the flyaways. I was ready to deal with whatever I would encounter as I left the safety of Naina's apartment. I needed to clear up some headspace. I needed to find answers. I wanted to run away from all the painful memories.

The faster I ran and stomped the earth, the more pain radiated from my heart and spread all over my body. My feet ached for mercy, but I conquered Central Park. At one point, I tripped and fell and got slight bruises on my arm. I got up and ran more. Five minutes after I finished running, the phone rang. It was Naina.

"Why are you panting?" Naina spoke at the other end.

"I just ran ten miles."

"Didn't Rohan and you get enough of a workout last evening?" Naina laughed.

I looked up at the sky.

"That's why I didn't call you sooner. Didn't want to disturb in case you guys—"

"Naina, please stop."

"What's going on?" She sounded worried. Her questions also meant Josh hadn't told her about Jay.

"I don't think I'll ever know how to pick good men, Naina. I just don't have it in me." I dug my shoes into the ground.

"What are you hiding from me?"

All of a sudden, I looked around and saw no one. Darkness started to creep inside of me. I was less than thirty blocks south of where the attack had happened. It was the middle of the day. But the fear of the unknown suddenly started to haunt me. I looked over my shoulders. "Can I call you once I get back home? This'll take a while."

* * *

Once I got back to Naina's and locked every door in the house, I washed my face. Looking at my reflection in the bathroom mirror, I wondered what Jay saw in me that convinced him I would believe him.

I called Naina. She was getting fitted for her *mehendi* outfit at an Indian clothing store in the suburbs of NOLA. When I told her about what Jay had done and how I had found out everything from Josh, she said, "I knew it! That son of a bitch!" She hissed and added, "You get on a plane and come to New Orleans right away. I don't want you to be alone even for a second, Ahana." I was surprised how non-judgmental she was for a change.

"But I have to straighten out a few things here," I tried to reason with her.

"It's not safe for you in NYC."

I cut her off. "I'll be fine."

"Come home. Or I am ditching all this wedding prep and taking a flight out to New York."

"Naina, you can't do that."

"You know me too well." She let out a loud sigh over the phone. "Jay's ego is bruised, and we still don't know when and how he'll retaliate."

"I didn't see through his stories!" I felt angry at myself.

"Ahana, I want you to remember this isn't your fault." She spoke in fragments and her words were punctuated by abrupt pauses.

"How can he do these things and yet be married, Naina? It boggles my mind."

"Who knows what the inside story is, Ahana. We don't know anything about his childhood or his marriage or if his wife is involved or if she has no idea he leads a dual life. What we do know is that Jay has no interest in emotional bonding or any remorse for how he's hurt other women in your online therapy group."

With my left palm over my eyes, I said, "I've been such a fool."

"I am going to fucking castrate that son of a bitch. You need to come home tonight."

"But...Naina...the conference."

"Tell Michael you need to head to NOLA and that you'll work from their NOLA office. There are too many people at home. I am going to book us a room in a hotel. I'll tell Mom to inform the others that your company wants you staying at the hotel until the conference. This way, she can still feed you to death, but you don't have to be around others."

"You can't do that. You have guests at home."

"Meh. No one is as important as you. We need to sort this Jay shit out."

I played with my hair as I sat on the sofa and told Naina about my date with Rohan. My voice cracked when I confessed my feelings. How much I missed Rohan. How much I wanted him. But he'd turned me down. And after the whole Jay experience, I was unsure of online relationships.

Naina spoke in a mellow tone. "I wish I was there with you."

"It all feels too sudden."

"Isn't that what *Masi's* death and your divorce taught you—life happens when you are planning it? Get on the fucking plane now, Ahana."

* * *

I didn't know where to begin. This was Saturday afternoon. Yes, Rohan, Crystal, Michael, and I were supposed to fly to New Orleans on Tuesday for the conference scheduled from Wednesday through Friday. Saturday was Naina's *sangeet* and the wedding was a week and a half later. I had planned to stay back in New Orleans after the *sangeet* and take the week off. Chutney was going to join for the *sangeet*, but Dad was going to reach New Orleans only three days before the wedding.

I walked around Naina's apartment. Ugh. I was letting my own unresolved issues with Rohan impact the conference. Or was I projecting my disdain for Jay onto Rohan? I meditated for twenty minutes and pulled out my laptop, which was lying on the coffee table in Naina's living room.

I needed to work on my speech for the closing reception at the conference. I wrote, deleted, and rewrote what I was going to say. Dev and Jay's smug certainty that I ought to be ashamed of myself, that I was their thing to use and manipulate...it stopped me from penning my truest words. I had nightmares about the last day of the conference, when I was ready to give the crisp, professional speech I had planned and practiced to perfection. In them, the crowd became a blur of faces. I opened my mouth and everyone started laughing, gasping, and gossiping about my dark secret.

I called Michael and told him I had to leave on Sunday for New Orleans because of a personal emergency. "I will inspect the event site on Sunday evening."

"Hope all gets better. Take care of NOLA until the rest of us get there." Michael was surprisingly calm. Or was he happy that I was out of his way? I couldn't care less.

After purchasing my ticket, I emailed Naina. I was flying out of JFK at 6:30 a.m. on Sunday. I packed my bags, cleaned up the refrigerator, and invented more chores to distract myself. But my mind kept going back to Rohan. I wanted to update him on everything. But it felt like he didn't want me. I didn't realize how much it could hurt to be in love and not have the man you loved be in love with you.

= 30 =

Naina picked me up at the airport and hugged me tight—NOLA was warm and humid but still comforting. I unbuttoned by fall jacket and pulled out my scarf.

People in NOLA dressed differently than in New York. There was no sense of urgency in the air. They spoke slower than New Yorkers and added "ma'am," at the end of their sentences. My mind was on Rohan. This was his city.

As I closed the trunk of Naina's BMW, I turned on my phone. There was a text from Rohan. "Hedick told me you're in NOLA. Since you refuse to communicate with me, I won't bother you further. My team will work closely with you. All the best for the conference." I was devastated. I didn't write back and wore my dark glasses so Naina couldn't see my tears.

The drive from the airport to the hotel felt painful. Rohan had broken up with me even before we started going out. Naina gave me the entire scoop on her dad's side of the relatives and how Masi, her mom, was getting frustrated with the demands of the in-laws' side of the family. "Good thing you aren't marrying an Indian guy," Masi had told Naina while smoking in her bathtub.

"I don't think you would have lasted a day in an Indian marriage." I looked at her.

"Why? I know how to wear a sari and say 'Namaste, aunty. Will you eat samosas'?" She got her hands off the steering wheel and pressed them together.

It took us forty minutes to reach the hotel. The *Intercontinental* Hotel near the French Quarter was lovely and away from all the hustle and bustle of the family activity. It was a beautiful day, but I was a broken record, repeating questions about Jay. "How did I not recognize that he is a psychopath?"

"Because Jay put you through an idealization phase until you were sufficiently hooked and invested in beginning a friendship with him. Slowly, once he had his tentacles hooked in you, he tried to discredit, confuse, frustrate, and distract you from the main problem, which was him, and made you feel guilty for owning thoughts and feelings that differed from his own," Naina explained patiently as I checked into the hotel.

I sank into the love seat next to the window in my room. I remembered how Jay smiled without any change in his eyes. His eyes

229

were dull and cold. You would think those eyes had never loved anyone. I mean, how can you not wonder about a man who went through life doing what he did yet not have any remorse?

The sun hit my face, so I got up and drew the curtains shut in my hotel room.

"Ahana." Naina turned me around so I was facing her. "Does Rohan know you are in NOLA?"

I shrugged.

"No. No. No." Naina paced around the room. "You don't screw up a good thing, Ahana. Rohan is a good guy."

"What am I supposed to do with that?"

"Maybe nothing. You at least owe him an explanation as to why you left." She folded her arms across her chest. "Or why you initiated a kiss and now you pretend like he doesn't exist. You are being emotionally abusive and evasive."

"Naina, please. He didn't want me."

"Stop making shit up! Rohan acted with propriety." Naina clenched her fists. "Rohan never once said he didn't want you. He was a gentleman. Ahana, you fucking led him on and now you won't acknowledge his presence. We are *not* in fucking high school!" She prodded her index finger into my chest.

I walked away. She followed behind.

"It seems to be that you don't want to be happy," she blurted out.

"You did not just say that." My eyes were misty.

"Yes, I did. You're the spiritual one, right? You believe in the universe making things even for us?" She looked directly into my eyes. "Huh?"

"Yes."

"Dev and Jay were assholes. The universe sends a good guy your way and you ruin it because you've decided what he feels even without asking him once. You assume all men are the same. You are being so fucking immature. I can't even talk to you." Naina threw her hands in the air.

"Rohan has never opened up to me. I walk around the periphery of his life story, hoping to take a dip in. What am I supposed to think, Naina?"

"He has shown you in a million ways how much you mean to him. Not everyone shares their feelings the same way, Ahana." Naina raised her voice.

"What are you saying?"

"You're a smart woman, Ahana. You want someone to send you a dramatic Hallmark card with rhyming, nauseating, lame-ass poems so you can believe how they feel about you?" Naina stormed out of the room, huffing. "Unbelievable." She slammed the door behind her.

I sat on the edge of the bed and breathed deeply.

* * *

I settled into the hotel room and unpacked my bags. I reached out to Rohan's team in NOLA and we decided to meet directly at the conference venue at 6 p.m. that evening. We were to go over the arrangements. The conference was a sold-out event. But given we had dignitaries, academics, and a huge variety of speakers, I wanted to make sure there was enough space for all of them to relax between sessions. Though we had sponsors in place for tea and coffee, cafes were yet to be set up near the big rooms where sessions were going to be held.

The streets were lined with people even around mid-morning. Drinks, beads, and chats occupied every nook and cranny. I almost bumped into a group of college kids senselessly drinking the potent cocktail Hurricane out of giant takeout mugs and vomiting on the side streets. The panhandlers wanted to start a conversation, in some way, to get you to feel sorry for them, and give them money. Rohan and Naina had warned me to keep my phone inside my bag, not walk in the middle of the street, and not carry a clutch because purse-snatching was a common occurrence in the French Quarter.

I finally understood Rohan's unapologetic stance on Bourbon Street. "Overpriced, watered down drinks, ill-behaved tourists, and smelly street. Bourbon Street is all about drunk people and neon signs. Even the buildings aren't well-preserved. I'll show you true NOLA, Matron! Walking distance away from Bourbon and the French Quarter is Frenchmen Street where the locals hang out. They have a wide variety of live music on any given night of the week! You'll love it. The pride of Louisiana."

It felt so strange being in NOLA for the second time inside of a month and not seeing it through Rohan's eyes. This was his city.

* * *

Rohan didn't make contact after the text he sent me. Except for messaging Tanya, I didn't post on my therapy group that I was in NOLA. But I kept a close eye on Jay. He had posted a selfie and the caption read: "I know you think this face is up to no good." There was a thud in my heart—was that message for me? Tanya had liked the picture and Amanda had written "#Thingsthatmakeyougohmm" and ended it with a wink emoji. *Maybe Tanya is the one who has* been updating Jay about my schedule and personal details without even realizing? He is quite the charmer!

Naina sent me a text. "Let me know your plans. Mom wants to come and say hi before you and I grab a bite. BTW, still fucking pissed at you."

"I would love to see Masi. I finish work at 7:30 p.m."

"We'll swing by your hotel around 8 p.m. You can spend some time with Mom and then dinner afterwards."

"Sure."

I went back to the hotel and did an hour of yoga in my room. I did backbend poses so my heart would open and I could find the strength to handle my feelings. I took a hot shower and made some tea as I went over all the contracts with the vendors for the conference.

I logged into the online therapy group and shared a new post. "I might not be online as often, as this week is busy with the conference."

Jay wrote a personal message right away. "I hope you'll at least check up on me, babe. The bruise from the punch still hurts."

Naina being in NOLA made me confident. I wrote, "Send me a picture of your bruise. I am a doctor's daughter. I might be able to help."

Jay disappeared.

I was persistent. "Hello? You there?"

"I know you are busy with the conference and you need to save other women. I'll be fine. Don't want to send you a picture of my bruised face and upset you more."

Jerk! That's because there is no bruise or swollen face! "You are so considerate. Thanks, Jay." I rolled my eyes.

After changing into a tight green skirt below the knees, but with a slit over the left knee and tucked in chiffon, and a sleeveless nude color blouse, I left for the New Orleans Convention Center. Rohan's team was courteous and smart. It made me feel his absence even more. We were supposed to do site inspections together. This was our event. The thought that Rohan no longer wanted to work with me made me feel worthless.

I inspected the venue and worked out a roster. Every team member was assigned a dignitary. The team members' job was to make sure the dignitaries' needs were met. I emailed Michael and Rohan with an update. Michael acknowledged the progress report, but there was nothing from Rohan. I also emailed them pictures of what the venue looked like. I was so thrilled that we even had sponsors for chilled towels soaked in eucalyptus oil so we could create a spa feel for our speakers at the end of their talk.

I found a quiet spot and meditated. I did nine repetitions of alternate nostril breathing to balance both sides of the brain. After Mumma, I had never taken anyone for granted until Rohan. The ease of comfort with him both scared and confused me.

* * *

Naina and Masi met me in the lobby of my hotel. It was so nice to see Masi—made me feel closer to Mumma. Masi's motherly touch and "at least eat these *laddoos, beta*" made me feel less alone. But *laddoos* also reminded me of Rohan. His eyes lit up around them. Little did I know that I would come to America to heal myself and would discover the man I love.

Naina, Masi, and I sat in the hotel bar. While Naina barely spoke, or looked at me, Masi filled the room with her laughter and jokes about her in-laws. She was stressed about Naina's wedding and asked whether we could go in an area where she could smoke. On her way out, she cupped my face in her hands, "I should go now, *beta*. But remember that you aren't alone. Whatever is weighing you down, ask your heart for the answer."

My eyes became moist as I said a good night to Masi. I lingered on the hug.

Later, Naina and I walked quietly to an eatery on Bourbon Street. Despite the noise outside, we ate in silence as Naina dipped her fries in ketchup, or was it her ketchup in her fries? Naina was so warm and loving, but when she got upset, you didn't want to be on her bad side.

I took a deep breath. "I know you are mad at me, but I..."

"You want my advice?" She wiped the corner of her mouth. "Rohan is the best thing that's happened to you in a very long time. Talk to him." She ran her tongue over her teeth.

"And tell him what?" I put my shrimp po'boy back on the plate. "Should I tell him I'm a weakling? That I keep waiting to heal and forget the damage Dev has done? That I don't fully believe that Rohan likes me for who I am? That I won't be able to take it if he turns me down? That I am unsure of my ability to judge men? That underneath this tough persona, I am scared?" I looked away.

"If you are scared, it means you're willing to take a chance." Naina put her food down. "Your silence has done more damage than good. Stop designing your life and fucking grab it by the horns, Ahana."

"Dev." One word that came out of my mouth in response.

"Will you stop bringing your past into your today?" She was clutching the corners of the table. Everyone around us stared at her.

The air felt too thick to swallow.

Naina got up and walked over to my chair. Her voice softened. "The future is scary; I get it. But you can't keep running back to your past, which gave you only nightmares. Stop assuming every relationship will turn out the same way. You met Dev when you were too young. And Jay, you always knew there was something off about him. Both the jerks exploited and demeaned you because *they* are psychopaths." She paused for a second. "You allowed yourself to *be you* in front of Rohan, because deep down you know he is a good guy. When you find someone who makes you happy and you want to keep around, you do something about it."

I looked down and spoke softly, as if confessing to a priest. "I miss Rohan, Naina. No one else can compare to him. I don't know how to make this all better." My tears ate up the rest of my sentence.

Naina cupped my chin in between her palms and wiped my tears. Her phone rang. She looked at the screen. "This will all be fixed." She kissed my forehead and left.

I sat stupefied, not knowing what to expect next.

Naina came running back in. "Sorry; I forgot to pay for dinner."

"Silly, I can take care of it." I smiled at her but still felt confused.

"Yes, you can. Thank you, sis." She started to run out again.

"But where are you going?"

She rolled up a bunch of fries and shoved them inside her mouth. "Meet you in the lobby of your hotel." She gave me a time. "Don't change." She kissed me on my cheek.

After Naina left, I sat with a glass of wine and looked around. People seemed happy. Rohan was right; New Orleans had a magical quality to it. It filled up hearts. But my heart felt empty. I couldn't stop thinking about Rohan. I guess, in life, you never end up where you think you wanted to be.

I closed my eyes and tried to picture what happiness would feel like—I saw Rohan. His words, his memories, his face. He treated me with so much respect and adulation. I missed his silliness. His way with words. The way he made me laugh. His handsome face. I hated myself for what I had done. I had completely misunderstood and misinterpreted his actions. I wanted Rohan back. I wanted a sign. Something. Anything.

The server brought me the check and at the bottom it said, "Follow your heart."

In that very instant, I knew what had to be done.

≈ 31 ≈

I took a cab instead of walking back to my hotel. "There are lots of ways to stay safe and still have fun in NOLA," Rohan had advised me once.

When I got to the lobby of my hotel after a long walk, I froze: there he was, Rohan, sitting on a brown leather sofa. Clad in a white shirt, blue denim jeans, and suede brown jacket, he looked exhausted. Naina was sitting next to him and using a lot of hand gestures in her conversation. Rohan saw me and got up from his seat.

I walked up to them and brought my eyebrows together. "What are you doing here?"

He shrugged his shoulders. "A client needed some help."

"Cut out the bullshit, you two." Naina punched Rohan's arm. "I am sorry to interfere, Ahana. I called up Rohan as soon as I left your hotel room this morning, and told him what was going on. He took the first flight out of JFK. Sorry I had to ditch you at dinner because his flight got in before time."

"Naina?" I couldn't think of words.

I walked closer toward them. A smile lurked at the corner of my lips, but I was still cautious. Rohan's eyes looked like he hadn't slept at all. I don't know what prompted me, but I hugged him.

He hugged me tightly like he was afraid to lose me. He ran his hands through my styled hair. The slight stubble on his face rubbed my skin; I liked it. It was wonderful to be close to Rohan.

"Ahem, guys." Naina put her palms over her mouth and leaned in. "Go up to your room."

I pulled myself away from him. "Naina." I spoke in an embarrassed tone.

Rohan asked Naina to join us in the coffee shop.

"This is your time with her. Have fun, you kids."

I kissed Naina on her cheek. "I love you. Thank you. I don't know what to say," I whispered in her ear.

"By the way, those *laddoos* that Mom brought, they are for Rohan too." She wiped my tears.

"Masi too was in on this?"

"She masterminded the whole plan."

Naina said goodnight to the two of us.

* * *

Rohan and I stood in awkward silence. I dragged my feet and stared at his shoes. I spent an equal amount of time on each.

He offered me his hand. "Come with me." He looked at me. "But you might want to change into comfortable shoes and leave your handbag in the hotel safe."

People were waiting in line to take the elevators up to the room. I stared at Rohan as he waited for me in the lobby. I marveled at the certainty and honesty of his words. I didn't want to live in the past, but it occurred to me that while Jay had deliberately made me walk into a precarious situation, Rohan was making sure I stayed out of harm's way.

"Why are you so *chup-chaap*? I mean, quiet?" I asked just as soon we got out of the hotel.

"Because I don't want you running out and not talking to me. It frightens me when you become this way—so cold and distant, like nothing matters. Like *we* don't matter." He looked at me intently.

We walked on a quieter street. Rohan took off his jacket and covered his Rolex. I noticed that we were the only couple on the road for quite a ways in any direction. But I didn't feel unsafe in his company.

I slowly told Rohan everything that Josh had revealed about Jay. "I should have told you sooner, but I was so embarrassed by my inability to see any of the signs in Jay. You and Naina had both warned me about him," I confessed softly.

As we turned on Poydras Street, he stopped. "I want you to remember that people like Jay are career criminals who dupe others. Don't ever blame yourself for whatever happened. I am grateful you are safe."

"But you said—"

"I am sorry for saying things the way I did. I was upset. I can't imagine what you must be going through. Instead of being a friend, I judged you. Forgive me, Ahana." Rohan scraped his shoes.

"I'm so sorry for the way I behaved. I got nervous."

We went for a walk by the Mississippi River. I could hear the water slap against the rocks. Though the night had cooled off, the air was humid and salty. We found a rock. He took off his jacket and placed it on the rock for me. "You could have said something instead of catching a flight and coming to New Orleans." I glanced into his eyes; he didn't look angry, just hurt.

After sitting down, I got out of my shoes and brought my legs to my chest. Rohan sat down next to me. We stared at the moonlight on the river. His eyes were moist.

I put my hands on his wrist. "Did you feel I had abandoned you, Rohan? That I didn't want you?" I touched his arm.

"What would you have thought if you were in my place?" He picked a pebble and threw it in the river.

I dragged my feet sitting down. "Then why did you cut the night short on Friday?"

Rohan put his hand on my thighs and gently rubbed my knees with his thumbs. "I was upset about Jay. You compared me to that jerk! That's the worst insult, Ahana." He stood up. There was a chilling confidence in his voice. "I knew you were vulnerable after the episode with Jay—I realized that if I didn't call it a night, then I might not be able to keep my hands off you." He let out a sigh. "I didn't want you to start our relationship with any regrets."

Rohan's patience these past few days told me the distance I needed to travel for us to connect.

I stood up and dusted my dress. "Then why didn't you say anything?" I took his hands and brought them to my lips.

He cupped my face. My heart beat faster. "Because you are not 'easy' as you say." He put his right hand firmly around my waist and cradled the back of my head with his left hand. "You had made up your mind about me. And only you could change your opinion."

I stayed quiet.

He ran his fingers through my hair and pressed his forehead against mine. "Ahana, can't you tell that I'm crazy about you?" He tucked my hair behind my left ear. "I've been dropping hints for the past few weeks that I am ready to make a commitment. Not just making out. Or going out to dinner. I want to be with you. I want to spend the rest of my life with you."

My entire body trembled. I started to feel breathless in a way I had never known.

He caressed my cheeks. "I fell in love with you the first time we met. There have been no women ever since."

I gently kissed his eyelids. "Sorry I've been so difficult." I paused and pulled away. "But we live in different countries, Rohan."

"My company's Asia-Pacific headquarters is in New Delhi. I can move—I've already spoken with the human resources department. Or if you want to live in NOLA, there are many options for you."

I couldn't believe Rohan was willing to make such a huge change for me.

"I know how important family is to you. Even if you were to move here, your dad can come visit whenever he wants. And we can go to India too!" He stroked my collarbones with his hands and my heart with his words. The memory attached to Dev dissipated in that moment.

I kissed his chin.

"And our dogs will have buddies for life."

"You've thought it all through?" I liked the warmth of his arms.

"We'll make it work, Ahana." Rohan gazed into my eyes. "I want to be with you, and I am willing to do whatever it takes." He caressed my frazzled expression.

He kissed me gently on my lips. Bringing his face back a few inches, staring into my eyes, he asked whether it was OK for him to kiss me. I kissed him back. With his warm lips on mine, I felt safe. I didn't know I had waited my entire life to be loved so unconditionally.

I whispered, "I love you, Brady."

He gave me a big smooch. "I love you too, Matron. More than you will ever know or believe."

* * *

Next morning, I woke up by 5 a.m., and after a run in the French Quarter, I showered and left for work. I had to confirm arrangements at the meeting site, rental stores, and caterers. Depending on the attendee registration, I had to adjust the amount of food and chairs and tables. A little later in the day, I had a meeting at the conference venue. I needed to make sure that members who had agreed to help on the day of the conference knew exactly what they needed to do and when. I also had to make sure that all materials and supplies had arrived and the conference packets were assembled. I had to set up the registration area and have a meeting with the people who were responsible for the registrations so that they all knew what was expected of them. I had to assign committee members as trouble-shooters for any problems that might arise.

With a pen in my mouth and paper in my hand, I was pacing up and down when Rohan and I ran into each other at the NOLA office around 7:30 a.m. "Hi!" I could feel my face beam upon seeing him.

He kissed my forehead. "Looking sharp, Matron. How is it going?"

"A little nervous, *yaar*. I went over the list of things I have to finish in the next forty-eight hours. Attendees are already hashtagging the conference and posting selfies of their airport look—it's real."

"Social media and social networking are what brought us together." He flaunted his dimple.

I smiled at him.

238

"How about I bring you some tea? And we figure out if you can delegate any of the work to my team?"

Rohan made me a strong cup of Earl Grey and we stood by the kitchen windows that overlooked the street. I thanked him and held the cup with both hands. "Rohan, I want to go to your favorite bar in NOLA."

"I'd love that. Unfortunately, I am at a client site during the day and won't be home until late. And I'll be at the lawyer's office all day tomorrow because Hedick wants some last-minute contracts negotiated. But we can go there tomorrow after confirming all the conference setup. Works?"

"I won't see you until tomorrow night." I stared at my feet.

He lifted my chin, "I will see you later tonight," and kissed me on my lips. "I have no intention of letting you sleep."

I punched his chest and blushed.

"If you'd like, ask Naina and Josh to join us tomorrow evening for an early drink after work." He gently ran his thumb on my cheekbones. "I will text you the address."

After instructing the reception committee and double-checking the airport pickup schedule for speakers, I walked to the Westin Canal Place. The hotel was a central point between the French Quarter and the convention center, and this was where all our panelists were going to stay. I made sure all the arrangements were in place. The AV, caterers, volunteers, microphones, podiums, and green room. The staff was helpful and brought me a cup of tea after the meeting. It was nice to look out the window and see the Mississippi River. The view of the Riverwalk, riverboats, and open space allowed me to breathe out my anxiety.

* * *

I walked to Rohan's favorite bar to meet with him; I saw him and Josh caught in a serious discussion. I hugged Josh, and Rohan turned to the bartender. "Can I get a glass of your Deloach pinot noir? Thanks, man!" He pulled up a barstool for me.

I put down my handbag full of conference paperwork. "What are you two talking about?"

"Jay's possible next move." Josh was in cop mode. He hadn't touched his single malt.

"He hasn't made any contact or said anything on the group recently." I adjusted my dress as I sat down. "But yes, I wonder what he might do next."

Rohan turned to Josh. "If Jay committed a crime, why would it be hard to lock him up?"

Josh swirled his drink. "Jay is not your blatant lawbreaker. There is little defense our legal system offers against sociopaths like him. Unless Amanda or Tanya press charges or we have more proof, cops can't get involved."

"Men like Jay just roam around, defrauding people?" Both of Rohan's hands were in fists. "And we can do nothing about it, even when it's clear he defrauded these women?"

Josh patted Rohan's left shoulder. "I know, man. I hate it as much as you do."

Ten minutes into the conversation, Naina joined. "Are we still talking about that shithead?"

"How did you know?" Rohan gave Naina a hug and ordered her a drink.

"Guys, you forget that I'm a shrink."

Josh rubbed her shoulders. "Hon, I want to run something by you. Rohan and I are wondering if Ahana should post the details of her talk on her therapy group."

At her startled look, Rohan added, "It might trigger Jay to show up and confront Ahana. We can catch him in action then."

For the first time in my life, I saw Naina patiently hear everyone out. She took a sip of Josh's drink and unwrapped her scarf. "Guys, Jay won't make the rookie mistake."

"What do you mean?"

"You are prepping for Jay assuming what 'regular' criminals do. *But* he is an intelligent and a logical man with a narcissistic personality disorder. He has probably figured out Ahana is on to him. He won't show up and risk being caught." She took a deep breath. "He has probably already lost interest in you guys and moved on to his next victim in another group."

"As a cop, I have dealt with every kind of bum and criminal. But this is fucking insane."

"Yes, and it's fucking common, too. We don't hear about it because women end up feeling ashamed and refuse to talk about it even when it's not their fault."

I bit my lower lip, uneasy and content to let Naina steer the men away from their gung-ho plan. And she was already diving into case histories: "I have a client who almost married a man who fabricated an entire life on Facebook using strangers' pictures and their information. He lured lonely women into making romantic connections. My client found discrepancies in the information he shared, so she questioned him; he got evasive. She traveled to this guy's house in upstate New York only to find that his wife and mother were in on the scam. This guy moves in with single or divorced women and eventually gets their property transferred to his name."

Rohan looked helpless. "How is that even possible?"

"Fucking charmer! Since the wife and mother were involved in the scam, his secret stayed protected. Thankfully, my client found out before he moved into her house. For Christ's sake, she has a five-year-old son. When she confronted him and threatened to alert the other women on Facebook, he vowed to hurt her kid. She backed down and blocked him."

Rohan's blue eyes narrowed. "How did Jay know things not just about Ahana but also Chutney's job with the Indian government? Ahana didn't share it with him. How did he get all of this info on her, including your schedule and address?"

"Rohan, my address is listed if you dig deep enough—that one was easy. Ahana's family is famous as shit. I swear, you can even find out what her great-grandfather did. Plus, the online world is not transparent. While some of us may be more discriminate than others, we live in a time when it's common to build online networks that include secondary and tertiary connections. Ahana won't even know if there was information on her in the online world posted by a friend, colleague, or even her shithead ex-husband."

Josh hadn't lifted his hand from her shoulders, rubbing absently, pondering what she said. "There are other women in the group. Why did he mess with Amanda, Tanya, and Ahana only?"

"From what Ahana has told us, these are the only three single women in the group—all vulnerable after losing a loved one. Go figure."

"Easy prey." Josh stroked his chin.

Rohan played with the peanuts in the bowl. "But wait; Jay's mother is alive. He is married. How could he pull any of this off?"

"Maybe his manipulations are part of a petty scheme to defraud women of their money? Who knows if he has any inside help."

I sat in silence and obsessively rearranged the napkins on the bar table.

"I'm sorry," Naina whispered, and put an arm around my shoulder. "I know you don't want to hear this, but you may never find out how Jay stalked you so well. How he found out about my schedule. Whether or not his mother and wife were a part of all this. Your entry into the online world seemed to have sent tendrils out that you cannot retract, and snakes like Jay know how to pick up on your scent."

As I heard Rohan, Naina, and Josh mentally recording new steps in my discovery process, it finally came to me. That the goal, maybe, is to achieve the same kind of oneness with someone that we only get once—with our own mothers, ideally. That goal isn't attainable, or at least it probably isn't, because even our mothers are their own imperfect people. Like my mumma who loved me unconditionally but didn't think I could make my own decisions or fight my own battles. Her love, which I will forever hold dear in my heart, at times made me vulnerable rather than strong. Truth: we can still strive for the best, and if we are lucky, we end up with a few real, great loves in our life. In my case, it was Rohan, Naina, and Josh. I was grateful for them. They made me feel safe.

⚡ 32 ⚡

On the morning of the conference's first day, it was humbling to bow my head to the morning sun and do eleven sun salutations. "If you want radiant and ageless skin, *surya namaskars* are the answer, not cosmetic surgery," Mumma would tell her bridge partners when they complained about the age-appropriate wrinkles on their faces.

I meditated for twenty minutes and set my intention for the day.

Naina and Masi sent me text messages wishing me lots of good luck. Masi had asked whether she could drop off any homemade breakfast for me on her way to work. *Indian moms and aunts, no one feeds people better,* I thought to myself. I said, "Masi, I'm too nervous to eat, but I'll get a green juice, I promise."

"*Beta*, when do we get to see you? Do you want me to stop by at your hotel in the evening?"

"No, Masi." My heart filled up. "Not at all. You have guests at home. I'll stop by and spend time with the family."

"Perfect. Bring Rohan along." Masi's voice was filled with affection.

"Ummm."

"Masi means—like Mom. While I might not be your Mumma, I am your mom's sister and will always know all the antics you and Naina are up to." She laughed. "You haven't sounded this happy in very long time, *beta*. I want to meet the man who has won my Ahana's heart."

"Love you, Masi."

"Love you too, *beta*."

I called up Dad and Chutney and got their blessings. When I told Chutney about Rohan, she teased, "Brilliant! We'll have blue-eyed grandchildren."

I laughed hysterically. "You are mental, Chutney."

"I love this boy already, Ahana."

"Without meeting him?"

"He made you come alive from the very first day he walked into your life. God bless him."

"Will you prep Dad about Rohan?"

"I have already started the process. I cannot wait to see you. Tell Rohan that I am bringing *laddoos* for him. Love you."

I checked my online therapy group forum and my emails. There was no message from Jay. Dev hadn't made any contact since I'd last screamed at him in New Delhi. Contact between him and Jay seemed more and more unlikely.

I looked outside the hotel room windows and whispered my gratitude to the universe.

I had so much love in my life. I was happy. I wished Mumma were alive. I wished she could see me handle the conference. I was a victim, but I had directed my pain in a way so I could help others. The last memory Mumma had of me was that of a sad, quiet, lonely, and broken woman in the summer of 2013. The divorce with Dev had dissolved my identity. I wished she could see how much I had changed with Naina and Rohan's help in less than a year. Dancing, sipping Sazeracs, standing up for myself, honoring my needs, and laughing. In Rohan's company, it was hard to remain sad. I wished she could have met Rohan. With their love for dancing and whiskey, they would have really gotten along.

I took a hot shower and wore Mumma's pearl earrings as my good luck charm. I slipped into a fitting blue silk blouse and black skirt. Seer pantyhose, stilettos, a pink lipstick, and pink blush to stay subtle through the day.

* * *

It was a beautiful day in NOLA. Clear skies. Slightly nippy. The city looked busier than usual—over 3,000 people had registered for the conference.

Since I didn't like stressing out about being late anywhere, I reached the convention center an hour before the scheduled time. I confirmed that everything was as I had requested. The last-minute booths and three registration tables were being set up at the entrance. The day before, I had met with the people who were going to do the registration so that they all knew what was expected of them. The temperature and lighting were perfect. The caterer was setting up shop. I personally checked the microphones in each room. The team responsible for greeting the speakers was on its way. Being organized, planned, and structured gave me a high.

I put my hands on my hips and looked at the massive venue. It's all worked out, Mumma.

Rohan arrived fifteen minutes after me. He looked breathtakingly handsome in his light blue, fitted, designer shirt, blue pants, and Hermes orange tie.

"How come you are here this early, Brady?"

"Good morning to you too." He gave me a kiss.

244

Rohan tucked my hair behind my right ear. "I know how important today is for you. Figured I'd grab a cup of tea with you first before I meet with Crystal and Michael."

I hugged him. "Thank you. I'm glad you're here. So nervous, *yaar*. I hope it all goes well."

"Oh, it will. You have worked so hard for it."

"Thanks for the faith. *Uff*, managing these fragile, academic egos, I couldn't have done it without you." I threw my arms in the air.

"There are better ways of thanking me." Rohan let out an evil grin.

"*Paagal*." I pinched his arm.

Rubbing his right arm, Rohan said, "The arrangements look great, Matron! Did you see the napkins in the breakfast cafes?"

"No, why?"

"They all have the logo *No Excuse* on them."

"Wow, we remind them right from day one of the conference the importance of *No Excuse*! That's true brand identity."

"Exactly."

Rohan and I walked inside each of the five rooms, set up for parallel tracks of different plenary sessions, to make sure all the projectors were working. The conference rooms had pleasant daylight and could seat up to 100 people. We tested the audiovisual technology and wi-fi.

We made sure the breakfast cafes were set up and that every restroom was sparkling clean. Cafes and water junctions were set up. The hotel staff was prepped and ready to go. We each got a set of walkie-talkies.

I paused in my steps and held Rohan's hand. "I wish Mumma was here, Rohan." I looked at the room. "I can't believe where I am today." My eyes welled up.

"She would have been so proud of you." Rohan pressed my hand. "You are spearheading the largest women's conference in the world, Ahana. You're calling attention to the heinous issue of violence against women that should be addressed. I am so proud of you." He put his hands on my shoulders.

"Thanks, Rohan. I wish she could have met you. You would have really liked her."

"I have no doubt! Let's go to New Delhi after Naina's wedding. Show me around all the places where your mom liked to hang out." He smiled and scratched his chin.

I noticed that he'd missed a tiny spot shaving. I kissed it.

He planted a long kiss. "I mean her bridge partners would like me." Rohan winked at me.

"Such a pig, Rohan."

"You laughed. For me, that is most important."

Michael and Crystal showed up seventy-five minutes later. It was almost disconcerting to see Michael ecstatic about the arrangements. "You have fucking massage chairs in green rooms? That's mind-blowing. Ahana, you should come work for me." He turned to Crystal. "Find out what it takes for Ahana to get her visa."

Rohan and I smiled at each other. Mumma was right: when you set your intention and you are truly honest about what you want out of life, the universe conspires to make it all happen.

At 8:30 a.m., we all attached our badges. Yes, it was time to address the crisis of violence against women. It was time to say "No" to bullying, being timid, policing, and the exploitation of women.

Video cameras were set. Photographers were in place. The social media team was ready with the hashtag #noexcuse and #womencometogether. Looking at some of the social media posts and pictures of buses full of women attendees, with a gigantic banner with *No Excuse* streaming across their bus, it felt as if the collective consciousness of the global society had risen that day. As if everyone had pledged to set an intention for a safer existence for vulnerable women.

The conference venue started to fill up with people and words. *No Excuse* started to trend on different platforms in twenty-five minutes of registration booths being opened. People posted selfies, quoted the speakers, shared their experiences, and commiserated with other women. Rohan showed me all the applause the press was giving me and the event.

"Let's see what Hedick has to say about that." I elbowed Rohan and bit my cheek.

Most events were focused around women learning and realizing how important it was to use their voices. So many victims, including myself, had stayed silent around our perpetrators, because we felt shame and somehow responsible for the crimes committed on us. So many women didn't know they had the choice to say "No" to violence and rape. Most victims lost dignity and *No Excuse* would educate them to hold their head high and speak up against violence. There were also safety and self-defense workshops.

Each interaction with an attendee or speaker, every post, started to fill up the hole in me and gave me courage for the speech I knew was coming.

Rohan took good care of all the speakers and their temper tantrums every day. He even managed to defuse any stress Michael's fricative personality created. Rohan was calm, and diplomatically handled all the complaints. I interacted with the speakers and panelists and made sure everything worked smoothly.

Sarah Goldstein did an excellent presentation on women policing other women. Dialogues around victims' lifestyles, wardrobes, and work hours violated them as much as the perpetrator himself. "Let's stand together as one. Accept and make *No Excuse* for why a woman is abused or assaulted or violated. The women who are oppressed shouldn't become oppressors. We, as women, need to unite to fight the epidemic of violence against women."

Professors and activists held workshops to teach women to recognize signs if they were in an abusive relationship. "Emotional abuse doesn't leave scars that can be seen with the naked eye," they reiterated.

Every now and then, Rohan checked in with me. "Are you all right, Matron?"

"Why wouldn't I be, Brady?"

"Given the theme for today."

I examined his face. "I am strong because I am a survivor." I held his hand. "You remind me of all the good in my life."

"I want to see all this gratitude translate into a lap dance." He smiled at me.

"You might get a surprise tonight," I whispered in his ears.

I was getting bolder—a first for me in my relationships. It was marvelous to see the surprise on Rohan's face. I felt empowered, being at the conference. I was listening to gruesome stories, but I didn't personalize them. I was surrounded by serious discussions, but I had carved out space for the man who made me realize that my vulnerabilities only made me stronger. I felt a shift in me and it felt good. In that moment, *No Excuse* came alive in every cell and pore in my body.

Despite the long day, Rohan and I spent the evening at Naina's. Masi overfed Josh and Rohan. And Rohan seemed pleased with all the maternal love showered on him.

* * *

The first two days of the conference went seamlessly. People talked about making the event into an annual get-together for the intellectuals, activists, social workers, and everyone who wanted to make the world a safer place for women.

On Thursday evening, the second day of the conference, after drinks with the heads of nonprofits, I went to Naina's informal *sangeet* and *mehendi* ceremony.

"Only in America can there be a rehearsal for *sangeet* or as you call it, 'a dance ceremony,'" I had told her laughingly.

"I didn't want to invite all of Mom and Dad's friends to the wedding, so we figured an elaborate pre-wedding, pre-*sangeet* dinner and dance will be ideal for them. We'll do the *mehendi* ceremony too that evening, so all the aunties can show off their henna tattoos, jewels, and silk saris." Naina had rolled her eyes. "But, *sangeet* will be just family and our friends on Saturday. This way, we get a break on Friday evening to bum out, show Chutney around town, and then have fun on Saturday, the day of the real *sangeet*," she had quipped.

* * *

I showed up clad in a red chiffon *sari* paired with a bright pink, heavily embroidered, short, halter neck blouse ending right below my breasts. My *sari* was unevenly pleated. Mumma used to help me drape my *sari*. She would get the accessories sorted out. I would literally just show up to functions and weddings. This was the first time in my life that I had organized an Indian wedding outfit, keeping Rohan's taste in mind. Love turns us into beautiful clichés.

The guests had yet to arrive. Most of the extended family members were getting dressed or fixing their makeup or getting the final touches on their henna tattoos. I found an alcove next to the dining room with no one around and a full-length mirror. I was standing in a quiet corner, trying to go unnoticed and pinning my *sari* to the blouse, when Rohan sneaked up behind me. "Aah, so a red *sari*." He kissed my neck and then my earlobes. "I like that someone is keeping their promise, but how did you make that happen?" His touch stole my breath and reminded me how every other time in my life someone had touched me, it had been wrong.

I turned around to respond, but the safety pin fell from my hands. The *sari* slipped from my shoulders and onto the floor. The more I tried rearranging my *pallu*, the long trailing part of the *sari* that was draped around and across my shoulders, the more it got entangled in the dozen bangles in my wrists and hair. Rohan quickly bent down to pick up my densely ornamented *pallu*. I tugged at it tightly and covered my exposed chest.

Pointing at my *desi* avatar, I whispered, "Tsk! I am not good at any of this. Such a mess, Brady."

Rohan spun me around; I could see our reflection in the full-length mirror. "You look amazing, and I like your style, Ahana Chopra." With his chin resting on my shoulders, his body pressed close to mine, and his arms circling around my waist, he moaned weakly, "How did I get so lucky?"

I wanted to breathe Rohan. I inhaled his scent and exhaled all the foul memories Dev had built inside of me. When Dev would travel, he would order me to wear lingerie and stand in front of the mirror in our bedroom. "I am not ordering a woman from a fucking catalog, Ahana. Describe yourself to me so I am turned on. Say, 'Sir, I am wearing....'" I took a deep breath. Dev was nowhere near me. He was no longer a part of me. Rohan made me a better woman. I had never loved or wanted anyone the way I wanted Rohan.

My right hand gripped Rohan's hair, pulling him closer. "I have never been happier, Brady."

Rohan caught my wrists and kissed my palms. Suddenly, he noticed my hands. He turned to face me now. "Matron, how come you got no henna thingy?"

"Because of my talk tomorrow. But I'll get the *mehendi* before Naina's wedding."

"What's the significance of it?"

"You know, the saying goes that the darker the color of the *mehendi*, the more your guy loves you." My cheeks turned the color of a henna tattoo.

Rohan lifted my chin. He traced the lines of my cheekbones. "Ooh, yours will be the darkest then, right?" He grinned proudly, like a troublemaker.

The sound system was on by now. The music was blaring. Glasses were over-flowing with alcohol. The aroma of *kebabs* impregnated the space. Aunties discussed their diamonds, mothers-in-law, and expensive vacations. Uncles talked about their investments, the money spent on their kids' ivy-league education, and how well their children were doing.

Funnily, the more I squirmed at the display of hubris, the more Rohan genuinely seemed to enjoy himself. I admired how he fit in everywhere while I was the perpetual misfit. He danced with everyone and quickly took to throwing his limbs like the others in the room.

Chutney had reached New Orleans with her larger than life New Delhi persona and dance moves. She put her embroidered *dupatta* around Rohan's neck and danced with him as the song *"chunar chunar"* played in the background. Rohan was a great dancer, and he picked up new moves in minutes. He indulged her, so politely. I was embarrassed and surprised. For once, I saw Rohan Brady blush, but genuinely blissful. There he was, indulging my aunts, playing with my nieces and nephews, joking and binge-drinking with all the uncles, and partying with the cousins. The natural tendency to draw in people and garner their attention was tattooed on Rohan's forehead.

Every now and then, he walked up to me with some excuse. "Lighten up, Matron. Join us."

"Nah. I'm a terrible dancer."

"Your shimmies aren't all that bad. I've seen them." He let out a burst of his evil laughter.

"Leave me alone, Brady." I crossed my hands on my chest.

"See, I can't do that. I never will."

* * *

On the last day of the conference, which was the biggest day as all the speakers were convening for the closing, I was scheduled to give my closing remarks. I was nervous and excited, so much so that I had told people in my online therapy group too about my speech. Jay hadn't said a word, but most others had written encouraging messages, saying they would root for me and send good energy to Room #303 at the time I was supposed to give my talk.

Naina had bought the one-day pass to hear my speech. I thought I saw a NY Jets hat fading into the crowd at the bar. I didn't know for sure whether it was Jay. When I told Naina, she said, "So what? You're powerful, and surrounded by powerful women and men who love you. Your mom would be proud." She massaged my shoulders. "You are a force. You've bloomed in this past year, and if you're still *vulnerable* at times, this isn't a bad thing." Naina reassured me that I had boundaries and discernment now, which I didn't have before. "Jay probably has no involvement in *this* anymore because he is a narcissist and might have moved on to some other drama in his life. You'll be fine, Ahana."

I was still anxious about Jay when Rohan appeared at the entrance. I waved at him. Rohan walked up to me. "Matron, I am so proud of you. We must raise a toast to your mom tonight. She is the one who started this journey with you."

I held Rohan's hand. "I'm glad I got to end it with you next to me."

Rohan kissed my forehead. "It's almost time for your talk. Break a leg!"

"You aren't coming inside, Brady?"

"Are you kidding me? I'm going to sit in the first row and whistle at the end of your speech."

His voice, laced with unquestionable support, gave me the last boost of confidence I needed.

I walked up to the podium. Michael Hedick introduced me. I was very nervous, but focused. I looked around the room. The entire auditorium was filled with speakers, attendees, sponsors, and volunteers. Their faces became blurry. It's the source of power that Dev and Jay had over me all this time: my own fear. Their smug certainty that I ought to be ashamed of myself, that I was their thing to use and manipulate. My cards were in my hand on the podium, full of the words of my nice, safe speech. But I put them aside. I pushed my glasses closer to my eyes and took a deep breath.

"Good afternoon, everyone. I'm Ahana Chopra, the organizer of this conference. But I'm in front of you today simply as a woman who left a marriage two years ago—a marriage where I was complicit in my own repeated rape by my husband, a sadist. It was a ten-year encounter that left me confused and wounded to the depths of my soul. I was very ashamed. I was ashamed that I had 'allowed this to happen to me.' For ten years, I asked myself if I had turned my ex-husband into thinking that my body was not my own. That he could violate me whenever he chose because my choices were meaningless. Truth: *No* is a complete emotion, word, and sentence. Rape is never OK. As a survivor, you are not to blame. It's OK to be angry, but it isn't OK to carry shame. Because the only person wrong here is the rapist. I am telling you this dark secret because I want each one of you in this room to know you are safe here. We are together and we are strong. We must call things out and say where things are wrong. Don't be afraid to use your voice for change. Shame will not exist if you can talk to people who understand your story."

As soon as those words left my mouth, the burden lifted. The faces in the audience became clear to me. Rohan, out there in the first row, his face full of humility and respect for me, was the first to stand up and applaud. Seated next to Rohan, Naina joined in. In that moment, I understood what Mumma meant by "Forgive yourself, *beta*; grow from your experiences. Know that you are more than your scars. Believe that you deserve love."

I took a deep breath as the entire auditorium joined Rohan in giving me a standing ovation. Just like that, Dev and Jay's power evaporated. The damage they had done, it didn't matter any longer. I was now too strong for them to hold any control over my life. I finally felt free.

Acknowledgments

Louisiana Catch is dear to my heart for many reasons, so I would like to express my gratitude to the many people who saw me through this book—those who provided support, talked things over, read, wrote, offered comments and assisted in the editing, proofreading and design.

I would like to thank my publisher, Victor R. Volkman, for enabling me to publish this book and encouraging me to write about topics that are uncomfortable and scary but need to be addressed. My editor, Sarah Cypher: Without you, this book wouldn't be where it is today; thank you for pushing me harder with every round of edits. Doug West, the best book cover designer, aka mind reader, any author could dream of working with.

To my yoga and Ayurveda teachers, spaces and organizations that use my yoga services, especially *Exhale to Inhale,* and my yoga students: Thank you for making it possible for me to do what I needed to do. Much gratitude to the psychology community for sharing its wisdom and encouraging me to write complicated characters reflective of the real world. Thank you to the lovely team and quiet corners at my co-working space, Grind, where I could revise my book.

I would like to thank Armaan Saxena and Aadil Saxena for their input as I wrote about dating, how men think, and *all things dude-ish.* Ginormous thanks to friend and writer Nancy Agabian and many of the crew members from her writing workshop, *Heightening Stories,* where I shared my raw thoughts about *Louisiana Catch.* Justen Ahren, Poet Laureate of Martha's Vineyard: Gratitude for creating a safe and nurturing space where I could write, and later edit, *Louisiana Catch* over the years. Cindy Hochman: Thank you for your ongoing support. Abha Shankar: Thanks for empowering me in more ways than you know. Deepika Mahajan and Aditya Srivastava: Thank you for all the kitchen experiments in perfecting the Sazerac recipe.

Ellen Goldstein, Catherine Jean Prendergast and Kristin Bock: You are the first group of people I read to from *Louisiana Catch* at Martha's Vineyard. It was pouring; my eyes were wet. The three of you made me feel so confident about my book. Thank you for raising a toast and for reminding me that relationships are what make us writers.

Leah Zibulsky and Neetal Adkar: The reason I was able to write about loss, grieving and healing in *Louisiana Catch* is because you both reiterated, at separate times, that I should feel my emotions, without any apologies. Shuchi Sethi and Vivek Yadav: you are friends I can run to with every nascent idea and know that I won't be judged. Thank you for being there and for your patience as life and this book changed me. Dona Pal: Friend, psychotherapist, fellow traveler and yogi: Thanks a lot for every article, debate, discussion and study about psychology, shared over tea, phone and vacations. Yogita Kulkarni and Kashmina Nath: For twenty-five years you have had my back and laughed at even my bad jokes; I am a lucky woman.

To my three musketeers, Jaya Sharan, Nirav Patel and Rashi Baid: Over the decades, you have seen me fall down and stand back up; you have witnessed my heartbreak and my broken pieces come together. You have held my hand when I didn't know I needed support. Thank you for always being there no matter what is going on in your lives. Thank you for defending my truth and giving me the courage always to remain authentic. I am indebted to you.

Dad, you recently said to me, "I am proud of you for being fearless and for standing up for your stories and principles." You have no idea how much that means to me in a world where writers are often shunned for speaking their minds. Thank you! To my brother, Shantanu; sister-in-law, Jyothi; and nieces, Diya and Sana: I am grateful to you for celebrating my writing journey with wholehearted-ness over the years. My cousins and cousins-in-law, especially Vinita, Jyotika, Jyotsna, Rakesh, Manoj and Arup: I love it that you look for an excuse to pop open champagne for me. I am blessed to have you in my life.

Above all, a big thank you to my dearest husband, Anudit. What would I do without your incredible heart? Thanks for supporting and encouraging me, despite all the time this book took me away from you and home. But now that I am back, I bet you are worried about football Sundays. Joking aside, it takes a lot to support a wife who is a writer and tackles issues of social change. Thank you for your unshaken faith and for letting me be me.

Last but not least: I beg forgiveness of all those who have been with me over the course of the years and whose names I have failed to mention. You are, with gratitude, in my prayers and good wishes.

About the Author

Sweta Srivastava Vikram (www.swetavikram.com), featured by Asian Fusion as "one of the most influential Asians of our time," is an award-winning author of eleven books, five-time Pushcart Prize nominee, mindfulness writing coach, wellness columnist, global speaker, and certified yoga and Ayurveda holistic health counselor. Sweta's work has appeared in *The New York Times* and other publications across nine countries on three continents. *Louisiana Catch* (Modern History Press) is her debut US novel.

Born in India, Sweta spent her formative years between the Indian Himalayas, North Africa, and the United States collecting and sharing stories. A graduate of Columbia University, she also teaches the power of yoga, Ayurveda, and mindful living to female trauma survivors, writers and artists, busy women, entrepreneurs, and business professionals in her avatar as the CEO-Founder of NimmiLife (www.nimmilife.com). She also uses her holistic wellness training to combine creative writing strategies with Ayurveda and yoga to help poets and writers improve their writing.

She lives in Queens, New York, with her husband, Anudit. You can find her on: Twitter (@swetavikram), Instagram (@SwetaVikram), and Facebook (http://www.facebook.com/Words.By.Sweta) and her own blog www.SwetaVikram.com.

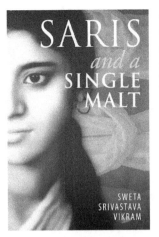

SWETA
SRIVASTAVA
VIKRAM

Saris and a Single Malt is a moving collection of poems written by a daughter for and about her mother. The book spans the time from when the poet receives a phone call in New York City that her mother is in a hospital in New Delhi, to the time she carries out her mother's last rites. The poems chronicle the author's physical and emotional journey as she flies to India, tries to fight the inevitable, and succumbs to the grief of living in a motherless world. This collection will move you, astound you, and make you hug your loved ones.

"There are few books like Saris and a Single Malt in which the loss of a mother, a homeland, and the self come together in a sustained elegy."
—Justen Ahren, Director Noepe Center, author *A Strange Catechism*

"In life, as in poetry, one must come from the heart. Sweta Vikram has done both with touching eloquence. Her work resonates deeply within one's deepest emotional sacristy."
—Sharon Kapp, Owner & Founder,
Houston Yoga & Ayurvedic Wellness Center

"*Saris and a Single Malt* is a fitting and delightful tribute of a writer daughter to her affectionate mother which goes deep into the minds of all children who love their moms."
—K. V. Dominic, English language poet, critic,
short-story writer, and editor from Kerala, India

Sweta Srivastava Vikram, featured by Asian Fusion as "one of the most influential Asians of our time," is an award-winning writer, Pushcart Prize nominee, author of ten books, and a wellness practitioner. A graduate of Columbia University, Sweta performs her work, teaches creative writing workshops, and gives talks at universities and schools across the globe.

Learn more at www.swetavikram.com

ISBN 978-1-61599-294-2